Hidden in Front of You

Robert E.F. Higgins

Copyright © 2019 Robert E.F. Higgins
All rights reserved.
ISBN: 9781687044044

DEDICATION

I dedicate this writing to my grandfather, who, since I could walk, shared with me the truths and cultural growth within San Francisco from the late nineteenth through the first half of the twentieth century.

ACKNOWLEDGMENTS

Even though my grandfather did no actual work on the manuscript, his life's teaching is embedded in each of the characters found in this writing.

Characteristically, the decisions, the actions, the understandings, the compassion, the empathy, the non-racism, the non-sexual deviance phobia, and the importance of saving the unfortunate came from my grandfather's personality and from the description of his life.

Paul Blair and I have different personalities. We worked together years ago in the software business and, in recent years, have gotten reacquainted. I had started writing, and he wanted to create a book or two. Paul worked endless days on getting my writings to a publishable manuscript.

Also, our differences seem to be a benefit for both. As we each brought to the table our own versions, we made good progress in joining our different opinions. Offering each other an idea and supporting each other has proven to be a benefit for both.

HIDDEN IN FRONT OF YOU

01 - THE JOURNEY BEGINS

It is a beautiful fall morning in the Bay Area. The weather is about to change from the foggy summer intrusion to the winter stillness. From a house in Marin County, a classy green Jaguar convertible traverses the curvy residential streets of Tiburon to the primary drive. It enters Highway 101 southbound. After merging with the 6:00 a.m. southbound traffic, the Jaguar crosses the Golden Gate within minutes. The Jaguar proceeds past Ghirardelli Square on its left and past Russian Hill on the right where the most crooked street in San Francisco is located, named Lombard Street. The driver turns right onto Columbus passing a grouping of Italian restaurants then past Chinatown to 3rd. The Jaguar turns left onto Market Street, then south to the Jessie Street parking garage. After parking and locking the Jaguar, the driver emerges from the structure carrying a black briefcase and takes a short walk to a luxury coffee shop on 2nd Street. 7:30 a.m. He enters the Gourmet Coffee House and orders a cup of Sumatra with a shot of Espresso and a freshly made cinnamon Danish. Sitting by the window, he sips his coffee and enjoys the pastry while watching the commuters. At 8:00 a.m. sharp, he walks to the 3rd and Market.

Commuters are walking from the Key System Terminal onto Market Street or using the citywide streetcars to continue their journey. All the city streetcars come to and through the Key System terminal receiving the trains from the east bay. These trains use tracks on the lower level of the bay bridge. The train-tracks take one half of the bottom level of the Oakland Bay Bridge.

The start of a new day in the big city has begun. Mr. Kenneth Able steps off his streetcar and starts his usual walk to his office, which is located just off Market Street near the Key System terminal with a view of the Oakland-San

Francisco Bay Bridge. People are walking briskly with a typical attitude of getting there, never mind the frills. They do not wander, do not look at buildings, do not look at the landscape, nor look at their fellow human beings beside them. They keep walking onward toward their destination. Each one of these hustle-bustle people has no time to spare. They only see the path.

The commuters are ignoring the street bums and the people sleeping on the curb; they step around the ones in their way. Anything seen lasts for only a fraction of a second before they move on. Constant is this fast-paced environment.

No one notices the stranger in the crowd, but this stranger is taking direct notice of Mr. Kenneth Able. This stranger is carrying his black briefcase, dressed in a dark blue suit, and is not in a hurry. This stranger is a person that has not been there before and will not be there in a few moments. He intends to alter Mr. Able's future.

For Mr. Kenneth Able, we need to remember that those clothed in good deeds are sometimes the very ones to be avoided. Mr. Able claims to be a religious man, he attends services regularly, and he donates to many community organizations, including his children's private school. He has a lovely and talented yet submissive wife.

Around the community, Mr. Able is prominent, accepted, and respected for all those who do not know him well. For those who do know him, when he barks, all those around him perk up their ears. When he is demanding, he wants things to happen right now. When he is judgmental, you do not offend him. Mr. Able has a healthy body. He is handsome, has a great skill in praising a pretty woman, has a black belt in karate, and is nimble on his feet.

Kenneth Able is not a classified narcissist in the full sense of the meaning. He does have some severe characteristics common to the narcissist of the class B personality disorder. Namely, I am most important, me first, and I am above all others. His personality would more closely be aligned with Stalin than Hitler yet not so pronounced. Like Stalin, there is severe cruelty found within Mr. Able's character, along with his above-average intellect.

He is successful in his business dealings. Mr. Able has generated wealth well beyond the average person and has placed himself into places of authority. He is uncooperative, uncompromising, and cruel. Mr. Able has ruined people's careers and their financial standings. In general, Mr. Able is considered a likable guy with his friendliness and attentiveness to detail for the person with whom he was speaking. In reality, it is buyer beware. For his attentiveness, he is nothing more than a narcissistic vulture type attempting to find out everything about you.

Upon arriving at his office, Mr. Able is welcomed by his secretary, Abigail. She hands him his black French roast coffee and a classic coffee cake from the nearby bakery. After a greeting kiss from Abigail, Mr. Able goes into his private office to review some client paperwork and make a few business calls.

Abigail is a beautiful woman with an air of sophistication, a stunning woman with a mind of her own, and her beauty catches everyone's eye. She has a close relationship with Mr. Able. She greets each arrival, filters all his calls and mail, and takes notes while attending every client business meeting. After each client meeting, Mr. Able and Abigail review the content of the conference together by evaluating the client by viewing the video from their hidden camera. Together he and Abigail review the meeting's video for body language information to help them find weak points in the client's personality or position.

Within the office space, there is a large separate room for

private use. This room has a window overlooking the Embarcadero and the bay bridge. In the distance is Treasure Island. The room contains a kitchenette, couch, king-size bed, TV, hot tub, and a full bathroom. The appearance is elegant. It appears to be an excellent place for a couple to spend time together.

At 11 a.m. Abigail steps out of the office for a luncheon engagement with her friend, a dental assistant from three floors below. Mr. Able has completed most of his initial business dealings this morning. He has a few moments to browse some client logs.

11:15 a.m., unnoticed by Mr. Able, the front office door opens and closes without a sound. From his peripheral vision, Mr. Able notices someone standing at his office doorway. He turns to see a man in a dark blue suit-wearing black leather gloves. Mr. Able reaches for his pistol in the top drawer.

He shouts, "Who in the hell are you. What do you want?"

A single psst sound from a pistol using a silencer, and Mr. Able is lying in a pool of his blood. Within seconds the front door closes without a sound. The stranger then walks downstairs to the next floor, steps into a janitor's closet, changes his clothes then departs the building carrying a sports bag. He is now dressed in a utility company uniform wearing a wig and baseball cap.

Unobserved the man walks toward the Jessie Street parking garage. Arriving at the Jaguar, the man removes his hat, wig, and work clothes, putting them into a black plastic sack then placing the bag into the trunk. He puts the blue suit coat back on. At 11:25 a.m., he climbs into the Jaguar, and drives away slowly, still wearing his black leather gloves.

At 12:30 p.m. Abigail returns to the office, puts her coat away in the closet, checks the mail, and then walks to the doorway of Mr. Able's office. Upon seeing Mr. Able lying face down at his desk, she becomes faint for a moment then falls to the floor.

First, she starts screaming profanities.

Then after a short pause, she continues at the top of her voice with "Ken is dead."

Contemplating her safe position, she thinks, "No one shot or hurt me. At least I have my car, my apartment, and my private funds. You're welcome for all those favors asshole, but now I need to find another egotistical sugar-daddy."

Abigail's screams were heard outside the office by a passerby. Someone from the hallway calls the police department. Before long, sirens are blaring, the red lights are flashing with San Francisco police officers running into the office looking for the bad guys. The crime has ended, the villain has departed, there are no clues, and most importantly, no one has seen what happened. A few minutes later, Detective Randall arrives. He clears the area and immediately posts an officer at the office door.

The investigation begins with Detective Charlie Randall in charge. With fifteen years of experience in homicide investigations, detective Randall pursues his standard plan of attack. He first interviews Abigail, who is surprisingly calm. Randall and Abigail discuss her working relationship with Mr. Able, her knowledge of the family, the number of years she has worked for Mr. Able, her financial position, her awareness of any known threats toward Mr. Able, and her personal relationship with the Mr. Able.

While the investigation continues in San Francisco, the stranger is returning to his daily life in Marin County. A few miles north of the murder scene, the Jaguar stops behind a small mini-mall. The driver wearing black gloves gets out and walks over to a garbage dumpster, throwing the black bag into the dumpster. He then returns to the Jaguar and drives slowly out of the parking lot. No one notices the Jaguar or the driver. Within a half-hour, this same Jaguar pulls into a parking structure in the city of San Rafael in Marin County north of San Francisco.

The driver parks his Jaguar in his private parking space. He walks to the elevator of a 12-story office building, rides the elevator to the top floor, and exits the elevator. Stepping from the elevator, he enters directly into his law firm's reception area.

He arrives at 1 p.m., greets several fellow employees, and has a short conversation with his secretary, Jennifer Hastings. He then enters his private office.

Who is this man that visited the city of San Francisco this morning to assassinate Mr. Kenneth Able? He is Arnold Pierce, a young man for his profession, but accomplished within his work. Mr. Pierce is confident yet not cocky. He is a trial attorney within a family-owned law firm with a history of over 100 years.

Within minutes of Mr. Pierce's arrival in the office, Jennifer brings him some fresh coffee and the daily mail. Arnold and Jennifer have a short conversation about his current day's schedule. They end their discussion after asking about each other's personal life. Jennifer leaves his office, and Arnold sits at his desk.

While sipping his coffee, he mutters to himself, "Another one completed."

Shortly after finishing his coffee, Arnold calls David Worth, a senior member of the firm. David is also heavily involved in the vigilante group that operates within the law firm.

They exchange hellos, and Arnold states, "Task completed, and no errors."

In return, David states, "Well done, Arnold, always pleased when you return safely."

Back in San Francisco, Detective Randall confiscates Mr.

HIDDEN IN FRONT OF YOU

Able's records and videos from within the office. Later in the week, Detective Randall will interrogate Abigail thoroughly about each client. Today, as a separate topic, Abigail is questioned about her relationship with Mr. Able and also about his wife, Mrs. Suzann Able. Abigail admits that the different room is where Mr. Able and she would spend many afternoons. She also admitted to having a continuous affair with Mr. Able since she started working for him. It appears to Detective Randall that there were only a few possible clients of interest. Mrs. Able might be potential persons of interest, but there is nothing conclusive.

Detective Randall soon removes Abigail as a suspect. Being close to all his business dealings, she had many opportunities for her financial gains. Abigail admitted taking advantage of every one of them. She had too much to lose with his death.

No dangerous suspects had surfaced his investigation. Throughout the queries, there was still something lurking in the shadows, something that almost comes out yet stays hidden. It might be more an intuitive feeling by Detective Randall. Randall believes this murder was a professional assassination. Information was sparse, connectivity to any thread was missing, and no one with a close association or proximity had a strong enough motive. Over the next few weeks, it will become evident that there is no new information. The case will be shelved and sent to the cold case files. Detective Randall will be disappointed with himself.

Back in Marin County, Mr. Pierce reviews the morning while relaxing on his office couch. He examines each segment of the task he just completed this morning. An assassination is never pleasant, but this one appeared to be necessary. Arnold was mainly checking for any errors, holes in his performance, or potential leaks. He then turns to prepare for an afternoon court session with his client Mrs. Harriet Powers and Judge Benjamin Rosko.

02 - LIFE-CHANGING EVENTS

This afternoon Mr. Pierce is representing Harriet Powers in the courtroom of Judge Benjamin Rosko. Mrs. Powers had a mild stroke the night before, and she is in the hospital for observation and tests. After an hour in court, the judge grants a postponement for two months. Still, a release by her physician must be submitted before the case can continue.

After returning from court, Arnold walks into his office, closes the door, and recounts his high school and college days with his love Alicia Holley Cummings. His loving memory of Alicia is sad and depressing for him. Occasionally, the memory of Alicia will haunt him. It reappears from time to time, yet his love for life and his profession helps him overcome. He has a typical type of relationship with his current girlfriend, Claire. She is also an attorney. He does not let his memory of Alicia ruin that relationship. However, the memory of his true love sometimes reminds him of the way it could have been. Arnold and Alicia met in the ninth grade and then dated throughout high school and college. They were inseparable and dedicated to one another. The 40.7-foot Beneteau sailboat named Alicia is named after Alicia Holley Cummings and is moored in the Tiburon marina.

On a return trip home after celebrating her birthday, Alicia was involved in a head-on collision on a two-lane road. Her girlfriend was driving their car. A gang-type cocaine addict was driving the other vehicle at approximately 55 miles per hour when he crossed the double yellow line and collided head-on with the other vehicle. Alicia was in the hospital for several weeks before she passed away, and her girlfriend died on the way to the hospital. A female passenger in Alicia's car was pronounced dead at the scene. The addict was rushed to the hospital with massive injuries and died within days.

After the accident, Arnold remained close to Alicia's parents. Whenever possible, he celebrated Alicia's birthday with them. Arnold was crippled emotionally by the loss. But, his interest in law, his performance in assisting the firm's vigilante group, and his sailing kept him busy. Staying so busy helped him diminish his feeling of depression over Alicia's death. Over time the level of severity decreased but was far from forgotten.

Arnold appears to be mild-mannered. But under that façade, lies a broiling personality and character known only to a few individuals. He is already wealthy, makes an excellent income, and derives a lot of bonus money from the firm's vigilante group. The basis for his personality is his love for his fellow man.

Arnold's parents died in an automobile accident caused by a drunk driver. Arnold was in another vehicle within view of the crash witnessed most of the collision. Arnold saw the DUI driver walk away and observed his parents being pronounced dead at the scene. Angered and almost driven mad, he wrestled with what he should do. Arnold studied the case, asked for aid from psychologists, asked for the church's guidance, and talked hours with his mentors David Worth and Frank Dulles. He could not get a handle on what was the best decision. The driver showed no remorse, was not convicted, and failed to provide any monetary support to the family. Arnold made up his mind on what he must do. Arnold decided to eliminate the DUI driver by creating the same type of accident. The DUI driver died in almost the same manner as Arnold's parents.

Arnold lives his motto in both his character and personality. His motto is:

"To save the good, you may need to engage in evil. Peace and fairness above all things. Thus, sometimes, blood must be spilled to obtain peace in equable and lasting terms."

HIDDEN IN FRONT OF YOU

This motto is in his wallet, displayed on an obscure shelf in his office, on his bedroom vanity, and on the base of steering platform aboard his 40.7 ft Beneteau sailboat. He has committed himself to live and die by this motto. His commitment to this objective overrides any personal desire or fear of death.

Arnold is seeing only one woman, Claire. She is also a lawyer in his firm. She is beautiful, cunning and a successful lawyer in her own right, but is not a good trial lawyer. They seem to work and play well together. As much as they enjoy each other's company, the relationship is not without some problem areas. The connection is nothing like the one Arnold had with Alicia. He is more energetic in his reaction to what is the proper way of solving an issue. Claire is more political and has a "cover my ass" attitude. To keep their relationship in place, both let many things about the other just slide by instead of addressing them. Occasionally though, an item does pop up that can't be corrected and is too meaningful to let slide. They both try to ignore the differences, but the relationship suffers.

Many years ago, when Arnold Pierce was a young boy, a bully was picking on a smaller and defenseless fellow student. Arnold discussed the situation with his father. Arnold's father supported the fact that if Arnold was bullied by him, then it was okay to kick ass. Arnold decided to extend that fatherly direction to any weaker person around him. Arnold found the bully and beat the hell out of him, settling the issue. Since then, he thought it was the right thing to do. His father supported Arnold in the principal's office after the incident. This type of thinking and behavior led the fellow students to appreciate Arnold's desire for fairness to all. From that point on, no one messed with Arnold's friends.

One of Arnold's many sources for his passion stemmed

from the memory of his favorite sixth-grade teacher Mrs. Olivia Stiles. She was one of those women with so much love for each of her students. The act of giving unparalleled sweetness and compassion is seldom found in life. While shopping for groceries one day, Olivia was attacked in the store's parking lot by three gang members. They held her at knifepoint, beat her, and raped her. Before leaving her, they disfigured her with knife wounds over her entire body. Arnold loved this woman as he would his mother. The guilt he felt was that he never had the chance to help her or tell her how loving she was. Olivia recovered from her attack but never returned to teaching. For years Arnold tried to find her but failed in his attempt until after he started working at the firm.

With the newly found capabilities within the firm, Arnold finally found her. She was living in Trinidad on the California Coast, about 275 miles north of San Francisco. One weekend Arnold and Claire drove to the area near Trinidad for a visit. Olivia's husband was retired by then, and Olivia had become a "stay at home" wife since the attack. They had a small house with acreage and a beautiful ocean view.

Olivia had scars over her chest, arms, face, and legs still visible to the naked eye after all these years. She had raised three beautiful children, currently had two family dogs, a few cats, and a botanical garden surrounding her home. One of the dogs was a female-friendly type, and the other was a male trained for the protection of Olivia. The male dog has bonded to Olivia alone. He never left her side.

Olivia was happy with her life and was so pleased to see one of her favorite students again. Arnold explained to her that he felt guilty for not helping her in her hour of need.

He said, "I was too young to help, but you were such a lovely teacher. I felt the need to help you. Also, I never got

HIDDEN IN FRONT OF YOU

the chance to tell you how much all of us appreciated you in your class."

Olivia blushed for a moment because of the beautiful remarks. She then hugged Arnold for a couple of minutes, crying in happiness. Soon they all said their goodbyes, and Arnold and Claire started back toward Marin County.

Arnold said to Claire, "Certainly worth the trip. I am going to return."

After the visit with Olivia, Arnold and Claire spent a relaxing day at his home. He cooked an excellent meal consisting of a filet mignon, mashed white potatoes with garlic, buttery broiled young carrots, a Caesar salad, and a classic Pinot Noir. The meal ended with Crepe Suzettes and a glass of imported French port wine. Claire found a work-related reason to leave, and Arnold was disappointed, but this behavior had frequently been happening.

03 - ARNOLD AND THE LAW FIRM

Arnold Pierce joined the law firm as an attorney shortly after passing the BAR exam and has worked for the firm for over ten years. He worked as an attorney, as a research paralegal, and has performed investigation procedures as a private investigator. Both his father and Frank Dulles would include him during casework and trials. His strong ethics, his steady work habits, his quest for justice, and his strengths earned him respect from his peers early on.

Arnold Pierce is the last surviving member of the Pierce family, so he owns the entire law firm. Because he is still a relatively junior attorney, the firm is currently managed by more senior professionals, including David Worth and Frank Dulles. He was delighted to join the firm's "charitable" group because of their desire for fairness and compassion paralleled his beliefs. Supporting a group with the same aspirations motivated him to excel. He has offered the group his maximum support from that day onward.

Mr. Pierce's first case was an investigation that included the research of holdings, interviews with neighbors, and stakeouts. A married couple had been holding a small housing community hostage by stating an obscure regulation that was not valid. They had driven property values down, generated incorrect information about the people within the community, and attempted to take over by buying up properties from the disillusioned owners. A class-action lawsuit was issued in the name of the property owners and won against the parties rendering the married couple ineffective. The property values returned to normal, and peace was restored. The troublesome married couple sold and moved on to another residence outside the community.

His second case was in defense of a wrongly charged client, Mr. Joseph Spooner, accused of the murder of a family member, Sarah Pfaff. Mr. Spooner has a temper and personality that would make him a person of interest in a murder case. When attacked, Mr. Spooner would strike out mostly because of fear. His actions otherwise were simple, generous, and he had exhibited a great deal of compassion for Sarah. Another family member, Mrs. Hillary Bland, could not wait for the natural death of Sarah Pfaff, who had monies, and Mrs. Bland wanted that money now. She tried to make it look as Mr. Spooner had murdered Sarah Pfaff. The facts showed that he had been assisting the older woman in her daily care for years. Sarah had always stated her pleasure in having Mr. Spooner around, and he had access to the lady's home regularly without any problems indicated by Mrs. Pfaff. Mr. Spooner's temper had been a problem and helped place him at risk.

After discussions with other family members, Arnold Pierce found that Mrs. Bland was far from honest. Through a few stakeouts and some examining of Mrs. Pfaff's credit card records, Arnold located some of Sarah's missing artifacts in different local pawnshops. He discovered that Mrs. Bland was always the recipient of the pawnshop funds. The police found incriminating fingerprints in Sarah Pfaff's home, and Hillary Bland had some of Sarah's personal items in her possession.

Mr. Spooner had been taking care of Mrs. Pfaff for a long time. All the known problems appeared after Mrs. Bland came onto the scene. It was proven that Hillary Bland had murdered Sarah Pfaff. As a result of Arnold's work, the District Attorney's Office dropped all charges against Mr. Spooner.

Within a week of closing the Spooner case, Arnold is driving his Jaguar one morning. Coming onto the freeway, Highway 101 South, from Tiburon, he drives up alongside a Corvette driven by a pretty woman. Arnold's Jaguar is built for speed and road racing. The two cars jockey for position, one, then the other, taking the lead as they both change lanes and deal with the traffic. Soon they are both in the clear, and they outright race each other. They are going about 135 mph, and Arnold's Jaguar pulls away. With traffic cruising about 65 to 70 mph, they catch the next grouping of cars quickly. As they pass by Frank Lloyd Wright's famous building on the left, they both wave and smile. Down the hill and around a slight bend in the road, they are running alongside each other. As Arnold pulls off the freeway onto Main Street in San Rafael, the woman blows him a goodbye kiss. She seemed to be there, but why? Arnold has no answer. She seemed too aggressive and arrogant, only to be just there. But this young man's ego has undoubtedly been boosted a peg or two.

Feeling quite right about the day, Arnold strolls into work, expecting the day to continue the way it has started.

04 - SAMMY

Jennifer calls on the intercom and says, "Arnold, Sammy is on the line, do you wish to take his call?"

Arnold says, "Thank you, Jennifer. Yes, I will take the call."

She replies, "Line one."

Arnold switches to line one and says, "Sammy, how are things going? Are you close? Maybe we could have lunch or dinner?"

Sammy says, "Arnold, I have some things to discuss with you. I want to share some of the recent events in my life. Some family things have changed, my schooling is going well, had some personal problems, and there is a girl in my life now."

Arnold says, "A girl! Now that is dangerous. Are your hormones flaming? Family problems we can discuss. Shall I pick you up or what?"

Sammy replies, "Could we visit with each other this coming weekend? I could meet you at the bakery on Powell between Sutter and Post on Friday afternoon?"

Arnold says, "Sammy, I will be there a little after 4 p.m. Good to hear from you. Bye!"

Sammy, Samuel Rodney Perkins, is a twenty-year-old that Arnold met one day. Arnold caught Sammy, trying to break into his Jaguar at the age of sixteen. Caught in the act, Sammy pulled a knife and threatened Arnold. Arnold just laughed at him and asked, "Why the knife."

Sammy launched an attack. Arnold twisted Sammy's hand and bent it backward until Sammy dropped the weapon. Then Arnold proceeded to beat the crap out the kid.

After being on the ground for a few minutes, Sammy looks up at Arnold and asks, "Why so rough, asshole? You almost broke my arm, and now it hurts like hell."

Arnold responds, "I caught you trying to get into my car.

You came at me with a weapon. You are lucky I didn't kill you, you little shit. Are you sure you want to confront me?"

Sammy says quietly, "Mister, who are you. You're one tough guy. I don't want to try to fight you again."

Arnold laughs, and says, "Good since your fighting isn't worth a hoot. You are boring. Now that you've had a chance to recover, let's have a bite to eat and chat."

Arnold can tell that this kid is in trouble, and maybe, just maybe, Arnold can make a change in his miserable existence. Helping him is indeed worth a try.

Sammy answers, "Okay, let's walk!"

As soon as they start walking together, Sammy breaks away and begins to run. Arnold throws his briefcase into his legs and brings Sammy down. Within seconds Arnold is on top of him hitting and slapping his face and chest. Arnold lets him get up but then dropkicks him with a shot into his testicles. The kid falls back to the ground and begins screaming in pain.

Arnold stats firmly, "Kid, when you decide to behave and follow my orders, things will become much easier for you."

Arnold then helps Sammy up, and they walk to the nearest café. Once inside, Arnold tells Sammy to sit at the back table and stay still.

Arnold opens the conversation, "First, what is your name?"

Sammy answers, "Sammy."

Arnold, with a louder voice, says, "Your entire name, lil shitface, and add your address. I do not like asking questions twice."

Sammy responds, "Samuel Rodney Perkins. I am sixteen years old, a school dropout. I have a drunk for a father, no mother, no siblings, a dog, and I have an attitude toward all you white boys. My address is wherever you find me."

Arnold responds, "First, I am not a white boy, and I won't

HIDDEN IN FRONT OF YOU

call you nigger. There shall be respect between us, or I will wipe the floor with you and hang you out to dry. Samuel, do you understand my statement?"

Sammy replies, "You are heavy, man. What can I do?"

Arnold says, "Young man, finish your food, relax, stay here and wait for me. I have some phone calls to make. If you are still here when I return, we might have a path that will be worth your interest."

Arnold steps away from the table and makes a phone call from a public phone booth.

He calls David Worth, "Hello, Arnold, this is David."

Arnold speaks, "Do we have some chores that are assignable to a little-retched kid?"

David responds, "Are you picking up lost souls again. You must have a heart of gold, sir. Damn you for always putting me into this position. Yes, we can always find some delivery, stakeouts, and some inside work for a young person. I do assume that this is a young one in trouble like the last kid. By the way, the last kid is getting ready to graduate from college. His family problems are solved, and he has a very nice girlfriend. You must be proud."

Arnold says, "Yes, I am extremely pleased with the outcome. Remember, if it were not for you in these matters, none of them would be succeeding as they are today. I will discuss the options with him, give him your phone number and turn him over to you for now. Thank you for your support, Mr. Worth. Good evening."

Arnold walks to the rear of the café, and Samuel is not there. He thinks there goes the chance that I offered him. Samuel comes walking out of the men's room.

He sits down and waits for Arnold to speak.

Arnold says, "I will be available for chatting and conferences. I am going to turn you over to my mentor Mr. David Worth." He has the resources and financing to help you. Then you will be given funds and guidance for your education."

Sammy says, "This is hard to believe. Why would you help me?"

Arnold replies, "A part of my life's motto is: Peace and fairness above all things. You will learn the other parts as soon as you earn them."

Arnold hands Sammy a piece of paper with David's name, Arnold's name, and their phone numbers.

He says, "Take this one to the bank, Sammy. I hope to hear from you."

Arnold leaves it to Sammy. If he fails to take up the offer, then so be it.

Arnold was quite pleased. He is a member of a sophisticated charity group. This group attempts to reach out to a needy person on occasion. This psychological match satisfies Arnold's desire. Mr. Pierce has his legal profession and personal life. He attends court actions, interviews clients, researches case law along with his paralegals, also has a fun night or two with Claire. Some weekends he spends on the San Francisco Bay on his sailboat, a 40.7 ft. Beneteau beauty named Alicia berthed at the Tiburon marina. On many occasions, Claire joins him on the boat for recreational sailing.

05 - RACING ALICIA

Arnold has an obsession with sailing. The Alicia has all the comforts of home, fully stocked with equipment for recreational sailing and racing, kitchen utensils, food, a fully stocked bar, and an automatic steering system for those casual nights on the bay. While sailing the bay, he sometimes takes note of the sailboat races within the bay itself. On occasion, Arnold calls for a crew by enlisting local bay area sailing people who are at least an expert, and some are professional racing sailors. He will often track the racing boats to study their maneuvering within the various tides and winds. Especially interesting to Arnold is how efficient they are in using the San Francisco Bay's winds. When rounding a buoy, the fastest path may be the longer path. Sometimes by swinging wide and taking advantage of the winds, a good sailor gets there first. During Arnold's night sailing, he enjoys the beauty of the Golden Gate Bridge, the Bay Bridge, and the ferry boats that are still running on the bay waters. They illustrate the picturesque northern portion of San Francisco Bay and the Sacramento River.

Arnold decides to put together a crew for the early December race out of the Richmond Yacht Club. He is known for his ownership of a beautiful boat but not recognized as an experienced sailor. The competition spans most of the San Francisco Bay from just north of Oakland-San Francisco Bay Bridge to Angel Island, using many of the shipping buoys along the way. Arnold has watched many a race, and he has run alongside a group of racing boats. He has ridden aboard two flying vessels during a race, but he has never actually raced before. His Beneteau 40.7 one of the better racing hulls. Arnold decides to enter his sailboat in the fall race.

The next morning as Arnold rises for the day, his thoughts are on playing sailor. No shower is needed, a healthy breakfast, and the usual coffee to start the day. He has contacted the crew. They are always happy to participate. Many of the crew members do not own a boat of this size and the speed of Alicia. It is a compliment to be invited.

He drives to the Tiburon marina and parks the Jaguar next to the Alicia. Most of the parking spaces are empty at this time of the morning. After stowing his gear, he starts the motor and checks all the gauges. He removes the sail covers then unties the mooring lines. Alicia moves gracefully into open waters.

Arnold's preferred racing crew list.

Bow: A feisty local woman named Raquel from the Richmond Yacht Club. Her credentials span the last 15 years of sailing. She is credited with many a win locally and has the talent required for this rigorous position. Her strength and willingness to stay aggressive throughout the race is a definite plus for her.

Mast: Cynthia, a lady from Marin County, owner of a San Francisco bar and an experienced mast sailor. In recent years she has been sailing for at least 14 days each month, is skilled and willing to go at any time.

Jib Trimmers: Two professional sailors from New Zealand, Paul, and Tim Coughey. Their resumes speak for them. The list of references seems endless, and their experiences are global.

Pit (Cockpit): Steve Palmer, is an experienced sailor from the Richmond Yacht Club.

Main Trimmer: Mathew, a paralegal working in San Francisco. He began in Oakland's Lake Merritt, from racing snipes at the age of 12, to racing 30 footers at 25, to becoming a pro sailor at 45. Mathew's life outside the legal firm's office is his sailing.

Helmsman: Arnold offered himself. It's the privilege of ownership.

HIDDEN IN FRONT OF YOU

Tactician (Navigator): Paul Harrison, a pro sailor with decades of experience. Paul is an expert in understanding the tides in San Francisco Bay. Still, more importantly, he has a creative interpretation of using the bay winds to his advantage. In many a race, Paul's boats will travel further and get to the finish line sooner than the others. He has a mastery in the use of the winds.

It is 5:30 a.m., and the Sunday morning winds have not yet picked up. The Golden Gate has the usual morning fog. The sun is just peeking over the east bay hills.

Arnold sets Alicia out for the Richmond Yacht Club. The crew should arrive by 9 a.m. Moving slowly across the bay waters, Arnold begins to reminisce about his love, Alicia. On a day like this, she would always be with him. Arnold can picture her sitting next to him with that beautiful smile, the shape of her image, and her calmness, plus that feeling of belonging together. He does not cry, but he does tear with these thoughts.

He slips behind the breakwater as he passes Angel Island and approaches the inlet just west of the yacht club. He pulls Alicia up to the external public dock and moors the boat. Before his crew arrives, Arnold starts considering the aspects of the upcoming race and who are the different teams in the competition.

Raquel arrives with her usual sparkly enthusiasm. She stows her equipment and sits with Arnold drinking some coffee. Soon most of the crew come, and they each stow their gear and grab some of the coffee that Arnold has brought along. As the rest of the team arrives, some of the other teammates are checking the boat's equipment and especially their area of responsibility.

With an hour to spare before the race, Arnold suggests that they go out and practice a couple of maneuvers. They leave the yacht club and venture out into open waters. The routine procedures go well; it seems that they are all on the mark today.

Within the hour, all seven boats are on the starting line. Every member of the crew is tense. They keep winding around and around in preparation for the start missing each other sometimes by only inches.

When the race starts, Arnold yells to the team, "Let's go, guys."

Arnold aimed for the pin end of the start line with 30 seconds to power up. They pulled the jib in tight and went for broke. These maneuvers put Alicia on starboard with all the rest of the fleet above Alicia. The crew's tacks were perfect as the crew members cut and tightened the jib. As Alicia headed for the first mark, she was sailing faster with a higher point than any other boat. The tactician kept an eye on the other competitors. Wind shifts, puffs, and tide lines were called from the bow by Raquel.

By the time Alicia made the first mark, they had clear air and were about ten boat lengths in front. The mast and pit folks hoisted the spinnaker sail as the bow person helped it out of the hatch as the boat did a standard bear away set. The Beneteau has three jibs, perfect every time with the dip pole. The bow and mast person was excellent with every move. This run was long and was when the competition was supposed to happen, except the Alicia was so far out in front that there was no one to play with. There was no one to duel with.

Alicia is heading toward the last mark. The jib went up on starboard. The crew was preparing to douse the kite to leeward. With the bow people ready, the tactician waited until the last second. He cautioned Arnold to expect the call before he turned the boat and yelled for a takedown. The pit person controlled the halyard. The mast and spinnaker persons pulled, and Raquel, the bow person, gathered the

HIDDEN IN FRONT OF YOU

spinnaker quickly. With the douse and the pole under control, Arnold spun the boat 2 feet from the mark and headed north to the weather and the finish.

As they were about halfway to the finish, they all looked back. Each team member was looking back to watch the knot of boats doing the rounding they just mastered. Two of the yachts collided, forcing the other one to run into the mark. These three boats now must do a penalty spin before crossing the finish. Arnold was not only comfortable with the win; he knew that the group's sailing was on fire this day.

After the race was over and the Alicia was back at the yacht club, they all congratulated each other on today's win. They also tried to make an extra effort to be humble to the competition. As a crew, they were used to winning. They just didn't enjoy rubbing it in any further.

Alicia's crew was given the trophy. The teams mingled while having a celebration lunch. Arnold stayed through the celebration. Afterward, he took Alicia toward the San Francisco piers, then under the Golden Gate and home to Tiburon. This was a good day with his friends, a day away from the worries. Today's sailing is his ideal environment. It has given him a day of relief.

06 - PROBLEMS AT THE LAW FIRM

Arnold notices new behavioral differences within the firm's charitable group. Some of these differences seem to pose a danger to the group's purpose, cohesiveness, and harmony. Arnold continues to seek an answer to this question. He studies the relationship he has with each of his more senior people in the group and keeps mental notes of the method of operation presented by each. Currently, there is no visible evidence of a rift between subgroups or individuals within the set of senior members. Arnold has gone so far as to study personality traits and personality disorders to understand the information he is gathering. As the study progresses, he is gaining a complete understanding of the senior members he is dealing with and can sometimes predict their opinions and even their actions.

Arnold calls David Worth, saying, "I am noticing some significant discourse within the office."

David replies, "Someone from the outside firm while thinking Frank was the owner, attempted to purchase the law firm. Frank Dulles is no longer the man you knew. He told them to go to hell. George Williams has taken over some of his duties because Frank can't make forward decisions and does not get along with anyone. Frank's wife, Lynn, has given us his last will and instructions of what to in case of their deaths. We are losing support staff to quitting, loss of life, and disappearance. Williams brought false charges against Rita. She is now in prison. Harriet, one of our attorneys, left due to threats for her trying to help Rita. We have a scary problem that seems to have developed overnight."

As he passes Jennifer's desk, she says, "Excuse me, Mr. Pierce, Mr. Dulles, has returned from his medical leave, and he wishes to meet with you today. He has you scheduled for 11 a.m. Can you make that time, sir?"

HIDDEN IN FRONT OF YOU

Arnold says, "I will make it if I must."

Jennifer says, "Mrs. Dulles says that Frank's neurological damage is irreversible."

Arnold says, "How sad, Jennifer, I'll see him right away."

He gathers his thoughts and then walks over to meet with Mr. Dulles, who became the CEO when Arnold's parents were killed. Arnold is the owner of the law firm, and Frank Dulles has been one of Arnold's mentors over the years.

Arnold says, "Welcome back, Mr. Dulles. I hope you are recovering well."

Frank Dulles replies, "The headaches are grueling, the neck pain is getting less, and the back may get better, but I am finding it hard to be patient. You are one of the attorneys that I needed to see.

We have, in the past, been very generous with picking up problem strays. There is no money in it, and I am to look at our bottom line only. Some of the cases that we have been doing for free or almost free. This needs to stop."

Arnold says, "But that was what you trained me to do when I started here. The group is for helping the under-protected. I seldom charge the group for my participation."

Frank says, "This is not a discussion of ethics, young man. It is a matter of profits."

Arnold interrupts, "So the first order of business is no longer a group to help people but a group looking for maximum profit? I am not sure that I have the same amount of interest in making you wealthy."

Frank replies, "I am the CEO here. I must make the calls. You do great work in court, you are one of the best with your clients, and I hope you continue here at the firm."

The fact that Arnold owns the firm seems to be lost somewhere in the discussion.

Arnold responds, "Frank, you are currently the CEO. I am only a group member, but I do own this law firm. I cannot say I agree with you. Being the owner and watching your change in behavior since the accident, I must request that you apply for your retirement immediately. Make it effective this coming Friday. I will have the paperwork ready for your signature on Jennifer's desk. We need to part before I say something I will regret. Good day to you, sir."

David Worth sees Arnold leaving Frank's office, and ushers Arnold inside David's office.

Angrily Arnold says, "The son of a bitch, Frank Dulles, just told me to stop helping people. What the hell happened to the man? Where is our legacy headed? If this continues, the charity group will be no more. Profits-profits-profits are all the bastard understands. I just washed him out. I requested his retirement to become effective this Friday."

David says, "I have been trying to deal with these changes for months. I have not been having any luck. We still have most of the older members on our side."

Arnold says, "I have been noticing the discontent recently. Frank seems to be part of it. I will be leaving early today after I handle a few phone calls. Maybe a little sailing on Alicia will relieve my frustration."

Harriet Williams calls Arnold and says, "After working with you for years, I feel I can trust you. You need my data on the Rita case, so I am sending you a copy of all my work on the case. Mr. Love and his family were threatened by McCarthy. I never worked with him, but my ex-husband George did. I suggest that you investigate the entire matter. Bye, for now, sweet man."

Arnold calls his mechanic, who answers, "Nick here."

Arnold says, "I need a favor."

Nick says, "I am one step ahead of you. I needed a part for a car just like the one your Frank Dulles had his accident in. I went to a wrecking yard and verified, the car to be Mr. Dulles's. I inspected the car. No one has told me why the accident happened. Do you know why and how the accident happened?"

Arnold says, "No, sir, I don't."

Nick says, "I inspected every part of that car. Excluding the damaged parts from the accident itself, there was some foul play. The left front brake line had been tampered with by something like a file to remove part of the front brake line, weakening the line. It burst when Mr. Dulles applied the brakes hard enough and made Mr. Dulles lose his brakes in an emergency. I am sorry to deliver this bad news because I know you were close to him, but you needed to know."

Arnold says, "Thank you, my friend. I do appreciate your efforts. Before we end this discussion, I have a few favors to ask. Both my parents were killed by a broadside collision. I want a ¾ inch steel plate installed in the driver and passenger areas, and on the firewall in each of my newer Jaguars. And, I want to increase the air intake in each of them, especially in the manifold."

Nick says I'll have that ready for the next Jaguar, and I just happen to have a new red Jaguar in stock

Arriving in San Rafael about 9:30 a.m. Arnold steps off the elevator on the twelfth floor. He stops by Matilda's desk.

Matilda says, "Mr. Pierce, you have a visitor in your office. He has been here since 8 a.m."

Arnold walks a little faster to Jennifer's desk.

She raises her head, saying, "You have a visitor waiting for you in your office."

Arnolds steps into his office. He is pleasantly surprised.

He says, "Colonel Matt Owens, it is wonderful to see you."

Matt doesn't waste time with pleasantries and says, "Young man, you are working in the blind. You see Frank Dulles misbehaving, and you demand an immediate retirement. You feel you have solved the problem. Frank's auto accident was no accident, it was attempted murder. Your office is in disarray. You do not know what is making your employees leave, end up in prison, disappear, having deadly mishaps, or just quit. Most likely, you have never been faced with this type of deception. You are in the first phase of a potentially violent takeover of your firm by a notorious group headed by a man named Kevin McCarthy."

"We must set up a system of protection for you, such that we can help protect you and win the war that is starting. At the same time, we must eliminate some of McCarthy's operators. My objective is to have access to everyone that knows where you are, and I will have someone near you. To communicate, we must use military radios or a secure telephone via Jennifer."

"McCarthy's MO is what is driving this entire war. He finds a city or county with a physical project that has politically selected attorneys. Then, he negotiates a contract that is full of holes while failing to have the required restrictions. He overcharges for work performed, and he fails to complete the work required. San Francisco is the eighth city he has done this to. Your law firm looks like it has a vigilante group that is not under any legal controls. If the owner or owners won't sell, he kills them and buys the company for pennies. He thought Frank was the owner. The list of cities with McCarthy controlled projects includes St Louis, Phoenix, Reno, San Diego, Portland, and Seattle. As he moves on, he dissolves the company and starts a new one. He employs low-income operatives to keep an eye on you. They are everywhere. If they are not willing to work for him, he threatens them, or he often kills them. Most operatives are afraid of what he will do to them."

Matt starts talking again, "You shall address me as Matt, with no last name. I do not want to be found. There will be no address or telephone number to talk to me. Here is the number to leave messages. You will always use a prearranged alias of Finion when leaving a message. Normal is #1, information #2 and an emergency is #3. I will call you back on the telephone you are calling from with a place and time to meet. You will use radio communications to speak with my operatives, who will be observing you on a 24/7 basis. You may ask why I am so cautious? Here are a few of the reasons. I retired after only 25 years. I had planned to stay until thirty. Still, since I will not kill children, I retired earlier. My objective is to take out the army of terrorists, namely one called the McCarthy Group. I have taken on some private contracts since I retired."

"The McCarthy Group wants to buy your firm. They believe you have a vigilante group that is free from police actions. They called Mr. Dulles to make an offer, thinking he was the owner. Frank told them to go to hell. McCarthy's MO is if you refuse to sell, they will kill you and whoever is nearby. McCarthy draws operatives from low educated and immoral groups."

Matt continues, "This is how we can work together. Along with that, I will provide you with personal protective assistance. You have a paralegal, Mr. Love, who rents an apartment from your friend, Al Frosini. Mr. Love has been threatened by McCarthy, and Love is a gold mine of information. Gather his info, and you will be able to use it to get Rita Kennedy out of prison. Your old classmate, Ron Burke, could be quite helpful in this endeavor. He is aggressive and not part of this office."

"That is the proper use of our hierarchy. If the authorities can identify me, they will try to arrest me. That shall not happen. I do not take out children, innocent women, or cops."

"From my sources, you have been having trouble with the McCarthy Group for a while. I took out a few of their contractors in several of their other companies. I warned them that if I would need to continue, there is a possibility that I would take them all out. Obviously, they do not listen. Because Frank Dulles was the CEO, they assumed he was the owner of the firm. When he wouldn't even discuss their offer, they simply attempted to kill him."

"It takes time to get it done without involving the police, but it is quicker and more efficient. If necessary, I may ask you to take some out yourself. I consider you my friend and an outstanding student in deadly martial arts. I have been watching you for quite a while."

"You have a McCarthy mole in your firm; his name is George Williams. He has installed listening devices in all the offices. I removed the ones in this office. I believe George may have been feeding information about Mr. Dulles and may have been working with McCarthy to set up Dulles for his accident. Williams is manipulating the firm's financial statements for McCarthy's benefit, and he thinks McCarthy will retain him as CEO. Mr. Williams is a fool."

"I know a good man you need to hire. His name is Julien Spence. He has been involved in many of my operations. He is an analyst, and I am an operator, so we never crossed paths. Spence is a good man to have on your team. Julien is a very hard worker, has the technical capabilities that you need, and he can be counted upon. Here is his resume, read it. Julien will be here at 3 p.m. I saw some pastries and more coffee by Jennifer's desk. I need to take a break."

Matt returns, saying, "You have become the prime target for McCarthy. First, all of this is at your expense. I don't have the funds to have you shadowed 24/7. We can draw in many of McCarthy's operatives by using you as bait. My group needs a twenty-five-foot boat available for trips to the Farallon Islands. That is where we will take the bodies. The best place to drop the bodies is at the edge of the fault shelf,

HIDDEN IN FRONT OF YOU

where a depth of 1500 feet drops past 5000 feet. I can't afford to maintain the boat and keep it ready on a 24/7 basis. In the past, you have used Josey to help you with your questionable charitable enforcement activities. He is reliable, trustworthy, and very loyal to you. I know he is your all-around dedicated workhorse. You are fortunate to have him. Put him in charge of the boat. I know we can both count on Josey."

"Another thing, your current dwelling is too open and easily attacked. I have someone else you need to hire as a contractor. His name is Sid Johnson. He is a cosmetology specialist, he is dependable, trustworthy, and a homosexual. He has a successful business and has many other qualities to offer. He has a retail shop and salon on Market Street and a commercial unit in the Mission District close to South San Francisco. He also has a working space within his home located on Filbert Street, two blocks from the Army Presidio. The customer traffic is too heavy downtown, and the commercial unit handles mostly mail orders. Neither of his business sites is suitable for you to come and go in stealth. The home next to his house is ideal, and it is for sale. Spence can install some monitoring gear and bulletproof windows. It has another big plus. You will not need to commute across the Golden Gate to the courthouse in San Francisco. Here's Sid's business card. Give him a call."

With no goodbye pleasantries, Matt gets up and abruptly leaves the office.

As instructed, Arnold places a call to Mr. Johnson, who answers, "Sid Johnson here. How can I help you?"

Arnold replies, "My name is Arnold Pierce, and I was instructed to give you a call."

Sid interrupts him and says, "I have been expecting your call. I suggest we meet at my home in the next few hours. We can discuss a business arrangement, and I can also show you the property next door. I have a set of keys. What time would be convenient for you?"

Arnold responds, "I will be on your doorstep at 11:30 p.m."

During their initial meeting, Arnold says, "Sid, I have a few things to straighten out before we even get started."

Sid pauses then replies, "Yes, Mr. Pierce, what are your concerns?"

Arnold says, "I am a straight heterosexual, I have no patience for a man's sexual activity concerning me. For us to work together, we must agree to respect each other's preferred position."

Sid replies, "Absolutely, total respect will be the name of the game."

Arnold says, "I believe it best that while we are working together that the area is completely free of other people. Meaning both within the same room and any adjoining areas within your house."

Sid says, "If that is what you want, other people will be excluded from my home and asked to stay away during our working sessions. One additional item, I have a spare parking place under the house that you may use. The first time you arrive, I will point it out and give you the key to the garage."

Arnold replies, "Thank you for your understanding and your cooperation. I will have the conversation when I move in next door."

HIDDEN IN FRONT OF YOU

07 - NEW HIRE WITH A PROBLEM

In Arnold's mind, after reading his resume, he thinks hiring Julien Spence should be automatic. With the recent problems and those that have not been identified, Arnold wants to start a healing process. The issues may be personal, software, lack of training, or the possibility of a mole. He is considering the mole, as the most probable entity. It appears that an outside entity is attempting to make an influence on the firm.

Julien Spence is a retired CIA contractor and an intelligence analyst. His position in the firm will be to use his analytical skills to help Arnold make decisions. His technical skills will be used to protect the staff and manage the firm's network of computers. He also has experience and expertise in operations and communications. Arnold feels that Spence could be a backup staff member to the troubled accounting department, which Williams is currently managing so poorly.

Mr. Spence is a software and hardware guru. He understands the system's physical properties, the actual and potential limitations throughout the firm's computer network. He has the rare ability to develop software in binary or Assembler, and this makes his value unchallengeable. With this capability, Spence can circumvent file protection, manipulate both hardware and high-level software protections, and communicate inward into the system or outward without detection.

It is 3 p.m. Jennifer shows Julien into Arnold's office. They each get fresh coffee and shake hands. Julien Spence is honored to be asked to become part of the staff. He feels that being retired is too dull for his liking, along with his daughter's new problem. Along with the assets of an individual, you inherit their problems. After fulfilling the HR paperwork, Julien is assigned an office and is officially hired. Julien recognizes Arnold's strong points and his honesty.

Julien is also aware of the vigilante element of the firm. He feels that he has a lot to offer yet brings along a problem that he is unable to resolve himself. Arnold may be able to assist him.

As Julien is preparing to leave for the day, Arnold asks Julien, "Do you have any questions, or is there anything else I can do for you?"

Julien states, "Arnold, I have a lot to offer, even more than I can say at his moment. I am pleased to join your firm, but, along with that, I have brought along a problem. If I do what I need to do to fix it, I will be the first to be interrogated. Being the father, I would be the most likely person of interest. The problem is that my daughter's husband was killed by a drunk driver, and the man obtained a lawyer who found holes in the police investigation. My daughter is left with a child to support, no income, and a need to finish school. I have failed to get the man's attention, and he continues to ignore our requests for compensation or to take responsibility."

Arnold replies, "My parents were killed by a drunk driver, and my girlfriend, Alicia, the love of my life, was killed in a head-on collision by a junkie. I do understand your pain. Sir, I am delighted to be able to assist you. Write up a complete description. List names, places, people, and get me the trial records along with the traffic investigation documents."

Julien Spence replies, "I already have the trial records and the investigation reports ready. My daughter will make herself available any day you have the time to meet. Thank you, Mr. Pierce, for your interest and willingness to help."

Julien leaves Arnold's office and heads off to the elevators.

After Julien Spence leaves, Arnold places a call to Josey and tells him that he has a little fun contract for him. First, Josey is to complete a preliminary investigation of Mr. Wise,

HIDDEN IN FRONT OF YOU

the DUI driver, his habits, house, house alarm, dogs, and any other information of value. He informs Josey that Jennifer will make copies of all the current data we have on Mr. Wise. Jennifer's package will be available by noon tomorrow. If Josey proceeds in his usual manner, the operation should happen within a week. At this point, Arnold's plan is to enter Mr. Wise's home after he goes to sleep and explain to him in an antagonistic manner, what he needs to do, and why. When Arnold sets his mind to correcting a severe wrong, like this one, things may get rough.

The next morning when Arnold arrives, all the information from Spence was sitting on Jennifer's desk. After reviewing the data again, Arnold asks Jennifer to request Mr. Spence's presence in his office for a discussion. Ten minutes later, Julien Spence arrives and is ushered into Arnold's office.

Arnold says, "Welcome back. I read through the data you presented. If we attack through the court, the weakness lies in the traffic cop's poorly written accident report. The driver, Mr. Richard Wise, lives in an expensive home within the Twin Peaks residential community. That means he could easily pay retribution. I knew this person through some legal dealings many years ago. He is vulgar, dishonest, stubborn, and certainly uncooperative. His wife divorced him on the grounds of cruelty. His children pushed him out of their lives, and he is not liked by his coworkers. I suggest that we pay this man a visit to inform him of his responsibility. Since you were a CIA operative, I feel it is okay to tell you this. To keep you safe concerning questions asked, lie detector tests, or court action, I should say no more."

Julien says, "I do understand. Can you give me some status along the way?"

Arnold replies, "No. There will be no need. We will be successful, and your daughter will get a call from Mr. Wise or his attorney first thing the following morning."

After a brief silence, Arnold says, "Thank you for acting so completely and quickly with the information. We will get on this immediately. We have enough information to continue. Presently there is no reason to bother your daughter. Do have a nice day, Mr. Spence. I have a specific job for you to do asap. I want you to install a movement monitoring system on my parking place in the building's garage."

Julien Spence is happy and stunned at what he was told. He stands, shakes Arnold's hand, and walks to his office.

A few days later, close to midnight, Arnold received a phone call at home.

He answered the phone saying, "This is Arnold, who's calling?"

The caller replied, "It's Josey. I have canvassed the property, the alarm is easily turned off, and I have been inside twice. There are three 9mm pistols in the house; one at his bedside, one in his dresser, and the last one in the kitchen drawer. There is no inside pet, but there is a guard dog outside. The dog loves hamburgers. I think we are ready to go. Give me a date and time when we can proceed."

Arnold replies, "Josey, I will bring my 22-target pistol. I presume you will be armed. We will dress in black with pullover hoods, wear gloves at all times, and finish within ten minutes. Okay?"

Josey answers, "How about we do it this Thursday night? We can meet at our regular location at about midnight."

Arnold says, "Sounds great, Josey. I'll bring a van, and we can review our procedures on the way. See you there. Thank you."

HIDDEN IN FRONT OF YOU

08 - ATTACK BY A BMW

Arnold now has a free day during the week, so he asks Jennifer to call Lynn Dulles to make an appointment. He wants to drop by for a visit rather than talking on the phone.

As Arnold is leaving the office, he starts questioning everything in sight. The main office space seems clear, with only staff members visible. When he leaves the garage, Arnold looks at all the cars parked on the street. All seems safe, so he proceeds toward home in his Jaguar. Arnold notices a BMW pacing him. He uses an overpass to change his direction from south to north on Highway 101. There are two occupants in the car. Arnold removes his 44-caliber Magnum pistol from the console and places the gun under his right leg as he drives north on Highway 101.

Without giving notice, he drives off the freeway, turns right onto an overpass sending him to the left over the highway and onto a very poorly maintained old logging road. In his younger years, Arnold often used this old logging road to lose cops. It goes straight for over a mile. Then, there are two choices. With no crossroads, he takes the Jaguar up to 150 mph. He then turns onto a curvy road, hangs a U-turn, and parks well off the roadway facing the oncoming BMW. Fifteen seconds later, the BMW is coming toward him at about 90 mph. He brings out the 44 Magnum, pulls back on the hammer, and waits. Arnold allows the pistol to be visible as the BMW drives by. Both men look his way. The BMW also hangs a U-turn then stops facing the Jaguar. Arnold moves the Jaguar further into the brush.

Both men jump out of the BMW, carrying handguns and rifles. They run into the nearby tree line. Arnold loses sight of them as they run into the forest. Moments later, a van pulls up alongside the Jaguar.

The driver says, "Don't shoot Finion."

Arnold and this stranger move away from the Jaguar

toward the two from the BMW. They both lie down among some bushes and wait. After fifteen minutes of waiting, they hear some rustling in the nearby forest.

Arnold says, "These must be real city boys. They are talking, making noise while walking, and are easily detected.

As the two-armed men get closer to Arnold's position, they are both standing and are clearly visible. They are carrying their loaded rifles. They have no idea where Arnold is located.

Arnold says, "Be my back up. Let me take the one on the left out. Then you can have the other."

The guy nods, yes. He has a 38-caliber long barrel. Arnold fires two rounds, and the other guy fires three. They run to the two now lying on the ground dead. They remove identification, money, weapons, and then anything of value from the BMW.

They are both are wearing gloves. They shake hands as Arnold says, "Thanks for the help."

Arnold drives his usual route to his home. Upon arriving home, he parks the Jaguar in the garage, closes the door, enters the alarm code, and then tours the entire house with the 44 Magnum in his hand.

All is clear, so it's time for dinner. Arnold boils some red potatoes, cleans the celery and cauliflower pieces, makes a fruit salad, and fries a filet mignon. He opens a fresh bottle of Pinot Noir. He assumes that today's incident is just part of the upcoming war.

09 - SAILING THE ALICIA

The next morning Arnold calls Jennifer to verify that the day is free. Jennifer validates the day is open and wishes him a good day of sailing. Jennifer has gotten to know Arnold's habits.

Arnold instructs Jennifer, "Please tell Matt where I am going."

He feels refreshed after a good night's sleep and is relaxed, looking at a quiet day ahead. On with his sailing clothes and he has a medium-sized breakfast. Arnold packs a small lunch and a thermos of coffee. He gets out his scoped 30.6 with a ten-round magazine, placing it next to his 44 Magnum. As he departs his home, the alarm is set, doors are locked, and he sits outside the garage, waiting for the garage door to close. With this day being unscheduled, Arnold believes it may be safe to sail without worrying. Although he feels caution is still advisable.

He goes down the hill and into downtown Tiburon. Driving south, he arrives at the marina where Alicia is moored. Storing his food and guns takes only a moment. The gas tank is full. Arnold unwraps the sails, unties the mooring ropes, and starts the auxiliary engine. As he pulls away from the dock, he takes a last glance at the surroundings, just in case. He raises the mainsail after leaving the marina. Soon Alicia is into open water and moving out into the bay waters; only a high-powered rifle could reach him. He starts to relax while enjoying the cruise.

The winds are moderate but consistent. Turning to port, Alicia passes Angel Island and is soon heading up the Sacramento River. On the left is San Rafael with its marina and the ferry dock. Further up the river is Vallejo on the left with the critical submarine site for World War II. Another fifteen minutes and on the left, are the hundreds of World War II ships in storage. A little further on the right is some shallows of San Pablo Bay prime for bass fishing just off the Rodeo shoreline. Arnold decides to turn around at Vallejo. Coming back into the bay, Alicia again leans to the port. As Arnold completes the turn into the channel, there is the Richmond Ski Club's site, which has a water ski slalom course and a jump anchored permanently just offshore. Arnold had skied there in years past with good old Al Frosini.

On several evictions, Al had been quite an assistant in getting the trashy renters out. Next on the left is the Richmond Marina. It is a private marina with a restaurant, trailered boat storage, and boat mooring. Just passed the ski sites are a breakwater with large rocks on the west side and a long sandy beach called Shell Beach on the east-side. There is another water ski slalom course running beside this beach.

Further southward on the left is the remnants of the World War II shipbuilding berths. After this long sandy beach on the right, there is an island purchased by Bing Crosby for quail hunting. There are dozens of ships along this stretch waiting for the scrap yard.

As the channel starts to turn into Richmond's main marina just off Cutting Blvd, Arnold decides to make a U-turn. Arnold is aware of the chance a large ship may be using this channel. The water at the end of the inlet gets too shallow for sailboats. The wind picks up speed with Arnold tacking to starboard, and Alicia is out into open bay waters within minutes. To avoid shallow water, Arnold steers Alicia straight across the bay toward San Francisco. Going around Treasure Island, Arnold maneuvers the boat west of Treasure Island and under the Oakland-San Francisco Bridge.

After passing the bridge, Arnold turns to port heading for the Oakland-Alameda Estuary. His destination is the foot of Broadway in Oakland. Sailing into the inlet, North Oakland

HIDDEN IN FRONT OF YOU

on his left. It takes only a few minutes to arrive at the Oakland public docking area at the foot of Broadway. Arnold ties off the Alicia and walks towards Luigi's.

Along the way, he remembers the tours his father would give him, citing the different houses of prostitution on Broadway across from Luigi's. Many times, over the years, Arnold and his father would come here for a meal.

Knowing the enormous amounts served for a full meal, he orders a spaghetti/ravioli dish along with a bottle of Merlot. Finishing as much as he can, he orders the remaining portion to go along with the half-full bottle of Merlot.

Walking toward the public dock, Arnold spots the Last Chance Bar, a favorite site to relax for Mark Twain. This is a day to relax and ponder, so let's have some fun. Upon entering the Last Chance, there is only one empty chair at a table. He orders a Triple Sec. The crowd was just finished applauding for the event from the women's bathroom. Watching the patrons' talk, smile, and get along reminded him of Alicia. It turned out that rather than being sad, he was reminiscing the good times together. After ordering a second Triple Sec, he decides he has had enough. Just before leaving, the bartender turns up the microphone volume in the women's bathroom. Two women were powdering their noses. The conversation wasn't too damaging, yet some little secrets were exposed. Upon their return to the barroom, the applause was rewarding.

Walking to the boat, he feels a little tipsy. Out of the mooring, he goes making a U-turn and tacking to starboard. The path of the inlet was about 30 degrees off the port bow. Once out of the channel, the winds are coming almost directly at him, so he must tack back and forth to get on the western side of Treasure Island. Once passed the bridge, Arnold notices Alcatraz on the starboard side. He has altered course, so the winds are now from his port side. From there, he points Alicia directly toward Tiburon.

Arriving at the Tiburon Marina, Arnold feels less tipsy. He lowers the mainsail, places the mainsail in the cover, and finishes tying off the Alicia. After rinsing off the Alicia, he walks to his Jaguar, carrying both the guns and food.

After sitting in his car reminiscing, he drives to his home in Tiburon, parks the Jaguar in the garage, and sets the alarm as he enters the upstairs area. Before going to bed, he puts on a tape of Mozart Piano Concerto #1. The concerto gives him solace. It has been a beautiful day, and he is exhausted, so off to bed, he goes.

10 - CORRECTING MR. WISE

The next day is a typical workday at the office. He has a regular breakfast with an extra cup of French roast with espresso. Upon leaving the garage, there seems to be no one watching. The drives to San Rafael in a few minutes. Arnold parks the Jaguar at about 9:30 and notices the monitoring system is already in place.

He rides the elevator to the twelfth floor and walks into the office. After greeting Jennifer and placing his coat in his office, he walks over to David Worth's office. David is reviewing the charity financials.

Arnold says, "Ask Spence to review it with you. He may be of some help. I need you to find a person with legal experience, that lived near San Francisco and has disappeared. I may need to disappear soon. Please make this request a high priority."

David says, "Speaking of Spence, I have hired his daughter, Juliet, and she is working out quite well. I will meet with Spence today."

Arnold then turns and walks to Julien's office, where he finds both Julien and Juliet.

Arnold says, "Sorry to interrupt, but I need to get an update on the phone situation. By the way, Juliet, welcome to the firm."

Juliet replies, "It's great to be here."

Julien responds, "No problem, Mr. Pierce. I have been one busy guy. Each office phone is now tapped with an automatic recording on each call. I can turn off the conference bugging quickly. We have an independent recording of each conference room and each office."

Arnold next asks, "Juliet, what about you?"

Juliet says, "I believe I have found one of my niches here. I am setting up an organized system to record, analyze, and report on phone calls coming in and going out with a time stamp. Already it is keeping me busy. Mr. Williams is making some odd phone calls. It is alarming to me that he is communicating outside the firm so often."

Arnold says, "Julien, I would like you to look at David's financials. I am trying to decipher them, and I believe there is fraud being done by Mr. Williams. When you are finished with the financials, please have some long discussions with Mr. Love, one of our paralegals. He has some additional info on the Rita Kennedy case. I feel he is too frightened to come out with it."

Arnold closes the door to the office while telling Julien, "Tonight is the night. The man will be far more helpful by tomorrow. Thank you for getting the monitoring system installed."

Arnold wanders throughout the office, chatting with the staff members about their items of interest. Both Dulles and Williams keep being mentioned in the negative sense throughout most discussions. After lunch, Arnold tells Jennifer that he is going home to rest. He makes it sound like he is just fatigued for some unknown reason. Arnold plans to get a few hours' sleep in preparation for tonight's visit to Mr. Wise's house.

As Arnold arrives home, the street is clear. He has a few glasses of imported Italian port. Arnold places the tape on the stereo that contains a long list of Beethoven's symphonies. He is off to bed at 3 p.m., and he sleeps until 7 p.m. Arnold prepares his clothes and weapons for the evening, then fumbles through his leftovers and freezer to fix dinner. Arnold is getting anxious to meet with Mr. Wise. He is already aware that his own anger is emerging.

He drives out of the garage, across the bridge, follows Lombard to Gough then ends up on 101 going south. The warehouse is located at the north end of the United Airlines employee parking.

HIDDEN IN FRONT OF YOU

He parks the Jaguar in the warehouse and grabs a company van. He transfers his equipment, sets the alarm, and drives out of the warehouse while triggering the door to close. It's now 11:45, and here comes Josey, who moves his equipment to Arnold's van. As they are driving north on the Highway101, then up the hill on Market Street toward Twin Peaks, Arnold explains his desires for Mr. Wise.

Josey says, "This guy is going to be a wreck when you get through."

Arnold says, "We will have gotten his attention. That is for sure."

Within minutes they park in front of the home. The guard dog comes to the fence to greet us but does not bark.

Josey says, "He remembers the hamburger I gave him earlier."

Josey hops out. He throws several hamburgers to the middle of the yard then shoots the dog with a tranquilizer.

As he gets back into the van, Josey says, "That dog will sleep for the next four hours."

Arnold puts his 22-caliber in his shoulder holster. It is getting close to 2 a.m.

All seems quiet. Josey unlocks the front door and immediately disarms the alarm system. The furniture is simple and not full of things to knock over. They both climb the carpeted stairs to the second floor.

There is Mr. Wise sound asleep in his bedroom. Josey retrieves the 9mm from the nightstand while turning the lamplight on. This does not wake Mr. Wise. Arnold gives him a light kick to his right leg, which wakes him. Wise grabs for the first 9mm.

Josey says, "I have your pistol, Mr. Wise."

Mr. Wise says, "What is going on and who in the hell are you?"

Arnold says, "Right now, we are your friends here to help

you correct a mistake you made. We have your financial records, your bank account records, a list with the value of each piece of real estate you own. You might just say that we have every piece of information about you, including your DUI charges."

"You left a young widow in distress. She has a child and no decent place to reside. You hired a lawyer, were found not guilty of a DUI, and didn't pay any restitution."

Mr. Wise says, "So what. That is the way the world turns."

Arnold says, "That was really the wrong thing to say, Mr. Wise. We are aware that your wife divorced you on the grounds of cruelty. Your children have disowned you, and most people dislike you."

The anger starts coming out of Arnold. He first does a 360 with his left leg breaking Mr. Wise's nose and a few teeth. Then from the reverse rotation with his right leg, he breaks Mr. Wise's jaw.

Arnold says, "You may not have gotten my point yet."

Blood has splattered over most of the bed and wall. Arnold next drives his right fist down on Wise's collar bone, fracturing it just short of breaking it into two pieces. Arnold then strikes his right chest with his left knee breaking several of Mr. Wise's ribs hard enough to puncture his lung. Arnold motions to Josey to hold Wise down across the bed. Arnold pulls out his 22-caliber. Carefully he shoots a bullet through the right side of his butt. The shot went in the front of his butt and excited the back of the buttock.

Arnold relaxes. Things are quiet.

Mr. Wise seems to be willing to listen.

He says, "Mr. Wise, you need to know that I do enjoy this type of work. If I must return because you have not cooperated, I will show you just how much I enjoy this type of work. It is my specialty. This young widow needs a San Francisco residence with a garage, located in a safe

HIDDEN IN FRONT OF YOU

neighborhood. She also needs a sufficient income guaranteed for life. Mr. Wise, do you understand me?"

Mr. Wise can't talk but nods yes. He is bleeding, can't move much, and can't speak. He has trouble breathing from the broken ribs. He is just moaning in pain and crying.

Arnold says, "If I need to return, the best you will have is a wheelchair or a life support machine. Do I make myself clear?"

Mr. Wise nods, yes.

Josey picks up the other 9mm pistol from the dresser. Arnold and Josey start to leave quietly. On their way out, Josey fetches the third 9mm from the kitchen. They drive away in the silence of the night. Josey is dropped off.

Arnold says, "Pleasure working with you, Josey. Good night."

Josey says, "You sure enjoyed yourself tonight."

Arnold smiles. He returns the van and drives his Jaguar home. Arnold showers and goes to bed.

The next morning is a bright clear San Francisco day. Arnold admits to himself that he took out some of his own personal vengeance on Mr. Wise. He deserved it. Arnold finishes breakfast and wanders into the office about 10 a.m.

Matilda greets him, saying, "An attorney is waiting to see you. She is with Jennifer."

Arnold thanks her and strolls to his office.

Jennifer says, "There is an attorney, Mrs. Alice Serveau, in your office waiting to meet with you. I have already served her coffee. Mr. Spence is walking around with the biggest smile on his face."

Arnold strolls into his office and hangs up his coat.

He turns to greet Ms. Serveau. Arnold and Alice shake hands.

Arnold calls Julien, who answers, "Hello, this is Julien Spence."

Arnold says, "Julien, please come to my office."

Julien arrives within seconds and sits down with his own coffee. He sits there as on pins and needles, smiling from ear to ear.

Ms. Serveau says, "We have a very different transaction to complete and finalize. My client, Mr. Wise, is in the hospital with multiple injuries and is scared to death. He called Mrs. Whitaker this morning, and she wants this firm to represent her. Just hours ago, I was thrown into this matter, so I may be a little slow in coming up to speed. I have been told by Mr. Wise to agree to any demands placed upon me by your client. The man was in so much pain and frightened that he could hardly speak."

Arnold says, "Your Mr. Wise is someone I have dealt with before. I have all the records from my client, Mrs. Juliet Whitaker. She is a widow because Mr. Wise killed her husband in a DUI auto accident. I have done a financial background check on Mr. Wise, and he seems quite financially comfortable. Mrs. Whitaker has a child she needs to maintain. Let me introduce Mr. Julien Spence, who is Mrs. Whitaker's father. He works for us and shall be included in any discussion and/or decisions."

"To start with, Mr. Wise is to supply a residence free of any debt, thoroughly inspected for any problems, and a warranty within a safe neighborhood of San Francisco, including a garage. Any expenses concerning this transaction are to be paid by Mr. Wise. Mrs. Whitaker shall receive a reasonable monthly financial support payment from Mr. Wise. There shall be guarantees held through liens upon Mr. Wise's other properties. Both Juliet and Julien shall sign for her, and at least two shall sign for Mr. Wise, including himself and a legally recognized witness. I shall have the right to alter and validate any contract that is the conclusion of the transaction. I am instructing my client to pick the

HIDDEN IN FRONT OF YOU

property she prefers. There it is pure and simple. Sixty days to completion should be enough. What happened to Mr. Wise? Did he get into an accident or what?"

Ms. Serveau replies, "I have no idea, but he seemed quite fearful. Since you seem to be the most up to date individual on this matter, I suggest you write the first pass at the agreement. I will inform Mr. Wise that we are working toward finding a solution and a formal agreement. Thank you for your cooperation and friendliness. My client will be pleased to get this behind him."

She gets up and shakes Arnold's hand, then walks out toward the elevator.

After the attorney leaves, Julien wants to hear about Mr. Wise.

Arnold asks, "Are you sure you want to know?"

Julien replies, "Yes, I need to satisfy my feelings of wanting to know. I am bubbling over with happiness."

Arnold says, "First a broken nose with the loss of some teeth, a broken jaw, a fractured collar bone, several broken ribs possibly puncturing his lung and a bullet hole through the right-hand side his ass. Then a message on how much I enjoy this type of work. I closed with a promise that if I must return, he will only be kept alive with a life support machine. Not much to it, just a friendly visit."

Julien comments, "Mr. Pierce, you are amazing. You must have enjoyed yourself."

Arnold responds, "Yes, sir, I did enjoy myself. I released a lot of my own anger."

Julien stands, shakes Arnold's hand, and says, "I can't thank you enough. By the way, Mr. Pierce, Williams, is stealing you blind. Those financials are totally fraudulent. I would fire the bastard immediately."

As Arnold arrives home, he opens the garage door. He waits for the door to open when a BMW flies around the corner, and the passenger starts firing a pistol at Arnold. The bullets break the right-hand side mirror and put several holes in the right door. Arnold backs up and does a 180-degree swap with the Jaguar and starts chasing the BMW. During the chase, he fires several rounds at the BMW with his 38-caliber snub-nose. The BMW does begin to swerve, meaning that Arnold might have hit the driver. Arnold sees the Tiburon police coming, so he turns around and heads for home.

After closing the garage door, he calls Nick, who answers, "Nick here."

Arnold says, "I need to bring my Jaguar in for repairs, and I'll need to rent a car from you."

Nick replies, "I'll be gone until about nine tonight. We can do it then. I have a light blue Mercedes coupe you might enjoy. See you at nine."

Arnold fixes dinner and waits for darkness to drive to Nick's. Within two hours, he returns with the light blue Mercedes coupe.

11 - WRONG CAR

Sunday morning comes as Arnold is attempting to get some extra sleep. The sun has been trying to peer through the windows, while Arnold keeps covering his head. The doorbell rings at 10 a.m. Arnold jumps up, grabs his 22-caliber, and walks to the door. Two men are standing there looking like detectives. He places the pistol on the ledge behind the door and opens the main door leaving the full-screen door fastened. He is standing behind the door with no clothes on.

Arnold says, "Gentleman, may I help you?"

The first man answers, "I am Sergeant Keith Brown of the Tiburon Police Department, and this is Officer Hause. May we have a few words with you?"

Arnold replies, "May I please see some identification?"

Sergeant Brown pulls out his shield and identification then lifts them toward the screen door. Arnold can see each one clearly.

Arnold says, "Thank you. Let me get some clothes on first."

He closes the door partially, takes the 22-caliber off the ledge, and heads to his room to dress. He puts on some pajama pants and his robe. As he starts back for the front door, he flips on the coffee pot. Reaching the front door, he lets them inside, showing them to the front living room.

The sergeant says, "Nice home, sir. Have you lived here long?"

Arnold says, "I have lived here for the last 3 years, but bought it along with my fiancée, 5 years ago, as a rental investment. I moved in after she died in an automobile accident."

Sergeant Brown says, "Sir, we are sorry to hear of your loss. We need to look at your car."

Arnold replies, "Let's go downstairs to the garage. Would

you care for some coffee?"

As they are walking down the stairs to the garage, Arnold is thinking what luck that he drove the Jaguar to Nick's last night. As they enter the garage, there stands a light blue Mercedes 450 coupe.

Sergeant Brown says, "That is not the car we are looking for."

Arnold interrupts, saying, "Let's go back upstairs where it is a little warmer."

Arnold says, "Coffee?"

They both decline as he pours a cup for himself.

Sergeant Brown says, "That smells so good. Maybe I will take a cup. Black, please."

Officer Hause still declines, and they all sit down in the front room.

As Sergeant Brown continues, he says, "Did you hear any shots around here yesterday?"

Arnold responds, "No, I was not here all day. I was in downtown San Francisco for most of the day with two of my clients. Sometimes I visit them during North Beach rehearsals. That is where I was most of yesterday."

Brown Replies, "We have arrested two foreigners' that claimed they were being chased. We are checking to see if your car fits their description. The driver died this morning of a gunshot wound, and the other was carrying a 9mm pistol. The passenger had outstanding warrants for attempted murder. Whose sailboat is that in the picture?"

Arnold replies, "That is my 40.7 ft Beneteau named Alicia. It is named after my fiancée. You're welcome to come along sometime."

Brown says, "You have been very cooperative. Thank you for your time and invitation, sir. We need to go."

Arnold says, "Any time, gentleman. Here is my card. Call me if you need anything more."

HIDDEN IN FRONT OF YOU

Arnold walks them to the front door. As they are walking to their car, Arnold leans against the closed front door with a big sigh of relief.

Arnold thinks, "They never asked me if I owned this car. No proof of anything was requested. They didn't even check my ID before I handed them a business card. Whatever it was, it worked."

Immediately Arnold calls Nick.

Nick answers, "Nick, here."

Arnold says, "This time it is an emergency. Paint my car a different color. Do a complete job hiding the green paint?"

Nick answers, "Arnold, you sound out of breath. What is going on?"

Arnold says, "Yesterday I was chasing a BMW that had a passenger who had been shooting at me. I broke from the chase when I saw the Tiburon cops. But the BMW folks got arrested. The driver died from one of my gunshots. The other gave a description of my car."

Nick is laughing, "Mr. Pierce, you always seem to have the luck of a leprechaun. I know how much you like my work. Last week I purchased a similar Jaguar a few years newer than your green one. I planned to build it like yours. If I take your engine and transmission and put them into this newer Jaguar, I could have it ready in about the same time. If I give you a good trade-in, would that be your choice? I have already cleaned up your green Jaguar."

Arnold replies, "Yep! You are a lifesaver, Nick, thank you. Please keep me up to date on things."

With all the times Arnold brought Nick cars with bullet holes, blood-soaked seats, and damaged auto bodies, there was no way Nick would not have known Arnold's pastime. Arnold knows that Nick is independent and bulletproof. He will keep the Tiburon police at bay.

Arnolds says, "One more thing Nick. In the next Jaguar, I

want a bulletproof windshield, a steel plate on the firewall, and a full metal cage around me, the driver and the passenger. The thickness of the Jaguar chassis and the steel bumper you installed is great. My parents were killed when their car was hit broadside. My enemies could be alongside shooting bullet after bullet."

Nick says, "You know that I will have to eliminate the backseat?"

Arnold says, "I don't use it, anyway."

12 - MOVE TO THE NEW HOME

What about the house on Filbert? He decides to go there and check on the movers, so he drives to the 101 South and enters the on-ramp. Minutes later, he is crossing the Golden Gate with his windows down, smelling the fog's wetness. As he approaches Divisadero, he is in the right-hand lane turning right. He continues the two blocks to Filbert, where he turns right again. The house is in the first block on the right-hand side.

As he arrives at the home, he gets out his remote garage door opener and opens the garage door. Stacked in the far end are the empty shipping boxes. He parks the Mercedes in front of the wooden crates and closes the garage door. Juliet is working in the kitchen area, Josey is directing traffic to all other rooms, and he sees an almost functional residence.

Juliet says, "Hi Mr. Pierce, I have the kitchen almost done. I'll get the bathrooms up and running next."

Arnold smiles and says, "When you are not in the office environment, would you please call me Arnold? Have you been here all day?"

Juliet replies, "No, I arrived about 10 a.m. Josey and his helpers had almost everything moved by then. I just unpacked the boxes and put items away. Then I broke down the boxes and stacked them in the corner of the garage."

Arnold says, "I'll take a look at the bathrooms."

Within minutes Arnold had most of the bathroom items stored and the sink, shower, bathtub, and toilet cleaned.

As he enters the front room, he notices that Josey is paying the workers.

Arnold says, "Well done, guys."

He then asks Josey, "Is the bulletproof glass installed?"

Josey says, "Spence already did that and the cameras earlier today."

Arnold hands each worker an extra twenty dollars. As they

leave, they thank Josey and Arnold for the work.

Arnold turns toward Josey and says, "Well done. I think it is time for dinner. I do have a place in mind. Please let it be my treat."

They all crawl into the Mercedes, and off they go south on Lombard to Van Ness. When they pass Ghirardelli Square, he turns right onto Columbus. As they approach the row of restaurants, Arnold makes a left turn and parks next to Telegraph Hill at the Washington Square Park. After locking the car, they run across Columbus to an Italian restaurant.

Arnold discusses the menu with the waiter in Italian. Arnold warns them not to overeat at the beginning. An hour later, which is perfect for Arnold's plan, they have eaten all that they can.

Arnold says, "We are ready for dessert."

Both Josey and Juliet put up their hands, and Arnold says, "Trust me, you guys."

He motions to the waiter to bring out the chartreuse, a French liqueur composed of distilled alcohol aged with 130 herbs, plants and flowers, and some strong black coffee for dessert.

Juliet says, "I like everything here tonight. Thank you for dinner."

Arnold says, "I have one more surprise in store for you, just be patient."

They each finish the chartreuse and coffee. Arnold pays the bill. Arnold is ready to go.

Both Josey and Juliet thought they were going home.

But Arnold says, "Follow me, folks."

Out the door to the right as Arnold walks fast. Two blocks later, they cross Columbus and are walking south on Broadway in San Francisco's North Beach. Arnold turns left, opens the door, and proceeds up the stairs to the second floor. At the top is a green metal cage where patrons pay the entry fee.

A nicely dressed female says, "Thank you. Have a nice visit."

They sit at a table just in front of the stage. The show is about to start. Both Joe and Eve sit down, joining them.

Joe says, "It is nice to see you, Arnold, and nice to meet you two."

Petunia is the lead again tonight.

Petunia stops by the table to meet both Josey and Juliet. She says to Arnold, "You know we are starting with your favorite program tonight, sweetie. Be prepared."

Petunia goes backstage to get some help.

They come out on stage with Petunia as she is saying on the microphone, "Folks, we have one of our favorite guests with us tonight. We are asking her to join us."

Before Petunia finishes speaking, two tall females come by the table. They pick up Arnold and carry him onto the stage. As they are removing his socks, they act as if they stink then throw them off stage. They place high heels on his feet and stand him upright, then they throw a dress over his shoulders and put a blond wig on his head.

Petunia announces to the audience, "She is so much trouble. We always need to dress her properly. Tonight, I know who I am going home with, and she is so sweet. We'll just call her angel for now. By tomorrow I may call her honey."

Arnold knows his part. The six ladies plus Arnold start by dancing, telling jokes about one another, and singing. When it comes to Arnold, alias Angel, he sings in a very feminine voice. Each time Arnold sings, the crowd applauds. Fifteen minutes later, the program is over for Arnold.

Petunia says on the microphone, "Thank you, sweetheart, for joining us tonight. Angel, you have my heart. Here are my keys; just be there when I get home. Oh, what a night this will be."

Both Josey and Juliet are still laughing when he sits back down. He takes off the wig then the dress. He sits down and removes the high heels.

Arnold is also laughing up a storm over the event. After putting on his socks and shoes, he places his legs under the table. Joe and Eve come by to compliment him for his performance and thank him for participating. After three more shows, the end of the evening, Petunia has all the performers gather on the stage. Arnold jumps up to join them. As each says in their words, the closing statements, it comes to the last one, Arnold.

Arnold says, "It is such a wonderful family to be a part of up here, and you folks in the audience add to that feeling, goodnight all."

Without anyone knowing, he sings one of his songs, "I'm in love with you." The audience again gives him a standing ovation.

Ah, shucks, the fun is over. On the way-out, Arnold, Josey, and Juliet pass by the green metal cage.

Out of the cage comes, "Good night" in a deep baritone voice.

It surprises both Josey and Juliet.

As they leave Finocchio's, Arnold leads the way north on Broadway and turns right onto Columbus. Three blocks later, they are at the Mercedes. Arnold drives up Columbus for three blocks, then turns north onto Broadway. After two blocks on Broadway, they enter the Robert C. Levy Tunnel. On the north end of the tunnel, the Mercedes comes out still on Broadway at the intersection of Hyde. Three more blocks on Broadway, they arrive at Van Ness, the downtown portion of 101. Right onto Van Ness then left onto Lombard Street. All left-hand turns at intersections from Van Ness north on Lombard are illegal. Arnold passes Divisadero. As

HIDDEN IN FRONT OF YOU

Lombard turns right for the bridge, Arnold goes straight toward the Army Presidio. He continues on Lombard for half a block then turns left onto Broderick Street. Two more blocks and Arnold turn left again onto Filbert Street. Home is insight. Into the garage, he goes.

Josey says, "It has been a long day. Your dinner and show were the greatest. Thank you, Arnold. It was a fabulous evening."

Josey goes down the driveway and drives off into the night.

Juliet says, "It looks like I need to go home, Arnold. This evening has been the best evening I have had in years. Your performance was outstanding."

Arnold says, "I have one more thing before you leave. Your father was jumping up and down the next morning after I met with Mr. Wise. I have not seen the document, nor do I have the particulars. Would you please explain?"

Juliet replies, "Mr. Wise has sent a document over to me. I get a house with no debt of my own in downtown San Francisco. Just what did you do to that man? His attorney said he was scared to death."

Arnold says, "May I have a copy to view. I just want all things to be fair for you and Alissa. What I did to him is not pleasant. Yet, sometimes, people are so selfish and corrupt that they fail to have any empathy or compassion toward others. Mr. Wise is not a nice or good person. Are you sure you want to know what happened to him?"

Juliet replies, "It is such a privilege for me that you went out of your way to help. Maybe I should let it lie. Thank you for your honesty. I do need to go. My dad has Alissa. Good night."

Juliet leaves through the garage.

As Juliet leaves, Arnold thinks what a beautiful woman she is. Bright, straight forward, friendly, a good mother, likes having fun, does not have a plan, just a lovely person. I need to know her better. Maybe a cruise on Alicia would be the right place to start. Each time I see her, I find something more I like about her. Perhaps I should say something to Julien. He seems to be there for her protection.

When Juliet gets to Julien's house, she walks in all bubbly.

Julien says, "Working this late?"

She answers, "No, daddy. Arnold took Josey and me to dinner then a show at Finocchio's. Arnold got up on stage during one of the performances wearing a dress, a wig, and high heels. He is talented, danced, made jokes for the audience, and sang like a female. At the restaurant, Arnold was speaking Italian with the waiter. He ordered a green chartreuse liqueur, which was perfect for a dessert. I am having trouble keeping my promise to you. I wanted to throw myself in his arms all evening."

Julien answers, "I can see why. This man is a person that stands well above most others. What I meant was bide your time. You have lost the father of your child. You are alone and lonely. As great as this man seems, you still need to give yourself time to know him well. Make sure his personality traits meet your needs. Remember, he is still in danger. I will do whatever I can to assist Arnold. Walk before you run my darling."

She says, "I'll try. I am not sure if I can hold back as you want me to."

13 - PERMANENT RETIREMENT

Lynn Dulles walks into David Worth's office and asks for an audience.

David says, "Hello Lynn, good to see you. How are things going for you?"

Lynn replies, "I am getting by. I have come here on business. Here are two envelopes for you to take care of. You should only open the one marked "my message in case of my demise." It will explain my position and let you know what to do. The other envelope contains our last will and testament.

Since the automobile accident, Frank has become a completely different person. Sometimes I feel threatened and do not know for sure if he is going to kill me or not. Then there are other times that I think I should take his life because he is so mean and dangerous to everyone. Frank has a new girlfriend. He seems to be defiant to all authority. He has become aggressive toward beautiful people like Arnold Pierce. Bullet holes in my car, dead bodies dropped off in our driveway, and many of Frank's sub-contractors have been killed."

"My world has fallen apart. I do not know what I should do. David, I am not asking you for advice. Just please be my caretaker for these envelopes. One more favor, would you please tell Arnold to call me sometime."

David answers, "Lynn, I will do whatever you request. My wife and I are always there for you whenever you want us to help."

Lynn turns and hugs David as she is sobbing with tears running down her face, then she leaves. David is ashamed that he is restrained from helping.

The entire office notices the changes that have taken place since the accident. David Worth is especially troubled since he is the second in command and in charge of the Firm's

Charity Group.

Frank Dulles was promoted to CEO replacing Arnold's father, Aidan Killian Pierce. He was a fierce man with little fear. Aidan Pierce served the firm from the early 20th century until his death. He followed the rule of law and served without limits to the citizens of the Bay Area.

Arnold has held his same motto plus his own values. Frank Dulles had a very similar approach to Aidan Pierce's ways of managing plus an almost identical set of values. Aidan Pierce's replacement by Frank Dulles was seamless. Before the accident, Arnold's working relationship with Frank Dulles was always productive and amiable.

At times, Arnold had stated, "It is almost like working with my father."

Later that day, Lynn drove Frank to the neural surgeon's office in the city, where she received a heartbreaking diagnosis of severed nerve damage. As they crossed the Golden Gate Bridge while driving home, Lynn decided to try going up Conzelman Road. Getting off the 101 North, taking the crossover road to Conzelman Road, she started driving along with one of their old haunts.

She parks the car in a position facing the Golden Gate Bridge with the back end of the vehicle pointing at the edge of the hillside.

Lynn says, "Remember all those times with the kids when we came here to investigate the gun positions that were started for World War II and never finished. They never fired one shot."

Frank says, "I do not know why we are here. What you are talking about is just history."

Before continuing, he swings his arm over, attempting to break her nose. Then, he tried again, but she raised her arm to block the second blow.

Lynn says, "We have had over thirty years together. They

were beautiful years."

Frank yells, "Take me home and get out of my life."

Lynn is crying so heavily she can't see clearly. The motor is still running.

She says, "I love you, Frank. I am so sorry."

He does not say another word. Lynn moves the gear shift knob into reverse.

She blows him a kiss, then steps on the gas pedal. The car starts running backward faster and faster till they are flying off the side of the hillside. The vehicle flies downward some 500 feet before hitting and then rolls for another several hundred feet. A passing motorist alerted the police, but nothing could be done to help either one of them.

That evening Arnold and Sid are in Arnold's home, and Sid is not smiling.

He says, "At 11 p.m., turn on the Channel 2 newscast. They will announce the information again tonight."

Arnold senses something is terrible. He pours more wine while waiting for the show to start. At the stroke of 11 p.m., both Sid and Arnold are watching Channel 2 news broadcast.

After about five minutes into the broadcast, the narrator says, "We reported the car that went off Conzelman Road on one of the hillsides at the north end of the Golden Gate Bridge. At about 3 p.m., the car flew off a hillside plunging some five hundred feet before hitting and rolling another several hundred feet. We have just received the names of the occupants, Frank and Lynn Dulles of Marin County. They had been married for well over thirty years. They are survived by their three children and many grandchildren. Frank had recently retired from the Pierce Law Firm, where he worked for over thirty-five years."

Arnold can't talk. He knew this might come to pass but is horrified at its occurrence.

Arnold excuses himself. He walks into his bedroom and

closes the door.

Sid leaves quietly.

According to Lynn's request, both Frank and she were to be cremated. The memorial is scheduled for Saturday. Arnold is expected to be the altar boy and to give a short eulogy. Arnold was Father John's altar boy for many years.

Saturday morning Arnold is up early. He lays out his new suit, shirt, and tie for the memorial. Father John's medium-sized church is in Novato. It doesn't take long for the funeral guests to fill it. Arnold notices that Claire did not attend. Father John Vincent is in charge of the ceremony. As the service flows, Arnold remembers being an altar boy for years under Father John. They work well together. Father John refers to the Dulles's many times in loving memory. Before Father John concludes, he announces that his altar boy has a few words to say. Arnold approaches the podium.

He says, "My name is Arnold Pierce. The loss of Lynn and Frank is like losing my parents again.

When my parents were killed, Frank and Lynn came to my side immediately. For many years Frank was my mentor. He would let me sit in on negotiations, client to attorney discussions and take me to court so I could observe. In every way, they both welcomed me into their family. As a fellow attorney, Frank and I worked together like well-oiled machines. When Frank replaced my father as CEO, both he and Lynn brought such love and harmony to our environment. When my Alicia was killed, they again stood by me. They continued to embrace me. I would not have proceeded through my young life without their embrace and total support. The loss of their loving company will be felt for the rest of my life. Please let us pray. Our Heavenly Father, we submit to you our beloved couple, Frank and Lynn Dulles. They are coming to you with our blessing. They will be with you in their last home. Please welcome them. Amen. Thank you for listening to my words."

Arnold leaves the podium and walks out of the back door. He is tearing. He has trouble seeing where to step. As the service comes to an end, Arnold stands at the back of the church. He has stopped tearing but has red eyes. As people continue to pour out of the church, the Dulles children walk back to visit with Arnold. They each hug him and assure him he is always welcome in any of their homes. Arnold feels blessed yet sad.

Arnold starts walking to the front where all the people are standing. Many come up to him and thank him for his words. Others say beautiful things about his relationship with the Dulles family. As they disperse, his group is standing there.

Juliet comes over to hold his hand.

Julien pats him on his back. David and Angela Worth give him hugs and condolences.

Josey says, "What a big loss, my friend. My heart is with you."

Arnold says, "I have a suggestion. Why don't we all go for lunch in their memory at the Tiburon Marina restaurant, and then Juliet and I can take a sailboat ride."

Julien responds, "Now kids, do I need to chaperone this trip?"

Juliet says, "No, Daddy, but thank you anyway."

Josey says, "Sorry, Arnold has me working long hours. I'll need to pass."

Arnold responds, "Josey, Matt says you have been tagged by McCarthy. Please be careful.

Arnold and Juliet jump into his red Jaguar, Alissa, and Julien go in Julien's car. David and Angela get into their vehicle. They go southbound on the Redwood Highway. As they enter downtown Tiburon, Arnold notices a traffic cop. He stops and walks over to the policeman.

Arnold says, "Hi, my name is Arnold. The other day Sergeant Brown and his partner jaywalked. Would you write them up on a phony ticket?"

The cop says, "This will be fun. But lookout, those Sergeants are known for playing tricks. You may be sorry."

Arnold drives on to the restaurant, and parks close to Alicia. After sitting down, Arnold orders a dry martini up, Juliet a rum and coke, Julien a double scotch with no ice. Alissa is looking around, wondering what she can order.

Juliet says, "Alissa, since it is illegal, you may not be able to get an alcoholic drink. How about a Shirley Temple?"

Alissa nods okay.

David and Angela choose herbal tea. Sergeant Brown walks up to the table before they order.

He says, "Anyone here named Arnold Pierce. I have come by to arrest him. The charge is vagrancy."

They handcuff Arnold and then walk him out the front door. As they leave, Arnold has a happy face on. He is smiling from ear to ear. No one at the table understands.

Sergeant Brown says, "Now Mr. Pierce, you are not yet completely off the hook for that chase. But you have covered it well. You need to realize that you can't play with the fickle finger of fate. Trying to write me up for jaywalking will just bring discomfort."

With that, he unlocks the handcuffs, slaps Arnold on the back, and says, "You are a good sport. Hope I can take a ride on your boat someday."

Arnold says, "Sergeant, you are always welcome, but bring a lifejacket just in case I push you overboard."

They shake hands, and Sergeant Brown walks away, smiling.

Arnold comes back into the restaurant and sits down.

Juliet says, "I would never consider being happy about being arrested."

HIDDEN IN FRONT OF YOU

Everyone wants to know what is going on.

Arnold says, "Sergeant Brown and I have a little joke between us. I keep writing him up for jaywalking. He keeps responding."

David says, "Another one of your jokes when you can get away with it."

Arnold says, "What can I say, David. It's fun. Now folks, let's be serious. The food is superb here, let's order."

As they are eating, most of them are enjoying the food so much there is little talking. At dessert time, Arnold orders green chartreuse for both he and Juliet. The rest order ice cream or pie and coffee. Arnold thanks everyone for attending the service. Then lets them know that he and Juliet are going for a sailboat ride. Arnold and Juliet walk to Alicia. Everyone else heads for their cars.

14 - SAILING WITH JULIET

With both Arnold and Juliet working together, Alicia is ready to go within fifteen minutes. Arnold starts the Auxiliary motor. After unhooking the mooring lines, they idle into the bay waters. Arnold raises the mainsail and points, Alicia, in a southwesterly direction. He remains close to the shoreline while passing Sausalito, making a 45-degree path through the bay passage. The Alicia is sailing on her port side, catching much of the winds force. The wind is from the west by northwest direction. This allows Alicia to pass under the bridge with the receding shoreline on her left without requiring Arnold to do any tacking. Alicia continues on this path for fifteen minutes past the Sutro Baths and Museum and the Cliff House. Arnold turns westerly toward the Farallon Islands. Arnold is sitting at the helmsman's position with Juliet wrapped in a blanket beside him.

He thinks, "Juliet was there at the funeral in support, and she joked with me the other day during a meeting. Doing things together is becoming more of a pleasure."

The distance to the Farallones is just over twenty-five miles. Alicia, with only the mainsail deployed, is moving just under twenty MPH. As they approach the islands, Arnold knows of an inlet on the east side that is shallow enough for anchoring and will protect them from the winds. Not having an experienced sailor aboard, Arnold lowers the mainsail early while continuing by the motor. He shuts down the engine while coasting slowly into the inlet. He drops the anchor, it catches the bottom, and they are parked. Arnold verifies the anchor is in place, turns on the running lights, then motions to Juliet to follow him to the cabin.

He turns on the small propane heater and the cabin lights, saying, "We are home here for as long as we wish to stay."

Arnold pours coffee for both. He offers some pastry items, but Juliet is still too full from lunch.

HIDDEN IN FRONT OF YOU

Arnold begins by saying, "We have a lot to talk about. This outside attack on the firm has some possible deadly consequences. To date, I have been very fortunate to walk away with my body intact. On a more pleasant note, I find you enjoyable to be with."

Juliet says, "I feel the same about you since the day I met you. I recognize the difficulties you face, and I understand why you can't walk away from the situation. Remember, my father worked for the CIA for many years, so I really do understand the situation. There is a high probability that people will attempt to kill you. But for now, let us talk about something else. Let me tell you about my late husband. Then maybe you could share your perspective of Alicia."

"When my husband came home from Vietnam, I could see that he had changed. Before he left, he wasn't comfortable with a lot of communication. Once he returned, it was hard getting even a couple of words out of him. The night he died, we had a mild disagreement about communicating. He was having his own internal thoughts of events in Vietnam. He was out driving around. Most likely, he was not paying much attention to traffic. Mr. Wise broadsided him after running a stop sign."

"My father and I talk about everything. I have grown up with that. I prefer it to be that way, and now I feel that I must demand it. I hope that you agree. I have heard that Frank and Lynn used to be that way before his accident, and David and Angela treat each other that way. I see you doing the same with all of us in the group. My feelings are that you and I are off to a good start."

Arnold says, "Wow! Someone that says what is on her mind. I do like that. My father and mother were also killed by a drunk driver. That may be why I understood your position so well. By the way, I did review and altered the contract from Mr. Wise. You are much safer after the changes I made."

She replies, "Thank you for looking out for me. It may be the right time to let me know why Mr. Wise was so frightened."

Arnold responds, "If I tell you, it will show the aggressive side of me. There are things that I have done that are hard to discuss."

Arnold says, "Thank you for understanding. It was slow at first. Now it seems overwhelming. Most days, I can't put it aside. The two comparisons I have are the Nazi's and the Viet Cong. This McCarthy Group is similar. They destroy the workings of the company at the top and within its environment. Then they try purchasing it with an offer that is like ten to twenty cents on the dollar. Now things are getting serious. To date, their tactics have not worked successfully. They will be changing tactics and ramping up the threat level. I have thoroughly ticked off McCarthy by getting rid of those two thugs. My chase in the city last week, I took out four other mercenaries, and the outside group took out two more. So here I am trying to alter my tactics while attempting to avoid Mr. McCarthy's attacks. I will be hiring my cousin Bridget, who will be one of my better misdirects. With me not coming into the office, I hope that they will not be able to find me. Negotiations will be hampered by a delay factor from me not being there. Matt is going to help us see McCarthy more clearly."

"With Mr. Wise, it was clear that a lawsuit would take years to complete. The cost and no monies upfront would have placed you in the position of settling for a lower amount. Having no choice, I went with Josey into his home in the wee hours. At first, he was arrogant. We found three 9mm pistols in his house. I broke his jaw with a foot punch. After a little conversation, I broke his nose and took out some teeth with my other foot. He was still holding back. I threw him down while explaining that if he does not adhere to our demands, we would be back to finish the job. He was more cooperative though not wholly convinced. I shot a hole in his right buttocks with my 22-caliber target pistol. It went in one side and came out on the backside. I also fractured his shoulder and broke some ribs that punctured his lung. He had lost his ability to communicate, so we left. Before leaving, I informed him that if we were to return, he might not live another day or if he did live, it would be with a life support machine. That is enough for now."

Juliet says, "I don't think I would want to make you that mad at me. Let's get back to your stories. Why don't we continue where you left off?"

Arnold says, "No rest for the guilty. Alicia and I met in high school. We were together similar to the Dulles and the Worths. We both wanted to be attorneys. She wanted to be a corporate attorney, and I wanted to be a trial attorney. We had plans for children, and we had made investments early. We purchased a couple of investment homes and put monies aside for a rainy day. On her birthday, she had gone to her birthday party with a couple of girlfriends. As they were coming home from the party, they were struck head-on by a doped-up teenager. His car came across the double line. Both the Dulles' and the Worth's were there to save me from destroying myself. After losing my parents to a drunk driver, Alicia's accident left me without hope. Do you want more in-depth information?"

Juliet says, "Thank you, no. What you have already said must hurt to recall the events. I am pleased that we communicate so easily. Come over here, Mr. Pierce. I would like to snuggle a little."

They lay there for the next hour, holding on to each other kissing and exchanging small talk. Juliet notices the scar on Arnold's ear. Arnold feels that it would be so easy for them to become intimate. Arnold remembers that he must also respect the fact that he works with Julien.

It has become dark, and Arnold thinks it may be time to start back. The wind is mild, the city lights are aglow, and the Golden Gate is shining in the evening darkness. The anchor is up and stowed. Arnold raises the jib first. After the jib is tied off, he raises the mainsail. Alicia is on her starboard, flowing with the mild evening northwest breeze. Juliet is sitting up against Arnold, wrapped in a blanket. As they turn toward the bridge, Arnold turns on all the running lights. After a little more than an hour, they are passing under the Golden Gate. The bridge lights are glowing, the traffic noise is easy to hear, some pedestrians are still loitering on the bridge walkway, and no ships are in the passageway. After entering the bay waters, Arnold lowers the jib. Alicia is following a course of about four hundred feet from Sausalito. As the Alicia nears, Angel Island Arnold brings down the mainsail while continuing by the motor into the marina. Together they stow the equipment, encase both sails and hose down the deck.

As they are walking to the car, Arnold asks, "Where do I drop you, Mrs. Whitaker?"

She replies, "At my daddy's, please, Mr. Pierce."

They are each pleased with the day together. They both would prefer to go home together. After a nice ride to Julien's home, Arnold walks her into Julien's house.

Julien says, "Did you two children enjoy your day?"

Arnold says, "Absolutely, Mr. Spence. One problem, though, I had this little buzz in my ear called a chaperone. What a pain he was."

Julien replies, "You know that he gets worse as time goes by."

Arnold says, "Nah! A little bug spray should take care of the problem."

HIDDEN IN FRONT OF YOU

Juliet walks over and says, "Good night, sweet Arnold." Then she gives him a big kiss.

Arnold says, "Now, dad, you did not see that!"

Out the door and to his Jaguar, Arnold is as happier than he has been in years. Arnold is home within minutes. Both Julien's and Juliet's homes are a few minutes from Arnold's house. After closing the garage door, he is alone. He notices the feeling that he has been with someone special all day.

15 - PLAYING WITH ALEX

Monday morning starts with Arnold staring at the ceiling. The most recent events and the new data have him totally involved in the topic of the firm's continued success. Last night it kept him from gaining a full night's sleep. This morning he is unable to turn it off. He rises with a lack of objectivity. He can't discard it, so he decides to find something enjoyable to do. Maybe an intense fight will do it.

Arnold calls Jennifer, saying, "Please tell Matt that I am going to Alex's Gym, and I may need backup."

Arnold calls Alex, who answers, "Hello, this is Alex."

Arnold replies, "Good morning, Alex, what does your day look like today?"

Alex responds, "Ah, yes, this must be lil shit. How are you, Arnold?"

Arnold says, "I am considering a visit to your gym today. Is your schedule open?"

Alex says, "For you, always. Come by, and maybe you would like to step into the ring with me today. You won't last five minutes."

Arnold laughs then says, "I doubt that. How is Sammy doing?"

Alex says, "Sammy is staying with me. His father is back in the hospital again. He fails to get it. Let's see if you can last five minutes with me?"

Arnold says, "Alex, you won't last five minutes, not a chance. See you soon."

After a light breakfast, Arnold puts on some workout clothes and some lightweight tennis shoes. Arnold drives out of the garage to Lombard, then right onto Van Ness. As Van Ness meets Mission Street, he turns left onto Mission. Within a mile into the Mission District, making a right turn onto 19th Street, and before getting to the Mission Dolores Park, there is Alex's Gym. He parks in the gym's driveway.

HIDDEN IN FRONT OF YOU

He walks toward Sammy, who is shooting hoops. Arnold holds his hand out to shake hands with Sammy.

Arnold says, "Are things looking a little better?"

Sammy says, "Yes, my tutor is teaching me how to learn. It is getting to be fun. My father is still a pain in the ass."

Arnold says, "I need to see Alex."

They both walk into the gym.

Alex yells, "Great. You finally made it lil shit. Hope you are ready for your ass, whipping."

Alex reaches out toward Arnold. He grabs Arnold's shirt and lifts him off the ground. Without hesitation, Arnold tags Alex, lightly in the testicles. As Arnold is dropped, he hits Alex a couple of times around his head.

Alex grins and says, "Ring time, Mr. Pierce."

Sammy yells to Alex, "I told you he kicked my ass."

Alex asks the two in the ring to get out. Alex climbs into the ring with two pairs of gloves. He tries to hand one pair to Arnold. Arnold declines.

He says, "I have no need for gloves."

Alex says, "Suit yourself, lil shit."

Sammy is standing by the bell. Alex puts on his gloves having Sammy tie the strings. Arnold is getting antsy.

Arnold, as he smiles, says, "Come on, old man get with it."

Alex steps into the middle of the ring, along with Arnold. Sammy hits the bell. Alex starts his dancing around while occasionally lunging forward. Arnold simply steps aside or moves his head out of the way of each attempted blow.

Arnold leaves his hands at his chest level.

Alex has landed nothing. Alex gets a little more aggressive, giving Arnold a few more good possibilities.

Alex comes in with two quick jabs then a big swing. Arnold eludes the punches, then as the right arm comes in for the big blow, he pushes the arm further, throwing Alex off balance. This opens up the right side of Alex's body.

Arnold comes in with two punches to Alex's right midsection. Alex turns further to the left, opening up his backside.

Arnold lands two quick hard strikes to the waist area just above the spleen. Alex is a little wounded by now and starts to get even more aggressive. Due to Alex's fatigue, Arnold notices that the intended blows are getting more telegraphed. Arnold begins his next set of moves by moving inside with some sharp punches to Alex's stomach then finishes with a chop to the throat. Alex is stunned at this point. Alex is now suffering from heavy blows to the midsection and the throat. Alex has yet to land a blow on Arnold. He tries to land some quick punches but misses.

Arnold notices that Alex has started to plant his feet somewhat apart. As Alex continues to increase his movements, he has his feet planted for that big one. Arnold moves in as Alex attempts a big swing. He pounds Alex's stomach heavily. As Alex lowers his hands to protect his midsection, Arnold comes up, landing a sharp blow to Alex's throat again. Quickly Arnold turns 180 degrees facing away from Alex. Arnold rolls on the mat backward. Halfway around the role, Arnold stretches out his right leg planting a stiff foot onto Alex's testicles. Arnold gets up quickly, then he walks over to Sammy and rings the bell.

Alex is on the mat, attempting to breathe and gritting his teeth to control the pain from his testicles.

Arnold says, "Alex, that was a little boring. I am sure you could step it up a wee bit."

Two to three minutes pass before Alex speaks.

He says, "Okay, lil guy, you win. Where in the hell did you learn how to fight like that? Do you know how to box?"

Arnold responds, saying, "I do not know how to box Alex. To me, boxing is a sport."

HIDDEN IN FRONT OF YOU

My friend trained me after I graduated from college. The first thing he taught me was situation assessment. It has saved me many a time. You see, Alex, my background in physics, along with the ju-jitsu logical control, allows me to interpret your moves and take control. I am watching your body language, and you are telegraphing every move. That time I punched you in your side and back, I had taken your big swing and altered its momentum. I pushed on the backside of your arm, and your momentum carried you past your intended mark, making you lose your balance. That left you open."

Arnold approaches Sammy saying, "Sorry that your father is so difficult. Finding how to learn from your tutor may be the most important step in your education process. Once you find within yourself the ability to learn, you have the whole world to choose from. When learning becomes fun, there are no longer any limits. This will give you the confidence required to make headway in all situations."

Sammy replies, "Mr. Pierce, I am starting to appreciate what you have offered me."

Arnold starts to say goodbye to both Alex and Sammy. Matt's number #12 is escorting Arnold. Without notice, a young black man enters the gym. This man is aggressive and angry, plus he is armed.

The young man says, "Is your name, Arnold Pierce?"

As he pulls out his weapon and threatens Arnold, #12 reminds him that there is a 38-caliber pistol pointed at him. Then #12 orders him to drop the gun or die. Arnold jumps over the ropes and confronts this guy. He kicks the weapon off the matt.

Arnold says, "I am here asshole, and we are now on even terms. What would you like to do about it?"

#12 has seen Matt in these situations before. He knows nothing about Arnold. As Arnold and this young man approach each other, Arnold is performing his assessment. The body movements are exaggerated, showing a lack of confidence and a lack of knowledge of martial arts. Arnold keeps his arms close to his chest and has his moves already defined. The guy quickly starts poking at Arnold's face. This is to hide his intention of thrashing Arnold with a leg move. Arnold first runs his thumbs into this guy's eye sockets. Next, he moves in close to pound heavily on his heart, which is deadly if continued and gives him a slash across the throat. The guy is now having trouble breathing and can't see. Arnold steps in turns 180 degrees and flips this guy with a ju-jitsu move while breaking two of his fingers on his right hand. The guy is lying face down. Arnold pulls his head back into a neck-breaking position.

Arnold says, "If you wish to continue, I will break your neck. It's your choice, asshole."

Arnold drops his head and leaves the guy face down on the mat. Arnold gives the weapon to Alex and tells him to call 911.

As Arnold leaves, he says, "Step it up a little, Alex. That was boring."

16 - PROBLEM TENANTS

The next day in his office, Arnold is thinking of some of his friends. Arnold remembers Alfred Frosini, known as an exceptionally friendly fry cook at his restaurant located in Point Richmond, California. This restaurant is open Monday through Friday from 6 a.m. till 2 p.m. and is managed by Al's loving wife, Hannah. She is straight with you but firm in her management style. Al wants to talk and play, but Hannah always puts him back into the kitchen while telling the customer not to bother Alfred. Al and Hannah have been together since high school. She is the mature one, and he is the friendly, helpful, happy go lucky one that never grew up. Al would always prefer to play, that means box, rather than have a serious talk. He would prefer to get into a good fight than walk away. To Al, a good battle was his fun.

A problem case was turned over to Arnold once it became evident that someone special must take the lead. Arnold needed some help evicting an ornery set of tenants after the usual court action had failed. Three young college men thought they would use the legal system to avoid paying rent. These students had not paid rent for the last four months they had occupied the unit. It was found that they had been doing this all over town. Their tactics included bad checks, false identities, false complaints, and a complete unwillingness to cooperate. Arnold's firm had fought them in court, yet the three kept finding holes in the judgment or getting postponements. Each event was full of falsehoods and lies. Each delay embarrassed the firm's legal team, along with costing excessive amounts of monies spent disproving each accusation.

Arnold had represented Al in a lawsuit brought by a criminal that attempted to rob Al and Hannah when they were walking home from dinner at a local restaurant. The criminal had come up from behind Al and knocked him down.

Al laid there thinking, "Shit not again, well whatever."

Then Hannah came over to protect Al and hit the criminal with her purse. She was met by a fist in the face knocking her to the ground. Al saw this while still lying on the ground. The criminal tried to get Al's wallet, but he had made the mistake of hitting Hannah. Al, from a lying position on his backside, threw three very exacting punches breaking the guy's nose and several teeth. The criminal was knocked back onto the hood of a car. Al was up hitting the guy several times with his full force. Lying there in the gutter, the criminal was bleeding from his nose and mouth. Al just continued walking home with Hannah. To Al, it was just another good fight. The criminal had a broken nose, three teeth knocked out, and several open sores on his face.

It appeared that Al had money, so he and Hannah were sued. Hannah had heard of the firm's ability to help people. Arnold took the case and won easily. During the meetings with Al and Hannah, Arnold realized that Al could be an asset to the firm. So, one day, Arnold visited the restaurant in Point Richmond. The place was full of Al's water ski buddies, truckers, and locals. Arnold had difficulty finding an empty seat. There he saw one meeting place for the patrons. Stories and jokes were flowing between the fry cook Al and the patrons. The environment was like a big party, active, funny, harmonious, and a joy to experience.

As the time approached at 2 p.m., the crowd had left, and Arnold had a chance to chat with both Hannah and Al. Arnold proposed that Al do a service for Arnold in payment for the legal services rendered. Both Hannah and Al agreed that it seemed like a good idea. Al was enthusiastic, yet Hannah was cautious and hesitant. Arnold explained the problem with the three students to both Al and Hannah.

In response, Al said, "I'll take care of it tomorrow on

HIDDEN IN FRONT OF YOU

Saturday. Leave it to me."

The unit had three apartments, and a long driveway and a flat lawn in front of the building. Al called several of his old buddies from high school. Al walked over to the site from his home. His buddies were there ready and anxious to start. One of the students had gone to the grocery store that morning. With two inside the unit, the group walked up to the front door. Knocking on the door, Al started to get pumped up. Al's friends were all ready for the fight, but Al took the lead.

The door opened with a guy saying, "Yes, may I help you."

Pow, one blow by Al, and the guy was out cold. Al had hit him with his right fist. The group entered, leaving the student on the floor. Al found the second student in the bathroom.

The second student screamed, "Don't hit me!"

One punch and he was unconscious. While the group waited for the third student to return, they started packing. As the third student entered the apartment, Al clobbered him with a left to the stomach and then a right to the head. He was out cold. Within fifteen minutes, the group had all the students' belongings piled on their car or on the lawn. The locks were changed, and the apartment was secured. Al disappeared, but his buddies remained to wait for the arrival of the police. Going to the same high school, each of the policemen knew the members of the group. When asked, no one knew anything. The cops knew better than to ask any further questions. Without a doubt, they knew what happened, yet they were not going to turn in their friends. The problem was solved.

17 - NIGHT WITH THE GIRLS

Everything seems quiet as Arnold leaves the house Friday morning. He parks his Jaguar in his reserved spot in the parking garage. Arnold is in deep thought while riding the elevator to the 12th floor. He sees Matilda as he walks into the office lobby. Matilda is the Pierce Law Firm's primary receptionist. She handles all calls that come to the office, greets each client, escorts them if necessary, and walks all incoming mail to its intended recipient.

Arnold stops at her desk and says, "Matilda, I have been busy lately, and my attention has been elsewhere. I am sorry if I have ignored you."

Matilda answers, "No, no, Mr. Peirce, I do not feel excluded in any way. I heard that you went sailing the other day. How was it?"

He replies, "Wonderful. I visited so many places in the bay. I had a wonderful time, got back late, though. You and your family are welcome to join an excursion sometime."

Matilda responds, "It is just my two daughters and me. I lost my husband in Vietnam."

Arnold stands there, stunned that he was unaware of the loss.

Arnold says, "Maybe we could make it a secretary day, including children. Would you be able to join a group like that?"

Matilda smiles, saying, "Mr. Pierce, that sounds wonderful and fun for all. Thank you for thinking of us."

He walks off, feeling sad after hearing this stunning news about Matilda's husband.

After a short day at the office, Arnold heads home. As he drives across the Golden Gate, he glances at Point Richmond's silhouette in the setting sunset, remembering the time Al and Hannah accompanied him to Finocchio's. Al had parked his Keaton ski boat on the shoreline of Shell

HIDDEN IN FRONT OF YOU

Beach on the east side of the breakwater. It was Saturday, the day that the Tsunami created by the Niigata earthquake in Japan that had raised the water level in the Bay waters. Before Al returned to his boat, the water level had receded, leaving the Keaton stranded some 30 feet from the shoreline. Arnold had sailed over to give him a hand while anchoring away from shore. It took ten men to pick up the back end of the ski boat. They carried the backend with the propeller and dragged the front end through the sand to the water's edge.

Afterward, Arnold invited Al and Hannah to San Francisco for dinner, but he failed to tell them what else he had in mind. They sailed to the famous Fisherman's Wharf. From there, it required a cab to Arnold's favorite Italian restaurant. Arnold placed the dinner order while speaking Italian to the waiter. Both Al and Hannah are impressed since they both spoke Italian in their youth and are direct descendants of Italian immigrants.

Arnold knew the Finocchios would be fun for Al. After having dinner at a Columbus Street Italian restaurant, they walked several blocks to 506 Broadway. Without a word from Arnold, they walked up to the famous stairs to Finocchio. As they entered, Al's eyes got as big as saucers. He was smiling from ear-to-ear. He was singing, patting the entertainers on the butt, and wanting to get on the stage. He was excited, just like a little kid. Arnold went up to Petunia, who was the lead for the night.

Arnold said, "Petunia, can my crazy friend come onto the stage."

She says, "No, but I'll drag his skinny little ass up here during the show."

She added a little wink as she walked away.

About 5 minutes into the show, some of the performers were mulling around the tables.

Two of them came by and carried Al up onto the stage.

Petunia takes the microphone saying, "You lil thing, you are all mine tonight. You are going home with me. I'm going to take your body and make it quiver. You will be the happiest man after I am done with you."

It didn't take long for old Al to catch on. Before Al could get started, a stagehand brought out a table and high heels for Al. The six performers picked him up and put him on the table while making a big deal out of his stinky socks. They huddled around him while putting his feet into high heels. Al was a little unsteady in heels but went along with it. He started dancing and singing along with the group, while pulling up their dresses to look underneath, pinching their boobs to see if they were real. Al had a huge nose and was sticking his big nose down the front of their cleavage. The girls were kissing him all over the face and neck until he had lipstick covering his face and neck. There were six performers on this show. Each kept passing Al around until the end.

There was a standing ovation by the crowd and prolonged applause. Both Joe and Eve Finocchio concurred with a thank you from their hearts.

As we were walking out, the girl behind the payment window said, "Good night" in a deep baritone voice. Both Al and Hannah were surprised.

By the evening's light, Arnold dropped Al and Hannah at the Pier in Point Richmond. From there, it was only a 10-minute walk to their home, which was just a block up from their Cafe. Arnold then headed to Tiburon. The entire evening was funny, exciting, and certainly different from what Al and Hannah had expected.

In retrospect, Arnold notices a decline in the size of the audience at Finocchio. Both Joe and Eve say things are doing well. Arnold feels they are trying to keep a happy face.

HIDDEN IN FRONT OF YOU

Being just past the mid-20th century, all the arts and tourist attractions of these times have had the same decline. With the introduction of television in almost every home, people are staying home more. This is contrary to the 19th century in San Francisco. The changes have already been felt throughout America's culture. Arnold remembers the late 19th century into 1925 when tens of thousands of locals would travel by horse and buggy or the early automobile over the sand-dunes to the San Francisco Beach, Sutro Baths, Sutro Museum and Playland on Saturdays, Sundays and holidays. Summer days were perfect for some sun and a little watery dip. The sloping sandy beach runs for miles from the Cliff House, past Golden Gate Park, past the San Francisco Zoo, and well past Lake Merced Park. If you continue southward, you find beaches alternating with the rocky shoreline. Between the beaches, the Zoo, the Cliff House, the Sutro Baths, and Playland, you would see tens of thousands visiting on the warmer days. With heated and non-heated freshwater and saltwater swimming pools, the Sutro Bath and Museum was especially inviting. Built by the Mayor of San Francisco, a corrupt and wealthy Mayor with an ego as massive as his wallet.

18 - THE JAYWALKER

Jennifer has called Matt with Arnold's plans for the day. Having no other appointments, Arnold starts driving toward the city. After crossing the bridge, he turns off of Lombard then left onto Filbert. Using his garage door opener, Arnold opens the garage door and parks the Mercedes. After a quick inspection, he goes to the Filbert home then drives south on Filbert to Divisadero Street. Turns left onto Divisadero Drive past Lombard to Chestnut, right on Chestnut. On the right-hand side, just before Scotts Street is the supermarket. Arnold has begun shopping there, anticipating that he will become a regular patron.

As he enters the supermarket, he starts making small talk with each clerk he encounters. He tells them that he just moved into the neighborhood and wanted to find a friendly place to shop. Everyone is cordial. It feels like one of the old-time San Francisco grocery stores during years past. He purchases some odds and ends and drops them off at the Filbert house before going to Tiburon.

Since it was Friday night, Arnold decides to stay in the Tiburon Hotel on Main Street. The hotel has an excellent bed for sleeping, an array of choices for food, and plenty of parking. For breakfast, Arnold is sitting in the outside open area in the front of the hotel. The small restaurant has a good selection of breakfast foods. He chooses a cheese omelet with sharp cheddar cheese, ham, French toast, grapefruit juice, and coffee.

Somewhere nearby is one of Matt's contractors, but Arnold can't pick him out. As he is finishing breakfast, Arnold spots an unmarked police car parked across the street. He moves his chair to be more visible to people on the road. Keeping an eye on the police car, Arnold hopes to chat with Sergeant Brown, who may share some more pertinent information. He has all day, so he waits. Thirty

HIDDEN IN FRONT OF YOU

minutes later, Sergeant Brown comes out of the real estate office across the street. Arnold yells out to Brown while waving his hand. Brown recognizes him. After waiting for traffic, Sergeant Brown and his same partner cross the street.

Arnold yells out, "Should I give you a ticket for jaywalking?"

Brown replies, "I don't think you're a traffic cop."

Arnold says, "You know there is never a cop around when you need one. How are you guys doing today? Would you care to visit my boat for a tour?"

Brown's partner says, "If I can have a cup of coffee first, I would like to take a look."

Arnold turns to the waiter and says, "Sir, may we have two more coffees, please?"

The waiter pours the coffees, and Arnold gets a coffee warm up.

Arnold says, "I have decided to get a second residence in the city since so many of my trial cases end up there. It's not that far except in rush hour. That always takes hours."

Both detectives stay while chatting about odd and ends. There were no official discussions.

Arnold says, "We have finished our coffees, I have paid the bill, so would you two follow me to the marina?"

Both nod a yes, so off they go. Arnold gets into his Mercedes, and the two detectives both jaywalk again to their car. As Arnold pulls out of the parking lot, the two officers pull in behind him. It is only a few blocks, and Arnold finds a convenient spot to park the Mercedes.

They stroll onto Alicia. She is floating there quietly with all the sails wrapped, the other gear safely stored below deck. As Arnold shows them around, he walks them through different positions while trying to explain the importance of each location. He unlocks the cabin door then enters the cabin below. Arnold describes the separate storage of foods and drinks. He then shows them the sleeping quarters if they were sailing in the ocean for days. He shows them a picture of his great crew that allows him to steer the bloody thing since he owns it.

Arnold says, "I feel like a novice when working with them. They are expert sailors."

As they leave Alicia, Arnold locks up the cabin.

While walking back to their cars, Sergeant Brown asks Arnold, "Sir, do you own any other vehicles?"

Arnold says, "Why yes, I do. I just sold a Jaguar two weeks ago. I always upgrade my running gear, tires, and suspension, especially the tires. The stock ones are not safe enough."

Sergeant Brown asks, "Could you get me the address of this vehicle?"

Arnold says, "Absolutely It's at Nick's Roadway at Taraval and 19th Avenue, in the city. Nick does all my automotive work."

Sergeant Brown says, "Thank you for the tour. It's a wonderful boat, and we may need to take a ride sometime. That guy we arrested is back in Arizona, where the warrant originated. Both guns found have been traced to other crimes in the Bay area. Viewing your vehicles will be our ending point in this investigation. After that, I will place this file in the closed case files."

Arnold says, "Good seeing you, gentleman. Hope to see you again on a trip through the waters."

As they pull away, Arnold walks over to the nearest payphone. He drops the required coins into the telephone and dials.

Nick answers, "This is Nick."

Arnold says, "Hello Nick, this is Arnold. Has anyone called looking for my Jaguar?"

Nick responds, "Funny that you would ask. Two police

HIDDEN IN FRONT OF YOU

officers are on their way to my shop to view your two Jaguars. My story is that the green Jaguar is mine since you sold it to me a couple of weeks ago and is a trade-in for the red Jaguar. On your green Jaguar, I have already replaced the windshield and the right mirror. There is no engine in the green Jaguar because I have installed that engine and transmission in the red Jaguar. Like many times before, you are leasing the Mercedes 450 daily. Mr. Pierce, have I covered all the points you are worried about?"

Arnold responds, "You are the greatest. You have everything covered that I was going to ask you to do. I just had a visit with the two officers, and I gave them your address. Everything you have just stated was what I told them. When do you want me to pick up the Jaguar?"

Nick answers, "Some other work came in, which makes yours take a back seat for a week. On your vehicles, I have already done the hiding of any history, but I am waiting for some parts. They are coming from England."

Arnold says, "Nick, all is fine. I'll wait for the parts. Talk with you in a few days. Bye."

Arnold's concern was justified. The Tiburon police were asking questions, yet Nick knew what to say.

19 - SOME BOAT UPGRADES

As Arnold parks his Mercedes, he notices a familiar Mustang parked across the street. As he reaches the twelfth floor, Matilda informs him that Matt is waiting for him. Jennifer offers Arnold a coffee and a fresh Danish pastry. Matt already has his coffee and Danish.

Matt says, "We have somethings to discuss. My people are leaving the engines run when they arrive at Farallon Islands. Josey is doing his job, yet he is not critical enough. I need you to have these items fixed. I don't want my people stuck out there in the Pacific Ocean due to a mechanical breakdown. There is water leaking into the bilge. Some gauges are not functioning, both motors are running less efficiently, and the left outdrive now making noises."

"We are not capturing many of McCarthy's operatives. Many more need to be taken to the Farallones. The set-up by your law school chum may be a good start. You need to be ready to kill the guy next to you at an intersection when he fires at you. Your metal cage should help you there. Try building a planned trip to the Zoo, the Aquarium, and the park. David says the hiring of Bridget is ready to go. He has no idea what you are doing there. Get these things fixed as soon as possible. Please, check them out yourself. That is all, for now, Mr. Pierce."

Arnold thinks Josey is just being Josey again. He is doing his job without analyzing the apparent status or giving it any forethought.

Arnold calls Josey, saying, "Meet me at the boat at 9 a.m. Be prepared to do some repair."

The next morning Arnold wakes with the boat problems on his mind. He wonders how to encourage Josey without killing his enthusiasm. Arnold has a full breakfast, pours a full thermos of coffee, and takes some fruit along. Arriving at 8 A.m. should give him time to inspect the boat without

HIDDEN IN FRONT OF YOU

Josey there. Test driving the 25-foot boat opens up piles of information that Matt was saying. Josey arrives at 9 a.m. Arnold offers coffee and fruit to Josey and sits back to break the ice and make Josey comfortable.

Arnold opens by saying, "I got here at 8 a.m., and have surveyed the entire boat. The cooling system outlet is above the water level, and you are not flushing the saltwater from the cooling system with the freshwater hose. The exhaust manifolds are not steel, saltwater deteriorates the aluminum. The steering cable is beginning to bind. The oil is filthy and needs to be changed. Increase the SAE value to 40, add some STP, and change the oil filters. I want you to install a Frantz bypass toilet paper filter and learn how to maintain it. When the boat is underway, the engines are always climbing a hill, so they must be protected. The automatic bilge pump keeps the boat from sinking. The fan belts have cracks, and the engine rubber water hoses are leaking. Both engines are running poorly. Now the I/O units. The right side I/O is a little noisy. It may be a simple fix like replacing gears. The left side I/O is growling. A possible replacement may be necessary. I suggest at least new wiring and a carburetor overhaul. If necessary, check the valves in case they need a valve grind. Each engine has a rubber insert for a water pump. Replace each one. Make sure the rubber blades are pointed in the correct direction as you install them and lubricate each one, so the first time you run the engine, these rubber blades don't run while dry. And, get it done asap."

Josey says, "You found all of that in one hour. Phew."

Arnold says, "Matt's contractors' lives depend upon returning. Please keep this in mind."

Josey says, "If the parts are available, I will have the problems fixed in three days, four at the most."

Arnold drives back to Filbert street and asks Sid to come over for a chat. Free food and coffee always seem to make him available.

Arnold starts by saying, "Matt and I have some surprises for McCarthy where we can take out a few dozen operatives. Yet, that is only a handful. McCarthy seems to have them everywhere. I am ready to implement your idea of having me hide. I don't like it, in fact, I hate it. Soon, I may not have any other options. The level of attacks will get more dangerous and certainly more often. As hard as I fight, I seem to be getting closer to losing the battle. The more I attack or misdirect, they continue to come at me and are getting more successful each time. With my experiences at Finocchio's and your skills, I might be able to pull it off. I value your opinion. I am on my way to see Joe and Ava."

Sid replies, "You are getting smarter by the day."

Arnold asks, "What's the status on the pink Mercedes?"

Sid replies, "As you requested, I am working with Nick, your mechanic. He is installing steel plates in the front doors and bulletproof glass all around. The car should be ready in ten days."

Arnold calls Matt with an update on the boat repairs and to advise Matt about the upcoming visit with Joe and Ava at Finocchio's show lounge.

When he enters Finocchio's, Joe and Ava offer him for a cup of coffee. It is early in the day, so most of the female impersonators are not present. Arnold gives them an overview of the help he is seeking.

Joe says, "The girls will be excited to help in every way they can. I suggest that you prep and work with them on stage."

During the next many weeks, Arnold practices and does the makeup prep for the show. Soon he joins the shows to improve his understanding. With their help, Arnold fits into all the skits and is one of the most active members. He develops his female voice.

HIDDEN IN FRONT OF YOU

Sid has hired a contractor to turn Arnold's home into a purely female residence with large closets, a king-sized bed with silk sheets with all-male clothes stored out of sight. Sometimes Arnold drives home dressed as a female to get Sid's opinion. The two of them start visiting the local shops and supermarkets. Sid introduces Bridget to Evelyn, a recent successful transsexual working at the supermarket. Arnold, as Bridget, is beginning to be accepted by the females in the local shops.

Sid says, "You need to work on your feminine actions like raising your female voice in laughter, excitement, and surprises. You are not sitting as a female. Cross your legs and keep them together. Start using the tuck I gave you, it will help you with the discomfort as you cross your legs. You also must accentuate your hand movements in a female way.

Your hair is getting longer, so I can easily shape it into a feminine hairstyle. You are getting there. Go out with Evelyn. She will be a great help."

After a session with the Finnochio girls, Arnold is still dressed as a female. He drives to the supermarket to find Evelyn. There she is in the produce department. Arnold walks up to her saying hello. Because of the new wig and the clothes, Evelyn has no idea who this woman is.

Arnold says, "I am Arnold. I am practicing. I thought we could go shopping, out to eat, or just walk around a mall."

Evelyn says, "Phew! You had me confused for a moment. I think I could help you with a couple of things. I am off work in thirty minutes. Can you wait till then?"

Arnold says, "I'll do some grocery shopping while I wait."

As he does some shopping and walks around the supermarket, he is addressed as ma'am. Arnold draws money out of his purse, and he pays with cash at the checkout stand. No one questions his gender.

Arnold is wearing a wig supplied by Sid. He has his nails

painted red, and makeup applied by the girls at Finnochio's. For the next two hours, they shop in together at local stores. There is a cosmetic solon where Evelyn shows Arnold lots of things she learned as a transsexual. Then they ate dinner at Ghirardelli Square in the cheese factory. Evelyn gives Arnold tips on hand movements. Walking while wavering his hands in a female way, and practicing walking in high heels. At the end of their visit, Arnold has gained insight into his future female impersonation.

20 - TWO CALLS

As he is driving the blue Mercedes home, he wanders around Tiburon, hoping to spot Sergeant Brown again. Up and down Main Street. Nowhere can he find Brown. He drives up to the house on the hill, thinking that was worth trying. He enters the garage, feeling that there is little chance he will be attacked for a few days. He packs his bags in preparation for the move to Filbert Street. Not in the mood to cook, he changes his clothes. After a couple of phone calls checking on the group's status, Arnold drives back down the hill to the marina area for dinner.

Sitting by the south window of the Tiburon Fishery, the view is spectacular. The sunset is sending cascades of light just before it falls behind the fog. The sight of Alcatraz is clear. The city is partially covered with fog. The outlines of the taller buildings stretch well above this light fog bank. He can see the Coit Tower in its 210-foot distinguished display on top of Telegraph Hill, which is just up the hill from North Beach's Finocchios. Coit Tower was built in 1933, using funds from Lillie Coit's bequest to beautify the city of San Francisco. For Arnold, this is a relaxing moment since he has been around San Francisco his entire life.

Today, Arnold took some time to look for new furniture for the firm. He thought, why not keep the business in San Rafael. Nothing found would match what is already there. While wandering around, he met up with a possible new and some prior clients. He started to hand his phone number to this one gentleman. He dropped the card, so he bent down to pick it up. As he bent down, shots rang out from the rooftop of a nearby building. The bullets missed him but hit the guy he was talking to plus two other people. All three survived. Most individuals in the area fled in terror. While lying on the pavement, Arnold kept searching for the source of the shot. He saw a male holding a rifle and immediately pulled out his 44 Magnum. He fired six shots, reloaded, and fired six more at the figure on the roof. The police arrived. He turned his pistol over to them and explained he had fired twelve shots at the person on the roof.

The police investigation found blood and a gun on the roof. The police returned the pistol.

Arnold had no doubt that the shots were meant for him. This was definitely a close call.

Arnold was back in the office early Tuesday morning. As he approaches the office, Jennifer sees him and tells him the Spooner documents are on his desk.

Arnold's second case with the firm was in defense of a wrongly charged client, Mr. Joseph Spooner, for the murder of a family member, Sarah Pfaff. If Arnold had not intervened aggressively, Mr. Spooner likely would have been convicted. After the charges were dropped by the District Attorney's office, Arnold started a countersuit claiming damages and attempted character assassination. The trial was held several months ago., and the court's final decision had just arrived.

Mrs. Spooner answered the call saying only, "Hello."

Arnold asks, "Is this Mrs. Spooner? This is Mr. Pierce."

Arnold answers, "I called to inform you of the results. The judge came back with a verdict in your favor. All court costs for both trials are to be reimbursed, and you were awarded damages for $250,000. This means that you and your husband are to be repaid for our charges, including court costs and legal fees. Plus, you get 60% of the $250,000 since we reduced our portion to 40% from 50%. I do hope you are pleased with the result. Both you and your husband will need to stop by my office, ask for Jennifer, to sign the acceptance of these amounts."

Mrs. Spooner says, "Thank you so much for your great work. My husband will be relieved. The monies will help us get back on our feet. We can now sleep at night. I must call Joseph to let him know. Bye for now."

As a person that loves his profession, Arnold sits back in his chair, smiling. This was definitely a pleasurable call.

21 - BUSINESS AS USUAL

Wednesday morning, Arnold wakes up just after 7 a.m. He showers and shaves before having breakfast. Pleased with his maneuvers of yesterday, he feels like he is making progress. The downside is that the road to success seems like it is getting longer than Arnold initially estimated. He leaves the house in the blue Mercedes, feeling freedom from danger.

On the 12th floor, Arnold walks by Matilda's desk and says, "Hi."

Continuing to his office, Arnold is still in the same mode he woke up in.

As he passes Jennifer's desk, she says, "Mr. Pierce. Do You remember your scheduled meeting with Judge Thornton this morning? Julien was looking for you, also."

Arnold had forgotten about the meeting. He grabbed some documents while hurrying off to the judge's office. Arnold returned hours later with a frown on his face."

Arnold says, "I must be getting sucked into this other stuff and losing my legal analysis. Judge Thornton just tore me a new one. My prep work was inadequate, my actions were faulty, and my conclusion turned out to be without the necessary basis. I must learn to multiplex better."

Jennifer replies, "Mr. Pierce, you are under a mountain of pressure these days. Please do not be so hard on yourself."

Arnold says, "Thanks, Jennifer," as he enters his office.

After laying out the preparation documents along with the investigation report, he calls Jennifer on the intercom.

"Jennifer, please order dinner for me. I'll be staying late tonight."

Arnold thinks that he must prep for his next meeting, even with the known danger lurking around the corner. He is carrying his 38-caliber long barrel pistol. Arnold finishes dinner quickly. He continues to work until almost 9 p.m.

HIDDEN IN FRONT OF YOU

Unknown to Arnold, Julien had stayed to backup Arnold. As Arnold walked out of his office on his way to the elevator, there was Julien in Jennifer's chair. Arnold is amazed. He jumps backward while grabbing his pistol. After a few seconds, he realized who was there.

Arnold says, "Phew, I almost shot you."

Julien answers, "But you didn't. Let's go home."

As they walk out to the elevator, Arnold says, "Quite a surprise, Julien, thank you."

Julien responds, "We need to look out for one another."

As they arrive in the garage, both pull out their weapons while checking for intruders. They get into their own cars. While driving out, Arnold waves a salute to Julien.

Arnold says to himself, "It is starting to feel like a family."

Thursday morning, Arnold meets with his client at 8 a.m. They go over details before going off to court. The client is a general practitioner suing for character deprecation. The defense attorney was not well thought of. After several hours, Arnold returns to the office. He stops by Jennifer's desk.

Arnold asks Jennifer to call David, Julien, Juliet, Mr. Love, Cecelia, and Matilda into the conference room. As they all file into the conference room, Arnold is sitting at the head of the long table.

He says, "You will never guess what happened during jury selection today."

Arnold then proceeded to describe his morning in court. As usual, each potential jury member first gave a short dissertation on their life, their education, and working experience. This one elderly gentleman had discussed his early childhood, his two degrees in mathematics, and his experience teaching at three Universities. Of course, each attorney gets to ask additional questions. The elderly gentleman had given a rather light overview of his work experience. Within his description was the fact that he had worked for the intelligence gathering community. He had stopped with any more information. The defense attorney asked him for whom and what had he worked on. The gentleman said I'd rather not say. The defense attorney got a little hot.

Then the defense attorney walked over to him while standing directly in front of him said, "Mr. Hankins. Just tell us for whom did you work for, and what did you do?"

Mr. Hankins says, "No, I can't tell you."

This attorney again badgered the potential jury member saying, "Ah come on, tell us for whom and what you did."

Mr. Hankins quietly says, "No, I cannot tell you. If I tell you, then I would have to kill you."

Arnold then told the group, "I laughed, the judge and the other jury members were in hysterics. Now you guys are all laughing. You seldom find a jury member being so honest in his answer. Mr. Hankins was immediately excused from jury duty by the defense attorney."

The group's conversations were plentiful and funny. After a few minutes of comments, everybody went back to their jobs.

HIDDEN IN FRONT OF YOU

22 - MATT'S BAIT

Arnold calls Matt #1. He leaves a message that the boat is ready for use. Josey has done a great job. All should be safe for Farallon Island trips. Starting today, as Matt suggested, Arnold will visit the Zoo, the Aquarium, and Playland.

Up early, a big breakfast, and a thermos of coffee. Arnold is driving the red Jaguar. As he is closing the garage door, an operative is parked facing south. As Arnold closes the garage door, the operator hangs a U-turn to follow him. The operative is driving an older four-door Oldsmobile. Arnold feels that this guy is low on funds and not too bright. Arnold takes Steiner to California. Turning right onto California, he continues to the beach near to Playland, then south toward the Zoo. The older poor handling Oldsmobile is staying closer than he should. Highway 1 separates into four lanes with a forty to fifty-foot separation. The Olds pulls alongside. Arnold has not pulled out his 44-magnum. The Olds driver rolls done his window and starts firing rounds at the Jaguar. With the Jaguar being much lower, the bullets fly through the convertible top.

Quickly, Arnold jumps on his binders, slowing and pulling in behind the poorly handling older Olds. He speeds up hitting the Olds back bumper at a 45-degree angle with his steel bumper. That forces the Olds to flip over several times, killing the driver.

As Arnold pays his entry fee at the Zoo, he sees a couple of Matt's contractors that he recognizes. Arnold continues to wander around like a typical tourist. Within the hour, four McCarthy operatives surround him.

One of them says, "You must come with us."

They certainly have no idea of Arnold's fighting skills. Within moments they are lying on the ground, unable to move and are yelling in pain.

Arnold asks Matt's contractors if they have someone at

the Aquarium and the Playland Funhouse. They nod, yes.

At the Aquarium, Arnold parks in the front row so the red Jaguar can be seen. He wanders around for almost an hour before he recognizes someone keeping an eye on him. He does see some of the same contractors from Matt's group. This time five McCarthy contractors walk up to within a couple of feet, and one places a knife against his back. Again, this group does not know Arnold's skills. Within seconds the five are lying on the pavement gasping for air. The guy with the knife now has his knife inserted in his own thigh. Matt's group runs up, showing police badges, and Arnold calmly walks to his Jaguar.

Now onto the funhouse for his next package of fun. Including the drivers, they have only snagged eleven, and they will all be fish food very soon. Entering the Funhouse brings back many memories of Alicia. Arnold tells Matt's group to wait at the bottom of the long wooden slide.

There are four more McCarthy guys. They are getting easier for Arnold to pick out. As Arnold climbs to the top of the slide, all four of McCarthy's operatives are right behind. Within moments they are having trouble breathing, and by using Snake Kung Fu, they can no longer see. The funhouse supplies gunny sacks for sliding. Arnold places each of them onto a gunny sack then sends them down the slide.

At the payphone, Arnold calls Matt on #2. Matt calls right back.

Arnold says, "Matt, I have a surprise. My school chum Glen Hardy called me this morning to set me up. There will be a pleasant surprise for you at the marina if your guys are on the public dock at about 3 p.m. Let Glen go with a warning, but the others are fish food.

Matt says, "I was about to call you. One of the captured operatives spilled his guts before diving into the deep blue. He confirmed the identity of the mole who setup your former CEO. This same mole is now offering a big bonus to the man that takes out Arnold Pierce. Be careful, it's a significant amount of money. Don't be surprised if the mole disappears. Bye."

Arnold thinks Williams will soon be visiting the fishes. After what he did to Frank Dulles, the sooner, the better

Arnold calls Sid, saying, "Sid, I need a ride to the marina this afternoon. Are you available? I can't take my Jaguar."

Sid says, "Sure, let's get there early."

Arnold and Sid are waiting in Sid's car by 2:45. There on the public dock are three McCarthy looking operatives looking guys and Glen. Matt and a few of his contractors' swarm in at 3 p.m., taking control of the public dock. Arnold leaves Sid in the car and strolls to the public dock. The weapons are taken from the three operatives, and Arnold walks Glen away from the dock to chat.

He says, "We were good classmates together in law school, yet you have broken my trust. They most likely threatened you since you have always been known to be a weak link. You may leave immediately, but if I ever hear or see you again, I will personally kill you. Don't look back, our friendship is over. Now get lost."

Matt walks over to Arnold, saying, "Thank you for a great day's work. My contractors were surprised with your fighting skills. This makes over twenty for the day. A good day's work. Your boat is running great again. Thank Josey for a job well done."

Glen runs to his boat and leaves the area. As Sid is about to say how generous that was, Glen's boat explodes, and it sinks from sight.

23 - MR. LITTLE FROM THE CHRONICLE

As Jennifer leaves, she says, "Mr. Pierce, please remember your appointment today at 4 p.m. with Gregory Little from the San Francisco Chronicle. He requested an interview related to the history and the background of the firm. He wants to publish a historical article on the firm with an emphasis on you."

Arnold says, "Thank you, Jennifer. I had forgotten."

Thursday at 4 p.m., Jennifer walks Mr. Gregory Little into Arnold's office. Jennifer introduces Mr. Little to Arnold and then leaves.

Arnold says, "Mr. Little, please give me an idea of your journalistic background. Why are you here? What do you want of me?"

Before they can continue, Jennifer brings in a fresh pot of coffee and some pastries.

Arnold says, "Thank you, Jennifer."

After taking a cup of coffee and one Danish pastry, Mr. Little says, "I have worked over eight years for the Chronicle after acquiring my BS degree in Journalism. I was born and grew up on the east coast. I have requested stories like yours from others. These stories give me a better sense of what makes this beautiful city click. If you watch the cultural changes of San Francisco, it is astounding. Your story is a modern-day event that, in some ways, follows the cultural changes but also the adaptation of San Francisco into the modern world. I am interested in your story since you are the last of your kind from within the original."

Arnold responds, "Do you always prepare an answer as if you are about to give a public presentation?"

Mr. Little responds, "No, Sir. I just speak my mind."

Arnold says, "Start with Jennifer, who will introduce you to the office staff. They will help you with your research. I do require that you let me review your article before it goes to print. Have an interesting day." Arnold waves goodbye as Mr. Little leaves the office.

After sitting in his office for 10 minutes, he still feels that he must have a conversation with Julien about his daughter. He walks out past Jennifer and goes to Julien's office. Julien looks up, and there is Arnold with a somber air about him.

Arnold says, "I have a personal topic that I wish to discuss with you. The topic is your daughter, Juliet. We always seem to enjoy each other's company. I would like to get to know Alissa too. But most important is what I feel for your daughter. The more I see of her, the more I like her. She is sweet, straight with me, has no hidden agenda, yet most important, we have a good time together. We enjoy similar things, she laughs with me, she is upfront with me, and I feel no discomfort with her. Concerning you, sir, I need to tell you that I am interested in her."

Julien responds, "Arnold, I have discussed this with her. She tells me that her feelings are like what you have just described. I have no objections to the two of you seeing each other. I have told her that, in my opinion, you are a man of high caliber. What I have also said to her is to wait, be patient, and be sure of her decision. I have no fears of you being my son-in-law. Are you comfortable with that?"

Arnold replies, "Thank you, Mr. Spence, I feel much better after talking to you. I do agree with your opinion about being safe in our decisions."

24 - DOWNTOWN SAN FRANCISCO CHASE

Friday evening, after a long day in a San Francisco courtroom, Arnold is physically fatigued and feels mentally drained. He decides to stop at his favorite Greek restaurant, the "Gyro Kabob," located at the corner of Larkin and Willow in San Francisco. During the dinner, Arnold begins to sense an uncomfortable feeling of being watched. Is it the maître de', or is it one of the waiters? One of the waiters did make a phone call shortly after Arnold arrived. There is nothing that Arnold can recognize or isolate, yet this feeling persists. It seems to Arnold that the waiters are paying too much attention to him. After finishing his dinner, Arnold asks the maître de' for a telephone.

He calls Sid, who answers, "Hello."

Arnold says, "Sid, tonight may be an evening that you need to be available. Is it possible on such short notice?"

Sid answers, "Have nothing else going on this evening. I am available."

Arnold continues, "I only have a sense of danger because some people here are paying too much attention to my presence. I am at the Gyro Kabob on Larkin. Please call Matt with this info."

Sid replies, "Will do. I did speak with Matt earlier, and he indicated he had one of his men observing you. Maybe he's making you uncomfortable. At any rate, I'll be on standby."

Arnold says, "Thanks for letting me know. Please remain available, and if you see me coming down the street, open my garage door. Bye."

Leaving the table and walking toward the door, he sees nothing that catches his eye. Yet his intuition is screaming at him from within. He turns around and walks over to the waiter that had made the phone call. Arnold grabs his arm, then using a Snake Kung Fu move, he disables the waiter. Arnold escorts the waiter to the rear alleyway where the

HIDDEN IN FRONT OF YOU

garbage bins are located.

He says, "You have a choice to Make. Either let me kill you here or tell me who you called on the phone."

The man says, "I am already threatened by a bunch of thugs that I did some work for, now you threaten my life. They said they intended to kill you, and I must call them if I ever saw you in the restaurant."

Arnold turns the waiter around then chokes him until he passes out but is not dead. He uses the alley to reach his Jaguar. This allows him time to get into the Jaguar without being seen except for the Jaguar's interior lights. As he gets in, he quickly starts the Jaguar while pulling away from the curb. Arnold notices two cars with at least two individuals in each vehicle waiting for something. The chase Mercedes and the backup Chevrolet Camaro are parked on the same side of the Street as the Jaguar. They are about three parking spaces behind the Jaguar. One is a black Mercedes, two-door sedan, and the other is a Camaro coupe. Evaluating the two vehicles, Arnold assumes that the Camaro must be the decoy vehicle, and the Mercedes is the chase vehicle.

Arnold unhooks the 44 Magnum from his shoulder holster. He then opens his briefcase and removes the 9mm semi-automatic. Arnold intends to get these chasing cars near the Presidio, where the traffic will be light. That will give him the advantage. From there, the path to Filbert Street is only a short drive.

He cocks the 9 mm, puts the hammer on the safety position, and places the semi under his right leg. He pulls out the 44 Magnum from the holster placing it under his left leg. The Jaguar's black ragtop is up since this day was a bit chilly in San Francisco. The windows are closed. He inserts the seat belt clip into the holder, places his shoulders under the shoulder straps, and puts on his gloves.

Putting the gearshift into first gear, he pulls slowly from

the curb. Checking and rechecking behind him, he notices both vehicles move out into the street behind him. The Mercedes and the Camaro are following about a half-block away. This supports his earlier opinion of the Mercedes being the chase car and the Camaro being the decoy.

Arnold thinks, "Now is not the time to panic and do not let them know you are aware of their presence until the time is right."

Arnold turns right onto Willow Street, and then north on Willow to Van Ness. As he makes a right turn onto Van Ness, he drives twelve blocks to Pine Street, holding a reasonable speed. The Mercedes has remained one and a half blocks behind Arnold. From Pine to California, Arnold increases his speed to almost 45 mph. He has a green light and quickly makes an illegal left turn onto California Street off of Van Ness. Arnold speeds up to 55 mph. This forces the other cars to commit, and after passing Fillmore Street, Arnold increases his speed to 65 mph.

He thinks, "Now is the time to commit."

Arnold has his senses on full alert, his mind is going a mile a minute, and he is starting to enjoy this chase.

Arnold thinks, "This will be your worst nightmare, assholes."

At the end of the next block, he makes a sharp right turn onto Steiner Street. Since the Mercedes has not stayed close enough, he suddenly parks and turns off all the lights. Both the Mercedes and Camaro fly by, and then they slow down since Arnold's Jaguar is out of sight. Arnold pulls out behind the Camaro.

Arnold says to himself, "Your ass is mine."

Like a fighter pilot in a dogfight, Arnold has come up behind the Camaro at the 6 o'clock kill position and has a sidewinder locked on his target. Using his steel bumper guard, he rams the left rear corner of the Camaro. The

HIDDEN IN FRONT OF YOU

Camaro loses control and smashes into a bunch of parked cars on Steiner. The Camaro is now disabled. Arnold considers the decoy to be damaged and out of the chase. He fires six 44-magnum rounds into the disabled Camaro, then reloads the 44-magnum. Arnold turns off all side and rear end lights with the switch Nick installed under the dashboard.

Starting from the curb, he drives up behind the Mercedes. The Mercedes had followed the Jaguar's path onto Steiner then lost sight of the Jaguar, and it is now only going about 25 mph. Arnold comes up behind the Mercedes then passes the Mercedes at about 80 mph. The Mercedes picks up the chase again. With various rates of speeds up to 65 mph, both cars traverse the few blocks in just seconds.

As a youth, Arnold lived in this neighborhood; he rode his bicycle, delivered newspapers, and delivered meds for a local pharmacy. He is aware of every corner and every alleyway. Within the area, there are fewer stoplights and more residential buildings.

Suddenly there is a shot from the passenger side of the Mercedes which misses the Jaguar by inches. The Jaguar has better acceleration than the Mercedes and pulls away.

Everything is clear in Arnold's mind, and he is thinking, "This is for real, but what fun it is."

With the rear and side lights turned off, the Mercedes is having trouble seeing the Jaguar clearly. If he stays on Steiner, he will drive straight to Filbert. Without using the brakes, Arnold hangs a left-hand corner. He increases his speed to almost 110 MPH and is headed for the hilly portion just west of the Army Presidio. Arnold commits to the San Francisco Hills. The Jaguar leaves the ground at each of the intersections. Remaining in control, Arnold continues to drive as fast as he can. The Jaguar is headed up a hill with the Mercedes in pursuit. The Camaro is not there anymore.

Arnold recognizes a siren in the distance.

Arnold says, "Good job, decoy, the cops are now busy with you."

The chase is now between Arnold's Jaguar and the Mercedes.

A second shot rings out. One bullet travels through the plastic back window, hitting the new metal plate's edge. The bullet shatters ripping a small hole in Arnold's right ear and then smashes through the right-hand portion of the windshield.

Blood is pouring out of his ear, and Arnold thinks, "Shit that hurt. These guys are serious. It is time to halt this charade."

Arnold quickly gains another block lead on the Mercedes, turning again and then slides a few feet sideways into an alleyway. Arnold stops, turns off the headlights, dives out of the car, closes the door, and leaves the engine running. He runs a few feet up the alleyway to the sidewalk alongside the roadway. He lays flattened on the street. Within seconds, the black Mercedes is moving slowly down the road with the windows open and two people shining flashlights looking for Arnold's Jaguar.

The Mercedes comes close to his position. Arnold fires all six rounds from his 44-Magnum into the right-hand door of the Mercedes. He puts the spent shells into his jacket pocket and quickly reloads the 44-Magnum. He again empties all six shots into the Mercedes. It slows but continues traveling past him. The black Mercedes continues slowly down the street until it runs into a parked car. No signs of life are visible in the vehicle.

The neighborhood remains quiet, yet some bedroom lights do go on. Arnold jumps to his feet, runs to his Jaguar his climbs in, and leaves the lights off as he drives in the direction of his house on Filbert. Arnold slows to average street speed, engages his seat belt, and turns on both the headlights and taillights. A minute later, Arnold is driving down Lyons Street toward Lombard Street. Arnold turns onto Filbert, and he pulls immediately into the garage. He gets out of the Jaguar and closes the garage door. Simultaneously, Sid with a pistol in hand opens the kitchen door, flips on the garage light, and welcomes the bloodstained Arnold.

Sid comments, "Welcome stranger, what brings you out this fine evening?"

Still excited, Arnold yells back, "Sid, I just had a fantastic ride. Two cars were following me from the Gyro Kabob Restaurant. The San Francisco Police Department got the second car, which was a decoy. The first car, a Mercedes, is sitting next to some parked cars with dead people inside. My Jaguar handled well. The cage protected me."

Arnold is hurting and, of course, still bleeding. He states, "Damn, that was a great ride. Those guys knew their business. Just wasn't their lucky day. Sid, I was partially prepared, but I was not 100%. With a cage, I am 100% protected in case of an accident. But, a head injury like that suffered by Frank Dulles is still a possibility."

He pauses to wipe some blood away. He starts to get a drink of water then decides to get a bottle of beer from the refrigerator.

Pulling a small piece of paper from his wallet, he hands it to Sid and says, "Read this, my friend."

Arnold's motto, "To save the good, you may need to engage in evil. Peace and fairness above all things are desired. Sometimes, blood must be spilled to obtain peace in equable and lasting terms."

Sid responds, "Sir, I do appreciate your boldness, your willingness to risk your body and soul. Yet I will leave this behavior up to you. I wish to protect my body whenever possible. Though I shall be here for you whenever you need my assistance."

Arnold uses his bathroom to clean up and grabs some extra clothes and medical supplies for his ear. Arnold gets up and walks out of the kitchen.

Sid continues, "Mr. Pierce, you need to know that I am aware of a little more than most about your firm's involvement in this town. Please, this is only to help you relax about my part in all of this. The firm has helped a couple of my friends, and I have worked for them on several matters. Doesn't it seem strange that I am so cooperative with you?"

Arnold replies, "That's good to know Sid, because I may need much more help from you shortly.

Sid asks, "What about the Jaguar? Do you want me to find someone to repair it?"

Arnold replies, "Thank you, but I do have a mechanic that can handle that. I will call him and have him come over here to pick it up. He may have a vehicle that I can lease from him. Thanks for your support tonight. I'll call Nick in the morning. There is one more thing. If I am ever in some hospital bed, call Josey immediately. I am a sitting duck there. Josey is under my instruction to get me out asap."

HIDDEN IN FRONT OF YOU

25 - WATCH OUT FOR THE DUMP TRUCK

After arriving mid-morning, Arnold parks his Jaguar. He enters the office area. Jennifer has some coffee ready.

Jennifer says, "What is that bandage for Mr. Pierce?"

Arnold fails to answer. He walks into Julien's office.

Juliet says, "Mr. Pierce, did the bed bugs bite you?"

Arnold says, "Alright, everybody, I got it during a car chase last night. It is just a little hole in my ear lobe."

Juliet says, "You poor baby. Do you want me to fix it with a new bandage and kiss it for you?"

Arnold says, "It is only a small scratch, Ms. tease."

Julien says, "Children. Get along."

Jennifer comes into Julien's office with a phone call waiting for Arnold.

Arnold walks to his office and picks up the call.

Josey says, "The Alicia needs its auxiliary motor prop replaced. I found one on the Alameda Estuary in Oakland. I don't have time to fetch it till the end of the week. Can you call, arrange payment, and have it shipped? I gave the address and phone number to Jennifer."

Arnold says, "Sure, Josey. Before I met Alicia, I had a few girlfriends in Oakland. It would be enjoyable to drive around over there."

Josey says, "Which high schools?"

Arnold says, "Oakland Technical High, Fremont High, Castlemont High, and one nice one at Piedmont High. I did my first sailing on the Oakland/Alameda Estuary, and my first sailboat race was on Lake Merritt there in Oakland. I could drive around, looking at my old haunts."

Unknown to both Josey and Arnold, operatives are listening to Josey giving Jennifer directions and the address. Jennifer does pass on the info to Matt. Both #11 and #12 check-in with Arnold by radio. This time McCarthy sends three cars to attack Arnold.

Arnold leaves for Oakland without a worry. He tours the schools and adds a short trip to Piedmont, where a wealthy girlfriend lives. Things are getting more crowded. He leisurely drives around Lake Merritt, where he had entered his first sailboat race in a sixteen-foot Snipe with a mainsail and jib.

He gets to the propeller shop about 3 p.m. Picks up the new propeller and pays for it by check. He is not looking out for operatives. He starts back to the 880 freeway in a southbound direction as if he has no troubles. He then notices a string of three cars behind him. They are pacing him. He gets out his weaponry, puts his shoulder straps in place, and puts on a helmet he recently purchased after almost losing his ear.

Arnold thinks, "You guys are at it again. This is where I lost that CHP that was 20 feet off my bumper. He thought he had me then like you do now. I lost him then as I will lose you now. Stick close to me, assholes."

Arnold calls on the radio to both of Matt's contractors, saying, "We will be turning north on Highway 880. Stay in the far-left hand lane to avoid the accident that I am going cause."

They respond by saying, "Ten-four."

Arnold is thinking of this small off-ramp on Highway 880 northbound just south of 23rd Avenue. He knows this off-ramp is about the size of a narrow driveway with a 35 mph exit speed limit, which he took at 65 mph in years past. Just like the past, he will position himself in front of a truck.

He enters the Highway 880, going south to the High Street overpass. By using the on and off-ramps, he makes a U-turn onto the Highway 880 northbound. Going north, he is thinking of the off-ramp as he will be approaching 23rd Avenue. He jockeys in front of a large semi-truck, which is going about 65 mph. The off-ramp he wants to use is still a mile or so away. The three cars box him in, which is what Arnold wants them to do. One is in front, and the other two are alongside on his left.

A CHP patrol car is following the speeding truck. Even with the CHP there, the operatives still begin shooting. The thick metal plates keep the bullets from hitting Arnold. The CHP now has two problems; the operatives are firing weapons, and the truck is speeding. And, there is a red Jaguar in the middle of all this.

Arnold thinks of the solid steel bumper Nick put on the front end and the metal encasement he has around him. As they approach the off-ramp, he accelerates and rams the car in front of him, knocking him hard enough that the driver must work to stabilize his vehicle. As the roadway starts a slow turn to the right, they are getting close to the off-ramp. He accelerates one more time. He purposely hits the left-hand side only, causing the car in front of him to go out of control. The truck driver sees what he is doing and backs off. The CHP pulls out beside the truck. The car in front goes out of control, causing the other two to attempt to avoid a collision.

There are many cars involved in a multi-vehicular accident. The operatives have stopped shooting. Arnold thinks there are about fifteen to twenty new bullet holes on the left side of the Jaguar. At the same time, Arnold takes the narrow off-ramp at 65 mph. He is safe and on his way to the residential streets by himself again. The CHP officer must stay with the accident and the illegal assault attempt. He was beside the truck anyway.

Arnold drives to MacArthur Blvd then onto Highway 80 and the 580 northbound to the new Richmond Bridge. Arnold is smiling from ear to ear all the way to the firm. After checking in with Jennifer, he decides there is not much he can do today. On his way through the parking garage, he inspects the bullet holes on the left side of his Jaguar.

He thinks, "Good thing Nick put that cage in last time he had the Jaguar."

Arnold wants to check on his home in Tiburon before it is rented out. Arnold stops by an old haunt of his, a coffee shop in San Rafael, for a cup of Sumatra and Espresso to go. After leaving the coffee shop, unnoticed by Arnold, a newer model black Mustang hardtop is pacing his car. He drives onto the 101 southbound. At Highway 131, Arnold takes the off-ramp. Turning left onto Tiburon Avenue, he makes another left onto the two-lane road into Tiburon toward his home. #11 and #12 are behind the Mustang. He finally notices the black Mustang. Arnold feels a little safer with the steel plate cage. He already has his shoulder straps on, and now he puts on his helmet and driving gloves. The Mustang is not trying to crowd the Jaguar; it just keeps a constant space between the two vehicles. This behavior should have told Arnold something, yet he ignores the info.

Getting closer to his former home, Arnold speeds up, and the Mustang stays about a half a block behind. Fast or slow, the Mustang keeps a similar distance. Turning the last corner before his home, Arnold no longer sees the Mustang. Arnold does not realize what is about to happen. Looking for a Mustang with guns blazing, Arnold slows and stops alongside the retaining wall by his garage driveway. He hits the garage door opener. The door raises, and no one is inside the garage.

It is odd to have a dump truck parked in front of the next-door neighbor's home with a driver and passenger sitting in it. Suddenly, from the right-hand side comes the dump truck bearing down on the Jaguar. With a horrible sound, along with a sudden movement to the left, Arnold and the Jaguar are thrown ten feet into the concrete wall. The Jaguar is pushed up against the concrete wall, partially crushing the

HIDDEN IN FRONT OF YOU

Jaguar. Arnold's cage helps protect him, and the helmet softens any head blow. The truck backs up and comes at the Jaguar again, making the vehicle a u-shaped piece of metal.

The truck quickly backs out of the driveway turns and drives away before anyone arrives. The black Mustang comes around the corner following the garbage truck. Arnold is barely conscious. Arnold feels like his right arm is broken, his right leg is almost useless, and Arnold's consciousness comes and goes. #11 and #12 empty their weapons into the cab of the dump truck, then it disappears.

Within minutes red lights and sirens are headed his way.

Once the EMT's arrive, Arnold says, "Please, here is my card. Call my secretary Jennifer and tell her what has happened. Please do it immediately."

Both #11 and #12 have already called Jennifer.

Within five minutes, Jennifer had the message. She calls both Josey and Julien to tell them that Arnold is being transported to the San Francisco General Hospital & Trauma Center on Potrero Avenue. Arnold passes out.

The E.M.T.'s check his vitals then place him on a gurney. After several hours in the ER. They move him to a private room. He has become conscious but cannot move due to the bandages and the pain.

Arnold has refused any pain-killing medication. He is concerned about being unconscious.

Julien and Josey are waiting in his room.

Julien says, "Hello Arnold, it sure didn't take long for you to get into trouble. We will be leaving in a few minutes. First, I need to place some cameras on the wall."

Josey has brought a collapsible gurney for Arnold's placement into a van. Julien finishes installing the cameras and then turns toward Arnold. He and Josey pull this stretcher on wheels close to the bed, and they slide Arnold off the bed. Julien snatches the drip system and fixes the blanket to make it look like Arnold is still in the bed.

Quickly Julien and Josey hustle him out of the hospital emergency entryway into a waiting van.

Julien stops to call Sid.

Sid answers, "Sid here."

Julien says, "Sid, I have Arnold with me, will you please have the garage door open at his house."

Sid answers, "Of course, Julien, I will leave the garage open. Just drive-in, and I will close the door."

On the way from the San Francisco General, Julien, and Arnold have a little discussion on the evening's agenda. Arnold tells Julien of his drive from Sid's house, through Oakland to his old home and the total surprise he received when he got there.

Julien starts laughing and says, "You're a stupid shit, the old fashion bait and switch was used on you. You should have picked it up when the Mustang failed to close in on you when there were opportunities."

Stunned with this information, Arnold sighs heavily and says, "Tricked by that old of a method. I just stated to someone how history is cyclic in nature. Maybe I should have listened to myself for a change."

Julien asks, "How bad do you feel?"

Arnold replies, "Three broken ribs, a cracked collar bone, a strained shoulder, a mild concussion, and some pain from bruises all over. Otherwise, it is nice to be above ground."

Julien responds, "At least you are a tough little shit. Do these people realize how tough you are?"

Arnold answers, "Let's hope not, Julien. I would like to keep them in the dark. I had just fended off an attack in Oakland by three cars, putting a least fifteen to thirty new bullet holes in the Jaguar. I felt quite excited when I was able to get away, unharmed."

Julien pulls into the garage. Sid is waiting at the kitchen

door and closes the garage door with the garage door opener. Josey and Julien lift the gurney out of the van roll it to the kitchen steps and carry it into the kitchen. They roll it to the large room just off the kitchen, which for the moment, becomes Arnold's new bedroom.

Sid says, "Mr. Pierce, have you decided to listen to me yet? These people keep coming at you. They don't seem to be willing to stop. You stated earlier that they have an excellent intelligence gathering framework in place. They may know you better than you know yourself."

Arnold replies, "Damn it, you have a good point. I still hate to creep away and hide."

Sid jumps in, "But Arnold, for what I have in mind, you would be right under their noses, and they would never see you. You will be close enough to be one of them as you stand there. Just how close do you want your enemies?"

Arnold asks, "Okay, Mr. Sid Johnson, I know what you have up your sleeve."

Sid asks, "How do you feel currently? Are you in good enough shape for this discussion, or should we wait until you gain some strength?"

Arnold responds, "Let's wait, Sid. I've had enough for one day. I will need to be more alert for what you are about to propose."

Both Julien and Josey grab a few hours of sleep. It is almost dawn. Sid fixes some breakfast and makes a large pot of coffee. After eating, Arnold falls asleep, and Julien leaves to check on the videos from the cameras he has installed in Arnold's hospital room. Josey goes to get the propeller from the damaged Jaguar so he can finish his work on the Alicia.

Arnold sleeps until noon.

First, he calls Nick, who answers, "Hello, this is Nick. I have a feeling that you need my services again. Can't you keep that Jaguar on the road? Is it your Jag that got smashed in Tiburon last night? The story is all over the news this morning. You must be the missing patient from San Francisco General."

Arnold says, "I got a little busy last night. Would you pick up my Jag from the front of my old house and try to save whatever? Do not call me. I will call you if anything becomes a problem. David has a power of attorney for all my assets. Sorry, I have no time to play. I must go. Thanks in advance, Nick. Bye."

Next, Arnold calls David.

Amy answers saying, "Good morning, may I help you?"

Arnold replies, "Good morning Amy, is David available?"

She switches the call to David.

"David, here, good morning, busy man."

Arnold says, "David, I did have a busy evening. They sent another one after me, and I was a little careless. There is a power of attorney made out to you for all my assets. Please fetch it from Jennifer's desk. It is there waiting for you. It is dated from last year, but of course, it is still valid. I will stay in touch by phone. I doubt that I will be coming into the office for quite a while."

David responds, "All right, Arnold. I hope you remain safe and we see each other again. I love you like a son, Mr. Pierce. I would hate to lose you. Bye for now!"

David hangs up.

Incoming is a call from Julien, "Hello Arnold. Stay awake, buddy. Your request to be removed was right on the mark. Do I have some great photos for you? The cameras worked well. I will bring them by this evening."

Arnold replies, "I look forward to seeing you, Julien. Thanks again for last night."

Each hangs up. Arnold settles in for a nap. Sid is monitoring the residential area surrounding Arnold's home and is watching over Arnold as he sleeps.

HIDDEN IN FRONT OF YOU

Sid helps Arnold clean up and put on some comfortable clothes. At 6 p.m., Arnold is sitting up in the front room sofa.

He calls Claire, who answers, "Hello, stranger."

Arnold says, "I called to tell you that I am not coming back to the office soon. I won't be able to see you for a while. I had a bad automobile accident. I broke some bones and had quite a headache."

Claire responds, sounding desperate, "Honey, I am here to help. Where are you? What can I do to help?"

Arnold says, "I am okay. I am in a safe place. I am going to leave town for a while. It seems that someone is trying to kill me, and I really do not know what to do, so I am going to get lost for a while. I need to go now. Bye!"

They hang up, and Arnold thinks, "Do I trust this woman? She has never shown that much interest in the past. David has said that he thinks she may have been buddying up with the bad guys. Maybe she is just covering her backside again."

Not knowing Claire's intentions, Arnold is going to keep her at arm's length. 6 p.m. arrives, and the doorbell rings. Sid answers the door, and there is Julien, Juliet, and Alissa.

Sid says, "Please come on in."

Arnold turns to Julien and says, "Julien, Juliet must have more of her mother's genes because she sure is a lot prettier than you."

From that point in the visit, each start into the conversations. Hours go by before Julien, Juliet, and Alissa must leave. Just before leaving, Julien hands a package of pictures of the individuals entering Arnold's hospital room.

Julien says, "I think you will want to see these."

The visit was most pleasant and rewarding to all. Arnold cannot walk, so he remains seated while Julien, Juliet, and Alissa say their goodbyes. Juliet runs over to give Arnold a big kiss and a light hug before she leaves.

Arnold appreciates the affection and says, "I am going to look forward to more of that in the future."

As soon as the girls are out of earshot, Arnold opens the envelope full of pictures.

Arnold screams, "Sid, I know these guys. They worked for me and were good contractors, but very mercenary. Basically, they are thugs for hire and have no morals."

Arnold says, "I just received more information about what would have happened to me if I had stayed in the hospital the other night. Not long after I was ushered out through the hospital back door, two guys came into my room to kill me. We have the pictures here. I was able to get out just minutes before their arrival. I know their whereabouts, I know them well, and I plan on grabbing them for a message to McCarthy. Their names are Jack Sare and Joe Mitchem. They most likely have no idea that I am aware of their actions. I could pretend to hire them for an event, and they would jump at the chance. They will do anything for money. So as soon as I regain some strength, let's pay them a visit."

Sid replies, "Business is picking up each time we speak. Keep up the good work, Mr. Pierce. With you continuing this way, we will be putting you in the ground soon."

26 - ARNOLD'S TRANSITION

It is an early evening, and Arnold is still mostly confined to sitting or short trips within the house. His headaches have diminished, he can now breathe naturally, and he feels more alert.

Sid says, "You look like you are in good enough shape to listen to me."

Sid pauses in case there was an objection.

Arnold says, "Ok, let's talk about your disappearing or hiding, whatever you wish to call it. You now add on to your compassionate personality an ability to require all things of me. You are just a downright resourceful smart ass."

Sid responds, "Ah, yes, but you have not heard all of it. You practiced with your friend at Finnochio's. You are already able to impersonate a female You shall live as a woman."

Sid continues, "They are getting better and getting closer to success each time they attack you. You stated that McCarthy has a better intelligence gathering system, has contractors that are totally subordinate to him, and the number of his operatives seems to be unlimited. His operatives are everywhere, and they have a system in place. He already has an army. You are limited in number and are starting to fight from scratch."

Arnold says, "Damn it to hell. You do have such good points, Mr. Sid Johnson, you are right this time and not wrong. Damn you. Your wisdom is showing me that I am just resistant. Good night."

The next morning David calls.

Arnold says, "Hi, David."

Sounding excited, David says, "Arnold, who else in the office knows anything about you and an automobile accident where you sustained serious injuries? I just received information that you have a possible concussion, and you may be leaving town for safety. This information came from Julien's bugging of Claire's phone. When I picked up a power of attorney, I was careful not to inform anyone of your position. Jennifer was expecting you back within a few days."

Arnold responds, "Claire is just being Claire. She is the only one I gave that information. I told her certain information that was not shared with others to test the waters. I have not felt relaxed with her for many months. This tells me that Claire has been one of my weak links."

"Let's not disclose this awareness to the group. Let's use it to our advantage. I will deal with it later. In fact, I want to deal with it personally. Talk to you soon. Bye."

It's now day one of Arnold's transition. Sid sits Arnold down to enlighten him on what is about to happen.

Sid starts out saying, "Arnold, you are now called Bridget Ester O'Conner. I got the name from David. He believes some contractor is coming in to replace you during your absence. You will drive a pink Mercedes sedan with steel plates in the doors and bulletproof glass. You will have a "C" cup breast; you are a clothes hound, you love classical music, you entertain as it is one of your favorite passions. You cook meals for the enjoyment of the meal."

"You are Arnold's first cousin. Your father, Sean, who died in the Pacific during the Second World War. Sean was Aiden's brother. You have known Arnold your whole life. You and Arnold used to sail, play, and hang out together. You helped Arnold when he lost his parents and Alicia. Bridget was a close friend of Alicia's sharing many days with Arnold and Alicia."

"You are quite feminine. You must put those feminine expressions into your communication. You enjoy showing your cleavage by presenting your large breasts to men. When you walk your ass wiggles. You love high heels, lipstick, and perfume."

"You are stubborn, hate politics, are strong-minded, and you and Arnold would argue."

"You have some of Arnold's fighting skills."

Sid pauses briefly and then continues, "Tomorrow morning, you will be going to Dr. Neel's Clinic for the first in a set of surgeries. Sometime after that, you will start with an electrologist for the removal of your beard. When you are in a bathroom with another woman, your presentation must be totally feminine. I will do your nails until you learn how, and I will always maintain your hair. Your hair is already long enough that I can shape it into a feminine style. You will periodically shave your entire body. You will always wear perfume and body lotion to help soften your skin. You will apply skin-softening cream over your whole body and especially on your arms and hands. You must feel soft and smooth to the touch. In every sense, you will dress and act like a woman. There shall be no men's clothes available to you."

Sid says, "Now Bridget, what do you say to me? Do you want my assistance in helping you implement this façade?"

Bridget replies, "Okay, you have convinced me, you bully. Do I get the opportunity to act as if I am helpless?"

Sid is smiling while saying, "You can complain, but it will be received by my deaf ears. You must think you're a woman 24/7 in everything you do. You are under my care, and you are my responsibility, so you shall do as I say. I am offering this to save your life, my friend. I will keep repeating this statement until you adhere to my demands."

"Your training at Finocchio's has prepared you well. A little more female to female interaction should do the trick."

It's Wednesday at 8:00 a.m., and Bridget is sitting in Dr. Neel's office. Dr. Neel walks in, shaking both Sid and Arnold's hands.

He says, "I understand we are going to perform some surgeries tomorrow and Friday."

Sid says, "Doctor, this is Bridget alias Arnold. We have an emergency. He has a very aggressive group that is trying to eliminate him. We must hide Arnold behind the illusion of a woman called Bridget. Arnold, alias Bridget, has been trained to crossdress successfully. These changes that you and I have discussed need to be done immediately, and for the time being, they must be permanent."

Dr. Neel says, "I do understand your need. I also want to be part of this to help you and to do some of my own research. Here are the medications. They include testosterone-blockers, estrogen, and painkillers. I have the breast implants scheduled for 9 a.m. tomorrow. You said, "C Cup" Is that the choice for the cup size? Why so large? Is it to keep the eyes off everything else?"

Sid nods, yes.

Dr. Neel continues, "The next day, Friday, the facial surgery is also scheduled for 9 a.m. I will provide the necessary pain medications today. Bridget, you will be quite uncomfortable and in some pain for many days. Please be patient. See you at 9 a.m."

The next morning, Bridget has not eaten. At 9 a.m., Bridget is waiting in the surgery room with everything prepared for surgery. The anesthesiologist arrives. She administers the necessary medication for the first step of the operation, Bridget feels a bit calmed down and little sleepy. As the surgeon enters, the anesthesiologist ups the dose. Bridget becomes unconscious. The surgeon works on each side separately, sixty to sixty-five minutes per side. When the surgeon is done, the anesthesiologist starts Bridget's reversal. By the time the surgeon has completed closing the incisions, Bridget starts showing signs of awareness. Bridget is wheeled into the recovery room to finish waking up. Hours later, Dr.

Neel came in for a discussion.

Dr. Neel says, "Everything went well. There should be no problems with this surgery. The question is, Bridget, do you want to go home and then return or just stay here tonight?"

Bridget replies, "I'll stay."

Bridget falls asleep.

At 9 a.m. Friday, Bridget is once again waiting in the surgery room. The setup is entirely different for facial surgery. The anesthesiologist arrives and administers the necessary medication for the first step. Bridget feels a bit calmed down and a little sleepy. As the surgeon comes in, he wants to discuss the surgeries for today.

The surgeon says, "We are going to make some minor changes in your facial expression that will be more acceptable in presenting you as a female."

Almost immediately, Bridget becomes unconscious. The surgeon works slowly on the facial features, then the nose, and finally on the chin bone. When the surgeon has completed the alterations, the anesthesiologist starts Bridget's reversal. By the time the surgeon has completed closing the incisions, Bridget starts showing signs of awareness. Bridget is wheeled into the recovery room to finish waking up. At 1:00 p.m., Dr. Neel comes in for another discussion.

He says, "Everything went well again. There should be no problems with this second surgery. My suggestion is for you to go home. As soon as you can start walking every day, walk as much as you can tolerate. Since you are trying to impersonate a female, you should have a discussion with Sid about tucking. Your crotch has a small cavity that will let you hide your penis and testicles. Sid can supply some specially made panties with additional aids to tucking along with the required pads."

For the first three days at home, Bridget has so much pain

that walking around inside the house is stressful. Bridget's face is still bruised and sore, but her breast area is very tender. Bridget complains to ole Deaf Ears that these breasts weigh too much and are always in the way. There is no reply by Mr. Deaf Ears.

On the third day, Bridget is getting stir crazy. The pain has reduced.

Bridget can at least move around, but her movement is impeded by her new breasts. Dr. Neel said that the breast augmentation patient usually resumes a healthy life at one-week of post-op.

Bridget starts to perform her duties as being feminine. Sid has pierced her ears. The studs are visible with tiny diamond looking glass.

Sid has supplied a rack of earrings. Bridget shows her dislike for many.

Bridget prefers silver single short shaft hanging earrings and long strings of small gold chains.

Bridget goes to the transgender salon to get make-overs. As they are applied, the technician helps train her in the methods of designing and applying makeup. As Bridget gains some experience applying makeup, she chooses a slightly darker base tone than that used by the technician. She uses a slightly darker tone around the eyes, with black mascara and a soft black eyeliner. She wants the eyes to stand out but not dominate. Bridget has chosen several lipsticks from Revlon, depending on the occasion. Bridget uses a lighter, almost neutral color around the house, a vivid darker red for wearing to work, and a bright red for evening dress. Occasionally, she will purchase another color and brand to test the lipstick appearance.

Bridget's trips to Finnochio's is starting to pay off. Many times, after practicing with the girls, Bridget stays dressed and drives home to have Sid check things out. His approval is helping Bridget's confidence. Evelyn's help is adding to Bridget's spirit.

Bridget is finding it more accessible to think of herself as a woman when she stays concentrated on it. She has started cooking and cleaning the house because, to her, it seems more like a feminine activity. Sid has removed every sign of a masculine environment. Sid has replaced the closets with a massive walk-in closet containing clothes along each wall. There are built-in dressers and jewelry drawers with a six-foot-high mirror at each end of the cabinets. The entire set is what most women would want.

Another few days go by, and Bridget is walking around, trying to exercise and taking long walks into the Presidio dressed as a woman. Sid mandates that she dress as a woman 24/7.

Sid keeps saying to Bridget, "Remember you are in my care, you are my responsibility, so you shall do as I say."

Bridget wears girl's tennis shoes, women's knee-high skirts, and frilly blouses. The breasts are still tender, yet she is getting accustomed to them. They are held up with a soft sports bra for now. In the last few months, Bridget has let her hair lengthen. Sid has trimmed Bridget's hair a little to be more feminine appearing, put in streaks of blonde, and then finally a curly perm. The many months of training at Finocchio's is showing signs of paying off. Each morning Bridget practices applying makeup, finishing her nails, combing out her hair, and using perfume. Currently, the powder is hiding the bruising of facial surgery. It is becoming clear to Bridget that presenting herself as a woman is much harder than she expected. Yet the illusion is starting to pay off.

Bridget practices the training everywhere she goes. She is in the local supermarket almost every day, and she will try to make it a point to talk to everyone. Her confidence level is increasing, and this total acceptance has given Bridget hope for success.

Bridget continues to make friends with the locals. There is a large built-in barbequing unit on the back porch, and she is planning her first barbeque. Bridget purchases some new pans and barbeque racks for the kitchen and the grill on the back porch. There is a woman cook at Ms. Brown's Hamburger Hut, who has agreed to stop by for the barbeque. Several salesgirls have shown interest in coming to the grill from the different apparel shops, and many of the employees from the supermarket have shown interest. Women are accepting her as a woman, and that is very promising. Bridget thinks that this barbeque should help things along.

27 - READY FOR WORK

Bridget calls the firm with a female voice and asks for David Worth.

David answers, "Hello, Ms. O'Connor. Are you ready to stop by the firm?"

Bridget replies, "Yes, sir, Mr. Worth. I thought I would drop by this coming Friday morning. Does that meet with your calendar?"

David says, "Sure, I'll make it work. What time?"

Bridget says, "How about 10 a.m.?"

David says, "Thank you for calling Ms. O'Connor. See you on Friday."

They both hang up. David is surprised to speak with Bridget, who he believes is a female contractor.

Bridget, like Arnold, calls Julien to explain the background, the scenario, and the objective of his actions. She tries to explain it in complete detail with Arnold's voice.

Bridget, using Arnold's voice, says, "Be prepared to manage the accounting department until we can find a suitable replacement for George. I'm sure, with minimal effort, you will do a much better job."

Then in closing, she says to Julien, "Am I asking you to do too much?"

Julien responds, "I'll be there for you, no matter what."

Bridget, again as Arnold says, "I may let Bridget take care of this one."

Julien becomes excited, saying, "Do you mean that Bridget has finally shown up?"

Trying to keep Arnold's voice, she says, "Of course. She will be in the office on Friday to meet all of you."

Julien says, "I was beginning to believe that she is a myth."

Bridget, as Arnold says, "Julien, I am renting her my place on Filbert while she is here, and I am moving to one of my other rentals in the city."

The conversation ends with Julien saying, "See you some time; please take care."

The months of hard work at Finocchio's is paying off again. Bridget continues to roam the shops in the area, practicing her skills. People see only a female, and Bridget feels the illusion is working. Many women are sharing their phone numbers. Occasionally, a woman will come by the house to see the closets and other feminine items like pictures, music assortment, the outstanding kitchen, and the barbeque grill. Sometimes they just come by to visit with Bridget. She is becoming more like a woman as she continues to chat with other females. She meets with them while sharing secrets. The one-woman visitor wanted to learn how to do her makeup like Bridget. Progress is definitely being made. Bridget is sitting, walking, raising her voice, and making hand movements in a more feminine way.

Occasionally Bridget will try on three-inch heels, a tight skirt, and a V-shaped blouse that exposes her cleavage. It may be only practice, but it is a significant change for her. As she revisits the local shops with her upgraded style of dressing, she continues to get compliments. She feels that it must be the right choice.

Bridget asks Sid for some help. She wants to know what to wear on her first day at the firm.

Sid says, "You will want to knock their eyes out. Let's choose some things to prepare you for that day."

They go through the choices. Sid picks an uplifting pink bra that will accentuate her cleavage and then selects a pair of three-inch black heels, sheer black nylons, panties with the butt pads, a tight-fitting grey suit with long sleeves. The skirt falls just past her knees, and the very expensive see-through blouse with full sleeves shows it all. Bridget tries the pieces separately. To her delight, they fit correctly and give off the feminine side. What else can you expect from Sid?

For the next few days, Bridget tries matching selections to become acclimated. She finally chooses a set that is close to what Sid had picked. Bridget is walking with her butt wiggling. It helps when she is wearing heels. Bridget has mastered the ability to walk in heels with her feet crossing over to step on a straight line. She has improved her hand movements and high voiced responses that are strictly feminine, along with her facial expressions. Bridget is aware that Bridget is actually Arnold, but it is coming up less often. As she tours the local shops, she is getting more men to notice her, and many more hits than before. Like a good actress, she must put herself into the character she is playing.

Sid keeps saying, "You are a woman. You must think you are a woman."

Bridget has restrained herself from contacting the firm's personnel. Why not let them believe that Arnold is in bad shape. Make it appear that Arnold is in hiding while recuperating. This will send a message to the McCarthy Group. They may consider that he is critical and unable to act.

Without the Finocchio training, Bridget would be working for months to get where she is today. Bridget is hoping that her quick turnaround will be a factor in misleading everyone, especially McCarthy.

Since Sid has introduced his friend Evelyn, a transwoman who works at the supermarket, to Bridget. No one at the market knows of Evelyn's transition. Evelyn spent over four years in her development with multiple failures along the way. Having gone through the change herself and having experienced many failures and successes has made it easy for Evelyn to present ideas to Bridget. Bridget begins to depend upon Evelyn's assistance.

Friday morning has arrived, and Bridget is anxious yet

only partially confident about her first appearance at the office. It is one thing to fool the law firm staff, but even more critical that she can mislead the McCarthy Group. Bridget has a medium breakfast with strong Sumatra coffee. She finishes breakfast by 7:30. A shower and a shave of her face and her entire body. As she dresses, she applies a little extra Chanel Number 5, and lots of lotion everywhere.

With a sense of confidence, she walks through the garage, clicking her heels all the way to the pink Mercedes. She drives leisurely onto Lombard, and then Richardson. Soon, the Mercedes is crossing the Golden Gate Bridge, and the window is already down, and she is smelling the wetness of the fog. For Arnold, this drive would be routine, yet this is Bridget's first drive over the Golden Gate. Other motorists are noticing the female driver in the pink Mercedes. This is quite a different feeling for Bridget. Driving past the Sausalito off-ramp, it also seems so new. Just before turning off for San Rafael is the turnoff for San Quentin. Still, it feels so different driving in a dress.

Bridget thinks she must appear to be happy, outgoing, and pleased to be at the office. She must let them know how much Arnold has told her about them, and she must act anxious to get started.

Bridget is still quite aware of the implants. The pain has lowered to an acceptable level yet has not disappeared. As Bridget drives into the parking structure, she automatically pulls into Arnold's parking space. Before getting out of the Mercedes, she reapplies her lipstick and combs her hair. Feeling uneasy, Bridget walks into the elevator. Bridget presses the button for the twelfth floor, and the elevator starts to lift upward. Her heart is pounding as she experiences fear.

She thinks, "How do I get away with this? Are they going to recognize me? Oh well, the proof will be in the pudding.

HIDDEN IN FRONT OF YOU

She calms down a little. Remember, honey; you are a female."

Bridget steps off the elevator and walks up to Matilda, saying, "I am Bridget O'Connor. I am here to see Mr. Worth."

As Matilda reaches over the counter to shake Bridget's hand, she says, "I'll walk you to his office."

Bridget follows Matilda to David's office.

Matilda says to Amy, David's secretary, "This is Ms. Bridget O'Connor, here to see Mr. Worth."

Amy says, "Thank you, Matilda. Ms. O'Connor, would you care for some coffee while you wait.? David should be available in a few minutes."

Bridget says, "Yes, Amy, may I have it black, please."

As Bridget is waiting for David, she says to herself, "No one has the slightest idea I am really Arnold. Shut up, girl, you are Bridget, a beautiful female. You are a sexy woman."

Within a few minutes, David is available. He walks toward her reaching forward to shake her hand. Bridget answers with her hand. Her hands are soft, allowing David to continue the impression that she is really a woman.

Bridget says, "It is a pleasure meeting you, Mr. Worth. Arnold has spoken of you often."

David says, "Arnold is the greatest. Do you know him well?"

Bridget replies, "I am Arnold's first cousin. Sean, my father, is the brother of Arnold's father, Aiden. Arnold, Alicia, and I spent a lot of time together. I believe that Arnold is a great individual and is as straight as an arrow. For me, it is a different story. I took the low road for a while until Arnold helped me. I have worked as a receptionist, a secretary, an assistant attorney, and soon, I hope to be a practicing attorney. I must advise you that my husband is MIA in Vietnam. If he were to be found, I would be gone in an instant. But what are the chances of that occurring?"

Arnold said that I could use his office and secretary until he returns. Is that okay with you and the firm?"

David says, "It is all just fine. We are happy to see you here with us. I have said that I had already interviewed you. Please do not let it out that I hadn't? Shall we wander around meeting some people?"

Bridget says, "I am looking forward to that. I'll leave my coffee here."

Bridget sets down her coffee and continues, "I have met Matilda and Amy. I am looking forward to meeting Jennifer. Arnold has rented me his house for my time here, and he says that I may as well have access to his secretary, parking place, and office until he returns."

David interjects, asking, "Do you talk to Arnold often?"

She replies, "We chat every day. He is trying to make my time here as productive as possible. I am to check in on Sammy and Alex on Monday. He also says I should find others to help, but I'll need to discuss each one with him personally."

They leave David's office. The first stop is Julien's office. As they walk in, Julien greets them each with a handshake.

Julien says, "Welcome aboard, Ms. O'Connor. This is my daughter, Juliet."

After shaking hands with Bridget, Juliet seems to stare at Bridget. She just won't take her eyes off Bridget.

Bridget says, "Juliet is everything okay?"

Juliet snaps out of her, staring and says, "You look very similar to Arnold, but you are female."

Bridget receiving her first resistance, says, "Dear, Arnold and I are related. We are first cousins. His father, Aiden, was my father's brother."

Bridget says to herself, "Phew. Juliet is so bright, and she says what is on her mind, I had not counted on that."

HIDDEN IN FRONT OF YOU

Next, David walks her to Arnold's office.

He says to Jennifer, "Jennifer, I would like to introduce Ms. O'Connor. She will be using Arnold's office."

Jennifer reaches out to shake hands and says, "Welcome aboard. It is wonderful to meet you. Do you have any special instructions?"

Bridget says, "Why don't we play it by ear. Arnold speaks so highly of you that I am sure that we will do well together."

Speaking to David and Jennifer, Bridget says, "I am planning a barbeque at my house a week from this Friday, would any of you be interested in coming. The party starts at 3 p.m. You do not get off on time for the start of it, but everything will be there for you to enjoy when you do arrive. Please let me know."

David walks Bridget to HR.

Cecilia says, "Hello, Ms. O'Connor. I have some paperwork for you to sign."

Bridget signs the papers and says, "Nice to meet you, Cecilia. Arnold has said very nice things about you. I feel like I already know you."

As Bridget starts to walk away, Cecilia steps up and shakes her hand with an accompanying smile.

As Bridget and David enter his office again, Bridget says, "David is the barbeque too much to ask? It is one of my pastimes. I love having people over for a meal and a good visit. Here is my personal telephone number. It is unlisted."

David says, "You say you chat with Arnold regularly. We have hardly heard from him since the accident. Is he alright, or is he just trying to play the tough guy?"

Bridget answers, "Arnold just started walking this last week. He is recuperating slowly, and under the circumstances, Arnold will be staying in seclusion for quite a while. He has left most things up to me."

"When I officially arrive, I hope my position will not offend anyone. I will be reporting for work on Monday after the barbeque. Please let me know if any of you want to come? Thank you for the introductions and discussions. Hopefully, I will see you on Friday."

As she walks out, she waves to Jennifer and Matilda. Riding the elevator down, she feels that it went much better than she expected.

28 - BRIDGET'S COMING OUT PARTY

Starting on Saturday and through the week, Bridget begins the process of putting the barbeque together. She orders several pies, some ice cream, and lots of liquor. She would be happy with just the drinks that Arnold prefers, but that would give a signal to the firm's people. Arnold's preferred items will be included, along with several more feminine offerings. By Saturday evening, she has all the meats, the sauces, the vegetables, most drinks, and a full rack of liquors ordered. It is getting to be fun for Bridget. She has never done this type of party, and maybe she will continue after Bridget is gone.

Bridget contemplates what she will wear. There are a couple of short dresses that are extravagant and showing what Sid has suggested. Bridget tries them on during her day at home on Sunday. She picks an outfit and the appropriate accessories that express her feminine side and lets those C-cup breasts show off. The facial bruising is significantly less than last week and is easily covered with makeup.

Bridget thinks, "It is a go."

As an after-thought, Arnold calls Juliet.

"Hello, this is Alissa."

Bridget, in Arnold's voice, says, "Hello Alissa, may I talk to your Mom?"

Bridget hears in the background Alissa calling her mother.

Juliet says, "Hello, this is Juliet."

Bridget continues in Arnold's voice, "This is Arnold. How are you doing? I am getting better as time goes by."

Juliet replies, "Mr. Pierce, you have made me wait for two whole weeks without saying hello. Did you forget that I exist? Right now, I am not in much of a mood to talk with you. You hurt my feelings."

Bridget, sounding like Arnold, says, "Yes, but there are excuses. I had trouble thinking for the first week. I am letting

Bridget rent my house while she is in town. I have information that the McCarthy Group is wondering where I am. Bridget is taking over some of my duties. Would you mind escorting her around? I should have called before this."

Juliet replies, "Yes, you should have. Remember our talk at the Farallon Islands. We promised each other that we would always be upfront with one another. I feel that you are not as upfront as you agreed. I am a little shook up right now. My intuition says something is wrong. I am not asking; I am telling you to straighten it up. I love you, Mr. Pierce. No way do I want to lose you."

Click goes the receiver as she hangs up.

Bridget says to herself, "I was without compassion. The poor girl is definitely hurt."

Bridget continues to prepare the foods for the big barbeque. Most of the pies were purchased. No one offered a rhubarb pie, so Bridget had to find the rhubarb and a recipe. Since she had never made one, it was a real learning experience. She thought that besides the green chartreuse, she would also include grey chartreuse with higher alcohol content and a black licorice flavor. For the rest of the day, Bridget tries to stay on target. Hurting Juliet's feelings keeps returning to her thoughts.

Monday morning is a sunny day with no fog. The bay waters have gentle swells like snow moguls throughout.

Bridget thinks, "If I were to go out into the bay, I bet I could find some nut water skiing. The water temperature is 55 degrees Fahrenheit, and the air temperature is about sixty degrees with no wind, a perfect day."

Bridget calls the San Rafael florist. She orders a dozen red roses to be delivered to Juliet.

The card reads, "I apologize. Love, Arnold."

For the next three days, Bridget keeps picking up new items for Friday. Thursday, Jennifer calls to accept the

HIDDEN IN FRONT OF YOU

barbeque invitation.

Jennifer says, "She is coming, but her husband must work. Matilda and her children are coming. David and Angela are both coming. Julien will be there at about 5:30. No word from Juliet and Alissa."

Josey called separately to confirm his arrival.

Josey says, "See you Friday, Ms. O'Connor."

Friday morning, Bridget gets out of bed early to start cooking the meat. The vegetables are each prepared for cooking in their own pans. The drinks are out, silverware, plates, and glasses have been out since Tuesday. The liquor is ready for serving, and the lineup of liqueurs is impressive. She only needs to put out some ice.

Bridget starts by showering, shaving, and washing and drying her hair, which is becoming second nature. She adds some eyeliner and chooses a bright lipstick for the party.

Bridget has food warmers placed on the kitchen worktable for food availability. A glass of the grey chartreuse floating on top of the green chartreuse is a good start. Bridget is considering a drink called the "Pouse Café" as a bonus.

While Bridget is waiting in anticipation, back at the firm, Julien and Juliet are having a discussion.

Juliet says, "But Daddy, I am not going. I am furious with Arnold, and I told him so. He sent me flowers on Monday, apologizing. My feelings are hurt. I do not want to go."

Julien says, "My sweet, he may have been unable to or did not feel well enough to call. There may be several reasons. Possibly he was under pressure, and it was overlooked. The man has the entire firm's future riding on his back. If he apologized, he must realize his mistake. None of us are perfect love."

Juliet says, "Daddy, are you sticking up for him? He and I agreed to communicate completely. Then he let two weeks go by without saying a word. I am sitting here worrying and feeling lost for two weeks."

Julien says, "Now you sound as if you are feeling sorry for yourself. It sounds more like that than anything he did."

Juliet says, "Daddy, I am scared."

Julien reaches over, hugging his beautiful daughter.

Julien says, "Trust your old dad. It will be okay."

Friday afternoon, Evelyn arrives first.

She looks around, saying, "My, Sid has made some major changes. You look stunning. Most girls do not look as good as you, dear. How do you like the C-cup?"

Bridget replies, "The C-cup keeps guy's eyes off the rest of me, and I get hit on all the time. To tell you the truth, it makes me feel a little uneasy."

Evelyn replies, "Isn't that what you want, sweetie? Keep throwing that femininity at them. I know that you are testing the waters, but you do not need to test. You are already fantastic looking and acting. You will pass."

A few minutes after 3 p.m., and most of the people from the local shops are now arriving. Bridget begins telling each person about the selections available. The barbeque smells are filtering in from the back porch whenever Bridget goes out to check on the meats. As each female arrives, Bridget tries to give them a tour of her closets. The party is moving along well.

Each guest seems to be actively talking with others and eating. Everyone seems pleased.

Bridget keeps moving around the room, chatting with each guest. She announces the different pies and ice creams available, plus the special Pouse Café drink. She also suggests an Irish coffee with a shot of chartreuse or Grand Marnier after the Pouse Café.

Some have families at home, and others have children or husbands to go home to, so they must leave early. As they are leaving, they each state what a wonderful gathering it was, and if there is another, they say, please invite me. And, there were several offers to bring something next time.

There is a short lull before the firm's staff start to arrive. David and Angela are the first to come. Bridget shows them around the apartment, the closets, and the food. Bridget explains the options, and Both David and Angela dive right into the food. Angela liked the closet space and full mirrors.

Josey walks in, and Bridget shows him around.

She says to Josey, "Unless you want to wear one of my dresses, the closet will not interest you."

Jennifer and Matilda arrive together along with Matilda's two children.

Bridget says to herself, "Give the children special attention."

Bridget walks over, introducing herself to them. She grabs their hands and escorts them to the food, explaining what is available. Then she fixes them an individual plate of goodies and offers each one an apple drink.

Moments later, Julien walks in with both Juliet and Alissa. Bridget goes directly to Alissa, and introduces herself, and then walks Alissa around to the food and drinks. She finds a seat for Alissa to sit and eat. As bubbly as Bridget can get, she walks over to Julien and Juliet, grabbing their hands and walks them over to the food and drink.

Bridget says, "Don't be bashful, eat all you want. If we run out, I'll get more. Here are the alcoholic beverages, and over there are the non-alcoholic ones. Also, I have an Irish coffee with or without a liqueur. I have both kinds of chartreuse, and I offer a Pouse Café. I also made a rhubarb pie for tonight."

Juliet's hand was shaking a little. Bridget pretends to ignore it.

Julien seemed a little overwhelmed. As they sit down to eat, Bridget walks over to Evelyn.

Bridget says, "What do you think of my co-workers?"

Evelyn replies, "They each seem to be comfortable except that young woman. Something is bothering her."

Bridget says, "That was my fault. I ignored her while making the changes. She does not know that I had to impersonate a female."

Evelyn says, "You are doing an excellent job. I enjoyed the barbeque, but I must go to work. Thank you for going to so much trouble. It was delightful, and I am starting to enjoy these gatherings. Good night Bridget."

Evelyn gives Bridget a hug then walks to the door, slowly saying goodnight to all on her way.

Bridget says, "Most of you are staff members at the law firm, and Arnold wants me to say hello to each of you. You will be hearing from him soon. I may be bringing messages from Arnold at times. He has asked me to take over some of his responsibilities, along with my new assistant attorney duties. I am not an owner or a committee member. But I am a family member. I am aware of some of the troubles we are having, and in a few weeks, I should be up to speed on the whole thing. Thank you for coming to my little get together. It makes me feel welcomed more than I can describe."

During the whole time since Juliet entered the house, she has been looking at Bridget intently.

Juliet says, "Bridget, what is a Pouse Café?"

Bridget says, "Let's make one. Choose your poison."

Juliet looks at the liqueurs picking out three. Bridget picks two more, making it five.

Bridget says, "Seven would be best though I am not as good a maker as an experienced bartender might be. Five will do me just fine."

Bridget takes a medium-sized narrow glass. She lines up the liqueurs in order of heaviest first, then the next heaviest next and so on. For each liqueur, she tilts the glass to about

30 degrees and gently pours the liqueur down the side. The heavier one retains its position with the next one flowing on top of the prior one. Once she completes the pouring, the drink is ready.

Bridget says, "Here you are a young lady, a delicious multi-flavored drink."

Juliet says, "Where is yours?"

Bridget says, "I have already had a few, another would be a disaster. I would order a Pouse Café at a restaurant, not to drink it, but to watch how much trouble the bartender would have preparing it."

Juliet has had a few sips, and although she is getting more relaxed, she is still starring at Bridget. After finishing the Pouse Café, she gets up then walks over to Bridget.

She whispers into Bridget's ear, saying, "Let's go powder our noses."

Bridget is shocked but does not want to let on her discomfort.

Bridget says, "Excuse us, folks. We need to powder our noses."

They walk into the main bathroom, and Juliet closes the door.

Juliet says, "I have been watching you ever since I met you in the office. There are little things I keep noticing about you, dear. I could understand if you are really Arnold's relative. You are clever, you are a beautiful woman, your breasts are really sticking out there, your story is based on fact, and you have all the right answers. You act very feminine, and all the female moves. But with all you have done, you have made one little mistake. Can you tell me what it is?"

Bridget starts fixing her makeup and lipstick and says, "I am at a loss, Juliet. I have no idea what you are talking about."

Juliet moves in close to Bridget while whispering she says, "I laid on a bed on the Alicia one night in one of the bays at the Farallon Islands. Arnold and I didn't make love. We just hugged, kissed, and talked for hours. Later Arnold had a bullet fragment wound. You still have that same scar, love."

Juliet reaches over, pulling Bridget to her face. She plants a big kiss on Bridget's lips.

She says, "I just smeared your lipstick love. Best fix it before you come back out."

Juliet fixes her own lipstick and leaves laughing hysterically. As she arrives in the front room, Julien wants to know what is so funny.

Juliet says, "Sorry, Daddy. You do not have enough estrogen to understand the joke. If you want to hear the joke, you would have had to put a microphone in the women's bathroom like the Last Chance in Oakland. Otherwise, I am not repeating it."

Juliet continues to laugh and giggle for the rest of the evening. Bridget returns shortly after Juliet's entrance.

After the noise lowers, Bridget starts talking shop. She asks each member to define their duties and any comments. Nothing is said that Bridget doesn't already know.

Much later, Bridget asks, "How was the barbeque? Anything we should have added?"

David responds, "Bridget. I had never heard of a Pouse Café. Can you tell us about it?"

Bridget says, "I had finished dinner at one of the restaurants at Fisherman's Wharf. I ordered a green chartreuse, and the bartender was making a Pouse Café. The entertainment I had was watching a shaking hand trying to retain the levels in the glass. At first, it was the entertainment that got me started. Then after drinking a few, I started enjoying the drink itself. You line up your liqueurs, putting the heaviest liqueur in first. Then you add in descending order the thickest to the lightest liqueur. Getting it right is like making an Irish coffee. You place heavy cream on top of a coffee or coffee-liquor combination. Then you use a spoon to deflect the cream from mixing with the coffee. With the Pouse Café, you need to angle the glass than run the next liqueur down the side of the glass. Sometimes it gets tricky. It is a wonderful multilevel flavored drink."

Bridget says, "Matilda, have you decided when it would be a good time to take a boat ride? Arnold did not get around to that before the accident."

Matilda says, "I feel like I am imposing. I can always wait."

Bridget says, "I am a moderate sailor, and I have sailed the Alicia before. We could easily get by with my skills, so please think about it?"

Bridget continues, "David, how about you. Would you and Angela want to go along?"

David says, "Most any time, Bridget. A weekend would be better for us."

The evening is about over, and people would like to get home at a decent hour. As people are wandering out, Juliet comes over to Bridget, giving her a big hug.

Juliet says, "I'll be back love. We will need to powder our noses again sometime."

Juliet walks away with a big smile.

After everyone has departed, Bridget sits down exhausted.

She says to herself, "What an effort to retain my illusion. I hope it gets easier."

Bridget puts the perishables into the refrigerator while leaving everything else alone. It's time to get some rest. Bridget removes her makeup and changes her clothes. As she crawls into bed, she is noticing the silk sheets and the nightgown she must wear to bed. Bridget thinks that Sid is a little overboard with his demands. Bridget considers Juliet's surprise as she falls asleep.

29 - THE CLEANUP

Saturday morning and Bridget feels a little bit of a hangover. It was a good meal and a good party. Except for Juliet, everyone accepted Bridget. Sid arrives early to check on Bridget, who had already put on her bra, makeup, lipstick, and perfume. She is wearing her nightgown under a lightweight robe and pink slippers.

Sid says, "Ms. O'Connor, how did it go last night."

Bridget says, "It was a total success except for Juliet. The scar on my right ear lobe gave it away." "But she did not blow my cover. Evelyn was a delight and helpful. We will be able to move forward."

Sid says, "Good show, Ms. O'Connor. You have done well, and you have stuck to my demands. Even this morning, you have dressed as a woman before breakfast. Are you cooking breakfast this morning?"

Bridget says, "Is that a food order? French toast, bacon, juice, and coffee sound, ok?"

Before Bridget gets started, the doorbell rings. Both Bridget and Sid are surprised. Bridget walks over to the door and sees Juliet and Alissa waiting to come in.

Bridget opens the doors saying, "Welcome back, you two."

Juliet walks in, giving Bridget a hug, whispering, "Good morning, my love."

Bridget says, "We are just fixing breakfast. Would you care for some?"

Alissa says, "Sure, I am always hungry."

Juliet says, "Maybe a little. I am still full from last night. How do you feel today, Bridget? You were one busy woman last night."

Bridget reaches for more eggs and bread. Into the bowl goes the eggs, a little milk, cinnamon, and vanilla flavoring. Bridget pulls out more bacon. Onto the skillet goes all the bacon. Within minutes everyone is sitting around the kitchen table eating French toast.

Bridget says, "Juliet, I appreciate you coming over to help. Alissa, how did you get roped into this?"

Alissa says, "I didn't get roped in, it was my idea."

"My Mom had a good time last night. She came home happy."

"My Grandpa is confused. He doesn't know what to think. You and Mom were in the bathroom telling jokes. Mom wouldn't tell Grandpa the joke, but she did say to him that he did not have enough estrogen. He feels left out."

Arnold's phone rings.

Sid answers the phone, saying, "Hello, this is Sid Johnson."

Alex says, "Sid, I need to talk to Arnold. Good to hear your voice, Sid."

Sid says, "Arnold is unavailable. He is recuperating from a terrible auto accident, and Bridget O'Connor, his cousin, is taking his place for a while. Would you care to speak to her?"

Alex says, "Okay."

Sid hands the phone to Bridget.

She says, "Hello Alex. We haven't met yet, but I will be handling some of Arnold's things for a while. What can I do for you? Arnold has brought me up to speed about you and Sammy. Is this something else?"

Alex replies, "Yes, I found a little girl being totally abused without a chance of escaping. We need to take care of this problem."

Bridget interrupts, saying, "Do I need to come over today?"

Alex says, "No, she is not available until Monday. This little girl is being abused daily. They do not feed her properly, the animal rapes her almost every day, and they will not let her go to school. It's horrible."

Bridget says, "Alex, who else can verify this information. The little girl, Sammy, and some neighbors will give you the same information. What if I arrive on Monday? Could we take care of this then? Will you and Sammy be available?"

Alex says, "We will all be at my gym at about 10 a.m. Thank you. I will meet you then," as he hangs up the phone.

Bridget says to Juliet, "Monday, I am going to search out the girl. Would you care to go with me? You and Alissa could stay at my house tonight."

Juliet says, "Yes, Alissa is off to a friend's house for the next few days. I would be excited to go with you."

Sid sneaks out as the cleanup starts.

As he leaves, Bridget yells, "Sid, you are always leaving when there is real work to be done. The breakfast was your pay."

Sid says, "It looks like girl time, I am gone."

He blows a kiss and closes the door.

For the next three hours, all three girls work vigorously. When they are done, all the dishes, pans, silverware are cleaned, dried, and put away.

Bridget says, "Ladies, you two are wonderful. You just saved me an entire day's work. Thank you so much."

Alissa walks over, giving Bridget a big hug and says, "It was fun."

Juliet is standing next to Bridget. She turns and gives Bridget a big hug while whispering, "As you said to me one time. You are stuck with me, love."

Bridget whispers back, "With you around, I have no other needs."

Bridget says, "You and I are about the same size, so you can just raid my closet for night clothes and whatever you need to wear tomorrow. The spare bedroom is already made up for both of you."

She shows Juliet the channel 97 street watching capability that Julien has installed. They prepare dinner together, and the three choose a comedy movie on TV. They go to bed at about 10 p.m.

Bridget feels that this is another positive day. She thinks, with Juliet here, it is even better. Bridget goes to her silk sheets, and both Juliet and Alissa use the second bedroom.

It's Sunday morning, and Bridget has breakfast ready by the time Juliet arrives in the kitchen. Some scrambled eggs with spinach, a waffle on the side, and orange juice. Sumatra coffee is included. Alissa walks in somewhat sleepy-eyed.

Alissa says, "Mom, what time are you taking me over to my friend's house?"

Juliet says, "Right after breakfast, dear. Is that what you want?"

Bridget says, "Why don't we both take her? It would be good for me to get out of the house."

An hour after breakfast, they are walking into the garage. The group gets into the pink Mercedes. Bridget, Juliet, and Alissa hook-up their seat belts. As the garage door opens, Bridget drives out of the garage. She stops to let the door fully close before continuing. Remaining vigilant, Bridget is not very talkative.

Juliet asks, "Are you watching for trouble, Ms. O'Connor?"

Bridget answers, "It is difficult to drive without being vigilant."

Alissa's friend lives on Pacific Avenue overlooking the Presidio. It is one the streets up from Filbert Street. All three walk to the front door of the residence. They meet the parents. The wife asks about the barbeque.

Bridget replies, saying, "It was such a wonderful time. We had some local folks come early then staff members from the firm, even some of my neighbors came over. It was pleasant. I was able to introduce the Pouse Café."

The wife says, "What is a Pouse Café?"

Bridget says, "A multi-layered after-dinner drink with five to seven different liqueurs. The flavor continues to change as you are sipping through the layers."

The wife says, "That sounds delightful, tasty too. My daughter and Alissa are going with us on Highway 1. We hope to visit some seashores and beaches on the way. I have both your father's and your phone numbers in case we need to call."

Juliet says, "We need to go. Thank you for including Alissa."

Bridget and Juliet get up and walk out to the Mercedes. As they drive through the Presidio, they pass many officer homes, the officer's club, the non-com barracks, the hospital, Crissy Field, and many support buildings.

Bridget starts talking, "I feel that I have made a great deal of progress. Without my prior training, there is no way I could have converted so quickly. Do you remember Evelyn from the party? She is one of Sid's successful transsexuals. Evelyn took four years with multiple failures before she was able to make the transition. We have not made too many mistakes. You are so perceptive that with all the massive changes I had to make, you saw through the illusion because of a small scar."

Bridget continues, "Your father gave me hell for letting them get me on the old "Bait and Switch" trick in front of my old home, but he and Josey got me out of the hospital in time. Two operatives came in minutes after I was transported out."

Bridget continues, "Impersonating a woman is one of the hardest things I have ever had to do. To me, it is an unpleasant challenge. Though on the positive side, it has taught me respect for a woman's position. I am looking forward to the time when I can be myself again and end this impersonation. The McCarthy Group is still a force I need to reckon with. They will sooner or later figure out how to breach our defenses. If I put them in a defensive mode with no choices, I can destroy them. Let's go back to my place and talk about us. I appreciate you for accepting my need to make these changes. I am having a tough time getting used to it."

Juliet says, "I would like it, Ms. O'Connor, you sweet thing."

Bridget says, "This transition has not bothered you why?"

Juliet says, "My father and I discussed the fact you had not called me. He pointed out that you have this heavy weight on your shoulders, and you are consumed with the firm's difficulties. Daddy said I was being selfish and feeling sorry for myself. He was correct. Once I saw you at the firm and saw the scar, I knew I was acting selfishly. The massive amount of discomfort must have been exhausting for you. Then you send me flowers in an attempt to apologize for something that was not your fault. I know that I can be a pain in the butt sometimes. My father usually helps me straighten myself out. Hopefully, you will, too, in time. Even with the danger, I want to stand beside you. I want to be someone you can rely upon. Is that a long enough answer for you, Bridget?"

Bridget smiles, saying, "Thank you, sweet woman."

By the time Juliet finishes, Bridget is pulling into the garage. She closes the garage door, walks into the kitchen while locking all exterior doors, and sets the alarm. Last, she calls Sid.

He answers, "Sid here."

Bridget says, "This is your rebellious daughter Bridget. I have locked the doors and set the alarm. Dad, I want to be left alone for the rest of today."

Sid answers, "If you are going to act in such a horrible way, I will need to punish you tomorrow. Children today just do not listen to their parents. Have a nice day, my loving daughter. Bye!"

Bridget says to Juliet, "That will allow us some privacy today. Let's take a shower and relax."

Juliet says, "You have only one shower."

Bridget replies, "You are correct again. You either shower alone or with me."

Juliet says, "No question there. Remember, you are stuck with me."

Bridget undresses and steps into the shower first. She washes the makeup off and washes her hair. Then she starts on her body. Juliet does almost the same thing but keeps stopping to view the bruises and scars on Bridget's face.

She looks at the breast area. The C-cupped breasts seem heavy.

She reaches out to lift one up. She is tearing during the time she is with Bridget in the shower.

Juliet says, "How could I be so selfish. You must have been in horrific pain."

Bridget answers Juliet by pulling her close and holding her tight.

Bridget says, "This is not your fault, just a little misperception. Would you wash my back?"

Juliet's eyes light up, saying, "Ms. O'Connor, I will wash you anywhere you want."

They continue to caress each other for another few minutes, and they both get out. After drying off, Bridget must put the bra on to keep the breast pain to a minimum. No makeup, no lipstick, just a nightgown and robe with pink slippers. Juliet searches through Bridget's closet, finding a nice knit chemise and a short silky robe.

There are several pairs to pick from.

Juliet chooses the fluffy white ones. They lay on the bed with the silk sheets.

Juliet says, "Should I complain that I had to sleep in the bed with cotton sheets? This is so nice, maybe you should sleep in the other bed tonight?"

Bridget smiles while she shakes her head, saying no.

Juliet teases Bridget some more by saying, "You don't think I am sharing these wonderful silk sheets with you. Do you?"

Bridget says, "This is so nice. I could forget my problems as I remember you said I was stuck with you. No, you are stuck with me."

The room is comfortable. The lights are low, and they are snuggled up against each other, they doze off with their bodies and arms intertwined. As they wake, both are involved with the other. They throw off their clothing. Juliet lies there on these silk sheets wanting to make love so severely that Juliet is almost hitting a climax before Bridget starts.

After entering her vagina, she says, "Don't stop. Oh, my god. Don't stop, oh my love, I have wanted this for so long. I am not giving you up."

For the next few hours, they make love, then stop in each other's arms and then start again. Finally, they get up for some food. Hunger has set in for both. As they are making dinner, they can't leave each other alone. They caress, kiss, hug each other, and hold on to each other. They are so happy that they could care less about the rest of the world. After eating a quick meal, they go to bed within the silk sheets. Feeling entirely at home with each other, they lay there in each other's arms as they fall asleep.

30 - FEMALE TROUBLE

Monday morning starts with the regular fog and traffic noises. Both are up to take another shower for the coming day. Juliet is much faster at getting ready than Bridget.

Once they are both in the kitchen for breakfast, Juliet whispers in Bridget's ear, saying, "Would it be nice to go back to bed? I could handle that one more time."

Bridget says, "You are unfair. You know that I agree yet can't. Maybe I should call you "Tease" for short."

As they finish breakfast, they continue to be engrossed with each other. Bridget is wearing a dark blue pair of women's slacks, black leather two-inch pumps, dark blue knee-length nylons, a long sleeve white blouse with a ruffled collar, and a matching dark blue top. Juliet chose one of Bridget's knee-length brown skirts, a blouse with a high neck collar, pink sweater, brown leather 2-inch pumps, and a matching brown jacket. They leave late that morning for the Mission District. When closing the garage, Bridget notices that the car with a guy watching Sid's place was missing.

Bridget continues on Filbert until Divisadero Street, left on Divisadero until Lombard Street, right on Lombard, then right onto Van Ness. Bridget turns south on Mission Street when Market and Van Ness come together crossing Mission. They are now entering the Mission District. As they drive south on Mission, Bridget points out different places of interest. For about a mile, they stay on Mission Street until 19th Street. Bridget turns right onto 19th Street and continues toward Delores Park. On the right-hand side is Alex's Gym. Bridget parks in the driveway and starts to walk toward the inside of the gym.

Bridget warns Juliet, "We are going into a very volatile and dangerous environment. I will be there for you, just follow my lead. If there is a confrontation, stay behind me and to my left. Do not look at anyone in the eye and stay quiet."

They both continue walking to the gym. Sammy is shooting hoops, and Alex is busy with a trainee. Two white ladies walking into a gym in the Mission District is noticed by all the local residents.

Bridget walks up to Alex and says, "Hello Alex, I am Bridget O'Connor. You called the other day about a young lady being mistreated. I am here to help fix the problem."

Alex says, "Good to meet you, Ms. O'Connor. Do you know where you are? This is a tough neighborhood. White folks are not always welcome here."

Bridget says, "They will need to get over it. Are you threatening me or warning me, Mr. Johnson?"

Alex says, "I am not taking that bait again. The last time I got my butt kicked by Arnold. I am just trying to be helpful, Ms. O'Connor."

Bridget says, "Fine, let's get started. By the way, this is Juliet. She also works for the firm."

Alex says, "This guy is mean. Can either one of you fight?"

Bridget says, "Don't try me, Alex. Let's get on with this."

Juliet is getting nervous. She has never been in this type of situation.

Alex says, "It's next door. I'll walk you over."

As they walk next door, a young girl is sitting on the steps, and Alex says, "Bridget, that is the girl. They moved here last month. Since then, I have seen the guy beat her on many occasions. He is mean and deceitful."

Sammy and Alex are standing on the sidewalk in front of the house. Bridget and Juliet are walking toward the house. A few neighbors walk into their front yards to watch.

A tall, slender, thirty-year-old black man comes running from the side yard, yelling, "What the fuck do you white girls want here? None of us niggers invited you. You two bitches turn around and leave, or I'll kick your little white asses.

HIDDEN IN FRONT OF YOU

When I get through with you, you will be blacker than white. Huh, black and blue-white girls."

The neighbors, Juliet, Sammy, and Alex, all are standing there, wondering what is going to happen. Bridget has just ignored all safety to walk onto this man's property.

Bridget says, "Your name is what, asshole?"

Juliet stands there frightened for her life. She has never seen a white woman with quite this much determination facing such a hostile man. Bridget continues to walk toward the man, and Juliet steps back toward the car.

The man says, "Ah, only one brave white bitch. Come on, sweetie, I like white girls."

The man reaches out for Bridget. She slams his arm sideways at the elbow, which causes his arm to hyperextend. He becomes more angered and takes a swing at her. Bridget moves inward, diverts his swing by using his own kinetic energy, forcing him to lose his balance, and he falls to the ground. The confused man lifts himself off the ground, mutters some swear words under his breath, and walks up to Bridget in a very cocky manner. He stands there, wondering how this little white woman could give him any trouble.

Then he says, "Bitch, I am going to kill you."

Those were his last words. Bridget steps twisting to the right jamming her left two-inch pump down his left shinbone. He reaches for his leg in pain then stands erect for just a moment. Bridget turns back around to face him directly and dropkicks him in his testicles. As he tries to remain to stand, Bridget has a couple of seconds to decide what she wants to do with this guy. He then moves toward her again, and Bridget steps into him using a Ju-Jitsu move throwing him over her shoulder.

Ju can be defined as gentle. Jitsu is using the opponent's force against himself, a martial art.

He lands upside down on the front stairs. The man is

yelling in pain. She rolls him back over, so he is facing her and, with a clear purpose, dropkicks his face breaking his jaw. He is out of commission and cannot talk and is bleeding profusely from his mouth and nose.

She bends down and says to him, "Now talk asshole."

He cannot talk. He is in pain and is crying and, for the first time, showing fear of this little lady. Bridget realizes a young black girl is standing on the porch, observing this activity.

The little girl says quietly, "He deserves every bit of that, Ma'am. He is a wretched person; he hurts me every day."

Bridget asks, "What is your name, dear?"

The girl replies, "They just call me Female, Ma'am. Are you the attorney that is going to visit me today?"

Bridget replies, "Yes, dear, but it appears that you need much more than a visit from me. Has this man been abusing you in any way?"

Female answers, "Yes, just an hour ago, he raped me, just like every other day. He beats on me for fun whenever he feels like it. Most of the time, I hide from him and my mother."

Angered and preferring to kill this man, Bridget calms herself and then calls 911 from Alex's Gym.

Bridget says, "I would like to report an attempt on my life and the rape and abuse of a child. The house is adjacent to Alex's Gym on 19th Street in the Mission District. You will see us all waiting for you in front of the house. My name is Bridget O'Connor."

Alex comes running up and says, "Are you as good as Arnold?"

Bridget says, "No, but almost as good. Arnold will hurt you and release you. I won't. I'll beat you and kill you."

Within minutes there are three police cars parked in front of the Female's house.

HIDDEN IN FRONT OF YOU

A policeman walks up to Bridget O'Connor and asks, "What is going on here, Ma'am?"

Bridget replies, "My name is Bridget O'Connor, but first things first. Over here is Juliet Spence Whitaker, she came here with me and is a witness to the attack. Ms. Female was on the porch when the attack happened. I want to report an attempted assault and an intentional attempted murder. That bloodied man over there came at Juliet and me from the side yard. He was threatening to kill us both. He then attempted to attack me and cause me bodily harm. I fought back, stopping his attacks. He verbally threatened to kill me and then continued his attempt to attack me. I fought back and disabled him for my own safety. I am filing charges on this man, his behavior in child endangerment, physical child abuse, and sexual child abuse on Ms. Female there on the porch. He has raped this young lady within the past hour. That will not be hard to prove with a sperm test. In my opinion, the mother should also be charged with abuse and abandonment."

Officer O'Malley introduces himself, "Ma'am. My name is Officer O'Malley; the 911 operator says your name is Bridget O'Connor, as you have told me."

Bridget nods, yes.

He continues, "In my report, I am going to write that this man is to be charged with attempted murder and child abuse, namely rape. You are making these charges because you were here and had a confrontation with this man. Is there anything else I should know before I interview Ms. Female?"

Bridget responds, "Yes, I am also Ms. Female's attorney and will be applying for the caretaker ship. I also have some knowledge of the martial arts, but I am not belted."

"We need to get the man to a hospital and then to jail. We also need to get the little lady to the hospital for a complete checkup. I won't be done here for hours."

As the officer walks away, Bridget calls David from Alex's business phone.

David answers, "Ms. O'Connor. What can I do for you?"

Bridget says, "David, another favor for Mr. Pierce. I am at the home of Ms. Female. There was a man that has been abusing her, and he attempted to attack me. The man is on his way to the hospital now and then on to jail. I am pressing charges. I am reporting child molestation and abuse charges. May I please have custody of Ms. Female with the blessing of the firm?"

David replies, "Bridget, as I said earlier, you and Arnold are like two peas in a pod. He would do the same thing to me regularly. I will start the paperwork with the South San Francisco Child Protection Agency. Proud of you for doing this."

Bridget turns to Juliet and says, "We have done it. I believe we have a chance of saving this young girl."

Bridget then turns to Female and says, "May we have a few moments with you, dear?"

Female replies, "Sure."

Bridget continues, "We are not perfect, nor are we the only salvation you may have. I believe you may want to listen to us through and allow us to assist you. We can relocate you, change the bad environment to a good environment, we can assist you in helping yourself. We are not welfare, and we are not just free money. We offer a person like you the opportunity to better themselves. What is your desire, young lady?"

Female answers, "I am twelve. Each time I leave and try to become someone, they send me right back into this."

"I do not want to walk the streets. I do not want to get beat up. I do not want to be raped whenever they get the thought. I want to be a good person supporting myself, and someday I would like to be a mother. But most of all, I want to be treated fairly and given a chance. I am not allowed to go to school, but I read everything I can get my hands on. I am usually crying and afraid, but with you being here, I feel safe."

Bridget says, "Sweetheart, we have the answer for you. I can offer the chance you have always wanted. You will work for it, you will struggle, and you will earn every step of the way. But I can guarantee one thing. Our group will always be there for you. Go to the hospital, get checked out, file your charges, and we will be there to protect you and fight for you. Here is my home number and my office number. I will be there whenever you need help, or when you just want someone to talk to."

The girl called "Female" asks, "Can I get a real name? I do not have one. Can I get a birth certificate? Can I get a social security number? I have never been to school. Can I go to school someday? Can I be taught to protect myself as you did here today?"

Bridget and Juliet both break down in tears and hug this little girl.

Bridget says, "What name do you want?"

The girl called "Female" says clearly, "Naomi Agatha O'Connor, after your last name."

Bridget says, "You make me so proud Naomi, for us to have the same last name. For me, that is my honor, thank you. Yes, you will know how to take care of yourself. We must leave you with the police for now. We will be back for you when the court makes its decision."

Naomi says, "Ma'am, you are a white girl, and I am black. Why do you want to help me?"

Bridget says, "Naomi, I do not see any difference between us. Black or white does not describe the person, their character does."

Bridget gives Naomi another hug, and then Naomi walks

over to Officer O'Malley. They both wave goodbye as she steps into the house.

Bridget and Juliet stop by the gym.

Bridget says, "Alex, it is done. She will be safe."

She now has a future, thanks to you. I am just the implementer; you are the savior. Any time you want to add to her future, just let me or Arnold know. You may want to become her friend. Naomi would appreciate your friendship."

Bridget and Alex shake hands.

Alex says, "I am not sure, but you might be as good as Arnold. That quick and deadly response is unique to me. He did not tag you once."

Bridget says, "For him, it is a good thing he didn't, or there would be a hearse instead of an ambulance waiting in front. Hope to see you and Sammy soon."

Bridget and Juliet walk to the car and get in.

Juliet says to Bridget, "Oh, god. That was so exciting, so wonderful. It makes me feel like jumping up and down. You mainly, but I was there, you are responsible for saving that girl's life. I want to be a part of that."

Bridget says, "You can be any part of this that you want to be. Juliet, that is what this vigilante group was all about when I joined. This type of activity was what brought me to the firm's vigilante group in the first place. Sometimes it requires an assassination. But most of the time, we help others."

Reaching Filbert Street, Bridget sees a few cars she does not recognize. She continues past the house, turns right onto Lyon Street then left onto Lombard Street straight into the Presidio.

Parking within the hospital parking lot, she calls Julien from a phone booth, "Julien here, and how are my two darlings? It did not take long for you two to get the attention of the firm today. I take it you cleaned someone's plow today?"

Bridget replies, "I did have a little disagreement with a tall man, but he is now in the hospital and soon to be in jail. We had a good time. Our efforts were received well, and Juliet enjoyed herself. Anything else you need to know about father? Have you been watching those other cars on Filbert?"

Julien says, "Oh, those cars. They have been there since about noon. They seem to be watching Sid, but they do glance over at your place occasionally. I'll keep watching those cars."

Bridget starts the Mercedes, drives back to Lyon Street, and turns right onto Lyon. In two blocks, she turns left onto Filbert. The cars are still there. She continues to the garage, opens the door with the clicker, drives in, and shuts the door behind her. Bridget pulls out her 38-caliber snub nose, disarms the security system, walks into the kitchen, closes the door, checks each room, and then rearms the security system. Bridget tunes the television to channel 97, so they can monitor the street in front of the house.

Bridget calls Julien and says, "Things are okay over here. Do you have any ideas about the cars out front?"

Julien answers, "The only chatter I have heard is they think Sid might be helping Arnold. There is no plan to hurt Sid. I have called Sid to give him the status."

"I believe you two are okay inside the house. I'll see you two tomorrow morning. Good night girls."

All is quiet. The silence of both Bridget and Juliet allows each of them to review today's events and the events of the last few weeks. They fix a meal together and sit down at the table.

Juliet finally talks, "Bridget, how long will this take? I mean, how much longer do you need to play this role? What needs to be done?"

Bridget responds, "We cannot become impatient. Identification and verification of the good guys and the bad guys will be the first phase. Remember my motto: 'To save the good you may need to engage in evil. Peace and fairness above all things are desired.' Sometimes blood must be spilled to obtain peace and lasting terms." But the most essential part is "that peace and fairness above all things are desired."

"Julien and Matt are gathering data. Once we can define the companies, the workers, and the contractor hierarchy, we will then be able to create our own strategy, as I have said before. Once we understand their authority, we can start solving the puzzle. It is unknown when we can do that."

As they go to bed, they are pleased to be together. Lying in bed starts another evening of happiness. Within seconds of getting into bed, they are wound together. Juliet is so delighted that she can't leave Bridget alone. She has never had such a desire for someone.

Tuesday morning comes, and nothing special is planned except going to work at the firm. Juliet and Bridget get up to shower, put on their makeup, and dress in things that are for lounging. Juliet is in a soft robe like material with built-in bunny mitten slippers. Bridget chose the flannel pajamas.

There is just one car in front of Sid's house. Julien has called to say that all fronts are quiet. David has called Bridget with an update on Naomi. She is doing well and happy in the foster home provided by the county Child Protection Agency. Bridget fixes eggs benedict, some ham, a bowl of fruit, fresh orange juice, and coffee.

Juliet comes in with her happy face and says, "You are making a fine breakfast, my love. You always have food prepared for me. Since I am getting used to this, I expect it every day from now on, sweetie."

Bridget says, "The price is too high for your budget. You

need to reconsider that my darling."

Finished with breakfast, they each get ready for a workday.

Before leaving the house, Bridget calls Julien as Arnold.

He answers, "Hello, Arnold. It is nice to hear from you. When will we be moving ahead?"

Bridget, as Arnold says, "I have briefed Bridget on McCarthy. Please meet with her today. If you can put together an initial plan, share it with her. I have good news, Julien. I was successful in killing that little fly. I used bug spray on the little guy. He is gone now."

Julien says, "I am lost, but I do hope it is good. I must go. You are not making sense."

Bridget says to Juliet, "I tried to inform him. He just does not understand my words."

Bridget says, "Juliet, it is better that you drive your own car today. Let's keep the real facts about us to ourselves for now. It won't be long before I can safely say something."

Juliet says, "Okay. I will support whatever you think is best. I would like to see my father's eyes when he finds out."

31 - ALISSA AND NAOMI

Bridget picks up Alissa from school on her way home after a productive day at the firm. Juliet arrives as soon as she gets off work. Alissa has a few ideas on how to help with the firm's charity work. She knows that her mother will be at Bridget's after work. She asks her Grandfather Julien to be at Bridget's so they may all talk about her ideas. Julien arrives a few minutes before Juliet.

Juliet and Bridget fix a delicious dinner. After dinner, everyone is ready to have a dessert.

Alissa says, "I am actively interested in doing something special, and I have a proposal. You have all been busy fighting this war, and I can't assist you there, but I could become a part of other things. I feel the charity group has not been offering much to the Petersons, Naomi, Sammy, and Alex."

"I just won a scholarship for my high grade-point average supported by my advanced courses. I could, with your help, put together a few evenings of family type fun. We could invite the Peterson family, Sammy, and Alex. They could accompany us when I receive my scholarship. Then on another evening, we could attend the ballet and symphony performance. If we were to make it a fun set of evenings, it would be the beginning of a group friendship. This way, I can become a part of your firm's work."

Bridget and Juliet say almost in unison, "These are great ideas. These will be experiences they would never have been able to have."

Bridget says, "Alissa, get together with Jennifer. She can help you with scheduling and logistics. With her, in the mix, it will sound more like it is in conjunction with the firm. Jennifer will keep me up to date."

Bridget says, "I agree that we have not put in enough time with our candidates recently. The scholarship presentation will help show the rewarding benefits being shown to outstanding students. Alissa, it is wonderful that you want to start working with the charity group. You will gain a lot of experience along the way."

Bridget calls Matt, "#1 Finion."

Seconds later, she receives a callback.

Bridget says, "Hello, my admirer. How did you like my mini skirt?"

Matt says, "A little more skin would do well. What is your question, sweet pea?"

Bridget replies, "Alissa has come up with a plan to try to include Naomi in some activities. She wants to show Naomi some friendship and assist Naomi with her future. Please give me your opinion. I have some bad feelings about this option. I can't explain why I have this poor outlook."

Matt says, "What a beautiful girl Alissa must be. Again, Ma'am, you are right on the mark. Some of the stepfather's friends have noticed the event between you and the stepfather. They have contacted Naomi's stepfather. Their objective is to try getting a bonus from McCarthy by attacking you to flush out Arnold. We need to end this immediately. It appears that we may also need to do something to safeguard Naomi."

"For starters, Naomi should home school and cancel any planned outings. Then at our convenience, we can take out the stepfather and any of his operative friends. Go to the Petersons and Naomi., and get their cooperation until it is safe. I'll assist in letting you break these asshole's necks. Okay, sweet pea?"

Bridget says, "As always, thank you for your involvement. I will be in touch."

Bridget calls the Petersons, "Hello, this is Jeff."

Bridget says, "This is Bridget O'Connor. Tomorrow is a weekend day. I hope that you and your family could be available tomorrow. We must get together for a discussion. May we come by your home tomorrow?"

Jeff says, "If it is that imperative that we talk, my family and I will make time tomorrow. How is 10 a.m.?"

Bridget answers, "That will be perfect. See you then."

Bridget says, "Well folks, we have an appointment to discuss things with the Petersons tomorrow. Alissa, I just received information that may change things. Some of the McCarthy operatives have hooked up with Naomi's stepfather. This means he may want to get at me through Naomi to flush out Arnold. I need to end this immediately."

Bridget calls Josey, "Hello, this is Josey."

Bridget says, "I need your presence tomorrow at the Petersons' home at 10 a.m. You will be one of my private investigators."

Josey replies, "I'll see you there at 10."

The three girls finish the dishes and ask Julien to take out the garbage. Then, Juliet and Alissa each give Bridget a big hug, and they all leave. Bridget is now alone again.

It's Saturday morning, and Bridget is up by 7 a.m. to prep for the day. She fixes a medium-sized breakfast with enough for Sid when he stops by checking on food availability. Bridget chooses a long sleeve full floral dress hanging to her mid-calf, light red nylons, 2-inch heels, puts her hair in a ponytail hanging to her shoulders with curls and silver jewelry. She is trying to present intimate apparel as opposed to the regular office dress code.

Everyone has arrived at 8:30 a.m. At 9:30, the group piles into Julien's car because the pink Mercedes would be too conspicuous, and they drive off to the Petersons. There aren't any eyes watching as they leave, and no vehicle seems to be pacing them. Possibly, McCarthy has no idea where the Petersons live or that Naomi has been living with them. As Julien drives, the group is still discussing this new problem.

HIDDEN IN FRONT OF YOU

McCarthy now has more reason to take out Bridget directly to enhance his chances of getting at Arnold. The stepfather wants to retaliate. When they arrive, Julien parks a few doors away from the Petersons even though there are parking spots closer to the residence.

After entering the home, Bridget starts explaining things to the Petersons. Josey is introduced as a private investigator, Alissa as Juliet's daughter and Julien as Grandpa.

Bridget says, "Alissa, please go with Naomi to her room."

After the girls leave, the Petersons appear distressed.

Bridget begins, "We have not been as attentive as we should be. Alissa asked to get involved by helping Naomi in her education and show her some of her own personal successes. Alissa has just won a scholarship based upon her high grade-point average in her advanced classes."

"The new problem is Naomi's stepfather is feeling retaliatory. He has started associating with some local operatives who are basically assassins. Through Josey's investigations, we think that we must protect Naomi and you folks as a family. Family Services will not release your name or address, so you are safe there."

"Our original idea coming from Alissa was to go out to dinner together and then go to the symphony at Davies Hall. Another idea was for Naomi to see the presentation of Alissa's scholarship. Alissa still wants to participate in Naomi's education and share it as a friend. The sad part of all of this is that Naomi must home study for now. She can't risk being out in public. Alissa can still assist, but Naomi can't be away from the protection of the home or one of us. Alissa drives her own car, so transportation is not a problem. For your safety, I shall not share with you what we must do to correct this problem. But we must get it solved immediately. Alissa will explain her scholarship and educational items to Naomi."

Bridget continues, "When we exercise our charity work, this type of behavior occurs on occasion. As you can imagine, some very terrible people in our world are just plain scary. We do have ways of dealing with them. For your safety, I can't share our actions with you at this time. I request that you have faith in us and trust us to do as much as we can."

Jeff and Betty look at each other with unhappy faces. Fear might be a better description.

Jeff says, "It appears we have no choice. We do very much appreciate your participation, your interest, and your willingness to protect us all."

Bridget says, "Thank you for your trust. Jeff, would you please get Alissa so we can go. I need to start working on this problem."

As the girls come back to the front room, Naomi runs over to Bridget, giving her a long hug and is tearing in happiness.

Naomi says, "Alissa and I are going to be great friends."

As they leave, Bridget and Josey are looking for operatives. None are seen.

Back in Julien's car, Bridget says, "I must get rid of this problem right now. It has too much of a chance of growing into large cancer."

As they walk into Bridget's kitchen, she dials Matt with a #3, Finion (Immediate action). Within seconds the phone rings.

Matt says, "There must be a problem, my dear. I am close by, see you in five."

Click goes the phone.

Bridget grabs her 38-caliber snub nose and opens the garage door. Within seconds Matt drives into the garage. Bridget closes the garage door, and they go up the stairs to the front room where Julien, Juliet, and Josey are all waiting.

HIDDEN IN FRONT OF YOU

Alissa is in the spare bedroom.

Bridget says, "I have an immediate problem that I need to take care of. I need your help, and I need you to make it look like you are responsible. Naomi's stepfather has joined up with some of McCarthy's operatives to find Naomi and take me out. In my opinion, this is meant to get to Arnold faster."

Matt says, "Sweetheart, you are panicking. The stepfather's five buddies only do work for McCarthy occasionally. They are not part of his permanent staff. They got together with the stepfather, hoping to get a bonus from McCarthy, who does not know what they are planning. They threatened both Sammy and Alex this morning, and they bragged to the stepfather that they could find Naomi. They all grew up in South San Francisco and had been getting into trouble together all their lives. McCarthy does not give a hoot about Naomi. He has never heard of her."

Bridget says emphatically, "I want them dead, and I hope you can take credit for it."

Matt says, "I'll tell you what I'll do. Have your boat ready to go tonight, and I will have all six of them delivered to you by 8 p.m. at the usual place. You and Josey can give them a ride to the Farallones."

Bridget turns to Josey and says, "Can we be ready for an 8 p.m. delivery?"

Josey says, "We are ready now. I'll see you at 7:45."

Both Alissa and Julien stay out of the conversation. Juliet listens intently. Without anyone noticing, Alissa listens to every word from the bedroom.

As Julien, Josey, and Alissa leave, Bridget and Juliet start to prepare for tonight's Farallon trip.

Bridget calls Alex, "Alex, here."

Bridget says, "Hello, Alex. What's new?"

Alex says, "Same old stuff. It's a weekend, so things are busy. I have the same old frustrations."

Bridget says, "What happened this morning?"

Alex says, "A couple of guys got a little nasty."

Bridget says, "If I need to come down there to wake you up, you will have trouble getting off the ground for the rest of the day."

Alex says, "They are local boys. They say things to scare you, but that is what I grew up with."

Bridget says, "But this time it had to do with Naomi. Where in the hell is your brain? Do I need to drop you from the program?"

Alex replies, "I do not understand, or you don't. Which is it?"

Click the phone call goes dead. Bridget hung up.

Bridget thinks, "These two have lived in this world their entire lives. When threatened, they feel like it is just another day. I must show them there is more to life."

It is a typical bay area day. Cool yet not cold. With the possibility of eliminating a known problem, the day has promise for Naomi's safety. Ridding the city of caustic individuals and Alissa coming up with ideas for Naomi's future has given her motivation. Juliet and Bridget fix a delightful dinner and relax by listening to Beethoven's piano concerto No 1.

Juliet says, "When you take in a person under the coverage of the Charity Group, you take responsibility for them from day one. I just may keep you around for a while. You do have some good qualities."

Bridget says, "It is like taking on an additional family member. They need help, and you have something to offer. The result is a new relationship, and it is quite rewarding."

Bridget calls Cindy, "Dogs for You, how can I help you."

Bridget says, "Hi Cindy, this is Bridget O'Connor. I am currently replacing Arnold. He is out on sick leave, caused by a serious accident. I require a special type of dog."

HIDDEN IN FRONT OF YOU

Cindy says, "I'll get you anything you want, Ma'am."

Bridget says, "I have a young girl that we have taken into our Charity Group that was terribly abused. She has lots of promise. She has a wonderful personality and sometimes maybe in danger."

Cindy answers, "I have the perfect young pup that is at its prime time for bonding and training. He is already house trained, loves a bath, likes children, likes to play games, and gets along with babies. He is a large black Lab with a friendly personality. He does lack protection training. Bring her by anytime soon. See you then. Bye."

Bridget thinks, "That was a good decision. I hope the Petersons agree to my intentions."

Bridget says, "It is time to start getting ready for tonight. Let's hope for success."

It's another black suit night, coffee and treats are packed, and Juliet checks her radio with Sid's. Juliet drives Bridget to the boat. Josey will bring her back after they return. Sid and Julien are informed of the event but are not asked to be backups. Bridget arrives at the boat by 7:30, and Josey has everything ready to go. Juliet gives Bridget a quick hug and kiss while wishing them both a successful evening.

Tonight has a full moon with broken clouds. The boat checks out and is full of fuel. The engines were already running and warmed up. Josey unties the mooring lines, and Bridget drives to the waiting position just off the public dock. Two vans show up at about 7:50 p.m. The first has three dead that must be carried. The other three are walked to the boat. Once aboard, two of the live ones are given an injection of Demerol. Bridget tells Josey not to inject the stepfather just handcuff him to the handrail.

Matt says to Bridget and Josey, "After disarming them, they thought six against two were good odds. I killed three, then they submitted to my requests. The stepfather was the most chicken shit of the bunch. Have a safe trip."

Bridget says, "Thank you for the presents and acting so quickly. It relieves me to have them out of the way. Naomi will be safe again."

Matt says, "It is always nice working with you, sweetheart."

Bridget pulls the boat away from the public dock, and the two vans leave. Between the broken moonlight and the headlamps, Bridget can still travel at about 30 mph.

Bridget radios Juliet, "We are on our way. The weather looks good. See you in a few hours."

The water is calm except for the mild moguls, no recent rains. The amount of debris is less than usual. Traveling at 30 mph takes a few minutes longer to get to the Farallones. By the time they arrive, Josey has already tied the weights to their ankles. Then the two injected guys are helped to the rear platform and pushed overboard. Bridget pulls her wool headcover off so the stepfather can see who she is.

She says, "It is a shame that we could not have gotten along better in your front yard. Shoving your penis into a helpless little girl's vagina must make you feel superior. Beating her with your hands must have given you the feeling of being big and strong. Just to provide you with solace, she is living with a loving family. She is brilliant, she is quick to learn, and she enjoys being treated with respect. She is going to have a beautifully full, enjoyable life without you. I could go on for a long time describing her new life without you, but you are about to be fed to the fishes."

Bridget and Josey move him to the platform.

He stands there, sobbing. Bridget pulls out her 44 Magnum. She then shoots him in the crotch. As he is waving his hands, she shoots one of them as he falls off the edge of the platform.

Bridget says, "What a shame. Let's have some coffee."

They pour some coffee, and each grab one of Juliet's treats. She lowers the right engine's rpms to an idle and turns off most of the lights.

Josey says, "I have never seen a person enjoy killing that much before."

Bridget says, "For what he did to that sweet little girl, it was easy to enjoy. When I cleaned his plow, I felt like killing him then. I have been sorry ever since that I did not do it then."

For thirty minutes of treats and coffee, they sat exchanging experiences of killing humans. Most were in the middle of firefights. As they finished, Bridget started the left engine and began heading back toward the city lights. The winds had calmed down, and the debris was light, so Bridget took a chance by upping the speed. The moon was out, and most of the clouds had cleared, so visual scanning was not as restricted. When they parked the boat, everything seemed in good shape. Except for fuel, everything is ready for the next trip. Josey said he would get the tanks filled tomorrow.

Josey drops Bridget off and says, "Each time I do an event with you, I learn something more about you. Sometimes you are a surprise to me. Good night, my friend."

Bridget says, "Thank you, Josey. As Arnold told me, you are a pleasure to work with."

Juliet welcomes Bridget home and asks, "Was it a good trip?"

Bridget says, "A nice large glass of port would go well with my feelings."

Juliet says, "What was so distressing?"

Bridget says, "My caring for Naomi and the horrific way she was treated by her stepfather angered me uncontrollably. I asked Josey not to give him a shot of Demerol. I wanted him to be aware of his last trip. We threw the others over the side, and then when he stood there listening to me, I riddle him with my anger. When I stopped talking, I used my 44 Magnum to shoot him in his crotch. The scary thing is that I enjoyed the entire thing. Never before had I ever enjoyed killing someone."

Juliet says, "That must really bother you. Your compassion for everyone is your normal way of thinking. Please think of it this way. You got rid of Naomi's problem. That should make you feel relieved."

It is past midnight. Bridget takes a shower and crawls in between the silk sheets with her arms wrapped around Juliet.

Morning has arrived, and the sun is up. There is no fog, just a calm morning. Bridget gets her coffee then calls the Petersons.

Bridget says, "I have good news and more good news. We need to talk without the girl's present. When is a good time?"

Jeff says, "I can take some time off this afternoon at about 2 p.m. How does that work for you?"

Bridget says, "I'll make that work. See you then."

Juliet leaves for work, as Bridget finishes dressing. Bridget decides to stop at Dogs for You and meet Cindy's puppy she has planned for Naomi. Cindy's animal facility is a few miles south of the San Francisco Zoo on Highway 1. Cindy has been an animal lover her entire life.

To avoid traffic, Bridget drives through the Presidio through the residential areas to Playland then south on Highway 1. Just as the roadway gets curvy is where Cindy's facility is located between the Highway 1 roadway and the ocean.

Bridget walks into the lobby in her 3-inch heels and asks for Cindy.

The lady says, "I am Cindy. You must be Bridget. Let me get Salty."

Without a leash, Salty follows along with Cindy wagging its tail and looking happy. Cindy stops, and Salty sits immediately and waits for instructions. Cindy kneels next to Salty, pets him, and talks nicely to him as she gives him a treat.

Cindy says, "This is the best dog I have to offer, and he is ready for the next stage in his training."

Cindy asks Salty to lie down and stay. As he lies there, he is watching both Cindy and Bridget.

Bridget explains a little about the firm and Arnold. She describes the information on Naomi and what she had to go through. Naomi is bright, wants to live a good life, is brilliant and friendly.

Bridget says, "Naomi is quite comfortable when people around her are the ones she trusts. She is having a hard time being left with people she does not know or trust. Naomi is very much afraid of being mistreated again. She is currently in a foster home with two other young girls, and they treat her well. She enjoys it there and wants an education. I have not introduced the idea of Salty yet because of what the foster parents may feel. I am meeting with them at 2 p.m. I want a dog that will bond to Naomi and will provide protection for her. I want the dog to be a service dog so he can go everywhere with her. May I have a few minutes with Salty?"

Cindy says, "Just call him and get to know him. Here are some treats."

Bridget calls Salty by name. He first sits up and looks to see if he should.

Cindy says, "Go ahead, Salty."

Salty comes over, wagging his tail, making friends with Bridget. As she pets Salty and plays with him, Salty seems very relaxed.

Bridget says, "What are the procedures for Salty to become a guard dog for Naomi?"

Cindy says, "If that is what you want and of course what

the parents and Naomi want, I would need to assist in training the dog along with the family. There will be a fee for that type of training."

Bridget says, "My firm will take care of the fees. May I have one of your business cards so I can give it to them?"

Cindy says, "If you get concurrence from the family members, we could try a meeting. I am open on weekends by appointment."

Bridget says, "I am on my way to their home. I will let them make any appointments."

Cindy says, "What is Arnold up to nowadays? I would have married that boy in a heartbeat, but Alicia was his first choice."

Bridget says, "That is a long story, and we may need more time than I have today."

It is about noon, and Playland is almost on the way to the Petersons. Bridget drives a little out of her way to the many parking spaces lining the Playland concession stands.

Bridget walks directly to the roller coaster.

She walks up to the ticket counter and pays. There is an empty seat in front. How lucky can you get? The roller coaster goes up the slow climb to the top. You're high in the sky. Then you start down and around. She knows they are about to close. This may be her last chance for a ride. The excitement is still there.

Back in the pink Mercedes, she continues to the Petersons. Bridget arrives at about 1:45 p.m. She knocks on their front door.

Jeff answers the door and ushers her inside, where Mrs. Peterson has coffee and snacks ready, and they talk openly.

Bridget starts off by saying, "You gave me your trust, and I have completed the task. Naomi's stepfather and his five friends will never bother her again. She will never see or hear from them in her future. Please leave the details to me. I can't discuss them. Girls that have been treated as Naomi has been treated will have fears that they try to hide, yet they are still there. When she is with me, my staff members, Juliet, and you folks, she feels happy and safe. Naomi may have repeating sessions of fear. Naomi is intellectually strong, and she is going to succeed at whatever she goes after. Yet, she is still going to remember being violated, threatened, and beaten. That will be the hardest fight of her life. How do you folks feel about getting a dog for when she is alone?"

Both Petersons look a little struck when they hear this. Jeff says, "We would like to get a dog, even two dogs, but we don't know where to start, so your choice will be fine."

Bridget says, "I just got back from meeting a dog named Salty."

Bridget hands them the business card and continues, "Here is the lady's name and address. I told her I would let you decide about meeting Salty and his training. Our firm will take care of those costs. The lady's name is Cindy. She will take care of your needs."

"This will help Naomi, and believe me, she needs lots of help."

"I need to leave for a meeting. Thank you for listening and joining in the solution. Off to work. There are many things on my list today. Bye for now."

Bridget stands and walks briskly to the front door. As she drives to Marin County, she feels like everything went well. Naomi will be safe.

Bridget says to herself, "There is that warm feeling again."

Bridget is running around the office with a smile on her face. Bridget is walking around, pushing those "C" cups out there to be noticed. Throughout the day, multiple things go flashing through Bridget's mind. One of those is the Naomi situation. The horrific way she was treated continues to keep Bridget's thoughts on that topic. Most of the week, there is silence from both Alex and Sammy on the Naomi situation. Bridget considers calling Alex, but maybe she will go by the gym instead. If she must go by the gym, some heads will roll. She picks up the phone and dials.

Alex answers, "Hello, this is Alex."

Bridget says, "Hello Alex, this is Bridget. Have you done anything about Naomi?"

Alex replies, "No."

Bridget asks, "Why? Have you not asked the Petersons permission to visit Naomi? Do I need to do all the work? I take this as a selfish response by both you and Sammy. Goodbye, Alex."

Alex turns to Sammy, saying, "Ah shit, Bridget is pissed. What the hell should we do?"

One hour later, the Pink Mercedes pulls into the gym's driveway. Bridget gets out dressed in workout clothes. She walks up to Alex and Sammy, knocks both of them to the ground, then pulls her 38-caliber pistol out of the holster as she saunters over to a group of six young black men.

She says curtly, "Anyone with weapons, place them on the table. All your weapons, guys, not just guns."

She checks their coats and frisks them.

Bridget then says, "Get your asses up there in the ring."

She places the 38 back into the holster and jumps into the ring with them.

Bridget says, "I am challenging you to show how tough you really are, and the odds are in your favor."

As usual, two brave hearts step up to take her on. They get ready to attack, and she takes them both out by pushing her index fingers into their eyes, followed by a quick slash to the throat, then a smash to their ribs. She hears some bones crack. Three more come running at her. She is attentive to their directions and kicks one in the throat, comes down from the kick, and takes out the eyes of the second then rolls

HIDDEN IN FRONT OF YOU

back into the third tossing this guy via Ju-Jitsu into the metal post in the corner. He lands on his head and is out cold.

The sixth guy sits down and says, "I am good. No trouble here."

Bridget walks to the picnic table where Alex and Sammy are sitting. She sits down and takes a swig of water from a water bottle.

Bridget asks, "Do either one of you want to get into the ring and argue with me? Do either of you have anything to say?"

There is a long silence.

She says, "I have a lot to tell you. Both of you are now on suspension. That means that your benefits have stopped. The firm's support is on hold. Remember, this is a two-way agreement."

"The only reason I have not to beat your asses to a pulp is that you finally did notify me of Naomi's abuse. You failed to call me on day one. You asked for help, and I offered to come here immediately."

"Alex, you chose to wait until Monday, and you continue running this gym with people that are trash. You are just coasting along because you are not in jail. What are you doing for Sammy? He is at least trying to educate himself. Will you succeed or fail if you continue in this type of environment? A family example is needed here. Sammy must learn compassion by helping others. The cleaning up of your situation and, most importantly, eliminating your lack of supporting a young girl is needed. She has already said she likes you two, but you are not her friends. What happened yesterday morning?"

"You and Sammy were threatened with Naomi in the middle of it. Naomi's stepfather is not here today, and his five friends are also not here either. Did you contact me with this information? No, you did not. What might you think if those six never come back here again?"

Alex says, "Did you have something to do with that."

Bridget smiles and says, "You know I can't answer that question. You know little of what I do when I am not here with you."

"Alissa has offered to be Naomi's friend and companion. Naomi now has a guard dog in training for her protection. Can you imagine the fear she has when trusted friends are not with her? There you two assholes are sitting on your hands, letting the courts take the blame for you not stepping up to the plate. Do either of you know how hard it is going to be for her to get past this horrific abuse?"

Bridget yells at the six guys, "Hey, you guys, it's time for you to leave, but do not try to pick up your weapons. Alex will be putting them into my car."

Bridget continues with Alex and Sammy saying, "You two are going to need to prove to me you're worth keeping. I do want you both to be happy and productive in your lives, but you are going to be required to work your way back into the group. Think about it."

Bridget stands without saying another word. Before leaving, she calls the office to inform Jennifer where she is and starts for home. Juliet and Alissa are busy at a school function. Bridget must stay home without the company of Ms. Tease. That is always disappointing. Since she still overbuys, making a leftover dinner is easy. She finishes a glass of port. Her workout made her sweat, so it's off to the shower. Last night with Naomi on her mind, she had a miserable night's sleep. So, she goes to bed early and has no love of her life to snuggle with.

In the morning, there is still no Juliet. Bridget is not pleased to be by herself. She preps her ponytail since she has received so many compliments. Bridget chooses a dark green suit with an arms-length to a see-through blouse, black nylons with gold jewelry, and white 2-inch heels. She is in no mood for breakfast., so she grabs an apple and banana. And heads to the garage.

No operatives are watching. Bridget shuts the garage door and drives leisurely to Lombard. A mild wind brings lots of fog across the bridge. Bridget enjoys the odor from the beginning of the bridge to the end. Upon arriving at the parking structure, she reapplies her lipstick.

As she enters the main reception area, Matilda says, "I like that dress too. You have such pretty clothes."

Bridget says, "Thank you. I found this one just last week."

She continues to her office.

Juliet walks into Bridget's office and asks, "What did you do yesterday afternoon?"

Bridget says, "I had a rather nasty visit with Alex. He and Sammy are now on suspension with the Charity Group. In my opinion, they both let Naomi down and had no intention of improving their actions. I had some fun fighting with six of Alex's customers all at the same time. I gave Alex and Sammy a decision to make."

Juliet says, "We do have different tastes in what we call fun. My father has most of the current research completed. You may want to meet with him."

Jennifer has Rita's paperwork copied and on Bridget's desk. Bridget reviews the data and determines that Rita was framed.

Bridget thinks, "Rita is a good attorney, and it was quite a loss, especially for Rita."

Bridget walks into Julien's office.

Julien says, "You and my daughter are starting to sound similar, always teasing."

Bridget says, "We girls need to stick together."

Bridget turns to Juliet, saying, "I am meeting with one of Arnold's friends from law school in the morning. Then I may go by Alex's Gym. Would you want to go with me as a witness? It may not be so friendly this time. I am somewhat angered by Alex and Sammy's reluctance to show friendliness toward Naomi. If necessary, I may be confronting the entire gym again."

Juliet answers, "Bridget, you must be angry about this."

Bridget replies, "I think about that nice little girl being tortured and then ignored. Alex and Sammy had better show some interest."

Juliet says, "I am willing to go with you, but I am of no help to you in containing those brutes. Some of those guys in the gym look downright mean."

Bridget says, "If you are going with me, be at my place by 7 a.m. Does Alissa have a place to be tomorrow?"

Juliet says, "Alissa will be in class tomorrow, then she will be staying at Grampa's."

Bridget walks over to Jennifer's desk and says, "Jennifer, I have made two appointments for tomorrow morning. 8 a.m. is with Ron Burke, confidentially, to pursue reinstatement of Rita Kennedy. After the meeting with Burke, I am going to Alex's Gym. I am trying to get Alex and Sammy to become friends with Naomi. She needs to be shown that she can trust other black people. Right now, most of the black people in her life have let her down except for the Petersons. Do you have Naomi's number?"

Jennifer writes it on a piece of scratch paper and hands it to Bridget. She walks into her office and calls the number and hears, "Hello."

Bridget replies, "Hello there. This is Bridget."

Screams come from the other end, "This is Naomi. I miss you, Ms. O'Connor."

Bridget is almost in tears while listening to Naomi and says, "Dear Naomi, how are things going for you?"

Naomi says, "This family is so nice to me. I'll be in school next week. There are two other girls here, and I feel safe."

Bridget says, "That all sounds wonderful, Naomi. What do you have planned for tomorrow?"

Naomi replies, "Nothing special."

Bridget continues, "Will, your foster parents, allow you to come with me for a few hours?"

She says, "I'll put them on."

Naomi hands the phone over to one of the parents.

"Hello, this is Jeff Peterson."

Bridget says, "Hi, this is Ms. O'Connor. I was hoping to visit with Naomi tomorrow and go by Alex's Gym to see both Alex and Sammy. Is that acceptable?"

Jeff says, "She will ready to go in the morning. She still never stops talking about you. She even wants to have your last name as hers. I will not be here in the morning, but my wife will. What time do you want her ready?"

Bridget says, "7:30 a.m., if possible."

Jeff says, "She will be ready on time. Thank you for paying attention to her. She is a sweet child. Bye."

Bridget again walks away with that warm feeling inside. She knows that it is worth the time spent on these children.

Bridget says, "Juliet, I'll be leaving tomorrow by 7:00 a.m. I am picking Naomi up at 7:30 a.m. on the way to Burke's office in South San Francisco. It sounds like things are going well for her."

Bridget says to all, "Good night. I am heading home."

Tuesday morning, Bridget is up by 5 a.m. and is showered by 5:15. She puts on the black panties with pads, a pair of legging pull-on denims, a sheer white Y necked blouse, with a white lifting bra, a denim purse, knee-high sheer black nylons and for shoes, it is the flat walking tennis shoe. Finishing her hair is a breeze. With one inch long dangling silver earrings and her makeup completed, Bridget is ready for breakfast by 6 a.m. Applying makeup is getting easier.

Bridget has a small meal and strong French roast coffee.

Juliet has not called, so Bridget does not know if she will be there by 7 a.m. Finishing breakfast, Bridget thinks maybe Naomi would like to visit with Alex and Sammy. Bridget has left Rita's papers in the pink Mercedes so she would not forget them. The time is approaching 6:55. Bridget starts down the stairs on her way to the car, as she opens the garage door in drives, Juliet. She grabs her donuts and coffee and runs to the Mercedes.

Juliet hops in, saying, "Would you have left without me?"

Bridget says, "Maybe."

The traffic could be worse for 7 a.m. The Embarcadero is reasonably clear, and Highway 280 is smooth with no delays. Bridget pulls up in front of Naomi's home. She walks up to the porch and rings the doorbell. There is Mrs. Peterson and Naomi, who is bubbling with happiness. They hug, and both have huge smiles.

The wife says, "Good to see you, Ms. O'Connor. Naomi has been excited about going somewhere with you. Thank you."

They both run to the car. As Bridget drives north, she finds the Highway 280 Mission Street off-ramp. As she turns north on Mission Street, she is about two blocks from Ron's office. They park in his lot and walk in together.

Barbara says, "Good morning, Ms. O'Connor."

Bridget responds, "Good morning, Barbara."

Bridget then tells Juliet and Naomi, "It may be best that I go in alone. I will not be too long."

Bridget steps into Ron's office, and they shake hands.

Bridget says, "I am here with some more data on the Rita Kennedy case. We still have a dangerous group that is trying to hack their way into our firm. Here are eight more pages on this case. It will be more productive if you read it first, and we talk later."

Ron responds, "Let me look at the data, then I'll call your office. Please say hello to Arnold."

Bridget says, "I sure will. Right now, we are going to take care of some business at a gym."

Ron says, "Nice to see you, girls. Have a good day."

All three girls exit the office and get into the pink Mercedes.

Bridget continues driving north on Mission Street. After a few blocks, she turns left onto 19th Street. Bridget pulls into the gym's driveway.

Bridget says, "Girls, this may or may not be a safe environment. Stay behind me and a little to the left. Naomi, you may again see the ugly side of me today, please forgive me in advance."

They each get out. The stepfather is not on the porch, and Naomi notices he is not there. Bridget walks boldly into the gym. As she enters, Alex is coaching some young fighter, and Sammy is sitting beside him. They see Bridget, and Alex stops working with the young boxer.

Bridget says, "What have you two done to see Naomi? She is here to have a discussion with you. I have given the Petersons your phone number, and they may be contacting you. Alex, do you have a car?"

Alex says, "Yes, it is behind the building in a garage."

A single officer walks into the gym.

Bridget says, "This must be your beat."

He says, "Officer O'Malley at your service. What happened this time?"

Bridget says, "Nothing has happened. We just came by for a chat. If you were not on duty, I would invite you to come along."

As they start to leave, Bridget turns to Alex and Sammy and says, "You don't see the stepfather today?"

Alex says, "All their friends are wondering where they

went. I think you know where. We have been discussing our suspension and what our options are."

Bridget says, "Maybe the two of you can work together on correcting your actions. If I took on six of your buddies so easily, think what else I can do. Playing with you two is like toying with babies. I am who I say I am. There is more to me than you can imagine. I still have a love for you, but you must produce in return. I'll let you know one thing. That girl is going to be one of the most important, talented and respected women in San Francisco. She has more to offer than most I have ever met. Now get your jalopy out of the garage and follow me."

Alex and Sammy close the gym and get ready to follow Bridget as the girls climb into the pink Mercedes. She drives back to Mission Street, left on Mission to Market, onto Market and over Twin Peaks almost to San Francisco State, and then westward to Highway 1. She heads north onto Highway 1 past the Zoo finally reaches Playland. For the next four hours, they drive the bumper cars, play in the Funhouse, and take a couple of rides on the roller coaster.

Bridget tells the group, "I used to come here and spend the entire day. What fun memories."

Naomi, Alex, Sammy, and Juliet are visiting this site for the first time.

Playland is almost gone, and there are already signs of it closing and being dismantled. Playland started to develop during the late 19th century. First, there was a railroad, then in a few years, trolley cars came along. Tens of thousands visited the site on warmer weekend days. Many rode their horse-drawn buggies and early automobiles across the sandy dunes so they could spend the day here.

Early afternoon and Bridget had to break off the rides and take Naomi back home. Alex and Sammy thanked Bridget for the exciting time and drove off toward the Mission

District. When Naomi got home, she could not stop jumping up and down, telling the Petersons about her exciting day. Bridget excused herself since she still had obligations in the office.

Driving toward San Rafael, Bridget and Juliet stop by the house for a change of clothes and to freshen up. Other than that, she had not broken a sweat or a nail. They both do a quick update on their makeup, lipstick, and perfume. No one is watching Sid's house today.

It is almost 1 p.m., so off they go. As Bridget crosses the bridge, the window goes down for the wet smell of the fog.

Juliet says, "Bridget, did I tell you that I actually talked to that lady the other day. Her name is Holley."

Bridget says, "Where did you see her this time?"

Juliet replies, "In one of the shops close to my house."

Bridget stays quiet for a while. It makes her think of Alicia. They arrive at the parking garage, Bridget locks the Mercedes, and up they go in the elevator and into the reception area.

After receiving a call from Officer O'Malley, Bridget calls the Petersons.

Jeff answers, "Hello again."

Bridget says, "Sometimes things happen in spurts. I just had a call from Officer O'Malley. That I can guarantee. Cindy has told me that you decided yes on Salty. I agree that it will be a benefit for Naomi. I have another decision you need to make. The arresting Officer O'Malley has obtained permission for Naomi to meet with another twelve-year-old with similar, yet less severe abuse experiences. There will be a psychologist present for assistance and legal reasons. I can have my private investigator Josey, Officer O'Malley, and Juliet's daughter Alissa ready to escort Naomi for this visit. This way, Naomi will be safe and comfortable, and it will help both girls. Naomi may have another friend in her life.

The question is, will you let this happen?"

Jeff answers, "My wife and I are amazed and thankful that you are doing so much to help Naomi. We are, but foster parents, and we have not had these kinds of experiences. We are unable to fix any problem that, for the most part, is unknown to us. Plan the meeting, and we will make sure Naomi is available."

Bridget answers, "We all thank you for your cooperation. I have a feeling that great things are going to come from these actions. Good afternoon Jeff."

Both Bridget and Juliet finish up at the office and drive to the Filbert house.

Juliet says, "Are you for real? Do you realize how generous you are being? I love you for it. I heard you took on six at one time. I may be a tease, but you are sometimes crazy."

Both Bridget and Juliet sit down to talk.

Bridget says, "Now my sweet, what about us? Where is Alissa?"

Juliet says, "Alissa decided to stay with Grandpa. He will take her to the friend's house in the morning. Poor me, I have nowhere to sleep tonight. You would not dare make me sleep on those horrible cotton sheets, would you?"

Bridget says, "You know I can't be that intolerable. But you best behave yourself tonight, another thought. I am getting more comfortable in these clothes. Second, my feeling of not being honest with my friends is starting to be not so wrong. Many things have changed for the better when they can't find Arnold. Telling my friends would put them in more danger. Maybe I should keep it this way until sometime later. Tomorrow will be stressful. We have some good preliminary data, and along with experiences, we have some good conjectures. The McCarthy Group is looking even more dangerous than before. In my opinion, after you take out the very top, the rest are nothing more than selfish money-hungry mercenaries."

Bridget continues, "I must go to bed early tonight. I am on my way to take a shower and sleep. You can stay out here if you are too embarrassed to join me."

Juliet says, "In your dreams, Ms. O'Connor. I want you beside me all night."

They both race to the shower then sees which one can get to the bed first. Juliet beats Bridget by a few seconds.

Juliet says, "I love you more each day."

For the next two hours, they are either making love or their bodies are intertwined. Neither one wants to get up the following morning as light shines through the window. The alarm goes off, ending the procrastination. The two are busy kissing each other.

Bridget plans to revive some old acquaintances today. The death of the Dulles, the disappearance of George Williams, and the lack of happier times is her motivation for wandering through the office and striking up conversations.

Both Juliet and Bridget know that their morning time is limited. They took showers last night, but Bridget must shave because she has skipped a few electrologist appointments.

Clothes are laid out. Bridget chooses 2-inch white heels and a pink dress falling just below the knee. By the time Bridget is ready, Juliet has most of the breakfast cooking. Bridget looks like she is going to the office to play. Juliet is happily moving through the kitchen, singing, and dancing as if the work is play. Juliet borrows a light blue dress with a comfortable white jacket. According to her, every day with Bridget makes life that much more meaningful. Together they still take the time to enjoy the morning meal. They spend some extra time for a second cup of coffee while looking at each other with those loving gazes. Soon they both start for the garage.

Juliet drives out while Bridget stops at the curb to close the garage door and check for operatives. The day is a little colder than most mornings. The fog is still there, and it reaches almost as far as San Quentin. As they park, Bridget updates her lipstick, and they ride up to the office together. Matilda is away from her desk, delivering the mail. Jennifer is her typical happy self with coffee in hand.

Jennifer says, "Please spend some time with David. Today is a good day because his schedule is mostly free."

Jennifer and Juliet have been working together, setting up a secret internal group that gives Matt continuous updates on Bridget's activities. Matt's men and women continuously track her movements. Juliet feels so much more at ease, knowing someone is looking out for her Bridget.

After enjoying her coffee and sneaking a little cinnamon pastry, Bridget begins wandering around the office, chatting with everyone that has time to spare. While David is busy, she spends time talking with Amy.

Harriet has been visiting with Julien after they went to lunch together. As Harriet is leaving, Bridget asks her to step into her office.

Bridget says, "All the wiring devices from Mr. Williams have been removed so you can talk here. I was surprised yet pleased that you came by. Have the pressures from the McCarthy Group eased?"

Harriet replies, "Yes, and no. They are recording what is said in my residence and sometimes when I'm out on the street. Arnold was a matchmaker for Julien and me. He insisted that Julien accompany me whenever I want to go out for dinner or to a show. I really welcome his company, and it has certainly helped put me at ease. We have been to Davies Hall for all the Tchaikovsky concerts and out to dinner several times. We are taking Arnold's advice and only talk like a dating couple, and never about business. I feel a little more secure now."

Bridget says, "I am aware of your concern for Rita. We have retained an outside attorney, and he believes Rita will be freed within a few months. Arnold may be returning in a few months, but it will depend on his recovery progress. Some injuries did not appear until he tried to move and exercise."

Bridget's intercom starts buzzing, and she says, "Business is calling. Let's get together again, maybe with Julien."

Harriet smiles and then walks out toward the elevator.

Bridget spends the rest of the day wandering about the entire office, talking with many staff members gathering information about their personal lives, and listening to their ideas about the firm. The day passes quickly, and soon Bridget is ready to head for home.

Bridget walks to the elevator past Matilda, who says, "Good night, Bridget."

Down the twelve stories, and all looks good. No black Mustang and no contractor are visible. Walking to the pink Mercedes, she notices the clicking of her heels again. Into the Mercedes and out the parking garage onto Highway 101 South. As she nears the San Quentin exit, she can see the fog well past Angel Island. The mist has intruded into the southern portion of Marin County. She must slow down due to traffic, and as usual, she rolls the driver's side window down for the full impact of the wet smelling fog. The fatigue she feels may be from the onslaught of the future. It is not a pleasant thought to have so many people depending on you while fighting such a relentless enemy. Arriving home, she locks the garage door and wanders upstairs.

It is quiet, peaceful, and comfortable in her brain. Bridget gets out Tchaikovsky Symphony #9 and places it into the player while grabbing the imported port wine. As the music starts, she turns up the volume slightly. Bridget is so tired that she kicks off her heels and relaxes while still in her business suit. Bridget falls asleep after two glasses of the Port halfway through the symphony. At the end of Tchaikovsky Symphony #9, Bridget wakes up to the clatter of pans and dishes from the kitchen. She thinks I must have forgotten the alarm, or it is Juliet. Better yet, it is Juliet and Alissa. Bridget gets up and walks to the kitchen. As she passes Juliet and Alissa, she gives them each a big hug.

She says, "I am changing my clothes, girls. Be right back."

Bridget returns in a nightgown and a light robe with her puffy pink slippers.

Juliet says, "We thought we should have dinner with you. By the way, you look like it is a good thing we came by."

Bridget says, "Thank you, girls."

Bridget continues, "Alissa, I have a trip for you soon. You will be accompanying Naomi to a discussion between her and another girl that has been raped. There will be a psychologist there, and Officer O'Malley and Josey will be your protection. Naomi's dog is still being trained, so he may not be ready for this trip. The Petersons are in full cooperation with what we are doing."

Alissa says, "Then I am in. Have I become a part of the Charity Group?"

Bridget says, "Not so fast, missy. You are now acting as a contractor. That is the only the first step as you work your way up the ladder. I do compliment you on your first step, though, and I feel you're certainly a welcomed contractor."

After dinner, the three girls clean up the kitchen.

Juliet says, "Time for us to head home, Alissa has school tomorrow."

Bridget replies, "Thank you for your company and your help this evening. I enjoyed your visit."

Alissa starts to leave. She stops and hugs Bridget. Juliet

gives Bridget a big hug and a kiss on the cheek. After they leave, Bridget decides the earlier fatigue must be saying something to her. Off to bed, she goes.

32 - THE FIRM GETS A NEW CLIENT

In the morning, there is no Juliet, and Bridget is not pleased to be by herself. After dressing, she grabs an apple and banana and heads off to work.

Around 10 a.m., Jennifer rings Bridget and says, "Claire would like to see you."

Bridget walks into Claire's office and says, "Jennifer said you wanted to see me. Is this a convenient time?"

Claire says, "Yes, please have a seat. I got a new client last Friday, and the case is very complicated. They came in looking for Arnold, but I explained that he was unavailable due to a severe automobile accident. I told them that I have spoken with Arnold on the phone, and he seems to be in a lot of pain while trying to recover."

"I may be in over my head on this one. It is a construction company with contractual problems. Also, there are some allegations of money fraud. They do not have a law office that has been representing them. The individuals seem more like convicts than businessmen. The company has a mother group that oversees their business transactions."

Bridget says, "What is the name of the mother group?"

Claire says, "Let me get the file out. Ah yes, there it is. It says McCarthy Group Investment, Inc. Do you know anything about them?"

Bridget is about to fall off her chair as she hears McCarthy.

Trying to remain unshaken, she says, "Let me get settled and schedule my assignments, then I could help you with this case. I could be your assistant."

Claire says, "Bridget, that would be wonderful. Thank you for the offer. I feel relieved."

Bridget stands and reaches across the desk to shake Claire's hand. As Bridget walks toward Julien's office, she is glowing with optimism.

She thinks, "Can you get anything better than that?"

Bridget changes direction. She proceeds to her own office.

As she passes Jennifer, she says, "Jennifer, please hold my calls and keep the door closed."

Bridget calls Matt and leaves a Finion #2 message.

Jennifer walks in, saying, "Julien is still waiting for you."

Bridget says, "Jennifer, I am having a difficult time calming down. I think I just hit a gold mine. Do you have anything that you need to do at this minute?"

Jennifer nods no. Bridget jumps up, motioning Jennifer to follow her. She is so excited that for a moment, she forgets who she is impersonating. Bridget regains her composure before arriving at Julien's office.

Bridget and Jennifer walk into Julien's office.

Julien says, "Bridget, I have never seen you this excited."

Bridget closes the door and directs everyone to sit down.

She says, "We have just struck oil. I have misjudged Claire. The fact that Arnold is not here is a blessing. Jennifer, can you support two attorneys?"

She nods, yes.

Bridget says, "Claire has no secretary. Let's move Claire to the Williams old office where Jennifer can be close enough to support Claire."

"You two are looking doubtful. Let me reduce your doubts. Since Arnold is on sick leave, Claire picked up a case for a construction company. They came in asking for Arnold. This construction company has a shell corporation controlling them. The shell is our infamous McCarthy Group."

"Julien does what you have found show that the companies under McCarthy each are active for some time, then they close down. Does the beginning generally start when a city or county attempts an infrastructure improvement based upon some set of politicians, not business folks?"

"Claire has agreed to let me assist her in this case. That means I will have full access to the most sensitive information."

"Julien, you may now see why I am so excited."

Julien says, "Phew, what a change in our luck! Yes, most of my data is pointing to something like this."

Bridget says, "Jennifer, continue to treat Claire like the enemy. Keep her happy and close. As Claire or I make new files, I want a copy of each one in my file drawer. Julien, monitoring phone calls is still a priority. Please make a log we can follow with as many names as possible. Identification is going to be paramount. I am so excited that I feel as if I worked for days in a row."

Julien interjects, "I recently just happened to install a metal detector at our main entrance. We may be needing it for these guys. I will double-check it before I leave tonight."

Bridget says, "Julien, please call Josey and have him here bright and early tomorrow morning. We may need his help and make sure he is armed."

Bridget is off to Claire's office.

She walks in and says, "Claire, I have requested some changes. First, Jennifer will be our secretary, and you will move to the old Williams office. By Thursday, we should be able to review the case together. Does that schedule meet yours?"

Claire says, "That is perfect. By the end of Wednesday, I should be completely transferred to the new office and have things worked out with Jennifer."

Bridget waves goodbye. She returns to her office. Before leaving, Bridget gets a call from Matt. He says the meeting shall be at 7:30 p.m. at Ms. Brown's Hamburger Hut on Lombard.

Click goes the phone.

HIDDEN IN FRONT OF YOU

By now, the workday is over, and Bridget and Juliet leave the office.

Bridget says, "Let's go to my place. I have a scheduled meeting tonight. We can talk at my place."

Bridget and Juliet drive separately to the Filbert house. As they put their cars away, Bridget closes the garage door. She does not set the alarm for now. Once in the kitchen, Bridget calls Sid.

Sid answers, "Hello, this is Sid."

Bridget says, "We just got back. Do you have a couple of minutes to spare?"

Sid says, "Maybe if I get some food to raise my sugar level."

Bridget says, "That means he is on his way."

Sid walks in without knocking.

Bridget says, "Again, without knocking. Such disrespect, am I going to be required to place a lock on that door?"

Sid says, "You trained me well, Bridget. What are you two lovebirds up to tonight?"

Bridget says, "Is it that obvious? No one else knows."

Sid says, "You don't need a sledgehammer for me to see. You call and tell me to stay away for an evening. Are you blind, Ms. Bridget O'Connor?"

Bridget says, "Everyone else is either accepting me or is damn confused. By the way, Mr. Johnson, it is your fault. Juliet spotted the shrapnel scar on my right ear the first time she saw me. We both overlooked that one."

Sid says, "When are you going to tell your little group?"

Bridget replies, "When it's appropriate, but not now. We have other things I would like to share with you, my friend."

Sid interrupts, "Oh, now I am a friend, not just a nosy neighbor?"

Bridget says, "Shut up. I have only a little time to tell you things. First, the McCarthy Group has requested legal assistance from the firm through Claire. I may have misjudged her. That is the first piece of excitement. Second, in a few minutes, I have a meeting with Matt, and between all of us, we should be able to take advantage of this windfall. I am bubbling over Sid. I am ready to celebrate before we start."

Sid says, "I am pleased that this is happening. Retain your outside appearance as Bridget, use Arnold's disappearance as leverage and be prepared for some mean folks to come at you."

Bridget says, "You are correct. My parting feelings are from the tremendous improvement in our position. Now that I have invited you over, I need to kick you out."

Sid replies, "No problem. You women are all the same. As soon as you get what you want, you dump us guys."

Bridget says, "Juliet, I am going to get into something skimpy. Then would you drive me to Lombard? I will duck down when we leave. The contractor will not realize I am in the car. Drop me off then drive around before parking nearby. I will walk back to the car."

Juliet says, "I like the red mini skirt, the pink low-cut blouse, red three-inch heels, sheer black nylons, and that sheer top. You'll knock them out, lady."

It is just past 7:00 p.m. Bridget puts on the set of clothes Juliet has set out, freshens some of her makeup, and applies the bright red lipstick. They exit the house through the garage. Juliet closes the garage door before driving away. To Divisadero, she turns left toward Lombard then left again onto Lombard. Within the block is Ms. Brown's Hamburger Hut. Bridget gets out, and Juliet continues on. As Bridget steps into Ms. Brown's, she notices that the female cook is not on duty tonight. Bridget walks over to a stool next to Matt.

Matt says, "Christ, are you trying to advertise something

HIDDEN IN FRONT OF YOU

with that outfit?"

Bridget says, "My name is Bridget. I am just looking for you to take me home."

Matt says, "Okay, sweetie, let's get down to business."

Bridget says, "It looks like Claire is about to acquire a new construction client for the firm, and it is a wholly-owned subsidiary of the McCarthy Group. According to Julien's research, various McCarthy subsidiaries have embezzled millions in city funds from over eight municipalities in the last ten years. McCarthy drops the company after they overcharge, fail to deliver, charge for work not done, and launder the embezzled funds."

"The San Francisco project has broken ground, but many of the local politicians have become concerned since the newspapers began running some negative stories. McCarthy wants to acquire my firm for two reasons. First, to represent his subsidiary in any legal actions by the city and second, to use our 'charity group' to quiet any political opposition."

"Matt, now that you are up to speed on the situation, you can begin to formulate some ideas on how we can take advantage of this development. I'm sure you will come up with some unique ideas. Together, I am sure. we can develop a plan to drive a stake into the heart of the McCarthy Group."

Matt nods his approval.

She continues, "I could use some direction on how to physically or legally to attack these people. I plan to continue with this façade. It seems to have brought out good things already. Julien and I will arrange this information along with our own and get back to you."

The cook comes by. Bridget orders two cheeseburgers, fries, onion rings, and two chocolate milkshakes to go.

Matt says, "Thank you, Ms. O'Connor. I must go. Good evening to you. See you soon. Love and kisses."

He walks out.

Soon, the cook has Bridget's order prepared. Bridget pays for the food, walks outside, and climbs into Juliet's car.

Juliet says, "Was it a good meeting?"

Bridget replies, "Great, and I even have our dinner. Let's head for home."

As they enter the garage, Bridget notices the contractor is gone. With the garage door closed, the doors locked and the alarm on, they sit down for a fast-food dinner. The cheeseburger was better than most; the fries and onion rings were okay, and the shakes were made with real ice cream.

When the next morning arrives, the girls are up and about preparing for a big day at the office. Bridget will be meeting the new construction client around mid-morning. The girls have a quick breakfast and leave for the office in their separate cars. When Bridget pulls into the parking garage, she notices a black four-door Mercedes parked with three individuals in it.

When Bridget gets to Jennifer's desk, Bridget says, "There are three individuals in a black Mercedes here in the parking garage. Please call the police. Also, ask Julien to stand by the metal detector."

Within five minutes, the police patrol car enters the garage. After the arrival of the police, Bridget walks into the parking area. Bridget walks up to the police car introducing herself to the two officers. She then walks over to the Mercedes. The driver rolls down the window.

Bridget states loudly, "If you are here for a meeting, you best go to that meeting now. If not, and you stay here, I will have you arrested for trespassing."

A voice from inside the car, says, "We are here for a meeting. We are early."

Bridget responds, saying, "You best go to the meeting now."

HIDDEN IN FRONT OF YOU

She walks over to the patrol car and says, "Thank you for your response, gentlemen."

Bridget walks back to the elevator, going up to the twelfth floor. As she gets off the elevator, she sets off the metal detector. Julien is standing there waiting for the group.

Bridget runs over to Jennifer, saying, "Call the police department and thank them for their fast response to our problem."

As each one of the three set off the alarm, Julien says, "You must be packing, hand them over."

Each one complies.

Then Julien says, "Please walk through the detector again."

Each set off the alarm again. Each hand over the knives.

Julien takes their knives and says, "Again, gentlemen."

The third time through, they fail to set off the alarm. Julien then escorts them to the setup conference room. Jennifer is there handing out coffee and pastries to the new visitors. After a few minutes, Bridget, Claire, and Jennifer walk in. Bridget takes the lead at the head of the table, with Jennifer beside her. Jennifer appears a little nervous.

Bridget says, "First things first, the garage. When you arrive, park your vehicle, get out, and walk directly to our reception area. We have had employees and clients bothered by people in the garage. Note the signs and believe what they say. This is your first time here. Weapons are a complete no-no. We do not care if you have a permit. Just do not return with a weapon. What I am stating here is mandatory. Any questions that we need to get out of the way before we start our business portion of the meeting."

Mr. Kayne asks, "Why do we need to pay so soon?"

Bridget, with delight, says, "Your company has no financial history. Most of the companies owned by McCarthy are no longer in operation, so no current financial records are available. This is not a contingency case where we are going to share in the winnings. You are merely hiring this law firm to help you with some accusations and disagreements. The comments and points in the letters are made by politically appointed attorneys. They are not basing their arguments upon the law or the statement negotiated in the contract. They are trying to cover their asses and make you look bad. That is why you hired this firm, and this is a 'pay as you go' situation. Keep us paid, or we stop. You are asking us to help you in some sort of disagreement, end of discussion. No letters will be sent until we are paid first. We will be papering them daily until the city drowns in paperwork."

Mr. Kayne asks another question, "What does your vigilante group do?"

Bridget says, "We call it a charity. We allocate funds from our before taxable income to help young people in trouble. Years ago, other competing law firms claimed that it was a vigilante group. They were simply jealous that we were obtaining new clients from our reaching out into the community. When you help a child, the parent is your close friend from then on. Just yesterday, a couple came in here thanking us for helping their son out of trouble. He is now a dentist in Los Gatos."

"It is a very strict two-way street. We will provide help to those needy people that will appreciate and work for an objective. I currently have two candidates that are on probation. They have been warned. We are waiting for their actions to prove they are still qualified."

Mr. Kayne again, "Where is Arnold Pierce?"

Bridget says, "Wish I knew where he is. I would like to go to see him. He calls me sometimes but will not tell me where he is. He sometimes gives me business directions, but otherwise, he is on long term sick leave from a severe accident."

Bridget says, "I suggest a bathroom break, then let's get talking about the case at hand."

As the three take a break, Julien is watching everywhere these three walk. As the three contractors once again sit down for the meeting, no one from the firm feels comfortable. Bridget has her 38 strapped to the inside of her leg.

Bridget says, "Gentlemen, we are waiting for your response to payment. Our work is at the point that there are three letters already submitted to the City of San Francisco by mail.

There are seven more waiting to go out. We have dozens more to create our response. If payment is received, these seven will go out one per day. We are literally papering them daily. If payment is not made, we stop here and say goodbye. You may take this either way you want. Full payment is due by noon of each Monday."

Mr. Kayne says, "We will pay."

Bridget says, "All transactions are on hold until after we are paid. If you pay by check, we wait for the check to clear, which could take two weeks considering stop payments, guarantees, and the banking system's processing. Cash would seem to be the best and fastest way. Jennifer has a contract for you to sign. Do you have any new data to share with us?"

She waits for a response before continuing, "Silence, I'll take that as a no. Let's plan a meeting in a week. Please bring any new information so we can get started on it. In my opinion, we are waiting for money before we can continue. As you sign the contract, please have your identification ready. We will need to make a copy. Also, Jennifer will be taking your picture."

The three each sign the contract, present their ID, and have their picture taken.

As Mr. Kayne is walking out, he says, "I'll be right back with the cash."

Standing by the metal detector, Julien hands back the weapons while commenting, "They are unloaded and do not return with a weapon."

Bridget has been staring at murder in the raw. On many occasions, she has listened to this type of mercenary brag about the people they have killed. She walks into Julien's office to see Josey.

Bridget says, "How was it from your position, Josey?"

He says, "You stood a good firm line with those three. They had no choice when you got through."

Julien and Claire enter the office.

Julien says, "They were a bit antsy throughout the meeting. They do not have any patience."

Bridget says, "That was a lot of pressure on us. We must keep the pressure on them. Claire, please finish the last few letters to go out. Hand them to me for mailing. I want a sequence of messages to go to the city with a scheduled period between each one. Please let me know if we do get any responses."

33 - REFLECTIONS ON THE BAY

Bridget feels that she acted in a typical law firm way in today's meeting. She gave no indication that she knew anything about McCarthy. But, sitting across the table from these McCarthy mercenaries has Bridget extremely upset. These people brag about how many they have killed, maimed, raped, or frightened people into submission. Dealing with these cutthroats has put Bridget in a foul mood.

She says, "Sorry, folks, I need to take a break."

Bridget walks out through the reception area where Matilda's desk is, then to the elevators and down to the parking garage. The pink Mercedes is parked there waiting for her.

As she is driving out of San Rafael, she stops at a local liquor store that is connected with a Marin County winery. She walks into the store and turns toward the deli section. She orders a pound of sliced salami and pound of sliced extra sharp cheddar cheese. She walks over to the wine rack and chooses a bottle of Shiraz. She grabs a medium-sized loaf of sour French bread, mustard, a bottle opener, and a wine glass.

The counter person says, "Ma'am, you have made excellent choices. I wish I were joining you for this feast."

Bridget says, "I need to park my brain and review the last week. This seems to be the best way of doing so. If you see me out there, you are welcome to join me, or else I am going to be talking to the seagulls."

She drives south onto the 101, past the San Quentin exit, to the Sausalito off-ramp. First driving past the boat-related warehouses and manufacturing sites, she passes through the downtown portion with all its restaurants and shops. She rounds the corner just past the downtown section where the road is flat, and there are some old docks on the waterside of the street. Parking the pink Mercedes, she carries her bounty out to an old pier, finds a bench, and sits down.

The seat is old but sturdy. The view is spectacular.

San Francisco is across the bay water. Alcatraz is close enough to pick out parts of it. Angel Island is close enough to swim to, and the Tiburon Peninsula is just across from her. She pours a glass of wine and finishes it before opening the meat and cheese packages. Breaking off small pieces of French bread, adding some cheese, salami, and mustard, she makes a tasty treat. She washes it down with a sip of Shiraz.

Bridget says to herself, "The heavens have opened their doors."

Bridget's moment is peaceful. The sun will be going down in about an hour, the winds have subsided for the evening, and the bay waters are splashing on the rocks producing a rhythmic sound. Her personal contentment is without equal. She noticed the calm of being alone, the rhythmic sound of nature, and coupled with a good glass of wine. She sits there, enjoying the sounds of life until after dark has presented itself. The salami and cheese have been consumed. The wine bottle is empty. As the darkness takes over and the city lights shower the sites, Bridget decides to drive home to warm up again. She fails to notice a man observing her from a parked car. It is not a McCarthy operative, but one of Matt's men looking out for her.

Leaving Sausalito, Bridget drives five minutes to the Golden Gate entrance going south. In a few minutes, she is home opening the garage door.

Friday morning comes with Bridget postponing getting out of bed. The day has no meetings scheduled, no McCarthy mercenaries, and no parties. It is tempting to take the day off. Before anything, she needs some coffee to wipe away the cobwebs from the last night's wine. Strong freshly ground Sumatra will do the trick.

HIDDEN IN FRONT OF YOU

Finally, after her first cup of coffee, Bridget decides to go to work today. Scrambled eggs with shredded sharp cheddar mixed in before cooking, some leftover Crepe Suzettes with Grand Marnier mixed in the dough, fresh orange juice, and more coffee. Satisfied, Bridget takes a shower and shaves what little is left of her beard. Her makeup is going on faster and is more refined. She chooses a light blue business suit, black three-inch heels, and an off-white sheer blouse with a "V" neck. Dangling silver earrings and full silver flat necklace and light blue sheer nylons. The three-inch heels seem louder on the cement than her other heels. Getting into the Mercedes, she realizes that driving with heels has become more comfortable for her.

34 - CAT WOMAN

Bridget has loaded her grocery cart with her weekly selections. Meats, eggs, flavorings, cheeses, cantaloupe, fresh strawberries, coffees, liqueurs, pastries, and heavy cream for Irish coffees. Evelyn stops her as she starts for the check-out counter.

Evelyn says, "What is new with you, Bridget?"

Bridget says, "Recently, I had a nice luncheon with some of our staff, and I brought one of my charity recipients along. Remember the twelve-year-old that I removed from an abusive household? The luncheon was for the secretaries, and this young girl came along. It was a blessing to see her reactions."

Evelyn says, "You must be one of those bosses that have considered the support team."

Bridget nods yes, and then as she gets her wits about her, she says, "This coming Tuesday, I am planning a birthday luncheon for a special employee. We girls have been teasing him, and we may have hurt his feelings. My thoughts are that several girls dress up in sexy clothes. Say mini-skirts, boobs hanging out, heels, and whatever. As a surprise, the girls will grab him from his office, and escort him via a chauffeured limousine to the restaurant. There we will have Crepe Suzettes with flaming Grand Marnier on sugar, fresh fruit, and liqueur layered drinks. After we eat, each of us will go up to him. We will sit on his lap, kiss him, throw ourselves at him, and call him a French lover. We will give him lots of affection, and maybe even give him a gift. I'll be going as Cat Woman."

Evelyn says, "It sounds like so much fun. I could get downright vulgar with that kind of an opportunity. Guess what? I am off work during the daytime on Tuesdays. Could I come?"

Bridget says, "That's a good idea, as long as you don't

mind not knowing most of the other girls. But you must promise to leave his penis in his pants. I'll fill you in on the details as soon as the party is finalized."

After checking out, Bridget drives straight home. As she arrives home, she again notices that the group is not monitoring Sid. With Arnold now in hiding, Josey isn't being watched either. The group has apparently responded to some information. What could that be? Bridget is feeling less guilty about keeping her female impersonation a secret. Maybe Bridget has presented the correct image for now.

Bridget stacks the bacon, pork sausages, the ham, eggs, heavy cream, fruit into the refrigerator while leaving everything else on the worktable. Bridget is ready to sit down with a glass of Port.

The garage door opens. Bridget immediately grabs the 45-caliber out of the kitchen drawer and stands at the top of the stairs. The garage door closes, and here is Ms. Whitaker.

Bridget says, "I am starting to get used to these surprise visits. I'll try not to shoot first."

They fall into each other's arms and kiss as if it had been a year since they saw each other.

Bridget says, "I am happy to see you."

They sit down on the couch and start to talk. Bridget wants to share her idea about Julien's birthday. There is a knock at the front door. Bridget and Juliet quickly fix their lipstick, and then Bridget goes to the door. As she opens the outer door, she sees Officer O'Malley. Bridget invites him in.

Bridget says, "Now this is a surprise. Officer O'Malley, why are you here? Are you just lonely for us, girls? Come on in, would you like some coffee?"

He nods, yes.

Juliet goes to the counter to warm up this morning's coffee. Within a few minutes, Juliet and O'Malley have their coffee while Bridget is sipping her Port.

Bridget says, "Now we can discuss your visit."

O'Malley says, "You got me in trouble the other day. You left before I remembered that I should have had you sign as a witness."

Bridget says, "I knew that, but I was in a hurry to get to my luncheon. Sorry."

He says, "There is one more thing. Some of the neighbors are afraid of you. Some think you are an unstable person, and they wonder how a small person like you can seemingly dismantle anyone."

Bridget says, "Do you have friends that were stationed in Vietnam or Korea?"

He says, "Yes, but they will not talk about it. They are different people now, and most of them get a little spooky every so often."

Bridget says, "Years ago I was trying to protect myself. I could stand up to most girls and some men. But I was lucky that I did not come across a real mean individual. My cousin Arnold was being trained by a retired Green Beret Vietnam veteran. They shared the training with me. Since then, I do not live 24/7 in fear of my life. When things are peaceful, I am relaxed, and nothing changes within me. Like right now, you do not pose a threat, so I am calm. If I perceive a threat, I go into threat assessment. I automatically evaluate the danger and come up with ways to take you out. When that man in the ring started swearing at us, I went into that mode. I first noticed the weapon in his jacket when he was hanging nearby. I immediately did an assessment on him and his body language. By his stance, I knew what I could do at several different levels. At that point, he was done. I had my options planned and continued with them. I took the gun away from him. He continued to threaten, so I flipped him and broke his finger. He could not continue. He tried to, but I disabled him. Anything else you need to know?"

HIDDEN IN FRONT OF YOU

Officer O'Malley says, "I can see no malice from your side. You were protecting everyone in the gym. He just ran into the wrong person. I do need you both to sign this report as witnesses."

Bridget says, "Sir, we need to read it first before we can sign."

He says, "Of course."

Bridget and Juliet read the report. They make the appropriate changes and then sign.

Bridget says, "Juliet, will you please make a copy?"

As Juliet runs off to make copies, Bridget continues, "I used to run around with many blacks from the Mission District. I thought we were friends. Last month I tried to find some of them. No luck. They are either dead, in prison, or on parole. The racial hatred was much different when I hung out in the Mission District. I have no racial bigotry. The last three recipients in our charity work are black. I treat them the same as I would any person. I am deeply concerned at our drift into this racial profiling. You are mixed; what is your story?"

He says, "Black mama and white father. They are still together. We have a strong family history with love and bonding. I am proud of both of them."

Juliet returns and hands the report to Officer O'Malley.

Bridget says, "Wonderful. I would like to meet them someday. I have access to Arnold's sailboat in Tiburon. Let me know if your family would care to sail the bay waters."

He replies, "Thank you, and they may be interested. I do know that when a pink Mercedes comes into the area, the neighbors are aware. Good night Ma'am. I have enjoyed this visit with you."

O'Malley gets up and walks out to his patrol car.

Both Bridget and Juliet sit back down.

Bridget says, "I have one for you, Miss Tease. Your father

felt left out the other day. His birthday is on Tuesday. I have set up the restaurant to have a special Crepe Suzette lunch with sugars and flaming Grand Marnier, along with fruit and liqueurs. Then the fun starts. Each of us will dress in the most revealing outfits like mini-skirts, and we will show as much cleavage as possible. You need to steal his bag lunch, and all of you must not let him out of the office. Change into your outfits at about 12 noon. At 12:30, we girls will go into his office walk him out through the elevator to a waiting limo. All of us girls will hang all over him. I plan to come as Cat Woman."

"I have already invited Evelyn. She is coming as a slut. I think Jennifer, Cecelia, Claire, Amy, and Matilda may be enough. You may try Harriet since they had several evenings together. After lunch, we will have a gift presentation where each girl is hanging all over Julien while presenting her gift. We will approach this as Julien being the French name of one of those famous French lovers. The comments from that approach should set off some great ideas. That will be the fun part. What do you think of my plan?"

Juliet says, "My father will go crazy! He will love it."

Bridget says, "Can you handle getting it going? Any married woman may bring her husband."

Juliet says, "Consider it is done, my love. They will be asking to get onboard for this one."

Bridget says, "Now my sweet, what about us? Where is Alissa?"

Juliet says, "Alissa decided to stay with Grandpa. He will take her to the friend's house in the morning. Poor me, I have nowhere to sleep tonight. You wouldn't dare make me sleep on those horrible cotton sheets again, would you?"

Bridget says, "No, I couldn't be that cruel. But don't expect me to behave myself!"

They race off to the bedroom.

HIDDEN IN FRONT OF YOU

As morning light shines through the window, neither wants to get up. The alarm goes off while both are busy kissing each other.

Bridget says, "I have a surprise for you, my dear sweet woman. I only had a short meeting scheduled for this afternoon, and I will reschedule it for tomorrow. As busy as I have become, I have let housework and laundry take a back seat. Today, I think we should do some housework as girls should."

Juliet says, "You are always a surprise, Ms. O'Connor."

They give the home a good cleaning, do the laundry, drop off other clothes at the cleaners. Bridget has some long-playing Mozart's symphonies playing throughout their time at home. Even though they are working, they enjoy being together. After cleaning out the refrigerator, there are many options for a leftover dinner. No one comes by. Sid leaves them alone. While out running around, they find a movie to rent. That evening they watch a comedy with Toni Curtis as the main character. Then off to bed together to finish their lovely day.

Still intertwined, they are sleeping soundly. When the alarm goes off, neither wants to get up. Each starts preparing for the day. Bridget's clothes are laid out, heels, the pink dress falling just below the knee. By the time Bridget is ready, Juliet has most of the breakfast available. They have a quick meal and head off to the office.

All is running smoothly.

Juliet takes Jennifer off to the powder room. She tells Jennifer about the Tuesday lunch and the gags.

Jennifer says, "I am bringing my husband. This is downright exciting." They both start laughing and screaming as they return.

Julien says, "Another one of those jokes daughter. Can you disclose this one?"

Juliet says, "Sorry, Daddy, but I will get you some estrogen."

Both girls are smiling and smirking at each other. Juliet runs around, announcing the lunch to all the attentive female office staff.

When Tuesday arrives, all seems usual at the office throughout the morning, except Julien's lunch bag has been misplaced.

Bridget finishes the last comments for a homeowner's case and brings it out to Jennifer.

The time is 11:30 a.m. Jennifer is not at her desk. Juliet appears as she walks around the corner from the lady's room. She has this smiling face that says it all, playtime.

Juliet says quickly, "Cecelia was too embarrassed to come, so I invited Harriet. I hope that was alright?"

Bridget says, "Good idea inviting Harriet."

Bridget thinks, "I had better get ready."

She changes into the Cat Woman outfit. With the cap letting only the bangs show, it is a little less showing than she hoped. There is a sheer panel over her breasts, but the skirt is as high as you can get with a sizeable fussy tail. It's almost 12 noon, and the girls are ready. Julien is in his office, working away.

Julien says, "Who the hell stole my lunch? Now I have to go out for lunch."

As he starts to walk out, an army of girls is standing in his office doorway with broad smiles on their faces.

Juliet says, "You are coming with us, you big handsome man. We will take care of your lunch."

They hand him his jacket and help him with it. With Harriet on one side and Juliet on the other, they walk him to the elevator then ride down to the waiting limo. When arriving at the restaurant, the room is decorated, the happy birthday sign is up, and the chef is waiting to start. The chef has a four-burner table set up with the thin French pans for cooking Crepe Suzettes.

As they each sit down, Bridget gets on the microphone saying, "Julien was found wandering around the southern-most set of piers along the Embarcadero looking somewhat like a lost Tomcat. Arnold argued with him, but finally, Julien allowed Arnold to bring him home for a well-deserved bath and some food. We each know how these tomcats can be at times. It is said that he has at least three of his nine lives left. We can exercise our bodies in those last few lives."

She continues saying, "Meow, my lil Tomcat."

The chef has Crepe Suzettes served to each member of the party. The chef continues cooking the thin pancake mix with Grand Marnier. Each pan had olive oil cooking, and the chef empties the hot oil back in the original container. The oil is ready for the next step. When the setting of the pancakes is finished, the assistant chef takes each one pouring various sugars over the top then pour Grand Marnier over that while lighting each one. The dish comes to the diner in flames. On the table is an assortment of fruits and jams for each to use as desired.

With most people almost done with their meals, Bridget grabs the microphone. She walks up to Julien dressed as Cat Woman and starts by sitting on his lap. She turns toward him and snuggles up against him while kissing him on the cheek with fresh, bright lipstick.

She says, "You are a handsome Tomcat, but Julien is the name of a famous French lover. Are you also a French lover that can satisfy my needs? Think it over. You know how to reach me."

As she leaves, she gives him a jar of special cream for having sex with some new sensations.

Juliet jumps on his lap, saying, "Daddy, it is okay that you see all those alley cats. I still love you. I am leaving you a bottle of estrogen so you can understand my jokes."

Evelyn runs up and jumps on his lap. Evelyn says, "I am the alley cat slut. I see many of you Tomcat s all of the time."

She stops talking while reaching between his legs.

As she continues, she says, "Yep girls, he is a boy, we are safe. Now tell me, Frenchie, when shall we meet in the alley? I don't want to be with my other Tomcats when you arrive. I'll be waiting for you, sweetie."

Jennifer runs over and sits on his lap. She says, "You notice I brought my husband for this. He is very understanding."

Julien looks over at Peter Hastings, who waves back.

"Every time you come by my desk to see Bridget, I want to reach up and kiss you. But you just ignore me. Here are some condoms for the next time you come by my desk. Here is hoping we can get together."

Claire is sitting on his lap, caressing Julien and kissing him.

She says, "My sweet man, where have you been all of my life. I have the key for the upstairs suite with the hot tub and soft couches. I could always pick you up on the way. What a wonderful afternoon we could have."

Matilda sits on his lap, rubbing her hands all over him and kissing him.

She says, "I have never had a French lover. Would you like to try me out, sweetie? I am available every day after work, at lunch, and on weekends. I have brought you some French cologne for when we get together."

She ends with a big kiss as she leaves.

Harriet walks up slowly with a naughty look in her eyes.

She sits on his lap, saying, "Silly Tomcat. To think I had you in my apartment all to myself."

She is kissing him and running her hands all over his chest.

"I have everything waiting at my apartment. Here is the

key. Bye for now, my love."

As Harriet gets up, she leaves with a big kiss.

Bridget says, "Sorry, Tomcat, that is the end of your birthday presents. I never realized you got around so much. Here is your stolen lunch bag."

Bridget pays the bill, and they all help escort Julien to the waiting limo. The limo driver is laughing so hard he is in tears. He had joined the group during lunch. When they arrive back in the office, Julien is covered with lipstick. Everyone is laughing and giggling. It is at least an hour before things quiet down to normal. Bridget gets back into her three-inch work heels and business dress trying to get back into a work mode.

Jennifer rings Bridget and says, "Claire would like to see you."

Bridget walks to Claire's office, hoping Claire has heard something new from the McCarthy Group.

She enters Claire's office, saying, "Claire, you called."

Claire says, "I received a call from the McCarthy Group. They want us to continue, but don't feel like paying the bill."

Bridget smiles and says, "Call them back. Tell them that we have ceased any further work. There are still eight different letters ready to go out, and plenty more to create. We are ready to continue, but payment is required. Explain that this is not a case where we share in any monetary gains upon winning. It is just a contractual disagreement. The city must come up with proof for any of the possible charges. With no payment, there is no need for another meeting."

Claire says, "I don't have the total hours I have spent on this, but I can look it up for you."

Bridget says, "Good. I'll also get Jennifer's and my hours. In your discussion, make it clear we may go prepaid weekly. Thank you for staying in touch. See you later."

Bridget walks swiftly to Julien's office. As she walks in,

Julien looks up and nods hello.

When he gets off the phone, he says, "Cat Woman, what are you up to now?"

Bridget says, "Frenchie, many a meow. I need your help again. We are now starting down that path with McCarthy. They want us to continue yet fail to see why they need to pay the amount owed. I stopped work on their case until they are current in their payments. What I need is a meeting room that is wired and can be recorded. I need a video that can be watched and listened to by Josey. I also need a telephone or other device that Josey can say things to me during the meeting. The next meeting is scheduled for Thursday at 10 a.m. What do you think, Mr. Tomcat?"

Julien says, "That was one of the nicest birthdays I've ever had. You girls really did the trick on me. Whose idea was it?"

Bridget says, "That is for another day, Julien. By the way, has your FBI contact gotten back to you?"

Julien says, "He wants a meeting with you or Arnold. McCarthy is on their radar. They have one person inside but not at a high enough level."

Bridget says, "Good, I'll work with your FBI guy to see if there is any path there. One more thing, give me his name, so I can check him out before talking to him. Please do not tell him that we have other avenues to the FBI."

Bridget goes to David's office next. As she is arriving, David is saying his goodbyes to a client.

David turns to Bridget, saying, "That must have been quite a lunch you gave Julien. The girls were so excited before and after. I hear you went as Cat Woman, how appropriate."

Bridget says, "How come you didn't get into a dress and come along? The war is starting soon. McCarthy has rebelled against paying their bill, so I stopped any further work on their case. This should get their attention."

HIDDEN IN FRONT OF YOU

Bridget says, "Bye, for now, David. I need to find Josey."

Bridget walks back to her office. Jennifer is on the phone, so she continues into her office.

Bridget dials Josey answers, "Josey here."

Following the discussion with Josey, Bridget calls the number for Matt and a message of "#2 Finion".

Bridget wants to go home, so she finds Juliet.

Juliet says, "You look tired, Bridget."

Bridget replies, "I just feel fatigued. Maybe I have too many items on my mind. I think I will go home early. What are your plans?"

Juliet says, "Alissa has not gotten home yet, but I think I need to be a better Mom and spend some time with her this evening."

Bridget says, "Probably a good idea. I'm a little worn out today, so some extra beauty sleep can't hurt. See you tomorrow, love."

Bridget walks to the elevator past Matilda, who says, "Good night, Bridget."

Down the twelve stories, and all look good. Bridget gets in her car and drives out of the parking garage and then onto Highway 101 southbound. Passing through the tunnel at the top of the hill before the Golden Gate, she rolls down the driver's side window down for the full impact of the wet smelling fog.

35 - CHANGES FOR CECELIA

Today, Bridget will be spending most of the day observing and listening to individual interviews with each support staff member. Jennifer will be conducting the discussions, and the purpose is to correct any difficulties or weaknesses with the firm, not with the team member. Bridget will only be taking notes, and no entries will be made in their personnel record.

Bridget walks to Jennifer's desk and says, "What time will we be starting the interviews?"

Jennifer says, "The first one is scheduled for ten o'clock?"

Bridget says, "Good timing."

Bridget walks to David's office.

As she enters, David looks up, saying, "You sure are pushing the envelope with the McCarthy Group! Are you sure you are not really related to Arnold? You do some of the same things he would do."

Bridget says, "I am sure, David."

It's almost 10 a.m., and Jennifer is primed. Her working list is prepared, and Bridget is waiting for the first staff member. The first person arrives. Each person is offered coffee and a pastry.

Jennifer begins with, "We are here to correct current difficulties and find weaknesses with the firm, not you. Your comments will not go into your personnel file. Bridget is only here to take notes, so please relax. We realize how important our support staff is to the success of our law firm. We value your suggestions and comments."

As Jennifer finishes her introduction, Bridget sees the level of anxiety reduce within the individual. Many personal subjects like educational assistance, single parent problems, divorces, husband not returning from the war, and husbands with PTSD are openly discussed. Also, methods of communication when supporting an attorney, and emergency situations are discussed. The objective is to make

HIDDEN IN FRONT OF YOU

the workplace a more harmonious environment. Some new items start to appear like where do I go for assistance when a problem arises? By five o'clock, Jennifer has met with all the secretaries and paralegals.

Bridget reorganizes her notes then asks Jennifer to join her in Bridget's office.

As Jennifer sits down, Bridget says, "What more would you want in your job? You seem to enjoy your responsibilities, and you are quite effective when given a task."

Jennifer replies, "Fulfilling my support role is important to me. I work well with others and sometimes want to correct irregularities."

Bridget says, "Would a coordinator or first-level management position be of interest to you? You coordinate activities well. Things are always done ahead of time when you are assigned to them.

Jennifer replies, "Yes, I would enjoy some additional responsibilities, and I feel that I could make a difference. Thank you for considering me."

Bridget continues, "Good, but let's discuss Cecelia, our HR Director. Why was she resistant to joining our lunch for Julien?"

Jennifer says, "I usually stay out of personal problems, but it's time I said something about Cecelia. She has a gender problem, and it embarrasses her. She is afraid she will be made fun of, not be accepted by her peers, and even being fired. She would like to be a man but was born a woman."

Bridget says, "Jennifer, please ask Cecelia to stop in before going home. We may be able to help with that."

Jennifer says, "It's quitting time, so I better catch her right away."

Jennifer leaves and walks toward Cecelia's office.

Bridget calls Sid, "If I can get this person to come over to my house, can you and Evelyn have a meeting with her tonight?"

Sid says, "Anything for my beautiful daughter."

She says, "Go easy, you already owe me for several meals. I'll get back to you."

Cecelia walks into the office and sits down. She looks nervous.

Bridget says, "Cecelia, please relax. We are on your side. What are you doing tonight?"

Cecelia says, "I have nothing planned."

Bridget says, "Would you be willing to come to my house for dinner and then have a meeting with someone I want you to meet? Here is my address."

Cecelia says, "I would be pleased to join you."

Bridget says, "Great see you there about 7 o'clock."

Cecelia walks back to her office with a smile on her face.

Bridget calls Sid, who answers, "Hello, my daughter."

Bridget says, "7 o'clock dinner, you leach. I have a female with male tendencies, and she needs help. The woman is a real transgender candidate."

Sid replies, "Evelyn and I will be there for whoever needs this help."

As Bridget is running out of the office, she says to Juliet, "Dinner at 7 p.m., can you make it?"

Juliet nods, yes.

Bridget bounces out of the office in a hurry to get to the supermarket. She arrives within thirty minutes, parks the pink Mercedes, and runs into the store. The first stop is in the meat department.

She says, "Eric, I need some fresh salmon for six or eight tonight."

He picks out some fresh ocean salmon filets, wraps, and hands them over the counter.

She gets some condiments and virgin olive oil. Bridget

HIDDEN IN FRONT OF YOU

walks off to the produce department.

She sees Evelyn and yells, "Where is my hug woman? I am so excited. A female to male transgender is coming over tonight. I believe you and Sid can get her going in the right direction. Be there by 7 p.m."

Evelyn gives her a big hug and a kiss on the cheek and says, "Do you help everyone in trouble? I am excited to be of some help."

Bridget smiles and then picks some large red potatoes, fresh celery, cauliflower, romaine lettuce, tomatoes, and sprouts. Bridget is almost running through the store with her butt bouncing for little Eric's enjoyment. Stopping by the liquor department, she picks up a few bottles of Chablis and Grey Riesling. After checking out, she hurries to the Mercedes humming Pachelbel's Canon.

Arriving home, she places the groceries on the worktable, washes her hand in the bathroom, goes into the bedroom to put on something more comfortable for dinner. Sid has supplied so many items to choose from. By 6:45, the entire meal is ready except to cook the fish. A large bowl of salad is on the table, with the veggies already simmering. The lemons and tartar sauce are on the table. With fish as the main dish, Bridget opens the bottles of Chablis and Grey Riesling. Bridget feels that her female skills are improving. Shopping and cooking dinner is becoming so easy; she feels almost like a female. People start arriving, and Bridget begins cooking the Salmon. It's another grand display of Bridget's love of cooking. Around 7:15, everyone sits down for a quickly prepared but excellent dinner. The guests include Juliet, Alissa, Cecelia, Sid, and Evelyn.

Bridget says, "Enjoy; there is plenty for seconds."

During the meal, everybody is chatting about their home life, jobs, boats, and even about Bridget.

Juliet says, "I have this most interesting woman that I see

occasionally. We seem to meet in the happiest of places. We chat, have ice cream together, she asks questions, and I mostly ask her opinion. When she leaves, she seems to just disappear?"

Sid says, "It is not your imagination, is it?"

Juliet says, "It seems real to me."

Bridget remains quiet.

As most everyone is finished with dinner, Bridget says, "We have pie, ice cream, and a selection of liqueurs for dessert. Of course, there is fresh coffee prepared by Madam Juliet."

Bridget says, "Sid, I think it will be more comfortable for Cecelia if you take your deserts next door."

Sid, Evelyn, and Cecelia pick up their dessert dishes and leave for Sid's home.

Almost immediately, Alissa asks, "What is going on. Why do they need to go to Sid's house? Why is their meeting closed to us?"

Juliet says, "When Alissa has a question, I attempt to answer as thoroughly as I can. Even if I do not know the entire answer, I try to share what I do know. Alissa is quite aware of our reproductive anatomy, but she has not gotten to the part about our emotional involvement."

Bridget says, "That leaves some room for me to add to your education Alissa. The meeting is one that Cecelia will find emotionally draining and scary at first. We should stay out of her way at this time. If I were to be complete in answering your question, we would be staying up all night. But let me try to summarize the problem at hand. Cecelia's brain is what we refer to as wired differently."

"All living organisms have a primitive brain. For an ant, a fly, or a reptile, their total behavior is initiated and controlled by their primitive brain. As you move up to animals like dogs, cats, horses, most of their behavior is still based upon their primitive brain structure. They can also learn from their surroundings and experiences. Humans are at a higher level of brain structure and have cognitive thinking capacity. That is, we have a frontal lobe along with additional paths in our brain for telling time, learning, decision-making abilities, etc."

"Within the first four to six weeks of a human pregnancy, the portions of the primitive brain have set up the responses for breathing, flight and fright, initial aggressiveness, sexual drives, and gender preference. Most times, gender and sexual portion follow the developing fetus concerning male or female. The problem here is that the primitive brain is working asynchronously. Somewhere between 3% and 6%, primitive brains do not follow the resulting physical structure of the fetus. That is sometimes referred to as wired wrong. Some people, as early as five years old, find themselves in the wrong body. A male may want to be female."

"In Cecelia's case, her primitive brain makes her feel like she wants to be a male. That part of the primitive brain is not in agreement with the physical characteristics of the developed body. Cecelia's gender portion of the primitive brain tells her that it wants to be a man. The same explanation for homosexuals is true for sexual preference. Sid and Evelyn are going to help her on a personal level. In the office, we are going to help her be accepted as a man."

Alissa says, "Some of this makes sense with the information I have read from the school library. Thanks, Bridget."

Juliet says, "I learned a lot there also."

Alissa says, "All right, you two, I have a request. I am sixteen and drive my own car. Naomi is twelve years old and very bright, according to you. Both of you discuss being friendly and helping Naomi. It is time I get more involved. I would learn some new skills, plus my presence may be of some assistance."

Bridget says, "I like the idea. You are quite genuine and compassionate. It might be a surprise to you, but I support it, but you and your Mom should be the ones to initiate the relationship. If the foster parents agree, you two could be friends and go places together. Please keep me informed of what progress is made and the times and dates of any activities."

Alissa says, "Thank you. I think it will be good for both of us."

As Sid, Evelyn, and Cecelia return each present a happy face.

Sid says, "We have a go here. The meeting went well, and Cecelia will be smiling from ear to ear very soon."

Bridget says, "That's very good to hear. Cecelia, first thing in the morning, I want you and me to have a quick meeting with the HR department staff. I have another meeting for 10 or 11 a.m. on Thursday. Our meeting will be short and sweet, you might say. I'll see you tomorrow."

Cecelia replies, "I will be there by 8 a.m. Any time is fine with me. Thank you for dinner and for introducing me to Sid and Evelyn. I feel that there is true hope."

Cecelia starts to leave.

Evelyn comes over to Bridget, giving her a long hug saying, "Woman, you are the best."

Both Cecelia and Evelyn leave by the front door together, while Sid slips out the back door.

Juliet helps Bridget with the dinner dishes and then says, "Time for Alissa and me to leave too."

Alissa stops to give Bridget a hug. Juliet comes by Bridget and gives her a big hug and a kiss on the cheek. Bridget walks them to the door.

The looks on both of their faces say, "I want to be with you tonight."

HIDDEN IN FRONT OF YOU

After they leave, Bridget decides to go to bed and leave the kitchen until tomorrow. Perishable food has been stored, and the dishes are already washed in the dishwasher. Going to bed alone is getting quite unpleasant.

The alarm goes off at six a.m. Bridget jumps out of bed and starts her preparation for the day.

She is hurrying through every step of the prep. A quick breakfast and out the door. The one thing that keeps reminding her that she is a female is the clicking of the heels on the cement floor. She drives to the curb, shuts the garage door, checks for any eyes watching, and drives off.

Soon she is on Highway 101, and as always, the fog is enjoyable as she crosses the Golden Gate. When she is passing through the tunnel, the air gets warmer. Her arrival time is 7:45. The earliest she has gotten to work in months. She does a quick update to her lipstick and runs to the elevator arriving at the office by 7:50.

Off she goes to HR, and Cecelia steps out of her office to welcome her.

Bridget says, "Can you have your staff meet us in your conference room? I need to powder my nose. Then I'll be there."

She runs off the lady's room. Before returning, she updates her lipstick. When she returns, Bridget has a little talk with Cecelia in her office.

Bridget says, "With your permission, may I address the issue the topic the three of you worked on last night?"

Cecelia says, "I am ready, Ms. O'Connor. I see happiness just around the corner."

The meeting starts with Bridget sitting at the head of the table.

Bridget says, "I am here to support our outstanding staff member Cecelia. Her work is always spot-on, never is there a complaint, and we wish to help her feel more comfortable while working here at our firm. Each of you is most likely aware of the fact that Cecelia would prefer dressing and be addressed as a male. We of this firm want to help make this happen for her. She shall remain the HR director. It is time for us here at the firm to support her in this transition. Cecelia tells me that she wants the new name of Cecil. I am asking you, folks, to support Cecil in his future."

One of the employees says, "We have always known of her desire, and we all support it. We are pleased that the firm will also support her choice. There is no problem here for Cecil."

Bridget says, "I am so thankful. It seems that Cecil's happiness is guaranteed. We both appreciate your support."

As Bridget starts to walk out, Cecil reaches out to shake Bridget's hand, saying, "Thank you, Bridget. You have saved my life."

She has tears of happiness running down her face.

As Bridget walks away, she is thinking, "My, that was an easy fix for me. Not for her, but that will come soon."

HIDDEN IN FRONT OF YOU

36 - ARRESTING THE COPS

It's Saturday morning, and all is quiet. Bridget is thinking about how bored she is when the phone rings.

She answers the phone, "Hello, this is Bridget. Who's Calling?"

Juliet responds, "Who else would be calling you at 7 a.m. on a Saturday morning? You don't have another girlfriend, do you? Open the garage door, I have fresh donuts."

Bridget runs out to the garage, opens the door, and greets Juliet with a big smile. Of course, Bridget closes the door and resets the alarm system before they head to the kitchen. Bridget brews some French roast coffee to go with Juliet's donuts

After eating a few too many donuts, Bridget suggests that they drive over to the firm's warehouse so he can pick up some needed items for the office. Juliet is free, and she is happy to ride along. After putting the coffee cups in the dishwasher and ridding up the kitchen, they walk to the garage and hop into the Mercedes. Bridget closes the garage door and sees that there is no operative. The alarm is set, and channel 97 is recording.

They head off to Divisadero, then Lombard, Van Ness, and Bay Streets. Driving along the Embarcadero traffic is light. They pass pier 38 and drive onto Highway 280. Within a few miles, she switches over to the 101. A few miles after Candlestick, she turns off onto the airport service road. They pick up the supplies at the warehouse and begin a leisurely ride back home.

As she crosses Market Street while on the Embarcadero, she comes upon a vehicle driven by a very drunk person. The drunk driver is weaving from one side of the Embarcadero to the other. He is driving quite slowly, but he scrapes one of the parked cars and barely misses others.

He finally slams into a parked car on the east side of the

Embarcadero. Bridget had been following him while giving hand signals to other drivers. She stops and continues waving at traffic, so traffic will avoid the accident. Bridget walks to the nearest phone booth and calls the police department. After fifteen minutes, she calls again. Each time Bridget asks for the badge number of the person that answers and notes the time of the call. She then writes that information down on a page in her notebook.

From the phone booth, Bridget can see a black and white police car parked at a nearby restaurant. The motor of the drunk's car is still running, and the driver is passed out in the front seat. The accident is far enough off the main roadway that there is little chance of causing a new disaster. Bridget is hot. Her face looks quite firm. It has been thirty minutes with no EMT's or no police on the accident site.

Bridget storms into the restaurant. She observes two patrolmen having a bite to eat while they are both consuming bottles of beer. Juliet is right behind Bridget but knows better than to interfere. She stays behind her and off to the left.

Bridget walks over to the table and stands there, and her expression needs no explanation. It could be described as anger in capital letters, yet just angry would not cover the seriousness of her look. Both officers stop eating and look up at her as she slaps her business card down in front of them.

One of the officers says, "Ma'am, are you the one that kicked ass on 19th Street?"

Bridget says, "You can just shut up officer. I called your precinct twice, reporting an accident and a drunk driver in your district. "You can even see the accident from here. It has been over thirty minutes, and no one has responded. By your presence here, I assume that this is your district of coverage. Read my card, gentlemen. You are both under arrest. Do not resist me unless you want to lose your teeth. Place your guns and handcuffs on the table."

Pointing to the left one, Bridget says, "Stand up."

She turns him around and places the handcuffs on the officer's wrists snugly as she pulls his arms behind him.

She does the same for the other officer.

She frisks each of them for a second weapon. None was found. Bridget unloads the pistols and then asks Juliet to call the police department and explain the circumstances.

Within five minutes, two squad cars pull up, with a sergeant and a lieutenant. The sergeant asks what Bridget is doing?

Bridget says, "Sir, I have just arrested your two officers. There is an accident with a drunk driver within eyeshot of this table. Their radio was off, and they failed to answer my two calls for over thirty minutes. They were both consuming beer that I personally observed as I walked into the restaurant. I'll meet with you on Monday morning to file my paperwork. I plan to file a lawsuit against the San Francisco Police Department. If you think I am just blowing smoke, consider that this lady Juliet lost her husband to a drunk driver. And, my cousin lost both of his parents to a drunk driver. Through that window, you can see the car where this drunk is passed out in the front seat, the motor is still running, and we both are witnesses. Here is my card. See you Monday morning. I am leaving this in your hands."

Bridget and Juliet walk out of the restaurant to the Mercedes and then drive away.

37 - THE CITY LAWSUIT BEGINS

Monday morning comes early for the two love birds. They rise at 5:45 a.m. Jennifer has made an appointment with the San Francisco Police Department Commissioner for 8 a.m. As they are getting ready for the day, they both remain on the quiet side. Both know they will soon be discussing the death of loved ones. Bridget chooses a business suit for the day that will clearly show her breast size but no cleavage. Her skirt falls below the knees, and the long sleeve white blouse has a curvy collar flowing down the front. Black nylons and 2 ½ inch heels seem appropriate. Bridget puts on a little extra perfume along with a slender chain of gold for earrings. Juliet puts on what she had last Friday for work. With the possibility of an early lunch at the Spinnaker Inn in Sausalito, they agree on a light breakfast.

At 7:15, they walk to the pink Mercedes. As Bridget pulls out of the garage, they both look for operatives. None are found. Off to Lombard, then Van Ness to the Civic Center. Bridget parks in the police parking garage. She asks the guard for an escort to the Commissioner's office. One of the officers on duty is asked to escort the two ladies to the Commissioner's office. After going up three floors in an elevator, they are walking down a hallway full of high-level police staff and officials.

It is now 7:55, and the Commissioner's secretary is expecting them both. The Commissioner is in a meeting with some of his high-ranking officers and is not available until 8:15. The secretary ushers them into his office and offers coffee. She suggests that the conference room may be best suited for this meeting.

At 8:15, Mr. Trinity walks in carrying some folders that appear to be police reports. The secretary introduces Mr. Trinity to Bridget and Juliet.

Commissioner Trinity says, "I have read the reports, met

with the sergeant and lieutenant that were called to the restaurant, and met with both involved officers. I agree that there is a severe problem here. Before we get started, I have a question. Are you the same individual that has caused the ruckus in the Mission District in South San Francisco?"

Bridget says, "Yes, I am that problem, child. The first was a female child abuser. The second was a person that drew a gun on me. Both times I was defending myself."

Trinity continues, "The officers said that once they realized who you were, they became frightened. They decided not to draw their weapons. What would you have done if they had?"

Bridget says, "This is a little embarrassing. Under the circumstances, I would not have let them draw any weapons. They both would have ended up in the hospital. I identified who I was, the reason I was there, my intent to arrest them, and then I reviewed the reasons that lead me to that determination."

Trinity says, "Maybe I should hire you to train my recruits."

Bridget says, "Sir, your officers were in the wrong; they had jeopardized lives. They failed to respond to calls from the central office."

Trinity replies, "Ma'am, I do not mean to fight you on this. I merely am wondering if you could have completed your offense."

Bridget says, "I have no doubt that I would have succeeded. Their nightsticks were in the patrol car, and both had their pistols tied down. If either had reached for their weapon, they would have been taken to the hospital."

Trinity says, "Let's stop skirting the issue. You stated that you intend to sue the City of San Francisco. I have two misbehaving officers. Where do we stand on this?"

Bridget says, "Sitting with me this morning is Mrs. Juliet

Whitaker. She was with me that night and will be part of our legal offense. She lost her husband from an automobile accident caused by a drunk driver within San Francisco. The police report was faulty, and the drunk driver got off. Not until he was convinced by other means, did he take responsibility. My cousin's mother and father were killed in a drunk driving-related accident. That drunk was not prosecuted. He was later killed by another drunk driver in a similar crash. Both cases had shoddy police work and litigation that failed the victims. The other night, the driver was passed out in the front seat with the engine still running. He had been all over the roadway. I was behind him, trying to warn other drivers."

"After two separate calls to your department requesting assistance, I spotted your officers' two patrol cars parked in front of the restaurant. We have three incidences that are questionable in nature. Each can be shown to be weak and inadequate police protection and assistance. In addition to the poor security is the incomplete reporting for legal prosecution."

"I love San Francisco, the people, the diversity in the arts, the sights, and the weather. Most of us can relate by having relatives that lived their entire life in this city. My intention is not to ruin the financial structure of San Francisco, but to improve its procedures in citizen protection."

"Pardon me, but I require a bathroom break since I can see that this is going to take some time."

Trinity says, "The lady's room is out this door to your right."

Juliet and Bridget walk to the door and disappear into the lady's room.

Bridget says to Juliet, "I want him to review his options before I hammer down a solution. He is aware of his weak position. From the mayor on down to his sergeants, there is plenty of blame to go around."

Juliet says, "You are a schemer, all you wanted to be here powdering your nose. I think I will keep you as a woman. It gets more interesting along the way."

Back in Trinity's office, they are offered more coffee.

Bridget continues, "My opinion of the San Francisco Police is dubious. It is an apparent fact that the casual attitude and approach to police protection has been in place for years. Both Juliet and I work in a law firm, and daily we see that the evidence is both current and historical. We, as citizens, can't let this behavior continue. Our lives are continuously affected by your department's lack of proper actions."

"My lawsuit will start in the neighborhood of six to ten million. The damage will disrupt the entire police force for years. It will force the replacement of most of the city's politicians. What is your response to that position?"

Trinity says, "I feel attacked. You are saying that the leadership here has not done their job correctly. You wish to attack us, and the end result will be disruptive. Many people will lose their jobs and their professions."

Bridget replies, "Exactly. You have a situation that is easily proven to be faulty. Your guidelines and enforcement procedures have been inadequate for years. Your officers lack discipline. Two officers drinking on the job while failing to answer a call just a few hundred feet away must be embarrassing. I hope you are not anticipating that we are going away because you have extended this meeting to us?"

Trinity says, "You present the muscle that can take on the job, and I can't argue the facts. Internally there is an agreement with your accusations. We have been aware of the problems and are currently proposing changes."

Bridget interrupts, "You waited too long to implement those changes. Now we have become the leading force. If you want a fight, we are prepared. We do not lose many fights. Our firm has many cases in your legal system every month. Ask your District Attorney for information about our firm. Mr. Trinity, let's hear an offer from you to settle this painful dilemma."

Commissioner Trinity says, "I want you to trust us in solving our problems. I want you to know that freezing our monies via a lawsuit will cause a delay, a shift in our personnel, and a possible omission of some procedural corrections."

Bridget, in a very stern voice, says, "Mr. Trinity, you have not heard me. I don't wish to be ignored, nor pushed aside. You are presently disrespectful. If you wish to continue this confrontation, you have been told the result. Possibly we are wasting our time here. The attorneys that you have on your current city staff are either politicians or appointees of politicians. The arguments that they have presented lately have been embarrassing, to say the least. If those are the types of individuals you plan on fighting our firm with, you had better ask for retirement immediately. If this is going to be the way you handle the situation, sir, my firm will have the preliminary lawsuit filed by Friday. An open discussion will be on their front pages of the Examiner, the Chronicle, the Mercury, and the Oakland Tribune. The San Francisco Police Department will appear to be the worst in the state. Since you work at the mayor's pleasure, and he, being a politician, I can see where you will be in a short matter of time. It certainly will not be here."

Trinity jumps in to say, "Wait a moment. Things are becoming argumentative. I don't wish to start out this way. I see that you mean business and are not willing to back down."

Bridget says, "You are correct. Sir, in your CEO thinking, consider some of the alternate paths this action can and must take. Be creative. Be that creator that makes a great CEO. Don't be a loser. Think along the lines that caused this dilemma. Why am I here? Exactly what do I want? Why would I bother to come here to talk with you before filing the lawsuit in court? In other less friendly words, use the frontal lobes of your developed brain instead of the primitive portion of the brain at the base of your head. In plain language, get your head out of your ass."

Juliet reaches over to cool Bridget down. Bridget smiles and nods a thank you back to Juliet.

Bridget says, "I have left it open for a negotiated outcome. My motivation is an improvement in a police department that is there to protect its citizens. We will demand some initial bonus type of compensation along with expenses like payment for our monitoring staff hours. Upon a department upgrade and implementation, we are willing to drop the lawsuit after we are convinced the proper procedures are in place. Sir, it is up to you, Mr. Trinity. I have plenty of work back at our office, so it's time for me to leave. I hope to be hearing from you. I would suggest a department head meeting first, then your attorneys. Call my secretary Jennifer with your decision, or else I will be starting the lawsuit very soon. Good day, sir."

Bridget and Juliet walk out of his office without shaking hands.

On the way to the parking garage, Juliet says, "He does not enjoy being told what to do. You will need to hold his feet to the fire."

Bridget says, "Yes, until he figures out that I am there to help him."

Leaving the building, they walk to the Mercedes. There are no tickets or tow-away boots. Off they go to lunch in Sausalito. Bridget chooses the one-way Franklin Street to Lombard then out Lombard across the bridge. As usual, she rolls down the driver's side window to smell the fog. This time it is only light moisture. The skies are clear, and the air is warm today. Just past the rest stop for viewing San Francisco from across the bay is the off-ramp for the town of Sausalito. They turn onto Jefferson, pass through the Sausalito business area, and turn right onto Spinnaker Drive. As the main road turns north, Bridget turns right onto Spinnaker Drive. At the end of Spinnaker Drive, she parks the Mercedes, and they both walk into The Spinnaker Inn located at the end of the peninsula situated directly across from Angel Island.

As they walk into the restaurant, they receive some looks from the mostly male crowd. They are both smiling and are showing happiness as they walk into the restaurant.

Bridget asks the maître de', "Sir, may we take the table by the window?"

It is a two-person table looking out onto the bay waters. Angel Island, Alcatraz and the city are all in clear view.

Bridget says, "We should reward ourselves for this morning's work. My feelings are that I should have been more aggressive with Mr. Trinity. He is having a rough time being caught in the middle of this mess. As a CEO type, he should have handled the problems before they got to this point."

Juliet says, "I believe your performance was perfect. You took it to the top, and then you gave him wiggle room to negotiate. You may be disappointed at the response."

The waiter comes by the table announcing the special of the day. He hands Bridget and Juliet menus, water, and the wine list.

Bridget says, "Sir, I would like some port wine and a glass of Grand Marnier with coffee. To eat, I would like to start with a shrimp cocktail, then baked halibut for my main dish."

HIDDEN IN FRONT OF YOU

Juliet says, "May I have a crab cocktail, the sea salmon, a vodka martini up, and a bottle of your house White Zinfandel."

The waiter returns with the drinks and shrimp and crab cocktails. They start on their appetizers while continuing to review the morning's meeting. Both are aware of the tremendous job that has been created. If the department has been considering changes and it was not getting them done, then there must be politics getting in the way. Now they have no choice. The chance of their job loss, political turmoil, and faced with financial bankruptcy each will be playing a role in Trinity's attempt to cooperate.

Juliet says, "Bridget, you do start things. We could have driven passed that drunk without looking back. Then when you consider the personal loss, the heartbreak, and the pain that one might suffer, we can't walk away. I do agree with your decision. If we do succeed in upgrading the operations and procedures of this department, I have no doubt we will have saved many lives. What a wonderful thing to be a part of."

Bridget says, "I am here because I hope to make a difference. If Trinity is smart, he will be at our doorstep within days. Looking at the bay waters makes me want to take a few days off. I think you and I should revisit Finocchio's and spend some time aboard Alicia. Think about it. Dinner at an Italian restaurant, playing with the girls at Finocchio's then a cruise for a day or so. Could you schedule the time away from work? Ask your boss."

The waiter returns with their meals. They both start eating immediately. The light breakfast and an extraordinary intense meeting created quite an appetite for both of them. Bridget is done first.

Bridget says, "Oops, I should have eaten more like a lady. When hunger takes over, I revert back to Arnold."

She calls the waiter over to order desserts.

Bridget says, "May I have a second glass of Grand Marnier with coffee?"

Juliet says, "I'll stay with what I have. Thank you."

Bridget says, "Let's go to the office and get some of our offensive work done. I need to talk with Julien, Josey, Matt, and Claire."

As Bridget sips on the coffee and Grand Marnier, she says, "Some desserts are just delicious. It's nice that I can afford such luxuries."

As they leave, Bridget gets the feeling that someone is keeping an eye on them. What she does not know is that one of Matt's contractors is also having lunch. Similar to the San Francisco chase, where the two cars were just outside, the feeling is there, but for Bridget, there is no known reason.

Bridget stops her departure by slipping into the women's bathroom. As they enter, Bridget places her finger on her mouth to tell Juliet not to talk. They both use the toilet then update their makeup and lipstick. To not be obvious, they do start some small talk about the meal and the courteous waiters. As they get into the Mercedes, neither can tell if anyone is watching them. Bridget drives west on Spinnaker Drive to the main road and then turns north.

After they have driven away, Matt's contractor makes a phone call. Passing the warehouses for boat building and repair, Bridget continues to the on-ramp for Highway 101. There is no car pacing them. Still, the feeling is there. She thinks that the pink Mercedes is enough to acquire second looks. Fifteen minutes later, they enter the office parking garage. Bridget checks her makeup and gives her lipstick a once over. They get out of the car, Bridget locks the Mercedes, and they enter the elevator.

As they enter the main office lobby, Matilda says, "Ladies, everyone is looking for you two. Jennifer has the list by their

HIDDEN IN FRONT OF YOU

priorities."

Bridget says, "Oops, we may have forgotten to tell the office of our meeting. Thank You, Matilda."

Juliet walks off toward Julien's office. Bridget walks straight to Jennifer's desk.

Jennifer says, "Good afternoon, Ms. O'Connor. We have been looking for you and Juliet this morning, and we were beginning to worry. Here is the list of people that need to talk to you. I have listed their names in order of importance."

Bridget looks at the list and sees that Julien is on the top. She puts her coat and purse in the office and starts walking toward Julien's office.

As she enters his office, she is greeted by Julien, "Wine and Grand Marnier's before work. What kind of an example is that for my little daughter? Should I be calling Cecil from HR about this? Oh well, she is a big girl. I have a response from the FBI. Morgan Feetly wants to meet with you today. He is jumping up and down with anticipation of getting at McCarthy's records. Can you meet with him today?"

Bridget says, "I'll make time, if necessary. Yes, tell him, yes, but you've got to fetch him and bring him here in your car. Check and recheck the parking garage and then come up to my office. Keep everyone from seeing him except Jennifer. Ask him to change his FBI type of clothes and put on something less formal. Let's make it around 4 p.m. in my office. See you then."

She looks at the list, and Josey is next.

Bridget walks back to her office and calls Josey, who answers, "Josey here."

Bridget says, "You called, sir."

Josey replies, "Yes, we need to meet. I do not want to talk over the phone. When is a good time?"

Bridget says, "Here at the office until 5 p.m. or my place

after that. Would my place be easier for you?"

Josey says, "Tonight at your place is good. Bye."

Bridget reviews the list again, and Claire is next. Bridget walks off to Claire's office.

Claire sees her coming and says, "We have some things to discuss."

Bridget enters the office, closes the door, and sits down to listen.

Claire says, "I have answered more accusations from the city about the McCarthy matter in the same manner as you and I did with the first set. I need a schedule from you of when to send each one and maybe a quick review of the content. There are only fifteen letters."

Claire hands the first two to Bridget for her review. As Bridget reviews the first two, Claire is printing the others.

Bridget says, "Good work, Claire. These are fine. Mail them off to the city on day by day basis. Start the mailing after we receive the next payment on Monday."

"Tell the group that we are waiting for payment before continuing. I'll review the others later. Thank you for sticking with this. Talk with you tomorrow."

As Bridget leaves Claire's office, Bridget sees David motioning for Bridget to join him in his office. Bridget anticipates some concern by the firm about suing the City of San Francisco.

David says, "Please explain the meeting this morning in San Francisco. You have taken liberties that should have been discussed in advance. Is Arnold aware of this?"

Bridget says, "Arnold's name will be on the lawsuit. I have taken some liberties that may be considered sensitive from a political position. Are you saying that this is not the correct path to take?"

David says, "Politically, the shit just hit the fan. I have received calls from every high-level official in the city. If you are confident that we can come to some understanding, then I will trust your position, and I will support it. I do need to get briefed on the matter."

Bridget says, "My schedule today does not allow me to take the time for your briefing. I can devote the time required to brief you completely after 5 p.m. today or tomorrow morning."

David replies, "Thank You, Bridget. Let's make it around 5 p.m. today."

38 - HOT TIME IN THE CITY

Bridget is feeling smug by the time she walks into Julien's office. She realizes that the firm now has some real facts.

Juliet says, "Dad is not back yet. He should be here any minute."

Bridget quickly walks to Jennifer's desk and says, "Jennifer, please call Gregory Little of the Chronicle. I wish to talk to him, asap."

Bridget thinks it is time to fight fire with fire. She intends to light a fire under Trinity's ass. Then she walks into her office and dials Trinity's private number.

Trinity's office answers, "Hello, this is Mr. Trinity's line."

Bridget says, "This is Bridget O'Connor, may I be connected to Mr. Trinity?"

Click goes the phone then, "Yes, this is Mr. Trinity. May I help you?"

Bridget says, "Hello, Mr. Trinity. This is Bridget O'Connor. It appears that you have taken the political road for your solution. Would you please explain?"

Trinity answers, "No, I have not. I have spread the information throughout the Civic Center. I would like to make an appointment with you and your staff for 8 a.m. tomorrow morning."

Bridget says, "Fine, how many people are you bringing with you so I may choose the proper conference room?"

Trinity says, "No more than six individuals. Myself, three department heads, and two attorneys."

Bridget replies, "Fine. I may have the same number of people.

I consider this meeting to be an open meeting. No secret or behind the scene deals will be tolerated. My secretary will take the minutes that will be available to both sides. I have considered inviting a reporter. I will be representing the firm's owner, Arnold Pierce, during the meeting. I request

HIDDEN IN FRONT OF YOU

that all discussions remain open and productive. Thank you, sir, I am looking forward to our next talks."

She hangs up the phone, and a feeling of success rushes over her. Bridget feels like jumping up and down. Everyone around her sees her big smile.

Jumping out of her chair, she runs to Jennifer's desk.

Bridget says, "Jennifer, I am kicking butt today. With the information that Juliet can provide, we can put together a preliminary lawsuit for eight-million-dollars against the San Francisco Police Department. Please have it ready by this Tuesday. Have Mr. Love and Juliet assist you. There will be a meeting with Police Commissioner Trinity and five others on Tuesday at 8 a.m. I would like you to take the minutes. Please schedule David Worth, Julien Spence, Mr. Love, me, and Juliet for this meeting."

Jennifer says, "There is a call for you from Mr. Little. You may take it in your office."

Bridget walks back to her office, and answering the phone, she says, "Hello Mr. Little. Thank you for calling back. Your journalism on our discussion was excellent. Arnold was quite pleased, and so are the rest of us here. Are you available on Tuesday at 8:00 a.m.?"

Mr. Little says, "If you want me there, I will make myself available."

Bridget says, "Great. We will need to meet before the 8 a.m. meeting to brief you on the direction and content of the intended meeting. That is all I am free to say at this point. Please be patient with me. See you in the morning."

As Bridget walks out of the office, Julien is standing there with Mr. Fleetly of the FBI.

Bridget says, "Julien come on in and make yourselves at home. I need to run off and powder my nose. Have Jennifer bring in some coffee and pastries. See you in a few moments."

As she walks off to the lady's bathroom, her thoughts are racing. All in one day, things are starting to explode. She thinks that she could not have planned this day any better. On her return to the office, she stops by David's office.

Bridget walks in, saying, "I'll give a quick briefing after my next office meeting. Say before 5 p.m. You are invited to the Tuesday 8 a.m. meeting with the San Francisco Police Department. There will be a reporter there also."

David starts to say something, and Bridget is running out of his office.

He thinks, "First, my fantastic Arnold now this crazy female what a trip it is."

Bridget walks directly into her office, and she lets out a big sigh as she sits down. Julien introduces Mr. Fleetly, and Bridget stands and shakes Fleetly's hand.

Bridget starts to calm down, saying, "Mr. Fleetly, why don't you tell me how we can work together on these McCarthy documents. Is there a formal way of handing items over? Should we keep a copy for our records?"

Mr. Fleetly says, "When they are handed over, you are given a receipt, and we take total control of the documents. From that point on, we begin our own verification. We will probably sync up with the city's payment records. We have a parallel investigation already ongoing into other McCarthy illegal activities. We have a record of some of their attacks on your firm. When Mr. Pierce fired most of the financial department, all links to the McCarthy Group ceased and have dropped off completely. We noticed that your firm is representing McCarthy concerning the City of San Francisco and some political allegations."

Bridget says, "We do have some staff inside our firm working on this case. We also have some outside attorneys that are being helpful to our firm. We had you checked out. The info on you came back saying it is alright to talk to you.

HIDDEN IN FRONT OF YOU

From some of our outside contractors, we are told that within the near term, some of McCarthy's documents related to work charges and payments made by the city will become available. The crime being committed by McCarthy is the illegal charging for work not done and overcharging for work completed. And, since these records were mailed, there will be additional federal charges. We have decided to make copies before turning them over to you. We should have a sufficient number of records in about thirty days. Can you relate to us the current status? That may help us coordinate other operations we have planned. Our purpose is to eliminate the threat to our group. Can you stay in communication with Mr. Spence?"

Fleetly says, "All sounds good. We will tend to ignore some of your other actions. We have already come across a few in the last months. Arnold Pierce's driving exploits are fun to observe. Thank you, Ma'am, we will be waiting for your documents. Good luck."

He stands, shakes Bridget's and Julien's hands, then Julien escorts him out of the building.

Bridget is feeling letdown since this meeting did not provide an immediate solution. Yet, at least there is a connection with an FBI person that can be trusted. The FBI McCarthy probe is alive and well.

The last item for the day is to brief David. Bridget just bursts into David's office, feeling higher than a kite.

Bridget says, "David, this has been a day for the books. The accomplishments have been outstanding, and it all happened without me planning it."

Then she shares the phone call with Mr. Trinity and the planned meeting on Tuesday.

David says, "You, just like Arnold, drive me crazy. And, you have more going on than anyone in this office. I now understand the city police problem, our advanced solution, and that it may make us look like heroes in the end. No worries, crazy lady."

Bridget leaves David's office feeling better than before. Stopping by Julien's office, she invites Juliet for a ride to her car. Out the door, they both go. After reaching the San Quentin turn off, Bridget explains to Juliet that Josey is coming over to the house with information. They discuss how exciting the entire day has been. Across the bridge, they go with no fog. The day is a little warmer than usual with very little wind. No operatives on the street so into the garage they go.

Bridget closes the garage door and enters the kitchen. After putting her purse away, washing her hands, and changing into something more relaxing, she pours herself a tall glass of imported Italian port. Juliet has some Merlot from the cabinet. They sit there, reminiscing over the totality of these past twelve hours.

Bridget is thinking of what Josey has that he can't talk about on the phone. It is almost an hour before Josey arrives and comes in through the garage. Josey comes into the kitchen looking very weak, and as he sits down, blood begins dripping blood on the kitchen floor. Bridget and Juliet jump up to assist him.

Josey says, "Another dumb move on my part. They are both dead, but they got one shot in on me. If you take me to the hospital, their friends will just kill me there. You better get me to Dr. Neel's clinic. The wound is on the left side of his stomach. It appears to have missed his vital organs."

Bridget says, "Were you sticking your neck out again?"

Josey says, "I did not mean to place myself at risk. I was listening to some casual conversations. They were McCarthy operatives. They did not know who I was, so they jumped me. They must have thought I had heard things they wanted to be kept private. Let's get me fixed up first before I bleed to death. I do have information for you."

Bridget calls the clinic to let them know of their intended arrival. Juliet calls Julien to ask him to pick up Alissa and that Josey has a gunshot wound.

Bridget changes into some work clothes and grabs a 45-caliber pistol, her purse, and some cartridges. Juliet throws on her shoes while grabbing some towels to catch the seeping blood. Juliet and Bridget help Josey to the pink Mercedes.

They drive out of the garage, close the door and speed off in the direction of the clinic. Bridget drives to Lombard, then onto Van Ness west then east onto Mission Street. After six blocks on Mission, she turns south-east then quickly right into an alley between Mission and Howard.

The medical staff is waiting for their arrival. Josey is quickly placed onto a gurney. As they wheel him into the clinic, Josey is still alert but weakened. Josey is taken directly into an operating room. Within a half-hour, they have the bleeding stopped, no internal injuries are found, and he is free to go. They place Josey into a wheelchair while moving him back to the Mercedes. He is still dopey from the Demerol. For most of the trip back to Bridget's house, Josey is passed out. Juliet and Bridget get Josey out of the car into a chair in the kitchen.

Bridget says, "Let's get some drink and food into him. I am sure he is hungry."

While the girls are preparing his food, Josey falls back asleep. Even though it is evening time, they fix him a breakfast of scrambled eggs, pancakes, fruit, and coffee. They feel that he is too sleepy to have food like steak or raw vegetables. He may eat his cheek or tongue. As he eats, Josey is becoming more aware of his surroundings. He is getting some color back into his appearance, but his speech is still impaired.

Bridget says, "Josey, eat slowly. You could accidentally eat your tongue or cheek because of the drugs you were given."

Juliet continues to fix dinner for her and Bridget. They sit down with Josey while eating their meal.

As Josey starts to come out of his dopey phase, he says, "Bridget, remember the building in Marin County that was built in the early 1900s as a brothel? McCarthy has rented it for his mercenaries to have a place to play. McCarthy has hired some working girls to staff the place. The meals are only average; there is no gambling, the opium den is now a pot or heroin den. Matt could clean out a good amount of them in one shot. That is the information I heard when they realized I was there. I only shot the closest ones with my revolver. Not wanting to run out of shells, I tried to exit when a third guy got me as I was leaving. After getting out of the building, I turned and got him too. I do not know if he is dead or alive. They saw me in the distance. I hope they have not identified me. Your progress today must have kept you busy. I'll bet you ruffled some feathers."

Bridget shares the many happenings of the day. Josey laughs when he hears about the San Francisco Police Department. He is surprised to hear of Mr. Love's coming out with the truth and was happy to listen to the FBI contact was pleased that the two-pronged effort that is in place. Josey agrees with Bridget's decision to bring Mr. Love into the group since he has come out being so forthright.

Bridget says, "David now calls me the crazy lady. He was quite surprised with almost the entire set of San Francisco politicians calling him today, wanting to know the damages. He laughed when she told him about Julien gave her shit about arriving to work after some wine and two Grand Marnier."

Bridget says, "Juliet needs to get home, you need to get to your place, and I need some rest. Juliet will drive you home.

HIDDEN IN FRONT OF YOU

I will follow with your van if you think they did not identify your vehicle."

Josey says, "My van was not there. I can drive myself, thanks."

Bridget says, "Okay, you two, you better get going. But, let's check the street first."

They collectively view the street, and all seems to be clear. Juliet and Josey leave through the garage. After clearing the kitchen and washing the dishes, Bridget calls Matt's number. She leaves a Finion #1 message indicating a desire for contact with more information. Moments later, her phone rings.

Bridget picks up the phone, saying, "Hello."

Matt says, "You called the beautiful woman?"

Bridget says, "Look out buster I may stab your foot with my high heels. Thank you for calling back. I have several things for you."

Matt quickly says, "Stop. I'll be there in ten minutes."

Bridget's TV is still tuned to channel 97, so her TV is continuing to monitor the street. Matt will probably come to the front door, so Bridget changes into something more appropriate and pours herself a glass of port. She waits near the front door until the doorbell rings. Bridget answers the door, but there is someone she does not know standing there. He says, Finion, please open the garage door. She closes the front door and walks quickly to the garage entryway. After opening the garage door, a car pulls in. Bridget closes the garage door behind Matt's car. Bridget offers some coffee and pastries to Matt and his partner. They each sit down at the kitchen counter.

Matt says, "Young lady, you have been busy today. Your lawsuit was a big surprise. Josey got away by the skin of his teeth. They did not identify him, and the third guy died. What do you have for me?"

Bridget says, "Before Josey was shot, he overheard the McCarthy guys talking about a brothel in Marin County, the one that was in the early 1900s as a brothel? Apparently, McCarthy is using it as a place to play for his mercenaries. McCarthy has rented the place and has hired working girls to take care of his men. Josey feels that it would be an excellent place to take some of the bastards out."

Matt says, "We have heard about the brothel, but didn't know the location. Thank Josey for me. This is valuable intelligence."

Bridget continues, "On another subject, Mr. Williams did, in fact, have Rita Kennedy prosecuted based on false testimony and corrupt data. I have an attorney working on the case. The McCarthy Group is still monitoring Harriet Williams."

"Mr. Alfred Love came forward today. He, his wife and daughter had been threatened with physical harm by both Williams and the McCarthy operatives."

Matt interjects, "Look carefully at the information from this, Mr. Love. There may be some stuff hidden in there. Mr. Love may not realize all he knows."

Bridget says, "His information is being taken a little at a time because we don't overlook something important. It may take a week or longer."

After pausing to gather his thoughts, Matt says, "I need to put together a plan for the brothel elimination. With some help from your people, we may be able to pull it off. I would plan to put the contractors to sleep. Get the girls out without them knowing who we are, set charges throughout the building, open the gas valves, and trigger the explosion with a projectile type of grenade."

"Good meeting. Progress is being made, but please have patience. We will win this fight. Good night and thank you for your hospitality."

HIDDEN IN FRONT OF YOU

Bridget checks the TV for operatives. None are visible. As Matt and his partner head into the garage, Bridget opens the door. Matt pulls into the street quickly and speeds away toward the Presidio. Bridget heads off to bed.

39 - DEPARTMENT HEADS

Mathilda opens the office at 7 a.m. most mornings. This morning, Department manager Louie Fish is already there.

Mr. Fish says, "I would like to talk with Bridget O'Conner as soon as she gets here."

When Bridget arrives, she has no time set aside to discuss things with Mr. Fish.

She says, "Sit with Josey to observe the scheduled meeting at 8 a.m. Then you and I can have our discussion."

Bridget has no data on Mr. Louie Fish. She dials Judge Brass for his opinion. He is generally in his office by 7:30. The secretary answers and Bridget asks to talk to Judge Brass. The secretary knows Bridget from many of Brass's court cases, so she puts the call through to the judge.

Brass says, "This is Judge Brass, how may I help you, Ms. O'Conner?"

Before Bridget can answer, the judge continues, "I hear you are having the first meeting with the department heads this morning. These are the crybabies that are hoping to jump ship before being fired."

Then Bridget says, "I am calling about a Mr. Louie Fish, one of the department heads. He is anxious to meet with me, and I don't know anything about him. What can you tell me about Mr. Fish?"

Judge Brass replies, "Mr. Fish is an outstanding department manager with around twenty-five years of service to the community. He has been fighting for corrections in the procedures and implementation for years. He runs a tight ship. Your suit has disrupted the police department politicking. Have a good time this morning. Thanks for calling."

It is now 7:45, and no city personnel has shown up. At 8:05, the city group arrives. Jennifer has coffee and pastries placed at the conference room doorway. Ten minutes later, all parties are settled in their chairs. Mr. Trinity introduces the department heads and the city attorneys that are in attendance. He gives a brief description of each department as he does the introductions. Bridget introduces herself and explains that she is also acting in Arnold Pierce's behalf. Bridget introduces David Worth, Claire, Juliet Whitaker, Julien Spence, Jennifer Hastings, and Mr. Little from the San Francisco Chronicle.

Bridget starts by saying, "We have chosen to pursue this lawsuit based on the continual poor behavior of the Police Department in protecting and supporting the citizens of San Francisco. The Police Department is aware of its discrepancies. There are groups within your staff that are currently hoping to correct these very problems. From the outside looking in, it appears that politics are hindering your progress. After the deaths of Mr. Pierce's parents and Mrs. Whitaker's husband by DUI accidents, each DUI driver walked away free of any consequences."

"We are here with vital information and evidence of a recent shameful policing by two of your officers. We shall continue to pursue our lawsuit. Without much work on our part, we already have more than enough evidence to prove our case and literally dismantle the police department. Court records are in the public domain, and we have many hundreds of supporting cases at our disposal. Upon going to court, we are certain of winning a significant sum and doing severe damage to the City of San Francisco's budget. For most of you, your career is damaged, if not over. The politicians will have their way with you. We will start by asking for at least six million and upward upon gathering additional evidence. It may become a class action suit if allowed to continue."

"But, let's change the tone of my opening statement. We of the Pierce Law Firm love the City of San Francisco. Each of us often drives into the city for pleasure. It is such a beautiful city with so many options to enjoy. Arnold grew up there. I spent a significant part of my young life there. As initiators of the lawsuit, we are the entity that must be satisfied. We will be open to alternate solutions if under a formal contract, and we are compensated properly. That is all I wish to mention at this, our first meeting. This parallels the statement made to Mr. Trinity Monday. Now, Mr. Trinity, I give you the floor to respond to my comments."

Mr. Trinity stands to address the group.

He says, "Thank you, Ms. O'Connor. We agree with you in many areas. We are forced to respond immediately based upon your lawsuit. We do not deny the Police Department has some problems. We have internal groups currently working on solutions. We wish to avoid the totality of a six-million-dollar lawsuit. Solving the problems and putting this behind us would be preferable. If you ask any of these department heads here today, you will obtain the same opinion."

Bridget says, "Mr. Trinity, is your Police Department is willing to work in a positive sense toward recovery?"

Still no comment from Trinity, so she continues, "One of the resulting failures is the difficulty in representing the citizen during court actions. An investigation of this problem lays the responsibility for it on your officers' accident reports. Any solution that we find must be implemented firmly and efficiently. There shall contain compensation in the form of a bonus, terms of cash as a monthly fee, charges for our attorneys paid monthly, punitive damages, a monthly monitoring fee, operational expenses, and payment for our employee hours assigned to this effort. I have my plan created. I ask that you arrive here to work out the particulars. The lawsuit will still be filed for the protection of all concerned. I question your intent. Gentlemen, are there any

HIDDEN IN FRONT OF YOU

questions to be answered at this time?"

Mr. Dewey of the legal department says, "I hesitate to allow you to browse through our files."

Bridget responds, saying, "Sir, you have a choice. Cooperate with our demands or pay the six million-plus. The time to do your homework was yesterday before this problem ignited. We will not be playing politics. Mr. Little of the Chronicle is here at my request to let the public know what is going on, not to muscle you into anything. You are essentially dealing with Mr. Arnold Pierce, who is the most forthright individual you can find. You may trust your life with him."

Bridget then states, "This meeting is over. Mr. Trinity, our proposed working arrangement is available, and my assistant, Jennifer Hastings, will provide you with a copy before you leave. Thank all of you for coming today. Will the people from the firm please stay for a short review?"

As he leaves the conference room, Mr. Fish is asked to wait outside Bridget's office until the staff review is finished.

After all the guests leave the room, Julien says, "Ms. O'Connor, you sure can be a badass. You gave them no choice but to cooperate."

Bridget says, "The severity of their actions and their unwillingness to correct the ingrown problems are their fault. I am just pointing them out. Here is what I believe we should get.

The law firm receives a $200,000 bonus for our charity group, a monthly stipend of $5,000, staff and attorney hourly fees paid monthly, all office expenses, travel expenses, operating expenses, fully reimbursed. All department heads must provide details on any plans that have already been created but not implemented. The District Attorney's Office must supply the firm with case by case information and an overall charted evaluation of progress. The firm must have the freedom to start appellate court actions in past cases. Julien, will you please take Mr. Little to a desk with system access, a tape drive, and a printer. He needs to start on his reporting. Mr. Little, please share with me your report before leaving. It is only 10:30. Would anyone like to go to lunch and discuss this meeting? Mr. Love, please get together with Julien Spence now. Outline your information so we can get started."

After a trip to the ladies' room, Bridget meets Mr. Fish in her office.

Bridget says, "Give me an opinion of the meeting."

Mr. Fish says, "I have been working toward precisely what you have proposed. I am here to offer my assistance. You have my complete cooperation."

Bridget says, "I did call Judge Brass to verify your intentions and your work ethics. Judge Brass did say you have over twenty-five years in the police department. We only talked for a few minutes, which did not allow me a complete understanding. I do thank you for your presence and willingness to tackle this difficult problem."

Mr. Fish says, "I am personally demanding and run my department by the book. I would fire those two police officers and hold any officer to the same requirements. You and I will get along because we share a similar line of thought. Thank you for including me in your review meeting."

He gets up, shakes her hand, and walks away toward the elevator.

Jennifer says, "Bridget, you are requested at Mathilda's desk."

The guest says, "My name is George Stearns. I work for Mr. McCarthy. This morning we have had an emergency. Here is the money owed for services to date. Please continue sending your responses and related questions to the City of

HIDDEN IN FRONT OF YOU

San Francisco. I do not know when we will be rescheduling. We will stay in touch with Claire. Thank you."

Bridget is sitting in her office when Mr. Little enters and says, "Ms. O'Connor, I have a draft for your review."

As he hands the document over to Bridget, he says, "I need to take a break. I will return in a few minutes."

The document is a four-page journalist version of the morning meeting. As Bridget reads through it, she notices that Mr. Little has taken a position of support for the firm. He is not attacking the police department, yet he does hold them responsible. The conclusion points to the necessity of improving the department's handling of the areas Bridget stated in her presentation. As Bridget finishes reading the document, she makes a shortlist of suggestions. Mr. Little returns and sits across from her.

Bridget says, "You have done an excellent job of stating the facts in this case. I do hope that your editor will allow you the liberties you have taken. I have a few minor suggestions. I would like to see a little more specificity concerning the accumulated weakness in officers not following department procedures and guidelines. Add some cases that were mentioned during the offline chats. Show some examples of the difficulty in prosecuting cases because of poorly written police accident reports. Also, report my comment that many Bay Area attorneys agree with my assessment and are willing to testify."

Mr. Little says, "Thank you so much for this exclusive. I will put all my efforts into presenting the information as you have requested. I have already asked for some liberty from my editor. Julien has moved a copy to tape so I can download it to my system. Luckily, we have the same operating system and applications. I must run to get this on tomorrow's front page. This will be my first time making it to the front page. I hope I am invited back again. It has been a pleasure."

He stands and reaches out to shake Bridget's hand. After they shake hands, he walks directly to the elevator. Bridget hopes he retains his honesty while confronting his editor.

Bridget takes a call from Judge Brass, "Ms. O'Connor, when the lawsuit story hits the front page of the Chronicle, a lot of things began to happen at the Police Department. Mr. Trinity and three department heads put in for immediate retirement. They were sure to be fired anyway. Mr. Fish will be the interim Police Commissioner until Mr. Trinity's replacement has been determined. The story will hit the newspapers tomorrow morning. Do you have any news for me.?"

Bridget says, "Not at this time. But I suspect Mr. Fish will request more retirements among the remaining department heads. I think he would like to make their lieutenant's interim department heads. Perhaps you can help him in this endeavor."

Brass responds, "Fish is a good man. I'll do what I can. Have a good day, Ms. O'Connor."

About a week later, a second meeting is scheduled with the Police Department that will require a larger conference meeting room. Louie Fish is leading the effort and is bringing a new representative for each department. Mr. Fish introduces each department head and describes their area of responsibility. The law firm staff, along with and an English professor assigned by Bridget for English language exactness and correctness, are all presented.

Bridget starts the meeting by defining the order of events.

Bridget says, "First, each group will read and analyze the existing department procedures. Next, how they have been implemented, and then how they are to be modified in the future. Following that, replacement and new portions shall be added coupled with stringent rules of implementation. A hierarchy of responsibilities shall be well defined. This is our starting basics. We may find that additional paths may be required."

She continues by saying, "Both Mr. Fish and I will be visiting to review the work as it is completed. Redirections and items may be added or subtracted by either of us. The assigned English professor will also be visiting to check for correct English usage. All items with may, can, etc. Are to be replaced by shall. Mr. Little will be visiting your groups to gather information for his next article in the San Francisco Chronicle."

She continues, "First, I need to announce that Jennifer Hasting has accepted the promotion to a first level manager. She is here for staff support and solving any possible staff problem. She is easy to talk to and has a solution to any issue."

Bridget says, "I have the honor of announcing the promotion of Mr. Louie fish to San Francisco Police Commissioner. You can drop the word interim from his title."

The room ignites with applause. Mr. Fish is totally stunned; he is unable to speak.

The only adverse event of the day occurred during the lunch break. Bridget decided to take Mr. Fish and one of his department heads for a quick lunch at a nearby restaurant. There was a drive-by as soon as she left the parking garage by a black Mustang. The woman driver waved at Bridget and put her on edge. It was like a reminder that the woman knew who she was. Bridget also felt like another car was following her back to the office after lunch, but the drive was so short, she couldn't tell for sure.

Despite Bridget's discomfort about the events at lunchtime, the afternoon session was quite productive, and everyone felt like progress was being made. Bridget has had enough of the office for today and decides to head for home. As she pulls out of the parking garage, she does not see the Mustang, but Bridget does note two of Matt's contractors in a green Crown Victoria. They wave as she passes, then they begin to follow her home. Bridget feels reassured.

40 - MATT'S MISTAKES

As soon as Bridget gets home, she calls Matt's number leaving #1 Finion as a message. Almost immediately, the phone rings.

Bridget lifts the receiver, hearing, "Matt here."

Bridget says, "The lady in the black Mustang has reappeared. She did a drive-by at lunchtime when a group of us left the office in my car. Remember, she seemed to be lurking around just before my near-tragic encounter with the dump truck. And, I believe I was being followed back to the office after lunch. I have a feeling that something is about to happen. Do you have any intel on this?"

Matt says, "They are trying to figure out why they lost so many people this week. They lost three by Josey and five by us. They are looking for answers. Good intuition, pretty girl. We will keep an eye out for the Mustang lady, and I will call you tomorrow. Bye."

Bridget continues to stay alert for Juliet. Fifteen minutes go by before the telephone rings.

Bridget answers the phone, "This is Bridget."

Juliet says, "A black Mustang followed me until the bridge, and then turned off. All seems to be clear."

Bridget says, "I'll open the garage door for you. Drive-in and park."

Bridget still has her snub-nose 38-caliber. She walks to the stairs and opens the garage door. Moments later, Juliet drives in, and Bridget closes the garage door immediately. Juliet walks up to the stairs toward Bridget.

She turns and hugs Bridget saying, "That was scary. You don't know what is going to happen. Do you get that same feeling when they are following you?"

Bridget says, "I am used to it, and I generally have my leverage with me. Would you want to get a concealed weapon permit?"

Juliet says, "I have no training. It is hard for me to say."

Bridget says, "The McCarthy Group has lost eight people this week, three by Josey and five by Matt. McCarthy might be a little on edge this week."

The next day back in the law firm office, Bridget is expecting to hear from Matt.

She sees Josey and says, "Josey, please don't leave. I have a feeling we are going to have a change in plans."

Just as she stops talking, Jennifer walks in and says there is a call for Bridget. Bridget walks to her office and answers line one.

She says, "This is Bridget O'Connor."

Matt says, "Please go to your staircase entrance and wait for my arrival. I will be there in ten minutes or less. Bring your snub-nose with you."

Matt hangs up the phone. Bridget asks Josey to stand with her at the staircase entrance.

As they are waiting, she says, "Josey, there must be some big changes if Matt is coming here to talk. When he arrives, after checking to see if it is safe, go to Julien's office. Wait there for me."

In a little more than ten minutes, Matt and a second person come up with the back staircase. Josey runs off to Julien's office, and Bridget escorts them to her office. Jennifer has coffee ready for each person. As Bridget sits down, she has her snub-nose in her hand, and the 9mm with a silencer is under her desk. The phone rings.

Bridget answers the phone saying, "This is Bridget."

Josey says, "Don't mention my name. The man with Matt is one I have seen with McCarthy. Please check it out. You may be in danger of letting McCarthy know all about your activities."

Bridget says, "Thank you, sweetheart. We can take care of that this evening. Bye, love."

HIDDEN IN FRONT OF YOU

She hangs up.

Bridget says, "Who is this guy with you?"

The unknown man shifts his body and becomes uneasy. Bridget can see that he is packing. She pulls the 9mm from below the desk and points the pistol directly at the man with Matt.

She says firmly, "Remove your weapon and give it to Matt now. Be aware that my finger is on the trigger. Okay, Matt, now tell me about this guy."

Matt says, "This is Jerry Nelson, an outside contractor from the east coast. He joined us just two weeks ago, and I am trying to introduce him to our group. What is the problem?"

Bridget snarls, "He is from the McCarthy Group. He has been seen with other contractors from the McCarthy Group. You have blown our cover by bringing him here today."

Bridget calls on the intercom to Jennifer's desk.

She says, "Jennifer, don't come into my office. Get our French lover and our old friend to come to my door. Have them wait there for me to open the door. Do not speak, please."

She points to Matt, saying, "Take out his identification."

Matt reads the documents. There are two sets of id's, one for Jerry Nelson and one other.

Matt says, "I'll be a son of a bitch. Where is Jerry Nelson, Mr. Scott?"

Scott answers, "He is dead along with your other infiltrator, Sherry. McCarthy is keeping his eyes on you. He knows when and where you are going to act. He may not know much about this lady, but he will soon."

Bridget hands Matt some tape.

She says, "Tape his eyes."

After he can't see, she opens the door, and Josey and Julien walk in.

In a whisper, she says to Josey, "Identify this guy."

Josey says, "That is the guy that has been chumming around with the McCarthy operatives."

Bridget reaches out and hugs Josey saying, "You, wonderful little shit, you have just saved our lives. He got in under the radar. Only you were aware. Thank you from the bottom of my heart. Will you take him to a safe hiding place? Stay with him until I come to get you. Give him some Demerol if you have some with you."

Bridget and Matt stay in her office.

Bridget says, "That was close. I know how that feels. We've had a few in here for months."

Matt says, "This is embarrassing. After all the tasks I have completed, this is so stupid of me. I must be getting sloppy. I am so sorry, Bridget. I could have cost all of us our lives. I had better recheck my entire group. It sounds like there are others in my group of contractors that may be on McCarthy's payroll."

Bridget says, "Who is taking this Scott guy? You had better clean up your group before we continue. I will have this guy ready for the fishes."

Matt says, "I know the captain personally from Vietnam. I will be the only other guy there."

Bridget says, "My crew is clean. We will handle Scott ourselves and let you pick him up later. Let's hope he likes the fishes."

Bridget continues, "I do have an educated guess of where you have gone wrong. Like most entrepreneurs and previously military personnel, you already have a background on the incoming workers. Like many civilian employees, you take from the general crowd available. You can't do that, Matt. You must vet the people before you talk to them. Let's save our other discussion for later, maybe over dinner at my place. I can't get mad at you. We just need to protect each other."

Bridget gives Matt a big hug and says, "We must be able to forgive each other."

Matt says, "Thank you, my sweet lady. Let's try to keep our mistakes to a minimum."

Matt smiles as he leaves via the stairs. Bridget finds Josey in a storage room with Scott bound, gagged, and passed out from Josey's Demerol.

Bridget says, "We will need to take him downstairs to your van for tonight. We are going earlier than scheduled."

Josey says, "We were lucky that I had misbehaved by getting too close to these guys, but sometimes it works out. Thank you for your appreciation. By the way, Ms. O'Connor, this guy is a junkie. Look at the needle marks on both of his arms. He is addicted. I would guess heroin."

Bridget says, "We will be taking him to the marina. If he wakes, ask him all kinds of questions. He may be able to give us names of the McCarthy lieutenants."

Bridget walks to Julien's office and says, "Julien, can you stay to give us a hand with this character after. We need to take him to Matt at the marina tonight."

41 - MATT'S PRESENT AND HIS PLAN

As good as this evening has been, it has not taken away the heaviness of Bridget's feelings. McCarthy is responding to the attacks from Matt's group, and the threats seem to come from everywhere. McCarthy can pick up numerous operatives daily, yet as he draws from those who are still available, the quality he finds has decreased, and he is becoming hasty. Bridget's team is sound and of higher quality. They have togetherness, family, and are highly dedicated to one another. Bridget's staff keeps her protected by staying in touch with Matt.

Bridget says, "Juliet, let's take tomorrow off. Let's make a point to talk about us and stay here for the day. Is Alissa still on her trip?"

Juliet replies, "She will be away for at least another week."

Juliet tries to soften reality for Bridget by saying, "Look at what you have done. The McCarthy Group is becoming less organized. Some of the better lieutenants have been eliminated. The records of the city's payments to McCarthy are almost ready to turn over to the FBI. Matt is developing a plan to eliminate McCarthy's brothel. That should demoralize McCarthy and reduce the incentive for operatives to work for him. With Matt's group and some of us, we have taken on the McCarthy army and are not losing the war."

Sid comes knocking at the back door.

Juliet is closer, so she opens the door and says, "Password, please."

Sid ignores the request and walks in looking for food.

Sid says, "My dinner is not ready? What is wrong? You two know I am hungry, password my ass. Well, my daughter, tired of being a girl yet? I'll bet you are not much of a girl between those silk sheets."

Bridget says, "We just got home. We have no plans, and hunger has not set in yet. My mind is going around in circles,

HIDDEN IN FRONT OF YOU

and then some leach from next door comes in here demanding food. Maybe we should have gone to a hotel for a quiet evening."

Sid says, "Remember my daughter; you are not a real girl. McCarthy thinks something is about to happen, so he is lining up new operatives. Some of my older acquaintances shared that data with me today. Some of the contractors are seeing the writing on the wall, and they are leaving the group. He is throwing parties at the old brothel for the new recruits. I do believe this whole thing is getting ready to wind down. Remember, McCarthy is not foolish. He is very calculating."

The phone rings. It is from Matt.

Matt says, "Be in your garage in ten minutes."

It is starting to appear that the desired quiet time for Bridget and Juliet is not going to happen.

Bridget runs to get the garage door open and waits at the top of the stairs. Matt drives into the garage in less than five minutes, and Bridget closes the garage door. His passenger seems to be unhappy. As Matt pulls to a stop, he motions for Bridget to come over to the car.

Matt says, "My beautiful woman, I have a present for you. Meet Mr. Williams. I lost no one today, and McCarthy lost five members of his group plus Mr. Williams. I remembered you saying that you wanted to say your goodbyes to him. Here he is my sweet. Can you plan a trip to the Farallones tonight?"

Bridget says, "Let me call Josey."

She walks upstairs to the phone and calls Josey answers, "Hello, this is Josey."

Bridget says, "Is the boat ready to go?"

Josey says, "It is full of fuel, all checked out, but I am not available until after 9 p.m."

Bridget says, "No problem, my friend. I just need it for a quick trip to the islands."

Josey says, "You are going without me aboard, that would be a first. Is it a special package?"

She replies, "You are correct. I want you with me. Please be at my place by nine."

Josey says, "Okay," as he hangs up.

Matt says, "We have lots to discuss, so let me invite myself in for dinner. But first, I need to give Williams another shot, so he remains quiet. I am giving my crew a rest tonight, so this present is for you, sweet lady."

Juliet and Bridget quickly grab from a collection of the leftovers. Within minutes dinner is ready.

Good thing, Bridget always overbuys. Most of them stay quiet while filling their mouths. Matt is accustomed to eating in a chow hall, so he finishes first and starts talking.

Matt says, "Bridget, most everything is coming together. The FBI data will be here this week. We need to give them at least two weeks to absorb and verify. Tell Julien to make copies before he hands the file over and have him request that Fleetly to agree to get on it immediately. We also need some guarantee from the FBI that they will be ready in two weeks. I will need some help from your people."

Bridget says, "My folks can be snipers but not infantry."

Matt continues, "If your folks need some training with scoped rifles, I will provide the practice range. My people are all from my Vietnam days. They will handle the actual combat assignments at every site. The timing is critical for every move, including the FBI, the brothel, and McCarthy's office. Each of you must have a substantial alibi. For alibi flawlessness, you must all return to your normal routines, and go back to everyday life at the office. Bridget, it is getting close to your time to disappear and Arnold to appear with bandages. There will be multiple agencies investigating these issues. We must be oblivious to any facts related to the extermination. That is the overview you have been waiting for. It has finally arrived."

Matt stops for more coffee and a touch of Grand Marnier.

He continues saying, "Our planning and scheduling should take two to three weeks. Practice runs a week at most. Handing over the papers to the FBI starts the schedule. Intermittent Farallone runs will be as required when we obtain an operative or two. Timewise, the brothel and the office are more closely linked. The brothel will start at 03:00, and the office will begin at 07:00. This will keep McCarthy from regrouping. Both events must be total extermination. We kill the operatives while shooting up the real workers with Demerol, or we pick a day that workers are off for the day. I have a few thousand messages to place around as decoys to keep the agencies busy for six months or more."

"Bridget, you should plan your heaviest efforts for the restructuring of the police department about this time. That way, you will be too busy to have an opinion on the newspaper reports. Use Mr. Little of the Chronicle to give the image of progress within the city rebuilding process. Between that and normal office business, you will be very busy. Bridget, it might be a perfect time for a family boat ride. Include the staff, Sergeant Brown, Naomi, and her foster parents, Matilda and her children, Harriet, Julien, and Juliet. Initiate the start of Rita's case on that same day. Things will be moving quickly, and McCarthy will have no interest in the firm."

The existence of Matt's group is, in some ways, like the vigilante section of the firm. Throughout history, when one clan or collection of people gather and execute using terror, it is a natural response to shut down or control the original faction. McCarthy has come out of the European prisons. His arrival has such ruthless acts of violence and terrorism that, when observed and understood, it is natural for an opposing vigilante group to dedicate itself to McCarthy's extermination. Matt, coming from the tunnels in Vietnam and execution death squads, makes him the perfect leader in this case.

Matt says, "McCarthy knows something is happening. He doesn't know what or when. If the schedule develops fast enough, McCarthy will be on the defensive for a change. The plan for the brothel will not leave any McCarthy operatives alive at the site. There may be others from his on-call collection that will go up in flames at the same time.

Matt plans to drug the girls and move them out of harm's way and strap military-grade plastic explosives to the operatives. This should reduce any other hopefuls from joining McCarthy, who will now be on the defensive and shorthanded. The explosions will be heard as far away as San Francisco. It will happen at 3 a.m. By 7 a.m., the business will be a tomb with McCarthy, his girlfriend, and close lieutenant's either dead or on their way to the Farallones. McCarthy shall be corralled by his own methods."

A quick thought popped into Bridget's mind, "Arnold will need a car that fits his personality, and a pink Mercedes just won't cut it!"

Bridget calls Nick, who answers, "Nick, here, may I help you?"

Bridget says, "This is Bridget O'Connor. Is Arnold's Jaguar ready for delivery?"

Nick says, "Ma'am, I have all of the parts but have been sitting on my hands till I heard from Arnold. That last accident must have taken him out of action. I could have it ready in a week. Does that fit your schedule?"

She replies, "That will be fine. Arnold would like to have enough time for some test runs. Has it been painted yet?"

Nick says, "No, not yet. What color does he want this time?"

HIDDEN IN FRONT OF YOU

Bridget says, "A metallic Pearl within a bright white cover and a clear coat over that. Do you require more time for this request?"

Nick says, "Maybe a couple of days. How abundant does he want the pearl to show when in the sunlight?"

Bridget says, "As brilliant as possible. Let's make the pearl predominant."

Nick says, "I'll call Jennifer when it is ready."

Bridget says, "Thanks, Nick. I'll let Arnold know."

Bridget remembers the last few Jaguars. Driving the Mercedes has been quite a step down in performance.

Sid has gone home. He has already offered to be a backup. Matt says he will help get Williams onboard at the yacht club. Bridget feels that a substitute is not required tonight but accepts the offer. McCarthy is too busy setting up roadblocks for what he thinks is coming. He may be waiting for a direct assault on the business area without knowing about the brothel extermination. His group will be weakened and understaffed. Some of his current contractors may just leave.

Within a half-hour, Sid returns to be a backup at the yacht club.

Bridget says, "It may be a good idea to be safe. Thank you for considering that."

Bridget starts getting ready for the trip.

Juliet says, "Would you care for some company?"

Bridget says, "My love, you may not appreciate what is going to happen. It may leave horrible memories. I would feel more comfortable if you were to stay here. Thank you for wanting to help."

Bridget is dressed and ready to go by 8 p.m. Bridget includes a bulletproof vest this time. She has brought a new 9mm with a silencer, her 44 Magnum, and a snub-nosed 22 pistol. Bridget has handled all the shells with gloves. She feels that the rubber gloves may keep her hands warmer on the trip to the Farallones. Josey will have all the rifles onboard. Juliet starts preparing coffee, pastries, and fruit. Nothing fancy tonight since there's only one passenger. Bridget has been looking forward to this one. One question Bridget has not been able to answer. Why does a man with a family, a wife, accounting experience, and a law degree hook up with McCarthy?

Josey arrives early with questions.

Josey says, "What is so special about tonight?"

Bridget says, "Go look at Matt's passenger."

Josey comes back with a wide grin on his face.

Josey says, "I thought we would need to snatch him."

Bridget says, "Go park your van and meet us at the public dock. I'll ride with Matt."

There are no operatives as Bridget and Matt pull out of the garage.

Bridget says, "I know of some possible reasons why Williams joined McCarthy."

Matt says, "His marriage went to hell after he got caught cheating on Harriet. He fought to imprison Rita since she would not join the McCarthy Group. Harriet fought it the best she could, but the threats put her on hold. There was no way she could fight them successfully."

"Williams has no compassion or empathy. His kids have disowned him. Does that start your wheels going? You may want to consider he had no choice by having no other place to go. McCarthy is famous for that. Others are brought onboard by threats to their family, and/or blackmail."

As they roll up to the dock, there is a parking spot in front. Most of the yacht owners use their own docks. It is not surprising to find the public dock empty at this time of night. Josey has the motors running, and the boat is tied off. Matt and Bridget stand Williams on his feet and walk him to

HIDDEN IN FRONT OF YOU

the dock. Once onboard, they place him in the inside front cabin. He just lays there out cold.

Matt says, "We had a good meeting, and the food was great. I wish I had other groups like yours to depend upon. Have a good trip to your favorite site."

Matt shakes Bridget's hand, and they exchange smiles as Matt walks toward his car. Bridget takes control as Josey unties the lines and pushes them away from the dock. The temperature gauges show the motors are warming up. Soon the transmissions will be getting ready for higher speeds. Josey pours a cup of coffee for each of them. He stands close enough to Bridget so the two can chat. While they are idling along, Bridget briefs him on the meeting from the night before. Josey likes what he hears.

He says, "With Matt's help, there is now a good chance we can win this war."

Before increasing the speed, Bridget places a check-in call with the radios.

Sid answers, "They are working."

As the San Francisco Bay often does, it is showing off its beautiful nature. With almost no fog and calm winds, the conditions are breathtaking. The water temperature between 50^0 F and 55^0 F. The Golden Gate bridge lighting is intense, and the traffic noise is clearly heard as you pass under the structure. It makes Bridget wish she was on the Alicia heading out for a weekend on the ocean. Bridget increases the boat speed to about 35 mph. Josey and Bridget sit back for the ride.

Williams is starting to move around but is still restricted by handcuffs. The bouncing from wave to wave is beginning to wake Mr. Williams. Bridget is excited because she is taking Williams out to his grave. As they are leaving the bridge behind, they must slow down to negotiate the waves of a Coast Guard cruiser. Crews from both boats wave their hellos. For the entire trip, the waters are calm yet dark since there is no moonlight tonight. Going a little slower while using only the bow lights, they arrive at the edge of the shelf in an hour and fifteen minutes. Bridget idles the boat a bit further just because it is Williams. Bridget leaves the right motor running while shutting down the left that had run long enough to cool down. The steering wheel is locked in a position that enables the boat to make a continuous circle. The running lights are off, and the onboard lights are left on.

Josey pulls Williams out of the front cabin and starts prepping him for his journey. Bridget starts talking to him. Williams is so doped up that he is barely aware of what is happening. Bridget wants answers to just what was going on within the firm. In his medicated state, Williams gives answers to most of Bridget's questions. Williams answers the first set of questions, then begins to be more elusive. He admits being a part of setting up Frank's accident, forcing employees to run like hell and not look back, or killing some of them. He admits to forcing Rita into a conviction since she would not back down. Rita was too visible to kill outright. The reason he kept working with McCarthy was the possibility of pulling in vast sums of money.

Bridget had brought a 22 along just in case Williams was not as corrupt as he appeared to be. Bridget changes her mind to that option. She was going to let him end his own life. Her bulletproof jacket was for precaution. Josey has already placed cement weights on his ankles. With this nasty information coming out of Williams plus his connection to the Dulles family deaths, Bridget pushes Josey out of her way. She bends over, picking Williams up and standing him on the back platform.

Josey thinks, "I had better stay out of her way."

Bridget pulls out the 44 Magnum then says, "You bastard, you killed the Dulles's."

HIDDEN IN FRONT OF YOU

She fires two rounds into his chest. The force throws Williams off the deck and into the ocean. Bridget is shaking, crying, and walking in circles. Josey intends to let this behavior run its course. Her reaction is like a volcano erupting. After 20 minutes, Bridget starts to calm down.

Josey is sitting there like always having his coffee and pastries. He offers her a cup. She takes it but says nothing, and she continues to sit there in silence. Tears are still pouring from her eyes. It is almost another 20 minutes before things seem to have calmed down. Bridget packs the food, hoses off the platform, and starts the second motor. As they start moving toward the bridge, Bridget walks over to Josey and gives him a big hug.

She says, "Thank you, my friend. I lost it."

Now that they are headed back, things on the outside appear to be reasonable to Josey, yet they do not talk. The ride is just a long wait for Josey. Bridget isn't speaking, but she has cooled down and is acting like her usual self.

The bridge seems brighter than when they left. Still, no fog or wind is making the ride as smooth as it gets. After rounding Fort Point, Bridget continues to turn to the right. As she is passing the Presidio, she calls Sid on the radio.

Sid says, "You're a little late, my lady. It's almost time for breakfast. All clear here."

Moments later, she is pulling the boat into the berth. Josey has the boat tied off while Bridget starts hosing the saltwater off the decks. Sid joins them as they are walking to Josey's van.

Bridget says, "Sorry to keep you waiting. I lost my composure, so I shot the bastard. Williams admitted, setting up Frank's accident."

Sid had walked to the yacht club, so they all got into the van.

Sid says, "Except for the normal police drive-troughs,

there was no activity here tonight."

Bridget says, "I feel like a clock has started. We are headed in the right direction."

They pull into the garage, the kitchen light is on. Juliet has a midnight snack of Crepe Suzettes covered in Grand Marnier, fresh strawberries, whipped heavy cream, blueberries on top, and a side of hot chocolate ready to eat.

Bridget walks over to Juliet, giving her a hug then says, "A rough night. I will tell you later."

Sid says, "Juliet, you always have the answers. You can come to my house to live anytime."

As the group devours the Crepe Suzettes, Bridget looks at everybody, thinking there is a family here. If things go right, we could have this at home and at work. Except for Bridget, they continue to talk, joke, and tease each other well passed running out the Crepe Suzettes.

Sid says, "I need my beauty sleep. I should go."

Bridget says, "Sid, you can say that again, lots of it."

As the party breaks up, all the thanks go to Juliet. Bridget and Juliet start to clean up the kitchen together.

Bridget starts talking, but Juliet stops her by saying, "Tonight was a night that you may have needed me there. The hour longer on this trip says I may be correct. We can discuss this some other time. Let things simmer down a bit before you try to discuss this one. I will be there to listen."

Bridget turns to Juliet and hugs her tightly. As they stand there, embracing, tears start flowing from Bridget's eyes again. After a few minutes, Bridget pulls away and goes to the bedroom to change from black clothes. She takes a shower to get all the saltwater spray and dirt off then returns in a pink nightgown and robe. She grabs a glass of port and sits on the couch.

Bridget says, "Was it written all over me?"

Juliet says, "Your body language, your reactions to the

group, your eyes were red from crying, and Josey was trying to stay away from you. The event had to involve many of your emotions."

42 - A DAY TO THEMSELVES

Bridget says, "I have a suggestion. Let's make it Juliet Day. What do you want to do?"

Juliet says, "The day is not long enough. We could start the day by making love. Then we could have a nice quiet breakfast followed by one more trip to the silk sheets. After that, we dress up in sexy outfits for the Mozart/Beethoven concert at Davies Hall. Then dinner at the Cliff House with a table next to the west window, followed by a slow drive through the Presidio."

Bridget calls Davies Hall and the Cliff House for reservations then off to the silk sheets they go.

Hunger eventually sets in, and they decide that breakfast would be a good idea. They are both pleased with the idea of a personal day together, but for now, hunger has arrived. Juliet is happy that she is with her man for the day, even though he must currently present himself as a female. After having a pleasant breakfast, they both feel like extending the coffee time and just chat. Most of the topics discussed were together topics. Where would you prefer to live? When would you prefer having children? What type of house would you prefer? They both want to marry as soon as possible. All the indicators for personal support, understanding each other, and looking out for each other are in place. Suddenly they start smiling, and then both get up as they start running for the silk sheets. When they arrive, they are naked and jump into the bed. Again, their thoughts on the rest of the world are gone. They can only think of each other.

Before too long, it's time to get ready to go.

Juliet says, "You need to inform Matt."

Bridget calls Matt. Her phone rings seconds later.

Bridget says, "Today we are going to the Davies hall symphony production and then to the Cliff House for dinner."

Matt says, "No problem. That must have been a rough trip last night. Thanks for the call, beautiful girl."

Bridget responds, "Yes, it was. I lost it for a while. Josey was patient enough to put up with me."

They pick similar outfits for the day to show off their female attributes. Since they will be at the Cliff House later in the day, a matching coat seems appropriate. Juliet is no longer that much faster when they are getting ready. Bridget straps a 38-caliber snub-nose inside her right leg for safety. No operatives are watching as they leave in the pink Mercedes.

She decides on taking Lombard to Gough, right onto Gough to Grove, left onto Grove, then directly into the parking garage. They walk out of the parking garage, which is one block north of Davies Hall. Bridget grabs Juliet's hand as they jaywalk across Grove, continuing to the corner of Gough and Grove, where Citizen Cake is located. There is a separate counter to purchase candy, cookies, and cakes. There is also restaurant seating, but there is usually a long wait time. This is especially true during Davies Hall's symphony performances. As they enter, two customers are leaving. Knowing how long the wait times are, Bridget grabs the seats before anyone notices.

Citizen Cake is extremely busy. She hears the maître de' say it will least be a forty-minute wait. Juliet is surprised to see so many exquisite dishes being served. Bridget chooses the partially cooked spinach dish, which looks like it was just plucked from the garden, chocolate cake, and a Grand Marnier. Juliet orders the spinach salad with strips of filet mignon, no dessert, and coffee. These dishes are expensive yet can't be equaled in diversity or quality at most other restaurants.

As they are eating, Bridget has the waiter ask Esther to

come over for a chat. Within a few minutes, a lady dressed in a white chef's uniform appears.

Esther Hamilton says, "Bridget, it is so good to see you. Josey took care of everything. I am now relaxed and pleased. Thank you so much for your help. Your dinner is already paid for. If it were not so busy, I would be pleased to show you two around."

Bridget says, "This is Juliet, my closet friend. We are on our way to Davies Hall. I am so pleased for you. It is good to see you. Thank you for dinner."

Esther says, "Nice to meet you, Juliet. You two have a wonderful evening. Bye for now."

Esther rushes back toward the kitchen.

After finishing their great food, they start walking toward Davies Hall. They are walking with a crowd of some of the fanciest dressed patrons in the city. Many of them have mink stoles, expensive jewelry, and a new hairdo for the evening. With almost 45 minutes to spare, Bridget suggests that they pick up their tickets and find their seats. Bridget pays for the reserved tickets then they turn to climb the stairs. When they enter the main floor, Bridget says they should wait for intermission for the wine. Juliet is in somewhat of an uneasy mode. She has never been among such a crowd of classical music lovers.

Over the intercom comes an announcement that because it is a matinee performance, there will be a description of Mozart's compositions. The girls hurry to their seats. The seating is in the center about eight rows from the edge of the stage. Bridget chose this since she wants to be as close as possible to the musicians while having a direct view of the pianist. On the stage, there are two pianos, one for the conductor and the other for the invited pianist.

The conductor starts by describing the composition scheduled to be played, Mozart's Piano Concerto #27. First,

HIDDEN IN FRONT OF YOU

he describes the exact nature of Mozart's style of composing. He then compares Mozart to Beethoven. Beethoven injects variations where Mozart does not. Second, the conductor describes the primary and secondary portions found in Mozart's composing, which is somewhat unique. The first work is in front and usually more easily noticed by the listener. The secondary work is played behind the primary. It is complementary to the primary yet must be listened for. At the end of the verbal presentation, the conductor sits at one piano, and the pianist sits at the other. They chose a phase within the upcoming Concerto, #27, as an example. The pianist plays the first work, and the conductor represents the secondary portion. They present the same passage over and over to give the audience a good chance of distinguishing the difference.

After removing one piano, they were almost ready for the performance to begin. Within fifteen minutes, the orchestra has filled the stage. Since the piano is such a significant portion of the #27th Concerto, Bridget and Juliet are fortunate to sit in full view of the keyboard. Throughout the performance, nature and specifics explained earlier were heard by both Bridget and Juliet. The quality of the orchestra's performance was dazzling, and the musicians present in unison the beautiful imagination of Mozart's mind.

As the orchestra leaves the stage for intermission, Bridget and Juliet walk out to the mezzanine that all floors empty into. They each purchase a glass of wine and sit at one of the tables alongside the large glass windows facing the Civic Center. Juliet continues to observe the many well-dressed patrons that came for this production. They appear to be genuine classical musical lovers.

Back at their seats, Bridget is looking forward to one of her favorite composers, Vivaldi. She would prefer all four sections of "The Four Seasons," yet starting with Spring and concluding with Storm is quite a pleasant experience. As the orchestra begins Spring, they include the nature sounds of birds chirping and water flowing over rocks. Spring has a light and well-designed beginning. At the end of Spring, there is a short pause. The same violinist that led the Spring performance remains on stage for Storm, which is only eight to ten minutes long, but it presents striking energy. It is always a pleasure for Bridget to hear.

At the end of the performance, Bridget looks at her watch. They have plenty of time for the trip to the Cliff House, but not enough time for the Aquarium. They remain seated for about five minutes to avoid the rush. Their walking is more comfortable by waiting for the masses to leave.

They even must wait in the parking garage because of the congestion. Juliet is amazed at what she has just witnessed.

While they are waiting for the garage traffic to exit, Juliet says, "I have never observed a classical orchestra perform before. This is my first time. Love, let's do this again."

Bridget says, "Of course, we will."

After ten minutes, the traffic has become lighter, so Bridget pulls out of the parking place and heads for the Gough Street exit. Turning left onto Gough then right on Fell, Bridget plans to take a leisurely drive through the San Francisco Golden Gate Park, which was initiated in 1871. Mayor Sutro and the city council of San Francisco had to have a park because New York City created one. At the end of the park, she turns northward along the Great Highway that faces the Pacific Ocean. On the right is Playland, which started in 1913. Bridget continues up the hill to the Cliff House, which is next to the current operating Sutro Baths and Museum built by Mayor Sutro.

Bridget finds a parking space within a short walking

distance to the restaurant. Juliet is having the time of her life. She had never been through the park, and she had never seen the long beaches that extend for miles. From well before the 1906 earthquake, tens of thousands of San Franciscans would travel in their horse-drawn carriages over the sand dunes for a day at the beach.

Arriving at the Cliff House, Bridget and Juliet are welcomed and seated at their requested table looking out over the ocean. The view is of a large set of rocks with a collection of seals with the surf continuously bashing against the rock formations.

After ordering their cocktails, the waiter delivers water, bread, and a dish of antipasti. Shortly after that, he returns with their cocktails. As Bridget looks at the ocean, the lighting allows a reflection from the outer window showing the patrons in the next level of seating. Either because of the war or because of Bridget's paranoia, it appears that two men in the reflection seem suspicious. Bridget says nothing to Juliet but pulls her snub nose from her leg and places it into her purse.

The waiter returns for their main dish order. Bridget orders fresh cod and Juliet orders salmon. Bridget also orders a bottle of dry white house wine. Before the waiter leaves, Bridget requests one order of jumbo prawns to share.

Bridget excuses herself and wanders off to the lady's room. Purposely, she walks next to the table where the two men are seated. She notices they are wearing everyday clothes that do not fit in this environment. Their shoes are grubby and not shined. Their hair is messy, and they are unshaven. Their hands and fingernails are also dirty. As she gets closer, she can see that both are packing a weapon. Neither one looks at her directly as they had been, but by their body language, she has the feeling that they are aware of her presence. She walks on to the lady's room for a quick pee, a touch up to her makeup and lipstick.

Before returning to her table, she uses the payphone to call Matt. She enters #3, in the payphone number. The message means an emergency.

Bridget picks up the ringing receiver saying, "This had better be you, darling."

Matt says, "Hello, my beautiful girl. What's up?"

Bridget says, "I am at the Cliff House with Juliet, and I spotted two guys eyeballing us. I am about to take them out. Are these two yours?"

Matt describes the two perfectly and says, "They are two of mine. We do not need to kill one another. Drop a note on their table. Then meet with them after dinner on the cement walkway."

She walks directly by their table without looking in their direction.

As she passes the table, she drops a note that says, "You two look like shit. Meet me after dinner. You know where."

Not to spoil Juliet's dinner, Bridget says nothing.

Juliet says, "That was a long break, even for the lady's room."

Bridget says, "Some things take longer than others."

Their main course is delivered. Both enjoy the high quality and freshness of the food. Rather than a dessert, both request green chartreuse.

Bridget says, "My love, please excuse me, but there is something we need to do when we leave here. Follow my lead and stand behind me."

After paying the bill, Bridget and Juliet start to walk out. The two guys also get up and follow. They walk to the stairs and then down to the cement landing that has a clear view of the seals.

One of the men says, "We know you as Finion. Did we stick out that much?"

Bridget says, "She came to me asking to be a Charity Group contractor. The most important thing I could think of was Naomi. The Petersons don't know how to help other than to give her a safe and loving home. Alissa has an essential role in this excursion. By the sounds of my intel, she is doing an outstanding job. I have a hunch she will open a whole new subgroup for the firm's Charity Group."

The day arrives for Naomi's meeting with the doctor. First, Alissa and Naomi pick up Salty from Cindy's and bring him back to the Peterson home. This is Salty's new home, and everything is new for Salty. People will be arriving soon, and they are all strangers to Salty. Naomi must introduce each unknown person to Salty. This will be an interesting test for both Naomi and her young guard dog.

Naomi and Salty are in the laundry room with the washer and dryer. Alissa is off to the side away from the action. Officer O'Malley is the first to enter. Salty is sitting next to Naomi. He moves to a standing position in front of Naomi intently concentrating on O'Malley. As Officer O'Malley steps closer, Salty changes from a stance to attack mode and starts to growl. He increases his interest in O'Malley with his teeth now showing and preparing to charge. Salty is without question the guardian of Naomi. Naomi reaches down to Salty and assures him it is okay by touching O'Malley's hand. O'Malley then puts his hand near Salty so he can get O'Malley's scent. Salty allows O'Malley to pet him but stays between him and Naomi. This is repeated for Josey. Both O'Malley and Josey can be around Naomi, but Salty is keeping a close eye on both of them.

The other two daughters come in and play "throw the ball" with Salty. The whole time Salty plays, he is keeping his eyes on both O'Malley and Josey. Friendliness with Salty will come later. Naomi rewards Salty with some nibbles and some vigorous hugs.

43 - ALISSA'S EXCURSION CONTINUES

Bridget says to Jennifer, "Some time ago, I asked you to assist Alissa with her Naomi excursion. At first, we took care of the things she was unable to do. Now, I want Alissa to handle things on her own. She must make all the decisions and obtain the objective without outside assistance. You are very familiar with what Alissa is doing and what is planned. Would you share with me how she is doing? Have I made it too hard for her? Is she going to learn from this exercise? Will her labor bring her some type of positive growth?"

Jennifer says, "Alissa is amazing and 100% on the mark. She has already completed preliminary discussions with each party, including Salty. She has already gone to Cindy's to introduce herself to Salty and to learn about the special training required. The meeting with the doctor is scheduled this week. She has the dates and times for Josey's participation. She has visited Naomi several times and has the complete confidence of Naomi. The Petersons are impressed with Alissa. I can guarantee that you and Juliet will be impressed with her results. I'll leave it at that. Naomi has found a true friend in Alissa."

Bridget says with tears running down her new makeup, "Thank you, Jennifer. This is a wonderful tear-jerker. I need to go fix my face."

Bridget makes a quick trip to the lady's room, and then they lock-up and go home.

When Bridget arrives home, Juliet is already cooking dinner.

Juliet says, "Your assignment has stolen my daughter from me. She only says hello and goodbye as she flies in or leaves. Alissa has taken the lead in this assignment. From what I hear, everyone is pleased with what she is doing and the way she is handling the issues. I have never seen her put so much effort into anything before."

thought there might be more of them around, so I called Matt. When he called back, he identified them and said it was okay. It's another example of how much Matt is doing to support us. What did you think about the Presidio?"

Juliet says, "It's a beautiful place, it's so relaxing."

HIDDEN IN FRONT OF YOU

Bridget says, "If I had not already called in my plan. I would have to take you both out right here," as she draws the snub nose out of her purse.

One of them flips on a small flashlight and says, "Look up there on the top of the hill."

A blinking flashlight is shining.

He says, "You are good, but you were not in Vietnam with us and not under the colonel."

Bridget says, "Checkmate, thank you for looking out for us."

They shake hands and say their goodbyes. Juliet is in total surprise. Together they get into the Pink Mercedes, and they both snap their seat belts.

Juliet says, "Ms. Bridget O'Connor, why didn't you tell me?"

Bridget says, "Why, you were enjoying your dinner? Now you know what took me so long in the lady's room."

Juliet says, "Thank you for your consideration, my sweet. I was having a great time."

Starting for home, Bridget drives east onto Geary then left on 25th Avenue. They turn right onto Lincoln, which wanders through the rugged terrain and beaches on the northern shoreline. The road finally turns south as they approach the Golden Gate. The Presidio presents mostly open spaces in a forest of greenery. Exiting the Presidio, they are two blocks from home. As they drive into the garage, they are happy and content. Once inside, they both grab a drink and chat quietly about a wandering of topics.

Juliet asks, "How did you pick those two out of the crowd?"

Bridget says, "I had an additional view of them from the reflection in our window. Their eyes were on us too much for my comfort, and their clothes did not match the occasion. As I passed their table, I saw they were packing. I

HIDDEN IN FRONT OF YOU

The group starts driving to the doctor's office with Alissa and Naomi riding together and Josey riding with O'Malley. Salty is sitting next to Naomi. The second girl, Lisa, is already waiting at Dr. Keane's office. The group has no problem parking and walking to his office. Dr. Keane is finishing up with his last regular patient.

Dr. Keane suggests his conference room for starting the meeting. Everyone is introduced.

Dr. Keane says, "Today is kickoff day. We are going to start with a discussion. We will talk about how to help each other and discuss where this may go in the future. Alissa needs to stay so she can become a closer part of the healing and be an assistant to the girls. Lisa and Naomi are the main players. I, as a professional, will try to use my experience to guide Lisa and Naomi as we move along. Officer O'Malley and Josey, you need to leave. There is a nice coffee shop with ice cream and desserts just down the street to the left. You two can take your time. There is no known time when we will be done. Thank you, gentlemen."

As the formal meeting starts, Dr. Keane takes the lead.

He says, "Alissa, being the responsible person for this excursion, you should not just observe, you should get involved in the points of interest. You need to understand the hurt that these girls feel, the embarrassment, and the violations they have experienced. They will not learn what that all means until they are well into these many-many discussions. Lisa and Naomi, you need to open up with each other about your haunting experiences. You need to share and listen to each other about shared your fears. Which of you wants to go first?"

Naomi raises her hand. She presents the terrible daily routine, then onto the beating, the lack of socializing with a friend, not being allowed to go to school, the continual rapes, and on and on. Even though Alissa had heard about most of the events, she starts crying. Lisa begins with her experiences, which are similar to yet less drastic. Dr. Keane directs the girls to take a topic and share their fears and discomforts. They need to share their concerns with each of those that haunt them both awake hours and during sleep. Dr. Keane is an expert in these areas, so he helps the girls express themselves. It gets harder and harder for each of them. Alissa is amazed at the numerous topics and the amount of hurt that has occurred.

When Dr. Keane observes the decline in progress, he suggests they stop at this point for today and start again on a new day. All three girls are exhausted. They thank Dr. Keane for his insight, his participation, and patience.

Dr. Keane says, "Really, girls, I thank you. Being a part of these types of discussions makes me feel that I can be of help. I want to thank you for letting me be a part of what you are starting here. It appears that it is going to be successful for all involved. It will be an honor to a part of the solutions found."

Both Naomi and Lisa appear to be more relaxed. The guys are waiting outside, looking like they are full of desserts. They all return to the Petersons. Both Naomi and Alissa are very positive about the meeting. They show interest in continuing these discussions. Alissa is stunned and somewhat uncomfortable with the information she has just heard. Salty has proven himself to be a guard dog for Naomi. His training is almost complete. Naomi must now introduce him to her daily life. Alissa stays to visit with Naomi while both O'Malley and Josey leave.

Bridget calls, and Jeff says, "Hello, this is Jeff."

Bridget says, "We have met with the school administration. Salty will be considered a service dog. Naomi can now go to school. I can tell you confidently that Naomi will not ever be in danger again from her stepfather. That earlier threat has been eliminated. That should relieve your mind. Salty needs the exposure so he can be safely taken to school. Naomi is now off and running. Talk to you soon."

Jeff says to Alissa, "What a delightful family you come from. Is the firm also this friendly?"

Alissa says, "We are one big happy family."

44 - MATT SLIPS-UP AGAIN

As Bridget walks by Matilda's desk, Matilda says, "Two gentlemen are waiting for you, Ms. O'Conner."

As she approaches her office, she sees that Jennifer has them waiting just outside her office.

Jennifer says, "I have served them coffee. They will not tell me their names."

Bridget says, "Good morning, Jennifer. I'll take it from here."

As she walks toward her office, she motions for them to step into her office.

Bridget says, "First, one of you needs to get Matt's car out of the parking structure. McCarthy operatives do have an eye on this building. You are the same ones that I saw at the Cliff House. At least you do not look like shit today."

Bridget puts her things away, and Jennifer brings her some fresh coffee. Bridget sees Julien is waiting to see her.

Bridget says to Julien, "My meeting with these gentlemen should not take long. I'll come to your office once I am done here."

Julien nods as he walks off.

The second man sits while they wait for his buddy to return. As soon as the other man returns, Bridget closes her office door and pulls the curtain closed.

Bridget says, "The connection between this firm and Matt must be kept secret. Coming to this office must be done via the back stairway. None of your cars can be parked in the structure. Let's discuss the reason you are here. I don't need to know your names, but I do need to know the reason you are here."

The first guy speaks, saying, "My name is Cliff. We are here to hand over a sketch of McCarthy's business site. Basically, it is laid out like a fortress. We are going to require three times the manpower and some special equipment to complete this operation. A total surprise is not going to be possible. He has cement bunkers like the World War II bunkers on the Normandy Beach. His car is bulletproof. A collection of guards covers every inch of the ground. There is a motion detection system in place around the outside edges of the site. He has our position covered by four to six of his positions. Your people that offered to be snipers are no match for these guys. Matt thinks we should abandon using them. McCarthy sleeps in different places each night, and his guards are posted 24/7. He and his top people drive in together. There is no way of knowing which car McCarthy is in when the vans arrive. This may be his one weak point. These are symptoms of his earned paranoia. One plan is to take out all three vans at once. For that, we need to adjust our approach."

Via the intercom, Bridget asks Jennifer to come in.

Bridget says, "Gentlemen, this has been an informative meeting, thank you. This is Jennifer. She will give you her own number. The next time you care to visit, please coordinate and schedule through her. She can let you in through the back stairway."

As they are exchanging information, Bridget walks over to Julien's office. Bridget is not pleased with this carelessness.

Julien says, "You do not appear happy, Ms. O'Conner."

She says, "Things just got more complicated. McCarthy's business site is set up like a fortress. I noticed that your employee was a little late this morning."

Julien says, "She called ahead. She had an errand to run. As I have said before, I spoiled her early, so she is ready for marriage."

Julien continues, "I reached back through the personnel files, and the information is very telling. I am talking about murders and suicides. Employees with over ten years were leaving because of threats, and Rita was put into prison.

People thought Frank was behind this stuff, and all along, it was Williams."

Julien hands a list of his findings to Bridget.

She says, "This is appalling. The worst part is that we were not aware of this when it was in progress."

Bridget leaves Julien's office and walks toward Clair's office.

Mikey is one of the firm's charity group beneficiaries that Arnold rescued from Alex's Gym. Mikey is a clerical intern helping Claire organize and file a large backlog of legal documents.

Bridget thinks to herself, "Claire was never good at keeping up with her filing."

Bridget stops at Mikey's desk to say hello.

Mikey looks up and says, "Hello, Ms. O'Conner. I haven't seen you for a few days. I have something I need to tell you about. The other day, in the early morning, two of the guys came by my place, forced me into their car, and took me to a warehouse near Army Street. I've heard things around the office, and I'm seeing a lot of documents in Claire's stuff about some guy named McCarthy. I'm starting to think these two guys may work for him."

Mikey continues, "When we got to the warehouse, I noticed three vans parked outside. Each one of the vans looked like a bunch of stuff had been done to them. They picked me up at 5 a.m. and grilled me till 7:30 when people were starting to show up. They tried to be nice but seemed very anxious to get some information on this firm. Nothing I knew was worth much. I thought what I knew was something I could share without putting you in danger. By telling the truth, I figured it would be easier to remember. If I had to repeat it, they would want me to establish what I had already said."

Then he says, "Many people began to show up, including

HIDDEN IN FRONT OF YOU

a lady in a black Mustang. Some of them parked their cars inside the large warehouse and then got into the three vans. The vans all drove away with some of the guys following in their own vehicles. Then as more people continued to arrive, the two guys took me home."

Mikey ends with, "The whole thing was beyond weird, and I thought maybe you should know about it."

Bridget says, "Mikey, you just made my day. This could be an important piece of information. Could you find this warehouse again?"

Mikey says, "Oh, yes. I know that area."

Bridget runs to her office. She thinks this is the way McCarthy controls his operatives while protecting his business interests. She calls Josey.

Josey answers, "Josey here."

Bridget says, "I need your services asap. When are you available?"

Josey says, "I am ready to leave right now. I'll be at your office within the hour."

While waiting for Josey, Bridget calls Matt, and he calls back within seconds. Bridget describes Mikey's trip and the warehouse. They both agree that this is a weak point for McCarthy's security, and if Josey does a drive-by, he may be able to pick up more information.

Bridget says, "Those two shit birds over here parked in the parking structure and did not use the back stairs. I straightened them out."

She continues, "I'll find the location of the warehouse. Then you and your guys need to produce a plan to eliminate all these contractors at the same time. That must include the warehouse, the business location, and the brothel."

Matt says, "You are a lovely golden lady. After Josey does his scouting of the warehouse, we will survey the site for options."

Bridget thinks, "That old man still wants to tease me about being Bridget. He means well."

Josey walks right into Bridget's office. He is excited.

He says, "We must be getting close."

Bridget explains Mikey's morning at the warehouse.

She says, "Mikey can show you the building. Find any vital information.

Don't hang around. Get in and out as quickly as possible. Make at most a few passes by the building and then get out of the area. Either rent a truck with your false ID or use one of your nondescript vans with non-traceable license plates. Make sure everything is non-traceable. This may be the weak link in McCarthy's security system. Look for offensive positions and their defensive placements."

Josey and Mikey leave immediately.

Julien walks into Bridget's office, saying, "The payment records and work hours are on their way to our office. I would like to have two to three days to examine them and make copies. If there are any glitches, a fourth day may be necessary. You can tell Burke that the date is getting near. I will also identify cities where McCarthy has done almost the same thing in the past. This should show the history of McCarthy's actions."

Bridget walks out to Jennifer's desk, saying, "Call Burke and inform him the start time will be in 15 to 20 days."

Bridget walks into Claire's office and says, "Claire, call the McCarthy contact. We require another payment. All work has again stopped."

Bridget walks back to her office and calls Nick the mechanic who answers, "Nick here."

Nick says, "I have adjusted the caster-camber on the independent suspension for the new Jaguar like we had the green one. Arnold would not want it any other way."

Bridget says, "Thank you, Nick. When can I pick it up for

testing?"

Nick says, "It is ready now, just waiting on you. I took it out for a spin. I believe Arnold will feel very comfortable with this one."

Bridget asks, "If I drop off my best friend Juliet's car, could you do an overall inspection and fix any serious problems?

Nick replies, "No problem. Things are a little slow right now. I can get on it immediately."

Bridget walks over to Julien's office. She says to Juliet, "Arnold's car is ready, so let's pick it up in the morning on the way to work."

Juliet answers, "I need to drop off Alissa first, then I will be available."

Bridget keeps going over the options. Should it be total extermination, which increases the level of security? Without a leader and the money, would the operatives just walk away? In the sense of safety, total annihilation seems the more cautious outcome. These contractors seem proud that they kill people. Leaving only one alive may be a potential problem.

Jennifer calls on the intercom and says, "Harriet Williams is here to see you."

Bridget walks to the doorway to greet her. Right behind her is Jennifer with fresh coffee. Jennifer closes the door on her way out, and Bridget pulls the curtains closed.

Bridget calls Julien, who answers, "Julien here."

Bridget says, "I have a beautiful woman here that would like your company. You best come to my office."

Julien walks in and affectionately hugs Harriet and gives her a kiss. They both sit down.

Harriet says, "I must apologize. I gave you a copy of all that I thought I had. I just today found some early copies I had hidden away for safety."

Bridget says, "Thank you for going to the effort in sharing these documents. I am not at liberty to share with you the details, but soon you should feel much more relaxed. Julien, why don't you two drive your separate cars to the Spinnaker Inn for lunch? I'll foot the bill. I need to be here this afternoon. Get lost, you, two lovers."

HIDDEN IN FRONT OF YOU

45 - PREP FOR EXTERMINATION

Bridget has had enough for one day.

She thinks to herself, "I think I should go home a little early. I have a taste for a good steak and some relaxing music."

As she goes to her office, she picks up the personnel stats from Julien.

She says to herself, "We lost so much, and so many people were hurt. The stats are staggering, to say the least. How could we have been so blind? We need to assist those that are still here and were hurt or threatened by these actions."

Bridget calls Nick, who answers, "Nick here."

Bridget says, "What did you find on Juliet's car?"

Nick says, "It's a pile of junk. Arnold would never let her drive this vehicle. I had to repair the steering box, align it, do a complete brake job, and flush and clean the engine before putting in fresh oil and a filter. The rear end was dangerously low in fluid, I had to replace almost every electrical item on the engine, put on new tires and replace the radiator. It is ready to go whenever you want to pick it up. Today would be a good time."

Bridget says, "You might be a lifesaver, thank you. See you in about an hour."

Bridget walks into Julien's office and says, "Juliet, we need to pick up your car. Have you ever done any maintenance on it since you purchased it?"

Juliet says, "No, I just drive it and put gasoline in it."

Bridget says, "Arnold had better not find out about this. I believe he would be pissed."

Julien says, "Why would Arnold be pissed?"

Juliet says, "Daddy, I have talked to Arnold on several occasions. He wants to come back. That accident did more to him than most people know. He feels it is still too dangerous, and he is not up to it yet. But his return date is rapidly approaching. Please keep this secret."

As they are walking to the Jaguar, Juliet says, "My Dad and I have always been completely honest with each other. I wish I could tell him more."

They drive to Filbert Street, drop off the pink Mercedes, then drive to 19th and Taraval. During the drive to Nick's, Bridget describes the problems with her car.

Bridget says, "This will not occur again. Your safety is much too important. I will keep a closer eye on your vehicle."

Before they leave Nick's shop, Bridget calls Jennifer from Nick's office phone.

Before Jennifer starts to respond, Bridget says, "Jennifer, please call Mr. Little. I would like to have a meeting with him tomorrow at about 10 a.m. Were you able to find a caterer to fit our needs during the meetings and for my next barbeque? Have you kept a log of staff-related problems?"

Jennifer says, "Yes to the logs. Not much is going on there. The caterers are asking for a better timeline."

Bridget says, "Chat with the restaurant where we had Julien's party. He may be more flexible."

Jennifer says, "I'll get on it first thing tomorrow."

After arriving home, Bridget calls Josey, and he answers, "Josey here."

Bridget says, "Can you have the boat ready to go 24/7 for our near-term events? Did the operatives at the warehouse notice you the day you and Mikey went by?"

Josey replies, "There was enough traffic in the area that let us blend in. The boat is always ready."

Bridget says, "On the deck where there is white paint scrape it off. Prime the wood with three coats oil base primer, linseed oil, and one-quarter turpentine combined. Then put on a quality oil base semi-gloss of a darker color this week."

Josey replies, "This sounds like overkill, but you are most often right. Are you getting ready?"

Bridget says, "I have been ready for months. Good chatting with you, Josey, good night."

Bridget calls Sid, who answers, "Sid here, what can I do for you?"

Bridget says, "This is your lovely daughter calling. I am starting dinner, you leach, and I would like some company. The back door is open."

Sid says, "Now that is an offer I can't refuse. See yah in ten."

When Bridget goes to the refrigerator, there is enough leftover food to feed an army. She gets out a few pans plus some salad. As Sid walks in, the food is almost ready. Bridget pours some Merlot for both of them.

Bridget says, "Things are about to take shape. This McCarthy Group is much too big for us to handle without help. If we had tried to continue fighting them directly, we would be history. I am proud that I have impersonated a female and gotten away with it, but now I want to stop and go back to being me. I can't right away, but my second transition day is approaching. I even picked up a new Jaguar for Arnold."

Changing the subject, Bridget asks, "How is your business?"

Sid says, "It has been growing very slowly but consistently. Since last year I have three new employees, so you could say business is up. The only trouble I have is my neighbor. He dresses like a woman."

Sid brings the discussion back to the war by saying, "I am impressed with the way you got rid of that operative Sowers. Your transition to Bridget has worked well. Even your own people don't have a clue, and you have learned a lot since you started this. Your empathy and compassion have improved, along with your cooking skills. Thanks for dinner, my beautiful daughter. It's time for me to get some sleep. It is wonderful that this has worked out so well. Bridget, you have done a great job."

Bridget says, "Thank you, Sid. Coming from you, that means a lot."

After Sid leaves, Bridget pours some grey chartreuse into a medium-sized glass. She puts on the tape for Beethoven's 1st Piano Concerto and relaxes close enough to the bottle, just in case. The orchestra leads off with the piano, and it becomes paramount as the piece proceeds. 40 minutes later, it ends, and Bridget rewinds the tape and replays the piece again. Bridget is finally ready to go to bed.

46 - FAMILY HISTORY

The morning comes with high winds, rain, and a significant drop in temperature. The roads will be slick, and people will be in a hurry. Not a good day to test the white Jaguar. Bridget showers and does her makeup before breakfast. She picks out a grey wool skirt and jacket with a light cream-colored long sleeve wool blouse. She chooses 3-inch black heels with black nylons, silver jewelry, and a medium-sized black purse.

Breakfast is three poached eggs and espresso. Beethoven's 4th Piano Concerto is playing on the stereo. As she is leaving this morning, she looks around, sensing that living as a woman is not for too much longer. She has dealt with this for so long there are things that she may miss. Bridget walks with that clicking sound of her heels across the garage to the Jaguar.

After closing the garage door, she pulls up to the Lombard stoplight. The rain is heavy enough to slow people down. The light turns green, and she turns left onto Lombard. The wind is a strong westerly, which is pushing the usually stable Jaguar around. The wind is most influential as she is crossing the bridge. Once in Marin County, after the tunnel, driving is much more relaxing, and the traffic is moving along.

Bridget pulls into the parking garage, and as usual, she freshens her lipstick. Bridget has impersonated a female successfully for many months, but she is still sensitive to possible mistakes in her presentation. Occasionally she forgets to concentrate on being a female. Sometimes her thoughts are of being Arnold.

But then, something will remind her to listen to Sid's advice, "To succeed, you must always think you are a female."

Riding in the elevator, she is reviewing how to structure

her day. Who do I put in charge of what topic? She will be talking about the accident reporting since that is what started this whole thing, and it is the most visible.

As she steps into Matilda's area, Matilda says, "Mr. Little arrived early. He is waiting in your office, Ms. O'Conner."

Bridget responds by saying, "Thank you."

Bridget walks into her office, and Mr. Little is munching on a pastry and sipping his coffee. They shake hands as they exchange greetings. Bridget removes her rain gear, places her purse in a drawer, and hangs the jacket on the clothes stand. Jennifer has already brought in her coffee.

Bridget says, "Mr. Little, it is good to see again. Do you understand that you are receiving an exclusive on this topic? I still want to verify its content before you release the article."

Mr. Little replies, "That has been our understanding since the beginning. I do appreciate the exclusive."

Bridget says, "You earned it, Mr. Little. Your articles to date have been spot on. My purpose for this interview is to continue giving information to the public that is as truthful and complete. I suggest that you spend time meeting with some of our staff members regarding the firm's objectives in our lawsuit with the city. This way, you may be able to put together the proper perspective. Remember, before any of this goes to press, I want to verify the information."

Mr. Little says, "Absolutely. I am excited that you would give me this opportunity. Thank you, as always, for your trust."

Bridget says, "We will jointly visit some of my staff. I will explain my rules to them and give you an open door to visit with them without my participation. Let's do that now."

Over the next hour, Bridget takes Mr. Little around to the key players. She then leaves Mr. Little to start talking with each person on a more personal level. She does go over with each staff member the condition that the city lawsuit is the only topic to be discussed with Mr. Little.

Bridget says to Mr. Little, "Because of your full cooperation, I will also share some of Arnold's family history. In his search for food and money for his family, Arnold's grandfather, Jules Voisinet, ran into other young boys having the same dilemma. They all had a common interest and problem, so they became partners. If one found lots of goodies, he would share with the others. In addition to working together, the group also played together. One of their games was to borrow an already stiff corpse from the local morgue. They would transport it to someone's house and lay it tilted against the front door. One of them would reach for the doorbell ringer on the front door and give it a good twist, and they would all run like hell. The homeowner would open the door, and the corpse would fall into the house. They were lucky to live through this since many times, the homeowner would come out shooting. That was early 20th-century humor."

"Jules Voisinet's father, also named Jules Voisinet, was a barroom bouncer. He had no sense of responsibility toward his wife and children. One day, Young Jules, who had grown into a good-sized young man, tried to get some help from his father for the family. Things didn't go well. He punched his father, and a fight began. At least his father didn't get his knife or gun out because this was his son. They fought hand to hand for almost thirty minutes until both were too tired to continue. Together with his friends, young Jules Voisinet told his father that he no longer had a residence to come home to. There stood six to eight streetwise young men backing young Jules. This union was the beginning of what was to become the Charity Group. They would each attempt to find employment. Jules started a concession business at Playland and operated it for many years. His empathy and compassion were evident from his early childhood exampled by his taking care of everyone in his family, three sisters, and his mother."

Bridget continues, "Arnold and I were sharing information about you. He wants me to give some more examples that may be hard for you to find in your San Francisco history search. Jules Voisinet confronted a problem with a local resident being shanghaied. They had drugged his drink and were paid for his service aboard a ship. Crimping, alias shanghaiing, ran rampant through every Pacific Ocean seaport. This local family man with a wife and children was foolish enough to enter a poker game at a local bar. During the game, he mentioned that he had sailing experience. The next thing he knew was that he was aboard a ship ready to sail. His wife contacted Jules's office before the ship sailed and begged for help. The Charity Group fetched an opium drunk from one of the 300 opium dens in Chinatown, replaced the local resident with this drunk, and paid the Captain a fee for his loss. At that time, the city law prohibited a shanghaied member of the crew from getting off the ship. This is an example of many things this Charity Group would do in the late 19th and early 20th century. I hope you enjoyed that information."

Mr. Little says, "Thank you. I'll bet there were hundreds of more stories like that one."

47 - PREPARING ALIBIS

Arriving back at Jennifer's desk, Bridget asks Jennifer to chat.

Bridget says, "Reviewing the personnel stats is breaking my heart. We let our people down. How are things going since you have assumed your management position?"

Jennifer says, "I have had a few conversations. Our people have noticed the interest taken by both you and Arnold.

You have given me a straightforward task. Helping Cecil has shown them you mean business and will stand up for your employees. I feel that you and Arnold did all the real work."

Bridget says, "That's nice to hear. Let's keep going in the same direction."

A call comes in from Matt.

Bridget says, "This is Bridget."

Matt says, "I have some people that know several of the girls at the brothel. They say the contractors are treating them like crap, and they are now sharing intel with us. It is so bad the girls want to shoot the bastards themselves. We can't trust these girls, but we can make it safe for them. One of my guys cased the building. They are only using half of it. Can you folks afford sharing some cash with the girls?"

Bridget replies, "Of course we can if that makes it work better. I'll have some cash put together. Stop by and see Cecil in HR when you need the cash. We will remove any fingerprints before I turn it over to you."

Matt says, "Thanks. I'll get together with Cecil."

Jennifer calls on the intercom. There is an incoming call from Josey.

Bridget picks up the phone and says. "Hello, sweet man. I hope your day is going well."

Josey says, "I have finished changing the deck paint on the boat. I have found and corrected a few minor maintenance issues. The boat is ready to go."

Bridget says, "Thanks for getting on this so quickly. Talk to you soon, bye."

Bridget has a quick thought about the day of the events. Everyone at the firm will be busy with their lawsuit group meetings, and no time to listen to police reports or the news media.

Bridget calls Sid, "Hello, this is Sid. How can I help you?"

Bridget says, "Sid, I need someone to be my eyes and ears on that specific day. I need you to keep me informed on that day and, and most likely, several days following. I must, along with my crew, stay focused on the lawsuit."

Sid says, "I can keep calling Jennifer with details. She is a good one to pass on the information to you."

Bridget says, "That will work well. Thanks."

Bridget thinks about the items she has postponed recently. Things concerning Naomi are currently quiet.

Bridget calls Alex, who answers, "Hello, this is Alex."

Bridget says, "This is Bridget. Is there anything new from your end?"

Alex says, "Sammy and I have started working together more. We have been visiting Naomi. All three of us go out together along with Salty. Naomi is exceptional. She has handled Salty better than most."

"She is getting straight A's in school. All three of us are taking some karate together. Her parents welcome us into their homes. We have really grown. Mikey is happier than I have ever seen him. He keeps bragging about you guys. A couple of heavy-duty guys picked him up the other days and grilled him for information on you. Scared him, but he held in there. Sammy is learning how to be a student. I am learning how to be a big brother or even a Dad to Sammy. Naomi says she misses seeing you. Hard to believe, but I have installed requirements for my students like no weapons, no drugs, and be kind to each other. You would be proud of me. That's all I can think of for now."

Bridget says, "I am so happy for all of you. You make me feel proud, Alex. Thanks for the update. Talk to you soon."

The day of the big event is now about 8 to 12 days away. Sid has been assigned as the newsfeed for the group. Matt is busy planning three separate attacks. As experienced as he is at this type of warfare, he will be the number one individual that the agencies will want to talk to. Mr. Little will keep the firm separated from most of the attacks. The only connection will be the legal assistance the firm is providing the McCarthy Group. Each employee can honestly say that their time has been absorbed in trial prep and the manual rewrite. This will be a good alibi. Josey already has the boat ready for multiple trips to the Farallones.

For the first few days, Bridget is going from one group to another to monitor and realign their efforts. By the fifth day, each group is working independently, and most are ready for the department managers to start participating. Monday of the following week, the managers will start showing up and hopefully begin to engage. Mr. Little is there almost every day. His editor is overjoyed in his ability to get an exclusive. The story is on the Chronicle's front page every day.

Bridget starts reviewing the remarks of the outside attorneys that have responded. Not long into the statements, she finds almost the same problems addressed by both Arnold and Juliet. In cases that were lost or appealed unsuccessfully, the primary issue was the lack of completeness of the reports submitted by the police officers. Physical measurements were lacking or flawed. The description of the scene was almost always lacking. A blood test was generally not available because one was not requested, or because the driver refused to submit to one with no mention in the report. When comparing the information with the required police department procedures, there was a lack of clarity and poor execution of the stated process. This, in itself, would invalidate a substantial lawsuit in a DUI case. Within two days of studying the documents, Bridget had more than enough to proceed. Rewriting the procedures and making it mandatory for the officer to follow was going to be the work of Bridget's group in conjunction with each department head. Day after day, as Bridget monitors the working groups, the anticipation of Matt's big attack is on her mind continuously.

One morning she just can't stand the wait, so she decides to test the white Jaguar. The weather is still a little chilly. The old road built beside the entry to the bay waters for the World War II bunkers was put together in a hurry. It has improper slanting pavement with spots of gravel. During the week, the roadway has little traffic. The scenery is beautiful. A full view of the bridge, along with the inlet from the Pacific Ocean, is a lovely sight from Conzelman Road. She plans to test the Jaguar at speeds under 100 mph.

Bridget fixes a healthy breakfast along with some coffee to go. She does light makeup and puts on some leathers. For shoes, Bridget chooses knee-high boots. She prefers a warm jacket, gloves, and a wool cap. The air is clear, and the sun is shining brightly today.

Bridget lowers the canvas top. She like a kid with a new toy turning left on Lombard and then onto the bridge. As she approaches the off-ramp for Sausalito, she takes the road under the freeway and onto Conzelman Road. This is the same road Lynn Dulles drove off with Frank in the car, killing them both. Up to now, she has not pushed the Jaguar's attributes. The vehicle is handling well as she starts up Conzelman Road. At first, the road has some mild curves and is a reasonably stable roadway. Soon it is not smooth, nor are the turns banked to the inside of the curve. She ramps up the speed and the level of intensity. The signs suggest a maximum of 45 mph, and she is doing 65 mph. Soon she is increasing that to 75 mph. The added strength of the engine increases her ability to drive with the gas pedal. The wider stance holds the road with more stability. Ah, the golden goose is just ahead. Someone is driving a Porsche. Bridget plants the front end on the back bumper of the Porsche. The driver tries to get away, but Bridget is staying within inches. Occasionally the Porsche starts to slide. Bridget can tell this is not a beginner. After five miles of this rudeness, the driver waves off. The driver wants to talk with Bridget, so he stops the Porsche.

The Porsche owner asks what Bridget has under the hood. She replies to a shortlist of the components plus realignment of the tires, chassis lowering, and changes in the aerodynamics of the body. The Porsche driver said we were doing well over 100 MPH a couple of times. He asks what the Jaguar's top speed was.

Bridget says, "Before the changes and upgrades it was about 250, but now, I think it is a little faster. My mechanic asked me to keep it under 125 MPH for a while. Thanks for the chat. I enjoined playing around."

They shake hands and part ways with respect for each other. Bridget starts driving back somewhat slowly. She has had her fun for the day. After returning to her house, she calls Nick.

"Hello, this is Nick."

Bridget says, "This is Bridget. I took the white Jaguar for a little ride. I need to tell you that it drives so well. The paint job is outstanding. Arnold will love it. Thanks for your great work. See ya later."

Nick responds before hanging up, "That is the best car I have ever built. Glad you approve."

Bridget calls Naomi's home.

The mother answers, "Hello."

Bridget says, "This is Bridget O'Connor. How are things going for Naomi?"

The mom says, "Outstanding. She is enjoying the visits from Alex and Sammy.

Her attitude is always positive, she is respectful, and a very hard worker. Her approach toward school is outstanding. She has been receiving A's on everything. She loves learning."

Bridget says, "May I speak with her?"

Mom replies, "She is out with Alex and Sammy. I'll tell her you called. Thank you for calling, she will be delighted, but sorry she missed you."

Bridget says, "It has been nice talking with you. I am proud of Naomi. It is so nice to see her have a good chance at life."

Taking the rest of the day off, Bridget is just hanging around the house. The phone rings. It is from Matt.

Matt says, "Jennifer said you were most likely home today. She had no idea whether you were coming to the office."

Bridget replies, "Yes, Matt, I took the day off to test Arnold's new Jaguar. I just got back. The Jaguar keeps getting better each time Arnold destroys it. This morning I crawled up a Porsche's backend for three miles running. Arnold has a new toy, you might say. The organization of each group is going well. I have scheduled the department heads to start working with us next Monday."

Matt says, "Arnold's toy. Are you sure it isn't your toy?"

Bridget says, "I am so used to talking to people that don't know."

Matt continues, "Planning is going well. I would like to drop by and discuss it with you. Is today a good day for that?"

Bridget says, "Perfect. I am the only one here today. No

one else will be here so we can discuss any topics."

Matt says, "I'll be there in about thirty minutes. Please have the garage door open."

Bridget was going to fix just a snack. With Matt coming, she makes a full lunch and fresh French roast with some added espresso. Bridget grabs a pistol, and the garage door opener then walks out to the driveway to wait. Five minutes and Matt is rounding the corner from Lombard. Before closing the garage door, she checks to see if anyone was following. The roadway remains clear, so she walks into the garage and closes the door.

As she puts the gun down in the kitchen and puts the door opener away, Matt says, "You must be on high alert. Do you always carry a weapon to the door? Lunch, how special, thank you. Well, the job is beginning to look somewhat easier than we anticipated. Let's eat first, beautiful lady."

As they are eating, Bridget shares her ride in the Jaguar with Matt. The paint job is impressive, and the car is faster than before in both acceleration and top end.

They finish lunch and are sipping on coffee when Matt says, "First, I have rearranged the timing for the events. I have moved the time to ignite the brothel to 6 a.m. to keep McCarthy from getting notice of the event before he arrives at the warehouse."

"I have moved the business site to 4 a.m. There are only four on guard during the night. This will give us more time to place the assorted correspondences throughout the site. Also, my business site group can now backup the warehouse group more effectively."

"The warehouse event will turn out to be an all-out firefight. They have an effective defense system. The brothel and the business site are ready to go, but the warehouse still needs some planning. These contractors are mostly assassins.

Some have military training, which will not match my folks. The question we are currently considering is how big our weaponry needs to be? The building walls are double-walled. Some bullets will not penetrate. The vans are bulletproof, so those will only get knocked out by a direct hit. We may need to bring some actual artillery."

"That is a brief overview of where we are. Your part must be well organized and ready to start this coming Monday. I'll update you fully before the day we execute. Thanks for lunch. This is better than talking on the phone. The one thing I am counting on with Mr. McCarthy is a surprise. See you later, beautiful lady."

After Matt drives out of the garage, Bridget shuts the garage door.

Bridget thinks, "Matt, continues to enjoy teasing me about my female impersonation."

48 - SAILING THE DEEP BLUE

Timing is going to be essential for when Bridget leaves, and Arnold returns. Who better to ask than the next-door neighbor?

Bridget calls Sid, who answers, "Sid here."

Bridget says, "Please come over. I have something to discuss with you."

Bridget warms some coffee and puts out some fruit. Sid comes walking in as if he owns the place.

He says, "What no dinner?"

Bridget says, "Shut up, you leach. I can't serve you dinner every time."

"I am planning the time after the McCarthy event. We need to have a Bridget sendoff barbeque before she leaves for a trip to Vietnam. Arnold needs to move back into this house. I am giving the pink Mercedes to Juliet, and Arnold will drive the white Jaguar. Sometime before Matt's event, we need to plan a staff outing on Alicia. My questions are, how do we make the changes, and most importantly, what is the period before Arnold can reappear? Do you have an answer? Do you need to meet with Dr. Neel before you can answer?"

Sid says, "I have been dreading this for months. You are going to want an instant change, and that is not possible. We can do something that would mask the straight appearance. The best we can do will be two to three weeks if the masking is applied. That is pushing it to the limit. You know that you will be in lots of pain?"

Bridget says, "Sid, I need you to start working on this now. Get together with Dr. Neel so I can make the schedule and the plans."

Bridget calls Jennifer, saying, "Jennifer, could you set up a getaway for a few people on Arnold's Alicia."

Bridget reads off the list and then says, "I would invite

others, but the boat is only so big. We may need to purchase some child-sized life preservers."

Upon arrival, Bridget notes that the restaurant adjoining the marina may be the right place for a wedding party. On her way to Alicia, she stops to discuss her idea with the manager. Upon entering the restaurant, she asks for the manager, Mr. Glengary Lightal.

Bridget says, "Sometime this year there will be a marriage ceremony, and I am looking for a place to hold the wedding party. Arnold's boat is moored in the first berth. Would it be possible for your restaurant to cater to the event?"

Mr. Lightal says, "No problem. We would be honored to have you here. Do you have a date set yet?"

Bridget says, "Within a few months, but the date is not set yet. Good, that will be perfect for us. I'll stay in touch."

She starts counting the life preservers aboard Alicia. Some older ones should be replaced, and there are no children's jackets. Before long, Alicia will need to be pulled out and repainted. The running gear should be updated at the same time.

On her way back to San Francisco, she takes a ride by her home in Tiburon. Traversing the old roads with this new Jaguar is fun. The Jaguar's handling abilities are improved. Driving by the property all looks well cared for and clean. The only thing the home may require is a paint job within the next year or so.

Bridget feels that she did stay slow enough for Nick. As Bridget pulls into the garage, she feels the pleasure of the ride. That urge to race is as strong as ever.

Bridget has nothing planned for tonight. She had not heard from Juliet. Bridget did call a local sporting goods store and ordered the life preservers, which will be delivered to the office.

Bridget calls Josey, who answers, "Josey here."

HIDDEN IN FRONT OF YOU

Bridget says, "Josey, would you want to take charge of servicing the Alicia? Arnold would like a complete upgrade of Alicia. A full repainting with a copper solution of the bottom, sanding and scraping of the upper parts with 5 coats of oil-based primer mixed with turpentine and linseed oil as a sealer, then an oil-based semi-gloss as a finish. The mainsail needs replacing along with all the lines. I am taking the boat out this weekend. You could start after that."

Josey says, "No problem. I'll get it done."

Juliet should be home by now. Bridget calls Juliet.

"This is Juliet. How may I help you?"

Bridget says, "Hello, my sweet. Are you behaving yourself?"

Juliet says, "Oh, indeed. My boyfriend has been ignoring me, so I found a new one. I am $100 ahead from playing pool at the local bar each night. I found a new job at a burlesque show. Do you want the rest of the story?"

Bridget says, "I have enough here for dinner. I am lonely. I am alone."

Juliet says, "I have not had dinner yet. Alissa is spending the evening with Grandpa. If you are the one with silk sheets, I'll consider it."

Juliet hangs up the phone. Bridget thinks what a damn tease. Maybe she will stay the night. Bridget waits only a few minutes, and Juliet is opening the garage door. Bridget is standing at the top of the stairs leading to the kitchen.

As Juliet is walking across the garage, Bridget says, "Come on in sweet pee. I want you to meet my new girlfriend."

The apartment is empty, and there is no sign of another person.

Juliet says, "I was a little hard on you. You may not have deserved it. But I love you, anyway."

They stand there, hugging and kissing each other before they enter the kitchen together.

Bridget says, "What did I do to get such a harsh line of teasing."

Juliet replies, "You deserved it. I was getting lonely. With you so wrapped up in this lawsuit and the upcoming events, I feel neglected. Childish as it seems, I was selfish. You have so much riding on your shoulders that I wanted to give you some tender loving care. You never complain. I thought raising a stink might get your attention. Crazy, huh?"

Bridget says, "Busy, yes. Multiple things are happening each day that are keeping me busy, but you are on my mind 24/7. Today, I found a place for our wedding reception."

Juliet says, "Tonight I am available. All you need to do is stay close. My father said that I could go off to see Arnold. I am taking that as he approves. Will I agree with your choice for the reception? That brings up another thing. You have never asked me to marry you. Just making assumptions, huh?"

Bridget says, "Another piece of information. I have scheduled an Alicia trip for Sunday. How's that for keeping our communication lines open? I chatted with Matt recently. The plans are starting to take shape. One concern I have is will we get them all. Monday starts our meetings with the department heads. I took the Jaguar for a couple of test runs. What an exciting ride. Let's fix a meal and relax tonight. It may be our last chance for a while."

As they start to prepare a meal, Juliet says, "It is a good thing you overbuy. We have enough for several meals. You even have the dark chocolate ice cream for dessert."

In the middle of fixing dinner, Matt calls.

"Hello, beautiful lady. Are you two girls fixing dinner? I know that because I saw you two through the window. Don't pull the shades but do move your curtains over to block the view. McCarthy is getting worried because we have not been attacking him lately. We will take out a couple tonight just to put him at ease."

The line goes dead.

Bridget says, "I believe we should keep your car for now. It's now a good backup vehicle because Nick worked on it. It could also be available for Alissa. Safety is a factor that we need to address. The Mercedes is much safer and is in excellent shape. As soon as I start driving the Jaguar again, I would like you to drive the Mercedes."

Juliet says, "Can I start calling you, Arnold?"

Bridget replies, "Not yet, but I am looking forward to it. Once this event is over with McCarthy, Arnold will find his way back. Part of my reason for this weekend's ride on Alicia is to give people like Naomi and her parents a special experience. Still, more importantly, it's to get to know Sergeant Brown of Tiburon a little better. He still suspects me of killing that driver."

Bridget continues, "Sure is lonely around here without you. You have my permission to move in."

Juliet says, "Is that an invitation? How much time will you give me to think it over?"

Bridget says, "None."

The dinner is healthy, yet a hodgepodge of what was left in the refrigerator. None of that mattered since the two were so happy to be together. Finishing dinner, Bridget fixes her dessert with some green chartreuse poured over the chocolate ice cream. Juliet goes for straight chocolate. As they relax, Bridget puts a tape of Beethoven's Moonlight Sonata extended play into the stereo. For the next hour, they chat about what is on their minds. Their conversations stay away from work-related items. They talk about housing, family functions, associating with friends, traveling, comments on how to parent, children, and such topics. The best idea was concentrating on friendly communication. Cleaning the kitchen goes well and off to the silk sheets they go.

This morning has thick fog. The waters are relatively warm, and the air is chilled, perfect for a foggy day. Breakfast is lightly poached eggs, juice, fruit, bacon, freshly made biscuits, and brewed French roast coffee. They are both ready to leave by 8 a.m.

All seems clear as they leave the garage in separate vehicles. While Bridget is waiting for the green light at Lombard, she starts feeling watched. Approaching the bridge, she notices a Camaro pacing her. As Bridget speeds up and slows down, the Camaro stays close to the Mercedes. When she reaches the Richmond off-ramp, the Camaro turns onto the Richmond bridge on-ramp, and her old friend in the black Mustang appears. Bridget does not have a reason why they would be looking at her again.

Instead of going to the office, she drives to a nearby restaurant, parks her Mercedes, and walks into the restaurant. Bridget sits at a table and orders coffee. The lady with the black Mustang comes in after ten minutes.

She sits down next to Bridget and says, "You noticed me following you. I just want to talk. My boyfriend, Kevin, appreciates the work your office did for him. We noticed two individuals that visited you the other day. Will you tell me about the visit?"

Bridget says, "It was kind of quiet meeting. One man was named Cliff and the other's name I never received. Neither was dressed very well. They asked to speak with Arnold and only Arnold. I informed them that Arnold is still trying to recover from his injuries, but he does call me on occasion, so I could pass on a message. I said if they wait a few weeks, he may start visiting the office. I will be leaving soon to be with my fiancée in Vietnam. The armed forces have sent word that they believe he has been found. They hope he will be released by the Viet Cong after the next round of

HIDDEN IN FRONT OF YOU

negotiations."

The woman lights up and wishes Bridget's success.

She says, "My name to Troi. Maybe upon Arnold's return, Kevin can talk with him to fill in some gaps. Why are you so willing to answer my questions so completely?"

Bridget says, "My only interest is my fiancée. Arnold and I never got along that well. When he was in that accident, he contacted me for support. He knew I had enough experience to fill in for him, and of course, I am still under his direction. I am like the private following the sergeant's orders. How is your situation with the city now? Did it improve?"

Troi says, "They are still crying but are well aware they can't do anything until after the end of the contract. We are negotiating with a new city. Kevin would like your firm to write the next contract."

Bridget says, "Thank you for the trust. I am sure Arnold will be looking forward to it. I am off to prepare for our lawsuit with the city. We are prepping for next week's meetings with the city. If you care to learn more about the lawsuit, the Chronicle has a full write-up covering the issues. It was nice to talk with you instead of just watching you wave from the Mustang. Bye for now, Troi. I've got to get to work."

Upon leaving the restaurant, Bridget considers the ease at which this woman lies. She is always trying to con you. She is such a beautiful looking woman but indeed a wasted person.

As Bridget parks the Mercedes and does her lipstick update, she is thinking about the conversation she had with Troi. She is most likely acting out directions from McCarthy based on the sudden lull inactivity.

On the way up in the elevator, Bridget decides to call Matt on this subject. He is not keeping his men up to the necessary standards of behavior.

As she enters the main lobby, Matilda says, "Hello, Ms.

O'Conner. No one is waiting to see you this morning. I like your idea of a weekend boat ride."

Bridget says, "Good morning. We will have some fun out there."

Bridget keeps walking toward her office.

As she arrives, Jennifer says, "I have a surprise for you this morning."

Bridget continues into her office and puts her coat on the rack and her purse into the drawer. The holster holding her 38 is uncomfortable, so she walks off to the lady's room. One of the snaps had become disconnected, so she connects it, and all is well.

As she enters her office, a smiling Jennifer hands her a cup of coffee imported from Africa.

Jennifer says, "I do hope you enjoy this new coffee. It has both a different initial taste and a pleasant after taste."

Bridget says, "Thank you, Jennifer. Do I have any messages or mail this morning?"

Jennifer nods no and says, "The lifejackets have been put aboard the Alicia. I had the worker at the marina wash the hull and clean the cabin. I did not disturb the sails."

Bridget says, "You are beginning to do my thinking for me. Thank you."

Bridget calls Matt. Seconds later, she gets a return call.

Matt says, "Hello, beautiful lady."

Bridget says, "Matt, your lack of security in some of your actions is worrying me. The two guys you sent to my office did not follow any proper protection, and they were observed by the McCarthy Group. I was followed by my home this morning by McCarthy's girlfriend. She asked me directly about them. This is getting to be a pattern. I do not like it. We are too close to finalizing this McCarthy mess, and I am noticing a lack of procedures executed by your men. Yes, I am not perfect, either. I realize that I am only an attorney. These most recent actions are making me feel uncomfortable. I need to suggest that you do some basic security training before we go forward. Please inform me what you have done to correct this problem. See you soon."

As Bridget hangs up the phone, she is feeling irritated. She has put so much trust in Matt's decision making that, in her opinion, these actions should never have occurred.

Julien comes walking into Bridget's office and says, "I turned over Harriet's additional documents to Burke. He is happy. Combining the two groups of documents, it implicates McCarthy even further than before. They show that he and Williams were definitely working together. Burke is very pleased. Is my daughter seeing Arnold? That little shit has always found a way of getting what she wants. Is it serious?"

Bridget says, "It certainly sounds like it. When this McCarthy thing is over, you had a better plan on walking her down the aisle. You and Harriet could make it a double wedding."

For her group, the procedures are mostly in place, though they are weak in their definition, poorly written, and are far from complete. Bridget feels like it is a day of giving directions while being very bossy. Her people now understand the significant strength in a document is dependent upon the law it is based upon.

Friday night is going to be lonely again. Juliet has Alissa both Friday and Saturday nights. On the way home, Bridget stops by a gun shop. She purchases over a hundred rounds of 44 Magnum shells. Next, she stops at Ms. Brown's Hamburger Hut for a hamburger and chocolate milkshake to go. Bridget plans on using the Jaguar Saturday, so the pink Mercedes is parked in the rear of the garage.

Bridget puts on Beethoven's 4th symphony and relaxes on the couch. Within minutes she falls asleep. Her arms are throbbing after firing less than 50 rounds. She considers it the estrogen injections. Bridget thinks she may be losing strength while playing this female impersonation, or it may be the lack of exercise. Arnold would usually perform better. The tape plays out, and she remains asleep.

When the phone rings, she wakes and answers it.

Josey says, "The Farallones boat is moored in the slip and ready to go. You never did inspect all the work I recently did on it, including the darker deck paint. When do you want to check it out?"

Bridget says, "I can be there in 30 minutes. Will that be soon enough?

Josey replies, "I'll meet you on the dock.".

As she hangs up, Bridget says, "I'll bring some coffee."

She takes the Jaguar. Maybe she can show it off to Josey. After parking, she walks with the coffee in hand. Josey has the motors running. When Bridget walks onboard, she starts inspecting the changes. The paint is an improvement. It blends with the water. Josey has replaced the carpet on the rear deck with a new one that will be easy to keep clean.

She starts checking the dashboard. All the switches work, and all the instrument lights and gauges display correctly. She inspects the two motors. New wiring is in place, the oil leaks are gone, and Josey has installed a Frantz oil filter system. Both engines are running quietly and smoothly. As she puts it into gear, it remains quiet.

Bridget pours some coffee and sits back to discuss the repairs.

Bridget says, "We and Matt's men are continuously hitting debris that floats down from the rivers. We have been fortunate not to run into entire trees. I see it all the time when sailing Alicia. Thanks for the update, and many thanks for getting it back in service so quickly. I have a feeling that we are going to have some contractor leftover after our event this next week. Matt may be asking us to take those out to the Farallones, so let's give this boat a test run."

Josey disconnects the mooring lines, and Bridget puts both motors in gear. While idling out to open water, everything seems smoother and quieter than before. Bridget increases the speed to 35 mph, makes sharp turns, then "S" turns and other aggressive maneuvers. All seems correct. Bridget has Josey take over the wheel, while she listens to everything as she moves from one place to another on the boat. Bridget takes back the wheel and opens it up to top speed. The new maximum speed is five MPH faster. She slows to 35 mph, then shuts the left motor down and raises the left I/O unit out of the water. The speed lowers to 25 mph. She repeats this by running on the left drive with the same results.

Bridget says to Josey, "Ok, let's go home."

Bridget pulls the boat into the slip, and Josey ties off the mooring lines.

As they are walking to their cars, Bridget says, "Would you like to see Arnold's new toy?"

Josey says, "I'll bet it is another Jaguar like that white one over there."

She says, "That's the one Josey. It corners better, it is faster, it accelerates faster, and it is improved aerodynamically; what a joy to drive. Nick upgraded the paint. He also had the tires moved outward. It has a wider base on the roadway and an increased cantor setting."

Josey says, "Impressive. Please keep me informed when the big day occurs. I would like to have an alibi."

Bridget says, "How do you feel about taking a trip to Reno? I'll pay for it, and you will be out of town."

Josey says, "No, thank you. I've been to Reno. Niagara Falls, maybe."

Because the McCarthy operatives each have independent

living accommodations, Bridget feels confident that Matt will not take them all out. Will there be any of these operatives arrogant enough to retaliate? If yes, toward whom and where? With the boat in excellent working order, any of them that Matt does a catch can be taken to the Farallones. Matt claims to have a list containing each McCarthy operative. Bridget is still worried. Just one is easily overlooked.

Bridget feels she has done all she can for today. She heads home, fixes a small snack, and puts on Mozart's Symphony #40 & #41 conducted by Bernstein while she relaxes.

She checks the weather for tomorrow. The forecast is for gentle winds, a relatively calm the Pacific Ocean, and only a light early morning fog. With many untrained guests aboard, she feels that she must be cautious. Bridget has been on the ocean when there were fifteen-foot waves with gusting winds.

The meeting time is set for 10 a.m. This will give Bridget time to prepare Alicia and have a quiet breakfast at the marina restaurant. Arriving at the restaurant, she will inspect the surroundings for sniper positions. She will bring her 44 Magnum plus some additional rounds just in case. She tells herself to stop going over the data. After an hour and a half, she finally falls asleep but does not sleep soundly.

First thing in the morning, Bridget rechecks the weather. Bridget remembers to call Matt. She makes sure he knows about the group and the intended path of the boat ride. Calm seas are predicted. She has coffee and fruit for a start. A thermos of French roast freshly made coffee is ready to go. She wants to have Alicia checked out and ready to go by 8:30 a.m.

She leaves at 7 a.m., and the streets are almost empty. A quick stop at Lombard and away she goes toward the bridge. She is as excited to drive the Jaguar as she is sailing the

HIDDEN IN FRONT OF YOU

Alicia. The fog smell is pleasant this morning, but not pronounced. Bridget drives a little faster than usual because she can. Reaching the Tiburon off-ramp, it reminds her of her home on the hill. Bridget sees the officer who took the message for Sergeant Brown. She merely waves and keeps ongoing. If she were dressed as Arnold, she would have stopped for a chat. There is ample parking this early in the morning. She parks at the walkway to Alicia's slip.

Carrying her clothes and coffee to the boat takes only one trip. She removes the mainsail cover, unlocks the cabin, and unwraps the mainsail. She raises the mainsail halfway up the mast. That seems enough for now. She leaves the secondary sails wrapped since they will not be used today. She starts the auxiliary engine to check the battery and gauges plus to check the gas tank. The cabin is clean. She sits at the helmsman's position reviewing the instruments.

It is time for a formal breakfast, so Bridget walks the few feet to the restaurant and asks the maître de' for a window seat facing Alicia. Bridget asks for the specialty of the house with some Grand Marnier for her coffee. As she finishes breakfast, she thinks of a quiet, comfortable morning like this one is what she needed. Bridget says good day to the maître de' and walks to Alicia and enters the cabin. Everything seems to be in order. People should be arriving soon.

Officer O'Malley and his wife come first. Bridget fits them with life preservers then they sit inside the cabin for a chat. Alex, Sammy, and Naomi come next. Mom and Dad Peterson decided to stay home because one of the children was not feeling well. The life preservers fit well. Bridget informs them that they must wear them at all times.

Sergeant Brown and Sergeant Emerson arrive next. The new jackets fit them better than the older ones.

Bridget says, "Be careful not to jaywalk off the boat."

Matilda, with her three children, walks onto the gangplank. The new children's jackets fit them perfectly. Bridget tells Matilda that each child must be attached to a good-sized adult via the leashes she has provided. We are going to be leaning from one side to the other. It would be easy for them to fall into the water.

Bridget says to Sergeant Brown, "Here's a better life jacket than the one you brought. Arnold says I should push you in, so keep that vest on at all times."

Sergeant Brown says, "Is that white Jaguar with the beautiful paint job Arnold's new car?"

Bridget says, "Yes, I am test driving it for him. It is so fast, it's scary. I am sure Arnold will give you a ride. When you ride with him, be sure to fasten your seatbelt."

As she gathers her guests around, Bridget says, "You need to focus on two things. One is that we are going to be leaning from side to side. Keep your balance and hang on to something. As we tack or turn, the mainsail is going to swing from one side to the other side across the boat. Always stay clear of the mainsail. It could hurt you or knock you overboard. I will not be taking sudden turns, and the slanting of the boat will be moderate."

Bridget starts pulling in the mooring lines. The boat begins to float away from the dock as Bridget starts the motor. Slowly the Alicia is moving toward open waters. Leaving the steering in a locked midship position, Bridget raises the mainsail then sets its position. She immediately walks to the helmsman's place to correct the boat's path. The mild breeze catches the sail, moving Alicia to the port side. Bridget has adjusted the sail to capture some air while making Alicia lean moderately. The winds are coming from the west-northwest direction. To reduce the amount of tacking to get out through the gate, she steers close to the northern shoreline by the Coast Guard Base and Sausalito.

HIDDEN IN FRONT OF YOU

Everyone is excited about viewing the shoreline from the waterside. The entire bridge can be seen from the boat as Alicia rounds the point just south of Sausalito. Bridget turns 15 degrees more northerly to reduce the boat's speed. Alicia is only slightly leaning to port. Bridget locks the steering wheel and adjusts the sail inward.

The vehicle noise is evident as they pass under the Golden Gate. Bridget is steering the Alicia so that they are hugging the shoreline by Point Bonita. The faster open sea winds increase Alicia's speed. Bridget adjusts the sail outward, which makes Alicia's mainsail pick up more wind. Many fishing boats are anchored around Point Bonita. Bridget stays as far away from them as possible.

As they sail further into the open ocean, a person's perception changes. The water is not smooth. It has rising and falling waves. Alicia is now reacting to the movements of the water. Water is spraying over the bow. The ride is no longer just a gentle cruise. It is a boat responding to the influence of the conditions. A few miles into the ocean, Bridget decides to turn around. She yells that she is coming about and watching out for the sail changing sides. As cautiously as possible, she turns to starboard with the sail swinging to starboard. Bridget resets the sail to a new position.

Alicia is now leaning to its starboard side with the sail picking up more air than before. They again pass under the bridge. Bridget keeps Alicia sailing on the starboard side until pier 39. Before getting near pier 39, Bridget warns everybody that she is turning, and the sail will be a swing to the port side. They have already observed the Presidio, Fort Point, Palace of Fine Arts, and North Beach. After the turn, Alicia is sailing almost due south past Fisherman's Wharf, Pier after Pier along the Embarcadero, the foot of Market Street, and then sails under the Oakland-San Francisco Bridge almost to

Army Street. Bridget yells out a warning for a starboard turnaround so they can sail past Treasure Island and just west of Alcatraz on the way back to Tiburon.

Bridget can see that the group is starting to fatigue. They are still enjoying the view and the chance to see sights from the position on the water, but they are talking less. Treasure Island is still a Navy base for processing naval personnel. Passing Alcatraz is always unique. It appears to be such a secure prison. Its decline was due to the saltwater rusting the metal in the concrete buildings. The Alcatraz cost was $10 per day per inmate compared to three dollars per day per inmate for other prisons in the mid-20th century. The escape of three inmates changed the value of Alcatraz. It housed the most dangerous inmates from the other facilities.

Passing Treasure Island and Alcatraz, Bridget steers Alicia just west of Angel Island to the marina. As they get close to the marina, Bridget lowers the mainsail and proceeds into the slip by using the auxiliary motor. Quickly the boat is tied to the dock. People are shedding their life jackets. Sergeant Brown, Sergeant Emerson, and Officer O'Malley leave first. They each thanked Bridget for a beautiful ride. Sergeant Brown reminded Bridget that she had forgotten to push him overboard.

Brown's jacket is hanging on the railing drying. She trips him when he steps onto the gangplank and into the water he goes. The sergeant is swearing as he jaywalks to his patrol car.

Bridget yells, "Thanks for the reminder. Sometimes we girls forget."

Matilda gives Bridget a big hug and a thank you for remembering her and her children. They were all excited.

Bridget asks Alex to rinse all the jackets and other equipment, and then hang them on the railing to dry. Sammy is to vacuuming and straightening up the cabin. Bridget and

HIDDEN IN FRONT OF YOU

Naomi clean the sail and pack it into its cover, and then rinse down the entire boat with fresh water. Alex, Sammy, and Naomi are pleased they were invited. Naomi hugs Bridget and says how much she appreciates the world now. For Naomi, the prospect of a happy life continues to appear promising.

Bridget says, "Please keep that positive attitude. You are going to have a wonderful life. Love you, sweetie."

They hug again, and tears are running down Bridget's face. Bridget had to go into the cabin to redo her makeup.

49 - THE BIG DAY APPROACHES

Bridget puts all the equipment away. The boat looks fresh and clean. After locking the cabin, Bridget carries the leftover coffee to the Jaguar. There is no other way they can rid themselves of this McCarthy evil. Arnold found that to fight them by himself was like one man against an army. If Matt had not come to his aid, Arnold would have had to close the firm.

Bridget drives home and parks the Jaguar in the garage. She takes a shower, leaves the makeup off, and puts on a feminine workout outfit. It gives her flexibility. She starts reviewing her notes on Matt's training. The details run from moderate, through severe, to deadly. She has not had to use most of the fatal moves in recent years, but this may be the time to review the techniques. Only the meanest, most arrogant, and the most ego-driven operative will be retaliatory enough to cause the use of these techniques. Also, a contractor may be on drugs that may make him feel no pain. Only the deadliest maneuvers would be sufficient for that situation. The actions by the McCarthy operatives show that many of them are capable and seem to enjoy their vicious acts.

For the next several hours, she reads and rereads the notes then practices each maneuver. Only when each movement became second nature again, did she feel it was time to quit. Bridget remembers that repetitiveness is what changes our brain's structure. Bridget is also aware that repetitive practice gives her the ability to exercise those moves instantly. The brain's neuron matrices must be in place for the automatic mind to body communications to take place. Her movements must come from memory. It is like playing the piano during a concert. The pianist is playing strictly from memory. If the pianist must think about what to do, the piece will be ruined.

HIDDEN IN FRONT OF YOU

She puts a tape of Tchaikovsky Piano Concerto #1 into the tape drive and settles back with a tall glass of port. She is thinking of the long preparation for this extermination event. Now that the game is near, it appears scary. It reminds her of the many people that came back from Vietnam, saying it was that way for them every minute of every day. It is no wonder that so many were changed when they returned and diagnosed with PTSD.

She calls Matt, and he calls back in seconds.

Matt says, "Hello, worried lil girl. You should be getting nervous by now."

Bridget says, "I am so nervous that I have just spent the evening going over the extreme procedures you taught me. When is our final meeting before you start your event?"

Matt says, "Tuesday at your home will be our kick-off meeting. I will fill you in on our plans. I know there will be some things that slip through the cracks. We will be hunting them down and delivering them to your boat starting Wednesday night through whenever. Relax lil girl. Talk to you soon, bye."

It's been a full day, and it's getting late. After a shower, Bridget brushes her teeth and crawls in between the silk sheets.

50 - POLICE DEPARTMENT CHANGES

Bridget wakes about 4:30 a.m. with anticipation. Rather than getting up, she attempts to gain more sleep by dozing as much as she can. By 6 a.m., her mind is going through the importance of the day. She gets out of bed and fixes some fresh coffee. With a caterer at the meeting, there will be plenty to eat there, so she has a light breakfast.

She spends extra time showering, washing her hair, doing her makeup, then goes to her closet, looking for the sexiest dress that is above the knee, shows her breasts, and is a bright color. She finds a gorgeous red skirt and jacket with a pink blouse: red 3-inch heels, red nylons, and complementary gold jewelry, including her long earring chain.

Like Lillie Hitchcock Coit of the famous Coit Tower, Bridget loves San Francisco. She plans on being hard-nosed and bossy when announcing her attack and calling it like it is. The department heads have not taken her warnings seriously. She is ready to inform them that they either work with her to repair the system or suffer a $6-8 million lawsuit.

Bridget thinks, "There I go again. I'm reshuffling item after item that I have already made up my mind on."

With breakfast finished, she's out the door with her objective in mind. There is no operative watching today. She closes the garage door. As she is waiting for the light to change at Lombard, she feels the aggressiveness in her body. Turning onto Lombard, Bridget tells herself to enjoy the drive. While crossing the bridge, there is no fog and traffic is normal. Bridget is back driving the pink Mercedes. She misses the Jaguar.

Arriving at her parking stall, as usual, she updates her lipstick. She feels surprisingly calm while riding the elevator to the 12th floor.

As she passes Matilda's desk Matilda says, "Ms.

HIDDEN IN FRONT OF YOU

O'Connor, we all had a wonderful time Sunday. It was our first time on a boat of that size, and we have never been out on the ocean. Thank you so much."

Bridget says, "You are welcome. I am pleased you and your children came along. It was a pleasure having all of you there. You may want to do it again. I am sure Arnold will be pleased to have you as his guest."

Approaching Jennifer's desk, Bridget notes a look on Jennifer's face that she has seldom seen before.

Jennifer says, "It starts today. All we have worked for these last many months is coming to a conclusion. How do you tolerate the pressure of the entire firm on your shoulders, Ms. O'Connor?"

Bridget says, "Sometimes it is just part of the job. Please call our group together for a 9 a.m. meeting. Also, call Mr. Fish to verify that the meeting at 10 a.m. is mandatory."

She continues into her office and hangs her red suit jacket and places her purse in the usual drawer. She checks for her 38-caliber is under the desktop. The snub nose 38-caliber is always strapped to the inside of her leg.

Approaching 9 a.m., Bridget goes to the lady's room. Her entire concentration is on the business at hand. Bridget is always reminding herself that she is a female 24/7. She has decided to keep her makeup fresh. Today especially, she wants the department heads to be faced with a sexy appearing female.

Her lawsuit staff is assembled in the conference room. She walks in and takes the chair in the middle of the long conference table. Jennifer has made sure that everyone has a fresh cup of coffee.

Bridget has the door closed and says, "Let's start our premeeting to make sure we are all on the same page. I have worked with each one of you on your portion as it is defined. I am confident that you will do your best in following my directions. At this moment, I want to orchestrate one common approach. When you manage an effort, it is the lead person that has the responsibility. Collectively we have reviewed the errors and weaknesses stated in the current police procedures. Some portions of these procedures are missing, and some are poorly presented. Mostly the officers are not held to the required written procedures showing a huge part of this lawsuit is the lack of management. We must find a way of forcing that policy and procedures to become the main basis for the corrective action. Remember, Mr. Little has open-door access to enter and leave without question. Some of his perceived actions have not been a compliment. He is our voice to the general public. I have confidence that we will work together for our common goal. I do not trust those politicians that were called department heads. They cause this problem. Mr. Trinity was the worst since he did not lead his people with a true and proper implementation. Thank God, Trinity is gone. The be damned with the citizen attitude is about to cease. This is not the end of the nineteenth century, where everything was corrupt in San Francisco. Take a break and refresh yourself. We will have the current department managers here at 10 a.m. Thank you for listening."

It's 9:45 a.m., and Jennifer says, "A gentleman is waiting to see you."

Bridget says, "Show him into my office, please."

He walks into her office and says, "Hello, Bridget."

Bridget is surprised Sam is standing there. She feels that she needs to find a way to prepare him before her actions hurt him. She walks around the desk and gives him a big hug.

She says, "It is good to see you, Sam. It may be time for you to find out what kind of a bitch I can become. There is a lawsuit meeting scheduled for 10 a.m., a few minutes from now. I would like you to attend the meeting. If asked, say you are a private investigator. Walk-in with me and find a seat in the rear. I'll be right back."

She runs off the lady's room to check on her lipstick. When she returns, they walk to the conference room together. Bridget closes the door.

Bridget opens the meeting saying, "Mr. Fish and I are heading this investigation until Arnold Pierce returns. We have our working group with us today. Mr. Fish and I personally will be leading the DUI accident reporting segment."

Bridget then addresses each one in her group and describes their area of work.

She continues, "Collectively, we have reviewed, studied, and come up with our first set of objectives. Judge Brass has given the go-ahead to fix the problems collectively. This firm will be compensated for our work and expenses until it is considered completed. If that is not successful, I have filed an eight-million-dollar lawsuit that is a slam dunk win in court. My witnesses include over two dozen attorneys willing to testify about their similar complaints with the court. They have experienced accident compensation failures leaving family members out to dry. These failures were mainly based upon poorly written reports, incomplete accident reports, and sometimes missing reports. They were missing measurements of the accident itself, no measurement of alcohol in the driver's bloodstream, no description of the drivers involved, and on and on. We have court records that support every one of these accusations, and the attorney's all willing to testify."

Bridget continues, "Similar to Lillie Coit, who was responsible for providing the funds for the building of Coit Tower, our CEO, Arnold Pierce, loves San Francisco. He wants the problems corrected rather than causing a severe financial crisis for San Francisco coupled with no fixes. On many occasions, I have witnessed the top dogs, and the managers receive the hit when their subordinates do not follow formal policy. You, the top dogs, are the very ones responsible for your subordinates' actions. Ladies and gentlemen, you are the problem and also the solution. You alone are responsible. The degree in which it happens differs from one department to another, yet it is similar."

"The two officers that I arrested have been fired. They were two blocks from my call for help in a DUI accident that I observed. They did not have their radios with them, plus they were drinking an alcoholic beverage during an on-duty food break. We are going to make sure the procedures directing your officers are based upon laws that are on the books. This shall be managed in the proper order and with appropriate diligence. Deviations from procedures shall be dealt with immediately and firmly. Multiple occurrences indicate real political influences. Anyone that wants to be replaced or just won't cooperate should start on your termination paperwork now. If you choose not to work, I will have you replaced. Our objective is to save San Francisco from what we see as corruption, political manipulation, incompetence, and pure laziness."

"That is the end of my introduction. By now, you know your assigned staff members. I suggest you go with them to start work. Mr. Little, please come with me. We need to have a chat."

Mr. Little, Sam, and Bridget walk to her office. She closes the door and sits down.

She says, "Mr. Little, this is Sam, he is a private investigator. Mr. Little, what do you think of my introduction?"

He replies, "You were forceful and clear in what you want to happen. I'll lay odds that even some of these new or interim department heads are thinking about early retirement."

She says, "That is what I want to discuss with you. I expect some of them to retire or ask for another assignment. I am asking you to omit any leaving by them from your article until we agree to make that announcement. My reason is the embarrassment it will cause. This is going to be hard enough to hold together. Making them look like fools will just make the job more difficult for me. Please give me enough lead time to review your writings. Mr. Little, you have a large part in this work. I believe you are the right person for the job. Let's see how it goes. Thank you for your willingness and participation."

Mr. Little leaves.

Bridget calls Judge Brass's office.

Bridget says, "This is Ms. O'Connor. Is there a chance I could chat with Judge Brass?"

The secretary says, "Let me check."

A few moments later, she says, "I'll connect you."

Judge Brass says, "Hello, Ms. O'Connor. I have already heard about your introduction. Good for you. Your fact sheets, in this case, point to total incompetence. I am talking to the city council, the district attorney's office, and the mayor's office. If you were to take this to court, you would win easily. Keep up the excellent work.

I look forward to talking with you soon."

Sam continues to stay close to Bridget as she walks around, wanting to put her chest out in pride. But with "C" cups, it may be overdone. She walks into Julien's office to speak with Juliet. She is out, but Julien is there.

He says, "You sounded like General Patton of World War II."

Bridget says, "Has daddy given his child the day off again?"

Julien says, "She is most likely in the lady's room. Thank you for lunch the other day. We ordered the most expensive items on the menu just to make you happy. Hello, Sam, it's good to see you."

Juliet walks in, saying, "Daddy is your boss complaining about me again. Ignore her. She will just give up and leave."

Bridget says, "Juliet, I would appreciate it if you would come to dinner with Matt and me Tuesday evening. We are discussing his final plan. Afterward, we are going attempt to track each of McCarthy's operatives. You are the perfect person for that activity. You're the one with the cross-tracking experience. No matter how Matt performs, there will be some leftover McCarthy operatives at different locations."

Bridget says to Sam, "Let's walk."

As they are riding the elevator down to the ground floor, Bridget says, "Keep your eyes open. Take the strap off your weapon and take a good look at any cars driving by."

Sam says, "You can be quite demanding and strong-minded. You must have an excessive amount of pressure on you with all those nice people in your office under your protection. They all seem to like you."

Bridget says, "Sometimes, a person must do what is required. We may not agree or want to do whatever it takes. I have done it, and I will do it again. These things cause me nightmares. I have killed before, and in the future, I will need to kill again. That gives me what you guys call PTSD symptoms. My cousin Arnold owns the firm. I am here to protect him and his staff."

Bridget continues, "I lost my fiancée in Vietnam. I like your company, and I enjoy being with you. Can we be good friends and stop there?"

They walk back to the garage.

She says, "It is time for you to go. It was nice seeing you."

HIDDEN IN FRONT OF YOU

Into the elevator, she goes.

Bridget walks to Jennifer's desk and says, "Let's call it a day. I would like another 9 a.m. pre-meeting on Tuesday and Wednesday."

Bridget goes to her office. She grabs her purse, and red coat then walks directly to her Mercedes. Bridget realizes that the day went just as expected. She smiles when she thinks of the ripple effect that is happening at city hall. Once home, Bridget changes to her nightclothes, have a quick dinner, and watches a rented movie. She has decided not to fret about what is about to happen. Doing something about this problem is long overdue.

Tuesday morning, and today, Bridget pulls her hair back into a ponytail with curls extending to her back. She changed her jewelry to silver but with similar items. She chooses a black mini skirt with a reasonably tight white sweater showing off her C-cup breasts and a black jacket, black 3-inch heels, and black nylons complete today's ensemble. Make these policemen and policewomen envious. She fixes a moderate breakfast, thinking there is so much supplied by the caterer. Feeling sort of smug, she starts off for work.

The fog has that pleasant smell as she crosses the bridge. Traffic appears more forgiving than most days. This morning she notices the eye-catching fact that her Mercedes is pink with a female driver. It's an odd color for a Mercedes. Sid knew that when he acquired it.

Arriving in her parking stall, she again updates her lipstick. Walking through the main lobby, she says good morning to Matilda, and walks quickly to her office, to review her list of messages. The new Police Commissioner, Mr. Louie Fish, is sitting just outside her office. It is 8:20, so she has time to meet with him before the 9 a.m. pre-meeting. She nods for him to enter, puts her purse in the drawer, and hangs her jacket. Jennifer pours coffee for each.

Bridget says, "What may I do for you, sir. We have about twenty minutes to talk."

Mr. Louie Fish says, "As I said before, I have been waiting for someone like you to come along. The old department heads have all been replaced. The current group of new or interim department heads will do what is necessary. I had a meeting with all of them this morning at 6 a.m., and they all assured me that they are all on board. I reviewed my demand to begin following the procedures currently posted in the procedure manual. Anyone not following these will receive a two-day suspension without pay on the first offense and a two-week suspension without pay for the second offense. If there is a third, it is termination. The DUI accident reports are not clearly stated and will need updating. I will work with you making corrections, updates, and additions. Your intro yesterday gave me the chance to step out there and go for it. You have my pledge that this is happening and will continue to happen. Thank you for taking this action."

Bridget says, "Mr. Fish, I respect you for your patience and willingness to solve these problems. Getting rid of most of politics is one of my objectives. I thank you for your efforts and especially for your willingness to manage properly. We will see who shows today. If this works out, you have just made my life easier."

Mr. Fish leaves so he can be ready for the 10 a.m. meeting. Bridget takes a bathroom break and has a snack from the caterer.

Judge Brass calls, "Ms. O'Connor., do you have any news for me?"

Bridget says, "I had a brief meeting with Mr. Fish this morning. He had a meeting with all his department heads this morning at 06:00 a.m. Everyone is committed to getting things done correctly."

Judge Brass says, "Mr. Fish will be an excellent police

commissioner. Let's stay in touch."

Bridget and Commissioner Fish start the meeting by sharing data. Bridget reads Fish's logbook, and Fish reads Bridget's information. After a half-hour, they are both read through the other's opinions.

Bridget says, "We are close to a solution by simply merging our thoughts. Start writing up your merge while I roam around and check on the other groups."

Bridget calls Julien and says, "Please give Mr. Fish a login to our external machine so he can make some entries and give him access to the local printer here in this office."

Julien says, "Sure thing, Cat Woman. Us Alley Cats always come through."

Bridget starts her rounds with the other groups. She reviews what each of her staff members is working on. She feels that good progress is being made.

Mr. Little has a draft article prepared for Bridget's review.

She makes a few minor corrections and says, "Let's go to press. I must let you know that the ripple effect has already started. You and I seem to be putting together a winning scenario. I am going to make another call to Judge Brass before I head for home. See you tomorrow."

Bridget walks to her office and calls Judge Brass.

Bridget says, "Sorry to bother you again. This is Bridget O'Connor."

The secretary says, "I was told to pass you through if you call. One minute, please."

Brass says, "Good to hear from you, Bridget."

Bridget says, "Enthusiasm and hard work today is my assessment. Fish's replacements are fitting in well."

Brass says, "Thanks for the update. Have a good evening, Ms. O'Connor.

Bridget head to the parking garage and then drives directly to the supermarket. It's Tuesday, and Matt will be presenting his final plan to Bridget and her close associates at her home.

HIDDEN IN FRONT OF YOU

51 - MATT'S FINAL REVIEW

Bridget likes to tease Eric in the meat department, so, from over twenty-five feet away, she says hi to Eric so he can see her mini skirt and her "C" cups pointing at him.

She says, "Eric, could you find me some lean corn beef for sandwiches?"

Eric says, "Yes, Ma'am, for you anything."

He finds some corned beef with very little fat and even trims that off for her.

Bridget says, "Thank you, sweet man. We should ask the management to give you a raise."

As she is walking toward the produce department, she wiggles her butt with the mini skirt for his pleasure. Evelyn is stacking the celery. They see each other and run to each other for a big hug.

Evelyn says, "You enjoy wiggling your butt for lil ole Eric. You probably give him an erection every time."

Bridget says, "And."

Bridget gets some fresh romaine lettuce and vine-ripened tomatoes. Then she goes to the condiment section for some various mustards and horseradish. She also finds some real vanilla flavoring and some special chocolate syrup.

On the way to the checkout, she says to the manager, "I am still planning a large barbeque. I might need you to deliver this time."

He says, "That will be our pleasure, Ma'am."

When she arrives home, Juliet is already there. She helps Bridget with the groceries, and then they both start fixing the salad with various dressings alongside. Some antipasti and cheeses are put on the table with several types of shredded cheese. Bridget boils some spaghetti noodles, and Juliet has the corned beef ready to serve. They still have about a half-hour to spare.

Bridget says, "no-no-no you little devil. I need to keep my

mind upon the business at hand. But thanks for the thought. Those sheets will be there tonight."

Juliet says, "I have never heard you call Jennifer Mrs. Hastings before."

Bridget says, "I wanted her to know that she is of such value that she must be included. She is such a superb support staff person. I wanted her to hear about her importance."

The phone rings and Matt states he is on his way. Bridget opens the garage door and waits with her 38-caliber in hand. Matt pulls into the garage. Bridget closes the garage door.

Bridget gets out the paperwork on the department heads.

She finds Mr. Fish's home number and calls Fish, "Hello, this is Louie Fish."

Bridget says, "Mr. Fish, this is Ms. O'Connor. We had a productive day today."

"I have a thought, and I wish to make a suggestion for you."

"Starting on the first watch tomorrow requires each officer report to be reviewed for correctness and accuracy per the existing procedure manual. It is just a thought."

"By the way, Mr. Fish, Judge Brass, was already aware of your efforts. He thinks highly of you. Good night sir."

She hangs up the phone.

Bridget says, "I feel bad that on his first month, he has to contend with the McCarthy event."

Matt says, "It will show everyone that he has the fortitude to take on adversity."

Bridget says, "Alright, Matt, let's have it. How and what are you doing tomorrow?"

Matt says, "I hear that Sam came by to visit with you. He got an earful. I think he feels that he needs to let go. We are fixed on tomorrow being our day. A few of my men have infiltrated the brothel. We have decided not to let the girls know. We will just put them to sleep and place them at a safe distance from the fire. At about 5 a.m., each one of the men will be put to sleep with 150 Mg of Demerol. Those that do not stay asleep will be shot. Within the next fifteen minutes, the natural gas line will be cut open, and gasoline will be poured at the extremities, then we strike the match. There are about fifty percent newbies, and fifty percent existing contractors. My folks will go home to their regular jobs and such."

"The other two sights are a little more complex. This is where McCarthy has built-in defenses. A small group will clean out the business sight at about 5 a.m. Before they leave, they will plant evidence for all the agencies. The FBI has completed its review of the payment's schedules. They are ready to proceed with illegal money transactions. They know nothing of our events. Following this smaller attack, this group will back up the larger group from the warehouse."

"We will be using some outdated military ordinance at the warehouse that will knock out the wall defenses and blow the vans to bits. Even flame throwers will be used. Gasoline will be sprayed in and ignited with a small piece of artillery."

"These men will be transported to their jobs, their homes, bus lines, etc. The military gear will be moved to my storage facility."

"I have the list here of the current McCarthy contractors. Juliet, you and I will continue to update the cross-checking."

"There are two contractors on the list that are exceptionally aggressive. They are physically huge and strong. They are heavy drug users. The reason for considering them is that we can't find them. One is named Jason, and I do not know the other's name. They are two of McCarthy's assassins, and everyone fears them. Either will brutally beat someone for looking the wrong way at them. I have seen

Jason pick up a man your size and toss him twenty feet."

"The only two items that may make your firm become of interest is that Williams worked for the firm and that your firm represented McCarthy. Most questions will not be significant. With a little time and effort from you, the interest will soon dissipate. That is all for now. I feel it would be unfair to you if you had all the details. Thanks for dinner. I need some sleep, so bye, all."

Out he goes to his car and leaves the area. Juliet and Bridget clean the dinner dishes and pans then sit down for a glass of port.

Bridget says, "I am both excited about tomorrow and uneasy at the same time. Mr. Fish gets thrown into this in the first month of his new assignment. If we could help, I would offer it. By helping too much, we could get drawn into the mess."

Juliet says, "Why don't you wait for Mr. Fish to talk to you. At that time, he could ask for some assistance, and you are relieved of the problem."

Bridget says, "Good idea, sweetheart. By the way, how is Julien taking the fact that you are seeing Arnold?"

Juliet says, "He said that he knew it was going to happen. He was just trying to slow me down. He is surprised that I could find Arnold since no one else has seen him. This would be a good time to try out those silk sheets. I'll forgive you for turning me down earlier."

Both agree and head for the bedroom.

HIDDEN IN FRONT OF YOU

52 - THE BIG DAY ARRIVES

Sid calls at 7 a.m., saying, "Go watch your television on Channel 2. The shit just hit the fan!"

Bridget and Juliet put on their robes and go to the kitchen for coffee. Bridget turns on the TV to Channel 2. The only thing they are reporting is information on all three McCarthy sites. All other news has been set aside. The fire at the brothel is out, and they have found 24 male bodies, no women. The business site has 12 dead. All were discovered when people arrived for work. The warehouse is currently in flames and being fought by the fire department. One of the bodies at the warehouse was said to be Kevin McCarthy, the CEO and sole owner of the entire McCarthy empire.

McCarthy is said to have had continuous problems dealing with the city. Somehow the newscaster has critical information on McCarthy. The newscaster is implying a history with the McCarthy Group about other cities that have had trouble with his group.

The Marin County Sheriff's office reported finding a group of prostitutes that had been drugged. They found them in their cars a safe distance from the burning building. It is said that the building was being used as a brothel. Its original design was to be a brothel when it was built in the late 19th century. From the city's records, it was constructed around the end of the century at a time when building permits were rare. The identification of the bodies will be obtained from dental records.

The newscaster comments about what a way for Mr. Fish to start his first month as Police Commissioner.

Bridget says, "Let's have some breakfast, something special. Look out, Sid may be planning a visit."

Within ten minutes, there is a knock at the back door, and the phone is ringing. Juliet gets the door while Bridget answers the phone.

Bridget says, "Hello, this is Ms. O'Connor."

"Hello, my sweet lady, this is Matt. I have a present for you, but you can't have it until 9 p.m. tonight. See you, then at the boat."

Click goes the phone.

Sid says, "How does it feel to get this much done today? Bridget is no longer needed. No more "C" cups. What are we having for breakfast, Ms. O'Connor?"

Bridget says, "Eggs Benedict and Crepe Suzettes with Grand Marnier. If you are nice, we will let you have some. Let's hurry since Juliet, and I still need to go to work as usual. Anyway, you are our alibi this morning."

Sid slips away once they finish breakfast.

Bridget says, "Someday, we need to leave all the dishes for that man."

They clean up the kitchen and start getting ready for work. Bridget plans on keeping the same sexy look for today while Juliet dresses more conservatively. It is already 7:45, so out the door, they go, and for sure, there are no operatives. Traffic on Lombard is average, and the bridge is foggy. To Bridget's delight, the fog smell was as pleasant as it can get. The fog had stretched almost to the San Quentin turn off. This means an average day in San Rafael. Bridget does her makeup check then applies a brighter shade of lipstick. On her way to the elevator, Bridget expects quite a change in the office.

As she steps off the elevator, she sees most of the staff watching the Channel 2 broadcast. They all go back to their lawsuit assignments within an hour. Most are not concerned with the outrage by the agencies or any guilt. The remainder of the day, they stay quiet yet productive. Bridget appreciates the change in the office environment. The many months of anguish make it worth the fight. The setting is back to a calm and friendly atmosphere.

HIDDEN IN FRONT OF YOU

As she walks up to Jennifer's desk, Jennifer says, "Many people want your thoughts on this morning's events. This includes staff, reporters, and police investigators. How do you want to handle things?"

Bridget says, "Let everyone know that I will hold a press conference in our main conference room at 1:00 p.m. Before that, I will have private meetings with key staff members. Make sure Mr. Little attends the press conference."

Jennifer says, "consider it done."

Bridget walks into Julien's office and says, "Mr. Spence, I will be holding a press conference at 1:00 p.m. Can you get a video set up in the main conference room? That way, I can have others watch, which will reduce the number of times I need to answer the same question."

Julien says, "I don't know Bridget. It is a lot of work, and I am fatigued from watching TV all morning."

Bridget says, "Get it done, or you will lose one of the three lives you have left, Alley Cat."

Bridget calls Jennifer, saying, "Best warn the caterer of the changes due to this morning."

Jennifer says, "I already have it taken care of."

1 p.m. arrives, and many individuals are herded into the conference room. There are three policemen, and the rest are reporters.

Bridget says, "You will find a pad in front of you. Please state who you are representing and the state the question that you wish to ask publicly. I will hold private meetings for questions that are too sensitive or those that you do not want to share with the group."

Bridget continues, "We are a law firm with a one-hundred-year history. Our office takes pride in our support for its clients. We have a charity division that assists individuals that are willing to work and need help. That group is headed by Mr. Worth. You may talk to him if you need more details. Currently, the firm has an eight-million-dollar lawsuit against the Police Department of San Francisco. A compromise has been offered by the firm to help fix the problems. All released information can be found in Mr. Little's column printed in the Morning Chronicle.

"The firm represented the McCarthy Group concerning a contract disagreement with the City of San Francisco. The financial records and a list of nonfunctioning businesses forced us to deal with McCarthy on a cash pay as you go basis. Ladies and gentlemen, I can now take your questions. The first question should be from Sergeant Brown since the first event was in his district."

Brown says, "Please speak about your knowledge and history of the brothel."

Bridget says, "I grew up nearby and considered it my playground. I have skied on the site. I knew the owners. I rented the kitchen, front room, and gambling sections of the large building for parties when I was in high school and college. I have not been there since my cousin's fiancée was killed in an automobile accident. Mr. Brown, any more questions?"

He nods no.

Both the FBI and San Francisco detective agents say, "That was my question."

Sergeant Emerson from San Francisco says, "You have a beautiful boat, the Alicia. Why do you also have a twin I/O boat at the St. Francis Yacht Club?"

Bridget says, "Both Arnold and I learned the enjoyment of fishing from our Grandfather. It is not practical to fish from Alicia. Occasionally, I prefer to dive, especially around Point Bonita and at the Farallones, where the shelf drops to thousands of feet. Do any of the police officers have special questions?"

All three raise their hands.

HIDDEN IN FRONT OF YOU

Bridget says, "I intend to answer other questions, but it seems most important that I answer these gentlemen's questions first. I have hired a caterer for your pleasure. Make yourself at home. I will be with you as soon as possible. Sergeant Brown, meet me in my office in ten minutes."

Jennifer has Bridget's lunch ready, along with plenty of coffee. Bridget makes a trip to the lady's room, checks her makeup, and updates her lipstick again. When Sergeant Brown comes into her office with his hands full of food, she closes the door.

Sergeant Brown says, "I still think there is a lot you know and have going on behind the scenes that I will never see. Sometimes I feel like you are elusive with me, and at the same time, I feel that you are playing games. I have heard through my own grapevine that McCarthy was hassling the firm. Can we discuss this, please?"

Bridget says, "In all honesty, the connection was through Mr. Williams, who I have fired. The McCarthy Group intended to get rid of Arnold so they could take over the firm. Arnold is the sole owner. With the former CEO, Frank Dulles having severe brain damage, they must have thought it was going to be a slam dunk. Arnold is a real fighter. He upgraded each Jaguar and used his history in chases to avoid their efforts. This last accident proved to him that he was losing the battle, but he still wanted to win the war. He was severely injured in that accident. We were contacted by someone that has had a big problem with McCarthy. I do not know who this was, but both Arnold and I were told just to remain stable. When we noticed the errors in the books, Williams and the accounting group were fired on the spot. Does that answer your questions?"

Sergeant Brown says, "I still believe Arnold fired the shot that killed that driver in Tiburon, but I have placed the case in the cold case drawer. It is always nice talking with both you and Arnold. I hope I never have to ride with him. Good day, Ms. O'Connor, and thank you for your time."

He is finishing his dessert as he gets up to leave.

Jennifer calls on the intercom, "Mr. Fleetly is ready to chat with you."

Bridget walks to the door to greet Mr. Fleetly. They shake hands. He already has a fresh cup of coffee.

Bridget says, "Please tell me why we are talking?"

Fleetly says, "Julien Spence and I have worked together before. He asked me if he came across some financial paperwork by McCarthy, could I accept it. I said, yes. If the paperwork turns out to be incriminating, we could use your firm in gaining control of all of McCarthy's assets."

Bridget says, "When we were hired by McCarthy to fend off the accusations by the city, we found identical copies of the accurate billings. I do believe you are safe in using them. Julien searched the payments sheets and said he thought they were all valid copies."

Fleetly says, "We feel safe and plan on using them as evidence."

Bridget says, "We hoped you would have confidence in our findings. Thank you for coming by to chat."

Mr. Fleetly grabbed his briefcase and walked out.

Bridget then calls Nick as Arnold.

"Hello, this is Nick."

Bridget says, "This is Arnold. I took the Jaguar out for a drive, and you did a beautiful job. The performance is definitely improved. The widening of the tire placement makes a difference in holding the roadway. The paint job is gorgeous, but the windshield appears different. Why is that."

Nick says, "You are always getting shot at from behind. What if the guy shooting is in front of you? After putting in the metal cage, I realized it doesn't protect you from the front. I installed some new metal on the firewall up to the windows. Then as a gift, I put in the bulletproof windshield. It will take up to a 30.6 round, and your vision won't be restricted. Merry Christmas."

She answers as Arnold, "Thank you, my friend, bye."

Bridget decides that she has stayed at the firm long enough for this day. She grabs her purse and coat, then walks out to the elevator. Whoever wants to talk to her can do it tomorrow.

Most of the vicious McCarthy operatives have been eliminated, so Bridget is reasonably relaxed as she is driving home. Old memories begin popping into her mind. Arnold's life started to fall apart when his parents were killed, and then to lose Alicia as well, was devastating. Unable to fight this army of operatives alone, both Arnold and Arnold, as Bridget, had to reach out to Matt, Sid, and bring in other staff and friends. Some friends and coworkers have died or disappeared. Even Arnold was forced to withdraw. But Bridget feels that even with the extreme measures that she has taken, it has been worth the fight.

It has been a total stroke of good fortune that Juliet has become a part of Arnold's life. Many people never find even one right partner in life. Arnold has a second wonderful woman. Back to being female, Bridget wonders if she should believe in angels when Juliet talks about Holley when Holley appears.

Arriving home, Bridget pours a glass of French port and turns on the TV while waiting for Juliet.

The newscasters are still commenting on the three sites that Matt hit. The problem is there was no significant evidence left behind. Even shell casings were missing. A couple of low-level contractors and McCarthy are missing. The FBI has begun confiscating all the McCarthy holdings. The newscaster mentioned that the investigators are also looking at seven cities scattered throughout the USA that

McCarthy had dealings with. The investigators are not finding much to work with. Most of the evidence generally found at scenes like these have a standard set of clues. These sites don't. Most of the evidence at these crime scenes point to McCarthy's illegal activities. Saving the lives of the prostitutes shows compassion and careful planning. So far, each of the victims identified has a lengthy criminal record and outstanding warrants. The weaponry used is easily found on the black market. A police spokesperson states that isolating this action to a particular group or type of group is only a collection of guesses.

Juliet arrives a little past six, and they are fixing dinner when the phone rings.

Bridget picks up the phone and says, "Hello, who's calling?"

The caller responds, "This is Matt on the run. It seems that everybody is looking for me, and my men have made so many boat trips today that it is beginning to look suspicious. We found Jason, and it took four of my men and a stun gun to take him down. Two of my guys had to go to the ER. I have both his arms and legs chained, but he is still dangerous. We have four more for a total of five passengers. Can you handle the last trip later tonight?"

Bridget says, "How can I refuse a guy like you. The fueling docks are closed, and I have no fuel cans, so bring twenty gallons of fuel when you meet me at the dock."

Matt says, "Arrive at the dock right at 9 p.m. The passengers will arrive in a work van, and the transfer must be completed in a matter of seconds. Bye,"

They hang up, and Bridget immediately calls Josey.

She says, "I need to make a last-minute boat trip tonight. Can you come along?"

Josey responds, "Bridget, I can't be seen with you tonight. Too many people are watching me. Sorry friend."

HIDDEN IN FRONT OF YOU

He hangs up. Bridget thinks that he is probably embarrassed. He always shows up when he can.

Bridget calls Sid, who answers, "Sid here."

Bridget says, "Can you watch the marina this evening from 8 p.m. onward?"

Sid replies, "I can because of that nice breakfast you made for me the other morning. I'll be at the marina and ready by 8 p.m."

Bridget says, "The plan is to have a quick exchange at 9 p.m. sharp."

They hang up.

Bridget looks at Juliet and says, "Josey is being watched, so I am going alone this evening."

Juliet says, "What about me going with you?"

Bridget says, "I don't think you should see what I have to do. It would create memories that you may not want to have. I would feel guilty of bringing you along.

Juliet replies, "In case you haven't noticed, my dear, I am a big girl. My Daddy worked for the CIA most of his life, so I know a little bit about their unusual activities. I have the CIA in my genes. I want to be with you in both good and bad times. So, there will be no more discussion about it, you are stuck with me as your second."

Bridget knows Juliet has made up her mind, so it's time to be quiet and finish making dinner.

They finish dinner around 7:45, and Juliet makes another pot of coffee for the thermos and puts some snacks into a bag for the boat trip. At 8:00, the girls lock up and take Juliet's car to the yacht club.

As Bridget expected, the boat needs about twenty gallons of fuel. Josey has left plenty of cement blocks and tie-down lines in the boat. While Juliet unties the mooring lines, Bridget starts the engines and begins to idle out to the public dock.

It is approaching 9 o'clock, and there are only a few vehicles in the parking lot. A car pulls up to the public dock area, but it's not Matt's people. It is the police patrol making their rounds checking for the homeless or any children out late. They do not notice Bridget's boat floating about 100 feet offshore. After they drive away, the headlights of a work van turn on, and the van drives from the parking lot to the dock.

Bridget drives the boat to the dock and ties off the back-mooring lines. One guy empties four five-gallon cans of gasoline into the fuel tank. The gauge now reads almost full. Several individuals help four regular-sized males to the boat. They put the men in front of the small cabin and inject each one with Demerol. Then all four of them literally carry a huge man onto the boat. He does seem to settle down after he is given a shot of Demerol.

One of Matt's contractors says, "This big guy took on four of our best men., and two of them are in the hospital emergency room as a result. We finally knocked him out with a stun gun and a baseball bat. Here are some needles containing Demerol. If he starts to move, either kill him or shoot him with these needles. Take no chances. He literally threw two of our 200-pound guys ten feet each. If he wakes, he will kick a hole in the side of the boat. We are finding a few more contractors than we anticipated, and we do not want the agencies to find any bodies. They could work backward from the evidence. Have a good trip, Finion."

The motors have been running long enough. Bridget idles out past the entrance and goes to 25 mph with the headlamps on. Juliet is dressed warm and able to stand next to Bridget on the way out.

Bridget says, "Never go close to Jason. Here is a 38-caliber. Keep it in your hand at all times. If at any time you feel threatened, shoot him with all six rounds. Stay well out of his reach. The chains may not hold him, and he is known to break handcuffs."

The waters are still relatively calm. Along with the partial moon and the headlamps, Bridget can avoid the larger debris. Jason is laying half on the back platform and on the main deck. Bridget asks Juliet to steer while she ties a cement block to Jason's ankles. They arrive at the north end of the Farallone Islands in about 90 minutes. Bridget slows to an idle, turns the left engine off after letting it cool down, turns the steering wheel to the left, and locks it in place. She turns on the running lights and runs the right engine at about 1500 rpms to keep the batteries charged via the generator. With the brightness of the lights, Bridget can finish her work.

Juliet is staying as far away from Jason as she can get. Bridget tries to decide the safest way of moving him into the water. If he is playing possum, he could pull her in with him even with his hands behind his back. The safest way is to put a bullet into his brain. Bridget fires one round from the 44 Magnum into his head. His body relaxes. He may have been waiting for Bridget to get close enough. It takes both Bridget and Juliet to move him to the rear portion of the back platform. Bridget has Juliet stay away as Bridget makes the final push. One at a time, Bridget pulls the others to the back platform. Bridget shoots each one in the head with the 38-caliber and then rolls them into the water.

Upon dumping the last body, Bridget sits down and pours herself and Juliet a cup of coffee.

Bridget says, "I have the feeling we are getting closer to the end of this war. If all goes well, sometime soon, we will be free to live our lives as we have intended."

Bridget starts the second engine, puts both gears handles into the forwarding position, and changes the steering wheel. The boat is pointing toward the Golden Gate.

Bridget says, "I hope that wasn't too bad. I have always

wanted to keep you from this event."

Juliet comes over next to Bridget and says, "Thank you. I can now understand some of the traumatic feelings you must have experienced on these trips."

She gives Bridget a big hug. The trip back to the yacht club is quiet for both. The outline of San Francisco projects a beautiful scene in the darkness. Within the hour, they are home taking showers and slipping in between the silk sheets.

HIDDEN IN FRONT OF YOU

53 - BRIDGET IS OUTED

They sleep in until 9 a.m and are not fully rested but functional. After finishing a light breakfast, Bridget pours a second cup of coffee and sit there chatting about this and that. They continue talking about things on their minds while appreciating their time together. The two are in harmony, enjoying each other's company.

Bridget calls Jennifer.

She answers, saying, "This is Jennifer, may I help you."

Bridget says, "Please tell the people on the lawsuit to finish what is important and take off for a holiday until Monday morning. That means you too, Mrs. Hastings. Let Matilda take your calls. Have a nice time."

Jennifer says, "Thank you, Ms. O'Connor, you are a dear."

Bridget says to Juliet, "We are going to lunch at a special restaurant. I am sure you will find it interesting. Let's plan to arrive there at about 1 p.m. That way, the crowd will have left, and there will be a full staff of waiters."

They both take their time preparing for the trip. Bridget does her extra things to retain the appearance of a female. They both pick dresses fitted just above the knee for shopping. Into the pink Mercedes, and they go south on Filbert to Divisadero, left onto Divisadero, right on Lombard to Gough, right on Gough to California, and left onto California. They drive past the Fairmont and Sir Francis Drake hotels to the bottom of the California Street hill. They turn into the parking garage of the Bank of America Building and drive two floors down into the parking garage where a young man is waiting to park their car.

After a few steps, they are standing in the elevator. Bridget pushes the button for the top floor. It is encased in glass so the occupants can see the view of the city as they ride to the top floor. The door opens, and there in front of them, is an elegant restaurant with each table offering a view of downtown San Francisco. Bridget asks the maître de' for a table viewing the bay waters, Telegraph Hill and Coit Tower. You can see most of the financial district buildings, most of Chinatown, the famous Italian restaurants, the charming Embarcadero with the large ships moored at the piers, and Telegraph Hill with the Coit Tower.

A waiter takes their order after describing the day's dishes. No prices or specials are ever mentioned. The maître de' keeps a close eye on the service and, in particular, the satisfaction of the customer. Their water, ordered drinks, bread, butter, etc. all are placed in their proper position. Soon after, the antipasti, salads, soups, and main dishes appear as well. The waiters are silent, efficient, and close by, but never noticed. You are never interrupted, spoken to, or asked a question. You are treated as an elegant guest. After Bridget or Juliet is done with a dish, it disappears.

Bridget hails the maître de' and says, "May we have some of your custard and a glass of green chartreuse, please?"

Throughout the lunch, Juliet is surprised at the service. She wonders how they get things refilled, placed, and served with such efficiency.

She waits until they are in the elevator to say, "I've never eaten in a place like that before. It's nothing like Ms. Brown's Hamburger Hut!"

Bridget says, "That is where the upper crust eats and entertains. You just had a $125 lunch."

They get in the car and drive up California to Stockton and over Stockton to Union Square, alias the downtown San Francisco shopping. All the large department stores are represented around the park. Specialty stores and jewelry shops are everywhere. They park in the underground Union Square parking area. For the remainder of the day, they shopped for Juliet. In most of the jewelry shops, Bridget is trying to find out what type of engagement ring to buy.

HIDDEN IN FRONT OF YOU

Juliet says, "Sorry to break up our wonderful time together, but it is time to pick up Alissa."

Bridget says, "Oh, good, I haven't seen her in quite a while. We should have taken her to lunch with us."

Bridget parks the Mercedes next to the school while Juliet runs in to get her. As Alissa and Juliet walk toward the car, Alissa has a devious type of smile on her face. Juliet and Alissa get into the Mercedes with Alissa sitting in the back.

Alissa says, "I have been playing with trig identities most of the day. Those students that have depended upon calculators are having a rough time of it. The whole thing is fairly trivial when you know how to manipulate fractions. What are you two up to today, anything we should discuss? You sure do hang out a lot with each other. The people at the office don't see how much."

Both Juliet and Bridget look at each other and wonder what she up to.

Alissa continues, "You had me stumped for a long time, but when you kept putting me in front of the TV. What do you think I was watching? I was watching you two of course, not the TV. Why am I getting pawned off on Grandpa so often? I saw the bullet holes in the green Jaguar. Why does Arnold's Jaguar keep getting replaced? Sometimes Bridget's driving behavior is just like Arnold's. Pure coincidence, I am sure. Why do you two do so much together? Mom, I am assuming you are not a lesbian, and you are not bisexual. Arnold does not have a cousin. Remember, birth records are open to the public. I have been there looking for the birth records connected to Sean Pierce. Not until she was needed, does Bridget come into existence."

"I will need my own car, some awesome jewelry, an increase in my allowance, and some new rules for when I am out on the town. It may be time to sit down for a friendly in-depth discussion. Neither one of you needs to say a word. I believe we call this "I gotcha." Bridget, I do have to tell you that you are good at being a woman. You have all of the feminine responses of a female, you walk like an elegant female, your reactions and hand movements are feminine. No one at the office has the slightest hint of what is going on, and that makes my case much more powerful. Maybe we three girls can go out together. Bridget, may I use some of your perfume?"

Both Bridget and Juliet are both squirming. Juliet is blushing, and Bridget is not saying a word. Arriving at Bridget's home, Bridget closes the garage door. Juliet is nervous while they walk to the kitchen. Alissa is dancing around because, for once, she has the upper hand. Bridget pours a glass of port for each one of them. Bridget sits at one end of the dinner table.

Bridget says, "Would you please inform us as to the facts as you see them?"

Alissa says, "The first inkling was Naomi. Yet that was only a surprise. I could not get comfortable with a female having the superior fighting skills you possess. The second was the guy in Alex's Gym that was arrested for carrying a gun while on parole. It was still a question. Your behavior in the office seemed normal and showed me nothing. The most obvious indicator is that Mom is here so often. I know you are fighting a war, and it is supportive of Mom to be so helpful. One that everyone should have caught was you, Bridget, speaking Italian in Arnold's favorite San Francisco restaurant. That was blatant. Those are the indicators that only slightly affected my thinking. And, Mom now tells Grandpa that she is nursing Arnold back to health."

"Mom's claim that she is using the second bedroom is false. This one is the big one. I put pennies in that bed with the cotton sheets, and they have not moved. Mom, you are sleeping between Bridget's silk sheets. The main reason for my decision, though, is the way you two act toward each other when you think no one is looking. I'm supposed to be watching the TV while you two are in the kitchen. How boring. The other is the additional affection shown when we leave. As judge, jury, and decision-maker, you are guilty. I don't hear any denials or pleads of innocence. You two are officially busted. The first thing I want is to go out together as girls. I do promise to keep this between us. I realize the danger you two face daily. Remember, we are family. I love you both."

Alissa continues, "Okay, Bridget, this is our little secret, but I have a favor to ask. In my opinion, your charity committee could be used to help someone and satisfying my selfish desire. There is a boy I like that's been having a rough time along with his father."

"His name is Otto, and his father's name is Joe Fleming. Otto and I were working on trig identities today. He is a very generous and kind person."

"They lost his mother to cancer. In trying to save her, the medical bills took all the funds Otto's parents had collected over the years. Joe's company went out of business, and he is unemployed. He has a contractor's license but no funds to get started. I request that we assist them. In addition to that, I want Otto as my boyfriend. We get along well, he is kind, and he is going somewhere in his personal life. We have a good relationship, and we do not argue".

"Joe and Otto are not in debt over the medical bills, but it did use up what funds they had. Joe could be one of your contractors for boat repairs, building repairs, and remodeling the Tiburon house, with Otto being his employee. They could work on your speedboat and Alicia. What do you say, Ms. O'Connor?"

Bridget says, "How long have you been working on this? You have it all planned so well. If they are as good as you believe they are, I would be more than happy to give them a try."

The doorbell rings. Bridget grabs her 38-caliber and walks to the front door. She opens the inside door, and there is the Alley Cat. He walks in.

Julien says, "I got the day off, and I have no granddaughter or daughter to visit with. I thought maybe they were at Cat Woman's home. What are you, three girls doing this evening? Bridget, I heard from Burke. He says the judge reviewed the case and agreed that Rita should be out soon. I also talked to Harriet. Once it is considered safe, she would like to return to the firm. She is not being watched anymore, and we are considering living together. That really makes Arnold a matchmaker."

Bridget says, "Let's find out if I am on call for tonight."

She calls Matt. The phone rings back in seconds. Matt says, "Hello, beautiful lady."

Bridget says, "Am I on call tonight?"

Matt says, "We got one today, but I can hide that one. We have some leads on a few more, but nothing for tonight."

Bridget says, "Okay, then we are going out for dinner. I'll be available later tonight if you have any more gifts. Bye."

Bridget hangs up the phone then says to the group, "Let's try Tommy's Joynt on Van Ness. It's classified as an official historical site, so it's always busy during regular hours. Since it's early, we could give it a try, or we could also go Italian."

Everybody chooses Italian.

Bridget says, "Let's dress up for this one. Miniskirts for all, except the Alley Cat."

Alissa has not completely filled out yet, so Bridget gives her some false boobs from the Finocchio's practice. She also tosses her a miniskirt she wore during the female practice sessions. Alissa gets to choose anything else she wants from Bridget's closet."

Alissa says, "Bridget, you don't seem to be as rattled as Mom."

Bridget says, "I am surprised it took you this long to figure it out."

Alissa says, "Well, the Naomi project has kept me very busy, and I had to make sure. I wanted to be correct if I was to say, "I gotcha."

Bridget smiles and says, "Thank you for being so respectful. This has not been easy."

While Julien is sitting there with an empty stomach, the girls are doing their nails, makeup, picking clothes and fixing their hair. Bridget calls for reservations. They walk out together with Julien, who is ready to go alone.

"Let's take the Pink Mercedes," says Bridget.

Everyone gets into the Mercedes. Bridget takes Lombard to Van Ness past Ghirardelli Square to Washington Park on Columbus Avenue at the base of the Coit Tower at Telegraph Hill. She finds a parking space almost immediately. They start walking fast, and they cross the streets with the three girls holding hands. Julien is right behind them. They walk past Filbert to the Italian restaurant that Bridget prefers. As soon as they enter, Bridget is talking in Italian with the maître de'. They are escorted to a large comfortable table near the rear of the restaurant. The girls give an extra wiggle as they pass through the crowd.

Bridget says, "Let me order."

She continues talking with the waiter in Italian. The waiter is enjoying himself while writing the list on his pad. Drinks are ordered, and the waiter doesn't question Alissa's age. The drinks are Martini's up with a green olive. Bridget also orders a couple of bottles of Italian Merlot.

The serving style is similar to the restaurant called Luigi's at the foot of Broadway in Oakland. The freshly baked sourdough bread comes with the antipasti, and dishes are placed for each diner along with a bowl of salad. That is followed by the large bowl of the soup of the day along with individual soup bowls. When everyone has had enough soup, all is cleared, and the new plates arrive for the ravioli and spaghetti. After they finish the ravioli and spaghetti, the main course is served hot from the kitchen. Bridget gives the nod for the third bottle of Merlot.

Juliet is telling Alissa and Julien about their day at the Bank of America Building for lunch and the shops they visited after lunch. Juliet was amazed that nothing was said to the waiters at the restaurant. Yet, things appeared in front of you as they should, and she told them that you could see most of downtown San Francisco from the dining table.

As Bridget is sipping her coffee, she asks Alissa, "Why are you taking trigonometry."

Alissa says, "I like mathematics. I seem to do well with math.

All my classes are honors classes. I have a 4.3 average in a 4.0 system. At school, I am considered sort of a nerdy student. I don't really care what the rest of the students think. It's their loss."

Everyone is beyond full, so they all request a takeout box for their desert.

Bridget pays the bill, and they all leave the restaurant. They head for Bridget's house. Tonight, thanks to the girls for inviting him and leaves. Alissa will be sleeping alone between the cotton sheets. Julien the leaves.

HIDDEN IN FRONT OF YOU

54 - $40,000 REWARD

The phone is ringing. Bridget's answers.

Bridget picks up the phone and hears Matt say, "We may have a bit of a problem. Troi has offered a $40,000 reward to four McCarthy leftovers for your head on a platter. Two of them followed you home from the restaurant, and Troi was about a block behind them in her mustang. I would not be surprised if they show up at your office tomorrow."

He continues, "The reward includes both you and Arnold, but only these four have received the reward offer because they are so bold. Troi doesn't have many more to count on anymore. We have gotten rid of most of them. Troi would be a prize for you, darling."

Bridget says, "I hope you are backing me up tomorrow."

Matt replies, "As always, my dear. Sweet dreams, bye."

Bridget looks at Juliet and says, "Tomorrow, we start on the lawsuit again. Fish wants an 8 a.m. to 3 p.m. schedule. The mayor has pushed forward the demotions of the department heads combined with forced retirements. Fish has announced that any officer not following the new procedures to the letter, will be terminated. I can see our lawsuit success on the horizon."

Bridget calls Sid, and he answers, "Sid here."

Bridget says, "I need a lookout on tomorrow morning at the firm. Can you be that lookout and stay in touch with me by radio?"

Sid says, "Sounds like wartime to me. Sure, I'll be there, anything to protect my daughter and those wonderful meals. See you at the office before 8 o'clock, bye."

Juliet asks, "Now what about these new combatants."

Bridget says, "I almost want you to stay home. I am thinking the worst is going to happen. Let's talk later."

Bridget calls Josey, and he answers, "Hello, this is Josey."

Bridget says, "If the agencies are through watching you, I

could use your help tomorrow morning at the firm."

Josey says, "I am clear. My alibis and behavior, plus all the interviews, have taken the pressure off me. None of the agencies believe I had anything to do with Matt's extermination. But they sure want him. Yes, I am available."

Bridget says, "Tomorrow morning, bring weapons with silencers, and roam around outside the firm to see who may be there. At 7:45 a.m., call Jennifer and tell her you are coming up the back stairs. I believe we are going to get some serious visitors Monday afternoon. We will be meeting all day with the Police department heads. We really shook up the Police Department, and everything is different now. I suspect some left-over McCarthy contractors will try to hit us after the police personnel has left at around 3 p.m. It will be great working with you again. I almost forgot, bring some radios. See you tomorrow morning."

Bridget calls Julien, and he answers, "Hello, this is Julien."

Bridget says, "Do any of your guns have silencers?"

Julien says, "None of mine have silencers."

She says, "I'll bring a few extras tomorrow. I have information that suggests we are getting hit tomorrow. Get to the office early so we can map out our strategy. I want to set a trap and extermination. Do not put up the metal detector. It would warn them. Matt and his folks will be in the area to assist, and I have also asked Sid and Josey to be at the office before 8 o'clock. These contractors are supposed to be bold and deadly. They will most likely threaten to kill the entire staff. There is a $40,000 reward on Arnold and sweet little ole me. If it hadn't been for Matt, they would have caught us in the blind. See you early, Julien, goodnight."

Juliet says, "Why am I safer here?"

Bridget replies, "Because of our dangerous visitors. If you must go to the office, then stay in Julien's office or in one of the vacant offices in the back. I suspect that they are coming

HIDDEN IN FRONT OF YOU

armed and expecting to force Arnold's presence. I personally want all four in my office."

Bridget says, "Let's go to bed early tonight. We may need to be there before 7 a.m. We can live off the caterer's food."

The home is quiet and peaceful, which allows them to relax. The active day has exhausted them both. They go off to bed and fall asleep almost immediately. They lay there intertwined and sleep through the night.

The typical bay area weather is again pleasant. Long before the sunrise, Bridget is lying awake between the silk sheets. She is enjoying Juliet's presence while she continues going over possible events for the coming day. The visitors are going to use brutality. It is doubtful that they will be there to negotiate.

Bridget and Juliet prepare for the day. Juliet wears a full dress with her hair hanging past her shoulders. Bridget combs her hair into a bun, puts on a sexy pink blouse and tight dark grey pants with tennis shoes. She chooses the silver jewelry with a long chain for earrings. For today, the brighter lipstick fits her inner feelings. Everything she is wearing gives her flexibility. She thinks maybe she can kick some ass today.

Bridget prefers the Jaguar today. Out of the garage doors, they go. There is a set of operatives, and they follow her to Lombard and across the bridge. There is a truck stop before the Richmond bridge off-ramp. She puts the pedal to the firewall and leaves the operatives' vehicle behind. At a truck stop, she pulls in behind a truck to hide her position. As the McCarthy operatives pass the truck stop, she comes out from behind the semi-truck, and she starts to follow them. Bridget is still behind them as they are driving along the auto row coming into San Rafael. Juliet thinks that Bridget is wound up today and will not be surprised if Bridget kills someone.

The operatives park across the street from the firm where Troi generally parks. It appears that there are three individuals in the car Bridget pulls the Jaguar into Arnold's space, writes down the license number, and then updates her lipstick. Both Bridget and Juliet get out of the Jaguar together and enter the elevator.

On the way up to the twelfth floor, Bridget says, "Please stay safe today. I am ready for just about anything. I am as nervous as a cat on a hot tin roof."

They walk by Matilda saying hello, and Bridget walks past Jennifer's desk to her office, and Juliet walks on to Julien's office.

Julien says, "Good morning."

Juliet says, "Bridget did not let me drive to work alone this morning. We had operatives following us. Here is your pistol with an extra box of shells. It is a 38-caliber with a silencer. Bridget wants to meet with both you and Jennifer asap."

When Jennifer arrives, she tells Bridget, "Two men want to meet with you at 4 p.m. I told them you would not be available until after 3 p.m."

When Julien arrives, the three of them sit down in Bridget's office to formulate their plan.

Bridget says, "The heavy stuff will not start until around 4 p.m. There is a $40,000 reward for Arnold and lil ole me that was offered to a group of four operatives. Two are coming here today at 4 p.m. I believe the other two will be outside waiting."

"Troi, as she now calls herself, was McCarthy's girlfriend. She may be with them. Her rise to fame is through lying, being deceptive, and probably her many assassinations. I plan to exterminate them in my office if necessary."

Jennifer, you need to discontinue the janitorial service for a few days. Tell them it is because of the sensitive information in the lawsuit. If blood is spilled, we will replace

HIDDEN IN FRONT OF YOU

the carpet and scrub the floors with plenty of Coca Cola."

"Jennifer, I do not want you in this office when they are present. All four or five of these people are dangerous lowlifes."

"Julien, this is war, and service comes first. I will take the lead. If there is any doubt, kill first."

The department heads show up on time. Bridget starts the day with a short introduction.

Bridget says, "Our attorneys have much of the work already in document form. I suggest that you first read these drafts then start your discussions. One generalized approach is words like may, should, hope to, etc., are all replaced by shall. These are department-wide directives. We will succeed if we give the courts the proper descriptions and support to work with. Please keep this in mind. The officer in charge of transmitting the appropriate data determines the outcome."

Each group forms and goes to their assigned rooms. Bridget and Mr. Fish have already reviewed each other's writings and are in very close to alignment.

Bridget finds Mr. Little.

She says, "What is your take on our progress? Our attorneys are much better prepared, and everyone has a positive attitude. When I visit each working group, I am finding real compatibility, and the progress of the different groups is considerable. Do you have your article prepared for tomorrow?"

Mr. Little says, "Activity is looking up now. People appear more productive. I have the data in my head so far. I'll have it in written form by 2 p.m. See you then."

At 2 p.m., Bridget makes only minor changes and asks, "Mr. Little, please give Mr. Fish a little more credit for his leadership. You may now announce the demotions and forced retirements. Give them hell."

By 3 p.m., most of the department heads have left.

Bridget takes Josey, Julien, Jennifer, and Juliet into the conference room that is equipped with the recording devices. None of the groups have been using this room. It is perfect for the 4 p.m. meeting.

Bridget says, "Juliet, I would like to have you in the recording room. No matter what happens, that is the only place where I want you to be. Have a radio with you, and have the speaking volume turned off. Take the smaller 32-caliber pistol with a silencer, lock the door, turn the lighting down, and stay out of sight."

"Josey, you're carrying a 38-caliber with a silencer. Get a key for that room so you can come and go. Make room for Sam, from Matt's group to accompany you wherever you are. Sam will be armed with a silencer. Make sure he sees all that is going on. Use either the phone or radio to communicate with me. I may call you to come to or into the conference room.

Bridget continues, "Jennifer, I want you to set up coffee and eats outside the conference room. Sit at a desk near Matilda and watch for Matt. Direct him to this conference room. Knock if the door is closed. Do not come into the room, stay away from these people, and stay out of sight."

"Okay, I think we are set, let us wait for their arrival."

They don't need to wait very long. Two men walk out of the elevator at 3:45 p.m. Matilda welcomes them and escorts them to Jennifer's desk.

One guy says, "We are here to see Ms. O'Connor."

Jennifer walks them to the conference room and says, "We have fresh coffee and some pasties. Make yourselves at home, gentlemen."

Bridget is sitting in the middle of the long table with paperwork spread out.

She puts the paperwork into one folder and says, "Who am I talking to? What is your business?"

One of the men says, "I am Blue, and this is Red."

Bridget says, "So you are a Democrat, and he is a Republican?"

The guy says, "We are not here to joke. We want to meet with both Bridget and Arnold. If that is not possible, then we are prepared to start killing your staff."

Bridget says, "Here I am, and Arnold can be made available if needed. It will take a few minutes since he is still recovering from his accident. You don't need to get angry."

The phone rings before they get started.

Bridget answers saying, "Hello, this is Bridget."

Matt says, "You have two arrogant assholes in your conference room right now. We are bringing three more, including Ms. Troi, to your party."

Bridget says to Matt, "Thank you, sweetheart, for calling. It appears that I will be busy for a little while. Come make yourself at home. You might be able to help me."

The call is followed by Sid checking in with the same information. Bridget makes a call to the recording room.

She hears a whispered, "Hello."

Bridget's reply is, "Hi Josey, will you get Arnold up and bring him into the conference room?"

Jennifer calls, "Bridget, Matt has three people in handcuffs. What should I do with them?"

Bridget says, "Send them in when Josey and Julien bring Arnold to the conference room. Now please do what I asked you to do."

Red and Blue are stifled by the relaxed attitude of Bridget and their hope to get at Arnold.

Bridget has two 38-caliber pistols with silencers hanging under the table.

Bridget says, "Why don't you two just sit down. Things will work out."

They sit down, but they are acting uneasy. Someone

knocks on the door.

Bridget says, "Wait a minute, please."

She grabs both pistols.

Bridget says, "Now gentlemen, how do you want it to happen. My fingers are already on the triggers. These are 38-caliber pistols. Take all of your weapons out slowly with your fingers and drop them on the floor. Kick them over my way."

Bridget yells, "Okay, guys, come on in."

Matt and Sam walk the three around the backside of Bridget over to the far seats. Matt and Sam keep an eye on the three.

Bridget says, "Josey set your weapon on the table over here and pick up those on the floor. Check Mr. Blue, the one on the left first."

Josey finds two more handguns."

Bridget says, "You're missing the knife on his back near his neck and check his crotch."

Matt tosses Josey, a set of handcuffs.

Josey checks Red the same way until he gets to Troi. All five are handcuffed and quiet. Bridget first goes through Troi's purse.

Bridget says, "Forty-thousand dollars. Why carry so much? Oh, I see why. All the serial numbers are the same. Isn't that called counterfeiting?"

As Bridget runs her hands over Troi's body, she finds multiple guns and two knives. She then remembers that this girl is devious and dangerous. Bridget runs her fingers around her crotch and then slips her fingers into Troi's crotch. Something does not feel right.

Bridget runs her fingers into Troi's vagina. Bridget finds a five-shot 32-caliber pistol.

Bridget checks her clothing, finding two choke wires used for assassinations. This infuriates Bridget.

HIDDEN IN FRONT OF YOU

She turns with a scowl on her face and says, "Has everyone gone home?"

Julien checks and says, "Yes, everyone has gone."

Bridget can't help herself.

She says, "Josey, if Troi runs, kill her."

Bridget goes over to Troi and starts to release the handcuffs.

A firm set of hands stops her by grabbing her arms. It is from Matt.

He says, "You are not ready for this. Let me show you."

He pushes Troi forward and kicks her feet backward. She falls directly on her face. Matt drops on one knee, which is placed in the center of Troi's back. He pulls out the sharp-edged blades built into her boots. Then he turns to her head and pulls out several needles, which may or may not be poisonous.

Matt says, "I have not trained you for this. You are in over your head."

Bridget backs off and says, "Thank you, my friend. I was about to put myself in harm's way. She must be one of Kevin's most proficient assassins."

Matt finds several more needles in her hair. Josey brings some pliers to the conference room so Matt can break the knives off. Sam is backing Josey up throughout each event.

Matt says, "That is why she never needed a backup. I'll bet many people were surprised then quickly died."

Matt then walks up to Bridget and says, "Sometimes you have to let that anger out, but not right now. Perhaps, sweet lady, when you take a cruise later tonight."

Matt, Sam and his crew walk the five out to the elevator.

Bridget says, "Josey, I need to talk to you privately."

They both go into David's vacant office and close the door.

Juliet runs in, saying, "Bridget, you were brilliant and

operated with nerves of steel. They thought they had you, and you had them the whole time. Other than Jason, those five were the most dangerous people I have ever seen."

The firm's crew locks the office, and Bridget and Juliet head for home. Bridget's driving this evening is subdued. The anxiety and aggressiveness have left. Even Sergeant Brown would enjoy this ride.

On their way home, Bridget says, "Both Kevin and Troi were in Ireland together and dished out extreme brutality. Troi was always around McCarthy's periphery watching. I am starting to assume that she monitored the behavior and associations of the operatives. She most likely had a lot to do with creating the accident in my driveway since I would always win on the open road. If Nick had not installed the metal protection, I would have been killed on several occasions. After being hit twice, the inside of the metal shell was still intact. Within hours they attempted to assassinate me again while I was in the hospital. Julien and Josey got me out of there just in time. These guys today were moments away from starting to kill our entire staff. I may have looked composed, but I was really getting ready to start killing them first."

When they drive onto Filbert Street, there are no operatives visible. Both Bridget's and Sid's houses look clear. Bridget pulls into the garage and pulls out her 44 Magnum. Bridget has Juliet stay in the Jaguar then climbs the stairs by herself. Within a few minutes, she comes out and motions for Juliet to come in.

They plan dinner and some relaxing time before Juliet must take Bridget to the marina.

Bridget calls Sid.

He answers, "Sid here."

Bridget says, "Thank you for being there today. I almost killed five people right there in the office."

HIDDEN IN FRONT OF YOU

Sid says, "Everyone said you handled it well. I also heard that Matt saved your ass toward the end. I like the fact that we are working as a family. Goodnight, my daughter."

The phone rings.

Bridget answers, "Hello, this is Bridget."

Josey says, "I checked the boat. Everything is in order. All we need is fuel. See you there at about 8:30 p.m. bye."

Bridget thinks, "How could we have succeeded without that wonderful man?"

Bridget and Juliet fix dinner together and have a pleasant early evening. From what she saw today, Juliet feels fortunate to have Bridget still with her. At 7:30 p.m., they start preparing for the cruise.

The winds are up, and there is a full moon. The boat may need to stay under 25 mph for the entire trip. Bridget has her warm clothes on and is carrying her conventional weaponry.

They take Juliet's car and drive straight to the marina. There is activity at the public dock. Juliet parks near the boat berth and walks out, carrying the food and drinks. The fuel has been loaded. The five passengers are there, and Josey is waiting for them with his pistol in hand. They check the radios then Juliet walks back to her car escorted by Bridget. Once Juliet is safely on her way, Bridget returns to the boat.

The engines are already running, the gauges check out, and all of the lights are functioning. Josey and Sam untie the mooring lines while Josey starts to idle the boat into the marina lagoon and then onto the open Bay waters. Josey waves goodbye.

Bridget says to Sam, "What did you think of today? Did you know any of those four guys?"

Sam says, "It is my understanding that they are recent imports from McCarthy's old Irish Mafia group. Real mean bastards. They were prepared to kill the entire office staff. I don't know their names or have any other information about them. There are still two more operatives that work as a team, but they are independent of the rest of the group. I heard some discussion about them from Matt."

When Bridget reviews her earlier mistakes today, she is angry with herself. This is a dangerous game she is playing and can never make that type of error in the future. She is still blessed with her many successes in other confrontations.

They are getting closer to the Farallones, and both Sam and Bridget are anxious to finalize this trip and get back safely. This is the roughest the water has been to date. The boat is stable because Bridget is busy picking different paths through the waves. The strong winds have raised the waves up to at least six feet. This is not the safest environment for this small of a boat.

Bridget slows the speed to 15 mph for safety. They arrive just north of the Farallones thirty minutes later. This trip is taking much longer than usual. Bridget stays at the helm, steering the boat with caution. Sam has already tied the cement blocks to each passenger's feet.

Locking the boat steering in a left circle would be asking for trouble, so Bridget leaves both engines running and makes a slow turn through the giant waves. She turns all lights on and continues steering in a full circle by hand.

Bridget asks Sam to unload the four male passengers and Troi. Sam tries to wake Troi, but she is out cold. He throws her over the back platform into the water. For the remaining four, Sam takes one man at a time and pushes him over the edge of the back platform.

After Sam finishes, Bridget points the boat toward the bridge and runs the engines just above an idle. He pours their coffee and gets out a tasty pastry.

Bridget says, "When this started, I thought I could discourage them by being elusive. When you count the number of individuals that we have killed, the number is well above fifty, not counting the extermination this last week. That was a small army. Both Red and Blue intended to kill our entire staff today. I was maxed out when I was dealing with them. I almost pulled the triggers on both. We have two more contractors with an intention to kill as many as possible. They are going to be much more difficult to deal with. Do you know what these next two looks like? Any hint to their names?"

Sam says, "I have no clue. I'll start looking around."

Bridget says, "We should look close by. Let's start back."

They have finished their coffee and are ready to start the return trip. Maneuvering during the return trip is much more difficult. Traveling in the same direction as the wind increases the danger. The distance between waves is more significant because they are going in the same direction as the waves. The wind has increased. Bridget reduces the speed to stay in control. The full moon and bow headlamps are still helping. The increase in the size of the waves is making it more challenging to navigate around any debris. Fortunately, the wind tends to eliminate much of the rubble by pushing it onto the shoreline. As they approach the Golden Gate, they both feel relieved to have avoided the numerous pieces of debris as large as a full-grown tree. Bridget turns a little to the right as the boat comes alongside the Presidio.

He calls on the radio to Juliet. Juliet now knows to pick her up. By the time Juliet walks up to the boat, it is closed, locked, and rinsed off. Both Bridget and Sam are ready to go, and they walk toward Juliet's car. They keep looking for contractors but see none.

Sam says, "Tonight, was a little bumpy yet we made it. While being careful, we need to keep an eye out for any pair of guys that are new in town. I don't think they will maintain a shallow profile, and I'll do the same."

Juliet says, "I have seen a suspicious car with two occupants. It appeared, and then, within moments, it was gone. I talked to Sid, and he said, that's how it has been all day."

Bridget comments, "They are most likely going to become a part of our daily lives. This will allow them to get close to us. People like a worker at the market, a waiter at the restaurant, or a mechanic at the gas station. This way, they will not stand out like so many we have eliminated."

The street is empty as they pull into the garage. Bridget starts thinking of her approach. A plan must be in place by the time Arnold comes back. Juliet has food ready for all three with a little extra if the leech shows up. Bridget starts explaining that the trips to the Farallones, the personal attacks, the constant pressure, the responsibility for the staff have made her feel very depressed. They finish their meal, and Bridget offers to drive Sam home in the Jaguar.

As they pull out of the garage, there is a black 911 parked on Filbert. She drives towards the 911, which is headed in the other direction. Bridget pushes the gas pedal down and flies by the parked car, turning left onto Lyon, she parallels the Presidio in a westward direction. Bridget turns off the tail and brake lights and loses the 911 within six blocks. She parks in Sam's driveway turns off the headlights while leaving the motor running.

Bridget says, "I think it's safe. Goodnight, Sam. See ya soon."

Sam gets out of the car, and Bridget drives away.

Bridget has an uneventful ride home, and Juliet is waiting for her with some coffee and pastries.

While sipping her coffee, Bridget says, "I am pleased with what we have done. Almost all the McCarthy contractors are gone. When this started, I thought being elusive and sometimes deadly in my response would send them on their way. But they kept coming and with improved scenarios. I fought Sid About this female impersonation until there was no choice. Sid had proposed the impersonation many months earlier. By getting me in my own driveway, I was finally convinced that another approach was necessary. I had run out of options. Implementing this female impersonation has given us time and helped to protect the staff. This kept the McCarthy Group at bay simply because the sole owner of the firm was unavailable. This last attack was without caution. Troi and her group had run out of options. We have verified that most of the would-be contractors have run to other places or have been eliminated. These last two new ones have time to spare. They must be confident planners. They stay out of the way while blending in. I did take these two for a little ride before letting Sam off at his place. I lost them within six blocks. I will need to use my imagination to flush them out. I must identify them before they act. If the firm's staff ignores them on the surface and go about our business as if we are safe, these operatives may relax and become a little careless. I am having trouble shutting off my mind. I'll make some changes tomorrow."

They prep for bed then climb between the silk sheets. Within minutes they are intertwined for the night.

The morning seems to come too early. Both would prefer to sleep in. There is no fog, just the continued westerly's and some heavy looking clouds on the western horizon. They choose their clothes for the day, shower, and apply their makeup. They both say it is easier to live off the caterer's menu, so breakfast will be at the office. Bridget takes the pink Mercedes, and Juliet takes her car. This morning it is just driving to work. The department heads are going to be there. Bridget pulls into her space and does the usual updating of her lipstick. They say nothing to each other on the way up to the twelfth floor.

Matilda says, "You two look rather relaxed this morning. Mr. Fish is waiting for you, Ms. O'Connor."

She walks directly into her office, and Mr. Fish follows her into the office. Jennifer brings in some fresh coffee. They sit down to discuss the documents they each have taken home for review. They are both somewhat amazed that their approaches are close enough to be merged and finalized.

Mr. Fish says, "I have a favor to ask. Could Jennifer rotate into your office each of your staff members so I may ask them some evaluation questions? I have some reservations about a couple of the new department heads I have chosen. I would like a second opinion."

Bridget calls Jennifer in and says, "Mr. Fish has a request. Would you please follow his directions? I will be in Julien's office."

Mr. Fish describes his request, and Jennifer is right on it. Within minutes the first staff member is in Bridget's office meeting with Mr. Fish.

Bridget says to Jennifer, "Talk to your friend from the house cleaning service. I need complete background information on each employee, including pictures. Please ask him to keep this information confidential."

HIDDEN IN FRONT OF YOU

55 - MIKEY GETS A JOB

Bridget decides to check out the restaurant in Tiburon, where she plans to hold the wedding reception. As she heads back to the 101-freeway southbound, Bridget is wondering if her guess is valid. Having the wedding reception at the restaurant to Alicia seems like the location of opportunity for an assassin. Alicia is right there, and Arnold will be there, so the restaurant would make a perfect site. The building's second story has an inline sight of Alicia.

As Bridget arrives at the restaurant, she scans the structure. She can see the roof along the edge facing Alicia except for the last ten feet. She walks around to the back of the restaurant then up a set of outside stairs. There is a place to sit, but there is no physical protection for a shooter. She finds a rifle stuffed behind some tar paper. It is a 30.6 caliber scoped rifle with a six-round magazine. Bridget alters the sighting adjustments using a cloth handkerchief, then puts it back where she found it and walks downstairs to the restaurant.

Bridget says to Harold, the restaurant maître de', "I would like to have a private conversation. We are still planning to have Arnold's wedding celebration here. We have had some difficulties at some of our recent gatherings. Do you research your employees by completing a background check?"

Harold, the maître de' says, "No, we found it impossible to maintain because of the high turnover. But we do attempt to keep a close eye on their behavior and verify their personal data. We just hired two that are working out well. We didn't need to train them. They have been efficient and polite to the customers. I do have several sets of pictures that we take when they interview. You are welcome to one of those. I agree that we should keep this confidential. If you schedule the event in the afternoon, our normal staff will be sufficient."

Bridget says, "Thank you for your cooperation."

Leaving Tiburon, she waves at the patrol officer but doesn't see Sergeant Brown. She uses the same route she did with Sergeant Brown but stays with the traffic. On her return, her guess seems more promising.

Back in the office, she calls Matt.

Bridget says, "I have a hunch, some data, and some pictures for you to review. When can we get together?"

Matt replies, "Tonight my beautiful girl, for one of those wonderful dinners. Open your garage door at about 7 p.m. See you then."

Bridget goes to Claire's office.

She says to Mikey, "Your work is almost completed with the lawsuit case. I feel like you have shown some good qualities, and we all appreciate that. I have a special assignment for you. Have you ever worked in a restaurant?"

Mikey says, "A couple of years ago, I worked in a small restaurant in downtown San Francisco. I washed dishes at first, then I was the cashier, and finally, they let me wait tables. It was sort of a unique place. They were busy from about 7:30 until just after lunch. There would be people standing outside waiting to get in by 6:30. It never had an empty seat. I left because the building was torn down."

Bridget says, "Your information on the warehouse did us a big favor. Your maturity level seems perfect for handling a special assignment. Are you up for that?"

Mikey says, "I'll do whatever you want. Appreciation runs in both directions."

Bridget says, "I want you to work at a certain restaurant. While you are there, I want you to be unnoticed. Do not get to know the waiters and get back to me with any intel you pick up. This is very confidential. People's lives will depend upon you."

Bridget walks to Julien's office and turning to Juliet, she

HIDDEN IN FRONT OF YOU

says, "Juliet, how is your day going? Is the collection of data coming together as we first thought?"

Juliet replies, "For most of the groups it is. I have a couple of groups that aren't."

Bridget says, "I'll be back."

She walks into her office. Mr. Fish is almost done with an interview, so she waits.

When the staff member leaves, she says, "I have some additional information for you. When do you want to receive it?"

Mr. Fish says, "I have interviewed all of your staff on this lawsuit issue, so now would be a good time."

Bridget says, "Be right back."

Bridget walks over to Juliet and says, "Please come with me."

They walk back to Bridget's office.

Bridget says, "Mr. Fish, this is Juliet. She is in charge of creating a cross-reference checking system for the court action. You may want to interview her about the cooperation from within each group."

Bridget leaves the two to share their information. Mr. Fish forgot to get back with Bridget before he walked out. Bridget realizes he is under so much pressure.

Bridget says, "Jennifer, please get Harold on the line. He is the maître de' at the restaurant in Tiburon."

Harold is on the phone within a few minutes.

Bridget says, "Harold, thank you for speaking with me. I have a candidate in our young adult program that is looking for a trainee position as a cook."

"He is a relatively new candidate and is proving himself very well. We will take on medical insurance and his uniform. He will work for minimum wage. Would you be interested in him coming to work for you?"

Harold replies, "With your recommendation and

assistance, we would be pleased to help him move along. Have him come in for an interview next Monday at about 10 a.m. Have him bring a resume and a couple of checkable references."

Bridget says, "Thank you, Harold. I look forward to working with you."

Bridget walks to Claire's office.

Addressing Mikey, she says, "You have an interview for a cook trainee at the Tiburon Restaurant. Have Jennifer assist you in preparing a resume and have both David Worth and Julien Spence write you a letter of recommendation."

"This assignment gives you two things. One is exposure to a restaurant environment. Second is an assignment for us. After you get the position, I will instruct you in the second part of the assignment. This must be kept confidential."

Mikey says, "I think I understand. There is some danger associated with it?"

Bridget says, "Yes, for all of us. I need you to do one critical thing. Let it be known that after a week or so following the going away barbeque for Bridget, you are finally going to meet Arnold Pierce. I'll give you more specifics later. I'll talk to you after your interview."

Bridget walks back to her office. Mr. Fish has finished his interview with Juliet and has left for the day, but Juliet is still sitting in the office.

Bridget says, "I had a hunch this morning. I have things going on to validate my hunch. Matt is coming for dinner to discuss the next step. What are your plans for this evening? Maybe you could join us?"

Juliet says, "Today I pick up Alissa; then I am available. My father is getting suspicious. So far, I have blamed my seeing Arnold. Should I get mad at Arnold for that?"

Bridget says, "That may hurt his feelings. You know how sensitive a man's ego is. The other day Julien asked me if I thought Arnold was going to marry you. I asked him if bears live in the forest. See you at the house."

Bridget drives home with no incident. It is always comfortable driving against the commute traffic. It's also comfortable not to have someone following you. When Bridget arrives home, she notices Sid is cleaning his yard.

Bridget asks, "Is my yard next?"

Sid answers, "Silly girl."

Bridget enters her home and relaxes with a glass of French port and Beethoven's Melody of Tears as she waits for Juliet. Within twenty minutes, Juliet is letting herself into the garage. They both go off to change for dinner, brush their teeth, and wash their hands.

As usual, Bridget has over purchased the food. Throwing dinner together is mostly grabbing leftovers. Within minutes they have dinner ready. Matt will arrive in a few minutes, so everything is prepared. Just before 7 p.m., Bridget opens the garage door. She stands at the top of the stairs waiting to close the garage door. Once Matt is inside, she closes the garage door.

Matt asks to use the men's room. Bridget directs him to her bathroom.

As he returns, he says, "Silk sheets. Now you really have turned feminine. What sort of items do you have for me today?"

Bridget replies, "The music, the food, and the quietness of the evening. There is no ice cream and no pie tonight but plenty of liqueurs and coffee for dessert."

Bridget continues, "I know where to find the last two contractors. I have pictures, I can partially control the environment, and I even found their rifle. Also, my mole will be in there with these two by next week."

"I based my analysis upon the track record. Remember how you taught me to evaluate the opponent. Are you finished with your dinner yet, ole Speedy Gonzales?"

He is not finished.

Bridget says, "I am not waiting for you, Gonzales. Just keep eating. They know where some of my homes are. They know about Alicia and where it is moored. They know of the pink Mercedes, and as soon as Arnold comes back, they will know about the white Jaguar. They know that Alicia will be a prime spot for gatherings, group sailings, and Arnold's personal trips. They are patient, so time is not their issue. They must be here for bigger things than Arnold. Waiting for Arnold to appear gives them time to lay low. McCarthy has probably paid them a bundle to take Arnold out while they are here."

Matt says, "They are supposed to be two of the most skilled assassins in Ireland. They arrived well over a week ago, and we haven't found them yet. We do not even know what type of car they are driving. We have found nothing."

Bridget says, "This afternoon, I had one of those gut feelings we all get on occasion. In my case, everything pointed to the same thing."

Bridget throws the folder of pictures and personal identification from The Tiburon Restaurant on the table in front of Matt.

Matt reviews each picture and yells, "You son of a bitch. These two are the assassins that were sent here to kill the Irish representative. Their names are Logan Malone and Garrett Hogan."

Bridget says, "I have more. Here is the car they drive. It is a black 911. They are waiters at The Tiburon Restaurant. The maître de' says they are doing a great job, and they are quite well blended in with the locals."

"I found their scoped 30.6 and reset the scope sighting adjustments. I will be getting my intel from my mole by next week."

HIDDEN IN FRONT OF YOU

"I have decided not to follow them because it may alert them. We must sit and wait for the right moment."

"I shall be a part of taking these two out. Matt, do these two know you?"

Matt says, "Oh, yes, they know me. They observed me killing the rest of their group. I have a few within my group that they would not know. I'll let you manage this one, Sweetheart. You seem to have a handle on it already. Do you have a plan started?"

Bridget says, "Yes, Gonzales, I have one in the works. My thoughts place my finger on the trigger as we speak. Arnold must return before my plan can go into action."

Matt says, "I believe you are on the right path. You did an excellent job gathering the information. Let me review the plan, the strategy, number of people involved, the number of my people that will be needed, and the timing before you kick this into gear. You will need to kill both of them. That will reduce the mafia's need to send replacements because of public opinion. Have Mr. Little leak it to the front page of the Chronicle. That way, word will get out on the main news. These two were sent here to kill the Irish representative that information they don't want to be known. Like I said before, I wish you were on my team. I must leave; it is getting late. I had a wonderful dinner. Thank you."

Bridget opens the garage door, and he is on his way. The three girls quickly have the kitchen cleaned with everything put away. Juliet and Alissa give Bridget hugs and kisses before driving away. Bridget is left alone once again. The silk sheets are not the same without Juliet.

56 - WRAPPING UP THE LAWSUIT

The next morning Bridget feels relaxed and productive. Operations at the firm are now almost back to calm. It is an active group with an increase in the number of clients. Each day is like working with a happy family. Time seems to pleasantly fly by each day. One thing after another is accomplished without working at it. It feels like playing. To Bridget, the days look like fun again. But Bridget still has a few things to tidy up. She decides to start driving the Jaguar and ask Juliet to drive the Pink Mercedes. It will take some time behind the wheel to get her old driving skills back again.

It is getting close to the time Bridget can be replaced with Arnold, but Bridget still does her entire prep for the day as a female. She chooses a navy-blue knee-high suit with black nylons, silver jewelry, V-neck blouse with ruffles, and matching blue two-inch heels. Soon she can go back to wearing male clothing and feel like himself.

Bridget warms up the Jaguar. It's another typical San Francisco morning, bright with the usual fog. The winds are variable, and the temperature is moderate due to the ocean's influence. The light on Lombard turns green, and away she goes.

This morning she brings along a set of flat shoes for driving. Bridget wants to prepare for that next exciting ride. You never know when that thrilling ride will offer you the opportunity to exercise your abilities. She is driving a little faster than she does with the Mercedes. As she crosses the Golden Gate, the smell of the fog is pleasant. Bridget is in the fast lane., and she is pushing the speed to 10 mph over the posted limit waiting for a moment when she can push the pedal to the floor. Arriving in San Rafael, Bridget slides into the parking spot. Makeup check, some lipstick update, and put her heels on then off she goes for the elevator.

Bridget walks into the main lobby.

HIDDEN IN FRONT OF YOU

Matilda says, "My, you look happy today."

Bridget says, "It is going to be a nice day. Good morning Matilda."

As Bridget approaches Jennifer's desk, Jennifer looks up, saying, "You look on top of the world today. I like your suit."

Bridget says, "You can have it after I leave for Vietnam. I'll be leaving soon, and I can't take any of my wardrobes with me."

Jennifer's face lights up in a smile.

Bridget steps into her office. Mr. Fish is waiting for her.

He says, "I have marked up your version, and I believe we are close. I think we can finalize our procedures this week, but I must take a break for a couple of days. I have replaced two of the new department heads, and that will cause us a slight delay."

"This McCarthy event has got me going all day. It is like analyzing a wartime engagement. We have bodies from only one side with some missing personnel. Check my procedure work, have it typed up, and we can haggle next Monday. I think we are at a point where you and I can finalize our portion."

Bridget says, "You may be working with Arnold Pierce soon. I am leaving for Vietnam. He and I have gone over this together, and he and I agree. No worries."

Mr. Fish reaches across the table and shakes Bridget's hand as he is leaves saying, "It is wonderful working with you, Bridget."

Bridget impolitely demands that Fish to come back into her office, saying, "I have something on my mind that is essential to our success in this lawsuit repair. That is communication. Your officers go to work risking their lives every day, and that is something that has been hitting me in the face, yet I have not seen it until recently. Some of these department heads have inferior academic writing skills. Their poor performance suffered because of that, not their desires. In conjunction with that, they have not learned to listen; that is actually hearing what is said. We must add both of those requirements and add specialized training. Without that, we are failing are creating an essential portion of our improvement."

Fish says, "Damn Bridget, you are absolutely correct. Now that you mention this, I have to say it I have also noticed it. Let's both write up our own versions then meld them together as we have in the past. Great suggestion."

The transition from Bridget back to Arnold seems to have no hang-ups. The city's group, the firm's group, Bridget's local friends, the firm's management, and Juliet are all anxious for Arnold's return.

Bridget thinks, "If we can just get rid of any significant evidence, we are in the clear."

Bridget walks out to Jennifer's desk and says, "Would you please see if the caterer that is now serving the office would take on my barbeque and prepare it at my home. Ask for some additional waitresses. I will have the local market supply, whatever desserts and liquors are required. Let's set a date for the second Friday from today. Call Matt and ask him for some coverage during that event."

Bridget calls Matt. Moments later, the phone rings.

Bridget says, "Hello, this is Bridget."

Matt says, "You are absolutely correct about those two waiters. I agree with you that they are waiting for Arnold to show. They are packing some good-sized weapons. They are courteous to the clients but real assholes in the kitchen. They always go to the spot on the roof for a smoke break. Tell your mole to be extra careful. That means stay away."

Bridget says, "Thank you for your warning. I called to let you know that the boat has some bottom damage that we must fix before we make another trip. We should have it fixed in a few days."

Matt says, "Good to know. I have selected a few that may be candidates for a trip. I'll work on your schedule. Thanks for the notice."

The phone goes dead.

Bridget goes to Julien's office.

She says, "Juliet, I want you to start driving the pink Mercedes. I will be driving the Jaguar. That will make it safer for you."

"I will see what Mikey's needs are for transportation. I have asked Mikey to be our mole at the Tiburon Restaurant, where two contractors are waiting for Arnold to appear. They also plan to kill the Irish Representative before leaving for Ireland."

It is mid-afternoon, and Bridget decides to try another one of her gut feelings.

She drives to the Tiburon and walks into the restaurant. Not many patrons are present, which is perfect. Bridget orders a French roast with espresso, side glass of Grand Marnier, and a large bowl of clams with French bread.

She sits there, gathering information on the two waiters. They recognize her, which is making them a little anxious. They are not busy. They climb the stairs to the roof. It appears that they can be on the roof in a matter of seconds. If Arnold had been there, they would have pulled out their weapons and executed him on the spot.

Satisfied with her initial observation, Bridget feels she already has some ground rules for the confrontation that appears like it will be exciting, and possibly deadly. As large and heavy as a 44 Magnum is, bringing two may be a wise move.

Bridget goes back to the office, where she interviews each group. Her questions are mainly on status and progress. The rest of the week goes as planned, having growth and completeness in the procedure update. The replacement managers are doing well. The firm's staff and the English professors are on top of every decision. The finished work is being entered into the system, and a copy is placed into the appropriate folder.

Bridget calls judge Brass. His secretary answers and puts the call through immediately.

Judge Brass says, "Ms. O'Connor, I presume you have a status update for me."

Bridget says, "Mr. Fish was an excellent choice. He and I are almost done with our part. Each working group has similar progress in place. We should have a final draft ready for your review soon. May I release this status to the Chronicle journalist for printing?"

Judge Brass says, "That would be a good idea. It certainly will shut up some of the critics. With the minimum hourly wage at $1.25 per hour and the city facing a lawsuit of $8,000,000, it is incredible where the critics have their heads. Mr. Fish is doing an outstanding job. He has taken on the additional task of cleaning the house. We all owe you both a great deal. Tell Mr. Pierce, thank you also. Thanks for your update."

"I am looking forward to seeing the new procedures. Talk to you soon."

Bridget walks to Jennifer's desk and hands her an initial list of barbeque guests to invite.

Bridget says, "If I missed anyone, feel free to add them to the list. It won't be long before you get your Arnold back. I'll be moving on."

Jennifer says, "Ms. O'Connor, you have been an honor to work with. I will miss you very much. You and Arnold have the same magic. Is Arnold going to keep all the changes?"

Bridget says, "Every change has been Arnold's decision. I

follow orders, and he and I are in communication every day. We still have contractors with the sole purpose of killing him. I identified two contractors yesterday, and we may have a few more to eliminate. We no longer have an army to fight, yet the fighting is not over."

Jennifer says, "I have some messages for you. Harriet called and said that she no longer feels threatened. Mr. Burke called, saying that Rita is almost ready to be released with all charges dropped. She will be able to practice law again. Mr. Love wants to discuss going to law school. Cecil has made the most of his legal changes. He comes to work looking like a male, and he smiles a lot now. There is a call from Matt."

Bridget picks up the phone and says, "Hello."

Matt says, "Sweetheart, we just identified Eric at the meat market. He was an employee of McCarthy, and he died at the brothel. We have found three more guys having activities with your two waiters from the restaurant. We need to take them out the morning of the day before your event with the two waiters. See you soon. Love and kisses."

The document is getting more extended and more exact as it develops. Added to the report are qualified fines, jail terms, financial liabilities, loss of driving privileges, impounding of vehicles, extensive restrictions on repeat offenders, and limited driving rights. As the document matures, attorneys are brought in from other firms to review and inspect it for correctness. Mr. Love and Claire have been given the responsibility to verify that no laws on the books have been compromised.

Bridget is walking around with the feeling of success and pride in the firm's work. It was not the intent, but there has been a significant increase in new clients since they started this action. Bridget may need to request that both Harriet and Rita come back to the firm to cover the latest new cases. Mr. Love's responsibilities have increased well beyond the general paralegal level. This should help him in law school and with his own objectives. Juliet hired an assistant to cover her portion. Bridget is considering including Juliet's share as part of the final document.

They occasionally go out as three girls. Alissa thinks it is a kick. The three of them go to the Tiburon Restaurant one evening.

Bridget calls Harold over and says, "Thank you for everything. Bridget says she is leaving after her barbeque, and Arnold Pierce will be coming back again."

The two waiters are listening intently to what she has to say. She says, "I am going to Vietnam to recover my fiancée and bring him home. Arnold should be returning shortly after that. He wants to take Alicia out. He misses his sailing, and his injuries are almost healed."

Before leaving Tiburon, Bridget sees Sergeant Brown. They stop alongside his car.

Bridget says, "Where is the red light for your unmarked car?"

Brown answers, "I plug it into the cigarette lighter when I need it. You know for speeders, jaywalkers, felons, and shooters.

Bridget continues, "Arnold wants to meet you at the Alicia when he comes back. He probably wants to write you up for jaywalking, and he thanked me for helping you into the water. Good to see you, Sergeant."

The girls drive back to Bridget's home.

Juliet says, "You are up to something, my dear. It sounds like you have something planned for Sergeant Brown."

Bridget says, "He just likes riding in the Jaguar. His next ride may get him to crap his pants."

Sid comes in the back door as soon as the girls get home.

He says, "Bridget, we have an appointment with Dr. Neel. If we hurry, we can make it."

HIDDEN IN FRONT OF YOU

Both Sid and Bridget walk to the Jaguar. Bridget drives across town, through the Civic Center and out toward South San Francisco. They enter the clinic. The admitting nurse ushers them into the doctor's office.

Dr. Neel says, "Are we about to enter the next phase of this adventure? Arnold, it will be less painful. Some things that we modified are going to return slowly. You are using makeup, and that will no longer be necessary. The facial changes we are going to make are going to come back immediately. We may need some minor surgeries down the road. We can slowly, over time, replace some of them. Your beard is gone. When we made the first alterations, the intent was to return you to Arnold as easily as possible."

Dr. Neel continues, "I hear your impersonation went well. Your friends, your businesspeople, and the people in the courts are going to see a different Arnold. You must blame the restoration of your physical alterations on the reconstruction of your appearance. Luckily, we can point to the massive facial damage that you suffered. That will be the majority of the supporting evidence, but you will be required to convince some of them. Slowly but surely, your testosterone level will override your estrogen level. This will help with the appearance of the changes. I understand that you have continued to work out. That, coupled with the increase in testosterone, will fill out your masculine appearance. Do not wear thin or light clothes for the first few months. You want the appearance of more muscle mass to project your image. Your sexual activity may start to increase soon."

Bridget smiles.

Dr. Neel continues, "When I remove your breasts, I may also be able to do some facial reconstruction to improve your facial image. Leaving these bandages on for a while may hide some of the changes. At least it will help focus other people's thoughts toward the accident. The date will be on the first Monday following the barbeque Sid has told me about. That way, Bridget will have flown to Vietnam, all ties will have been broken, and you will be back on the scene. Sid tells me that you have a few more of these so-called operatives to deal with. I wish you good fortune. We don't want to do this ever again. Have a great day, see you after the barbeque."

A few days go by, and the staff and the city department heads have framed a document that they are proud of. The material has been reviewed by each individual and is ready for presentation. Mr. Little's press releases are keeping the public aware of the progress and the political critics at bay.

Mikey is now working as a support person to the cooks. He hopes to be promoted to assistant cook. Harold is pleased with his work. No one is aware of his severe dyslexia because all instructions are given by voice during the food preparation process. He feels at home in this environment.

The two waiters are still there. They were warned by Harold to be more polite to their co-workers. Bridget has stopped by to thank Harold for his cooperation and to say goodbye. She made it well known that Arnold will be returning in a few weeks right after she goes to Vietnam. It is a few weeks before he preferred, but Harold assured her that he can handle it. Arnold has not fully recovered, but he will be back anyway. The contractor-waiters seem pleased that they will get their chance to kill Arnold.

As the days keep creeping by, it is getting closer to the barbeque. The coordination between the supermarket and caterer has been worked out by Jennifer. It appears to be much too big for Bridget to do it by herself. Matt has offered to post some of his men for safety. Josey, Julien, and Bridget will be packing their weapons.

Bridget arrives early on Monday morning.

HIDDEN IN FRONT OF YOU

Jennifer has a meeting set up in the large conference room with refreshments available. The staff seems pleased and anxious.

Jennifer says, "We have the procedural document ready for delivery. Only minor changes have been added since you reviewed it last. Upon your approval, we would like to present it to Judge Brass for his approval."

Bridget says, "My personal opinion is that it is a well written and complete document. I elect Jennifer and me to hand it to Judge Brass. If approved, I want each of you and any of the participating attorneys to accompany me to the function. Mr. Little, you may let this go to press. Jennifer, let's go make a phone call."

As the group leaves, they are applauding and making helpful comments.

Bridget calls Judge Brass. She is connected immediately.

Brass says, "You have some news for me, Ma'am? I am getting feedback that the document is in its final phase."

Bridget says, "We have a final document prepared. It is ready for your review. May we drop it off today?"

Brass says, "If I had workers like you folks, the city would be run efficiently. I am anxious to review it. Bring it on by. I'll be here until six or so."

Bridget walks into Julien's office and says, "Juliet, I am going to invite Jennifer to go with me to Judge Brass's office. After that, it is commute time. I thought it would appropriate to ask her out for dinner. Can you go with us?"

Juliet says, "Of course. Italian, I hope. You know that Alissa wants to go with us."

Bridget walks over to Jennifer's desk and asks her if she is available for dinner tonight. Jennifer looks at Bridget with surprise and nods yes.

Bridget says, "Let's meet at my house, and then take the pink Mercedes, let's go girls. We have a judge to meet with."

They each drive separately to Bridget's home, where they update their makeup and get into the pink Mercedes. Bridget takes Lombard to Van Ness and parks in front of the Court House. They walk into the building as if they own it, heading straight for Judge Brass's office. His secretary ushers them into a conference room for the meeting. They are told it will be a few minutes. Judge Brass is still in court. As he walks in, he removes his black gown then sits down.

Bridget says, "Judge Brass on my left is Mrs. Jennifer Hastings. She is my personal secretary. She is the contact for any changes that may be requested after your review. On my right is Mrs. Juliet Whitaker, who is in charge of the cross-referencing that was utilized for this lawsuit. Next to Mrs. Whitaker is her daughter Alissa whose is one of our contractors. Only verified errors will be modified. You have my permission to call either Jennifer or Juliet directly regarding questions you may have. You will find Mrs. Whitaker's name in this portion of the document since her husband was killed by a drunk driver."

Brass says, "Yes, I have heard of that case. The DUI driver became very generous after a couple of mid-evening visitors had a talk with him. He cooperated generously after that."

Bridget feels that not all things stay under the rug.

Judge Brass continues, "I talked to him while he was in the hospital suffering from a hole in his ass. Mr. Wise was so scared he could hardly speak. Let me have some time to review your work. I will call when it is time to discuss the next move. Good to meet you, ladies. Alissa, Juliet, and Jennifer, you two have been essential individuals in this production. We must now head over to the city council meeting, where we will be seeking the adoption of all the new procedures specified in this beautiful document.

They enter the San Francisco Council Chamber, where

HIDDEN IN FRONT OF YOU

every councilman is in attendance.

Judge Brass says, "The Pierce Law Firm has the new procedural document prepared. Ms. Bridget O'Conner and the staff members of her law firm, and Mr. Louie Fish and each police department manager, have jointly prepared this document. I have thoroughly reviewed this document. We, each and all, recommend that you vote for its acceptance."

The council votes 100 percent for its adoption, and Bridget feels a huge weight has been lifted off her shoulders.

Bridget says to all, "We thank you for your trust in our work, and we feel as if we have saved the city from further damages."

Bridget calls Mr. Little from a council chamber phone, and says, "You may go to press with the results. Enjoy yourself, and thank you for your assistance."

They walk out of the council chamber and out of the building with their heads held high. Bridget drives east on Van Ness to Broadway, right onto Broadway and a left turn onto Columbus. Feeling like she just won a marathon, she hangs an illegal U-turn parking right in front of the Italian restaurant.

Juliet says, "Jennifer, look out when she has things going her way. I think she learned that from Arnold."

A motorcycle cop stops and says, "If you ladies weren't so damn pretty, I would write you up. Bye, ladies."

Bridget gets out and walks straight into the restaurant as if the motorcycle cop had never stopped. She starts babbling in Italian to the maître de'. They are seated immediately in Bridget's favorite table next to the kitchen.

All four order martinis up with green olives. Bridget has ordered a typical Italian dinner that is not on the menu. The foods are delivered sequentially. The bread comes first, then the antipasti, followed by the soup and the salad. Each is provided separately in large bowls so that any diner may choose seconds. The table is cleared except for the drinks, and the main course is served. By the time they are done with the main course, it has been ninety minutes.

Bridget says, "This is a small victory dinner. Every department in the San Francisco Civic Center has been on pins and needles in hopes that we don't take $8,000,000 from their financial accounts. They had damn well better thank us. The minimum hourly wage is currently at $1.25 per hour, and the average wage of the lower middle class is about $1.86 per hour. We would have bankrupted them. Our actions could not have been more forgiving. To be kept between us, I feel that it may have been Arnold who put the hole in that guy's ass. He will not admit to it when I ask him, he just smiles." girls drive back to Bridget's home. When Jennifer leaves, it is well after commute hours. The trip is an easy one for her.

After Jennifer leaves, Juliet says, "Just what exactly did you do to that DUI driver?"

Bridget says, "Scared the shit out of him. I promised to come back if he were not generous with you immediately. That meant Mr. Wise would be alive but suffering severely for the rest of his miserable life. He had an active alarm system, a trained attack dog that Josey fed hamburgers. The dog went to sleep after being shot with a tranquilizer. Wise had three 9mm pistols. There I was talking to him at 3 a.m. in his bedroom. The most fun was putting a hole in his ass. As I remember, he lost some teeth, had a broken jaw, a broken collar bone, and a few broken ribs. He had no clue who I was or where I came from. He did know that I would be back if he did not fulfill his obligations. He did spend some time in the hospital. Was I to ask him for his friendly cooperation?"

Juliet says, "I know you had no choice. Yet that side of you is a little scary."

HIDDEN IN FRONT OF YOU

Bridget changes the subject, "The barbeque seems thoroughly planned. There will be many people you don't know. They will be there for our protection. Then think of it. Your lover will no longer be pushing "C" cupped breasts up against you. He will be telling you to hurry up with your makeup, or we'll be late. He will no longer wear a matching dress. That reminds me. I had better work on modifying my voice. What would people say if they knew your husband used to wear dresses."

Juliet says, "I'll take what I have."

The evening seems much more relaxed than the last few months.

Bridget says, "The Tiburon house will be a great starter home for us. What do you think of the changes that we should be made before moving in?"

Juliet says, "I agree with the landscaping and opening up the view. The addition to the entertainment area and the small pool is questionable. For the inside, you have overlooked having children. We will need to work on that."

"Another topic is my father. He will be getting older and less mobile. Someday he may need to be included in the house and be maintained. He loves the family connection."

Bridget says, "We will make Julien and Harriet feel welcome and definitely part of the family. We will help that Alley Cat becomes a house cat."

57 - GOODBYE BARBEQUE

Bridget feels the home on Filbert is ready for the barbeque. Many of the neighbors offered their driveways for parking. Bridget tells each neighbor that they are welcome. Preparation seems complete.

The caterer has brought extra chairs and tables along with the necessary cooking and serving utensils. Invitations have been sent to office staff, supermarket workers, local employees from the shops Bridget visited, and law firm clients. The three from Matt's group arrived early. They are wearing light-weight white jackets, so they fit in with the caterer workers. They will participate in the serving, letting them mingle freely. All three have dealt with these two McCarthy contractors before. The three are armed and prepared for the worst. Late morning the two contractors were seen driving by the home. Bridget's memory of Frank Dulles and his wife remind her of the loss. Under normal circumstances, they would be joining this barbeque. They were family.

Juliet's, Julien's, Josey's, Bridget's, and Matt's cars have been parked in Bridget's large garage to reduce the parking issue. By 8 a.m., the activities begin. The catering staff is working on the preparation of the foods. The cooking smells are filling the home and the neighborhood. Juliet stayed the night to help. Both girls take early morning showers and prep trying to give the best look possible. They are both wearing low heels because they will be on their feet most of the day. Both intend to mingle throughout the crowd as time and space permits.

It seems that the two contractors think Arnold will be at this function. They each have current murder warranties issued on them. Their presence would show a complete disregard for the law. In the early afternoon, as the size of the crowd grows, both operatives enter the premises. They see the three men from Matt's group. They also see Julien, Josey, Sergeant Brown, and Officer O'Malley, who are all well-armed. The city had provided uniformed officers to direct traffic. The contractors decide to leave since their odds were not looking as good as they had hoped. Arnold was not present, at least not as Arnold.

Inside the home, it is getting more and more crowded as the day progresses. The caterer has a hat, coat, and purse check-in station near the front door. This saves a lot of seating space and clutter. Bridget stands in the middle of the room with a loudspeaker in hand.

She says, "I want you to know that we have hired a fleet of cabs to take anyone home that may have consumed too much of the good stuff. We have many special liqueurs that may meet your fancy. The cab companies are under contract to fetch you and return you back here tomorrow so my friends you are safe and hopefully more comfortable. Thanks to Commissioner Fish, our officers are going to check you out on your way home."

Bridget continues, "I wish to thank all you wonderful folks for sharing our barbeque. I am so excited that they found my man in the jungles of Vietnam. He has a few minor holes in him, but he is otherwise looking healthy. For his heroism under fire and years of dedicated service, he has been promoted to Major. He has been credited recently with saving the lives of over twenty of his men, a little bragging there. I have been told that the food will be ready to serve in about thirty minutes. The bar is open. Appetizers and a variety of liqueurs are available along with your choice of any other drinks. I will wander around to chat with each of you. It is an honor to have you here with us. I have placed a picture of my darling husband to be over the fireplace."

Juliet pulls Bridget aside and whispers, "He is better looking than you and maybe a better lover too."

Bridget replies, "Maybe my love, but you are stuck with lil ole me. Where has Holley been these last few weeks? You could have invited her."

Juliet smiles and walks away.

The caterer has picked USDA choice meat, a selection of quality bread, fresh vegetables, and appetizers. Everything is first class and the top of the line. Bridget had requested the best possible, and the caterer has produced just that.

The desserts include pies, fresh fruit, ice cream, and a variety of freshly baked homemade cookies. The guests are busy gorging themselves and happily talking with each other. Bridget is attempting to visit each member as she mingles. She is happy in a bubbly way while kissing many of the visitors. This event will be remembered by everyone for years to come. Many local neighbors came to join in. They were surprised at the size of the crowd and were pleased to be included. The barbeque appears to be a great success.

After several hours of eating, drinking, and chatting, Bridget gets her horn out again, saying, "I thank you all for coming. It has been an honor to have your presence. Mr. Lee, our caterer, has done a marvelous job. I hope I didn't miss anyone saying goodbye. Being a part of this firm has become like family to me. If it weren't for my fiancée's release from the Viet Cong, I would prefer to stay here with you folks. You all have made my stay a joyful event. I love you all. Please forgive me for leaving."

The crowd applauds along with many sayings, "Bridget, we love you."

Many are still eating their desserts. Bridget grabs a tall glass of port as she starts walking toward the front door. She positions herself at the front door and personally thanks people for joining the barbeque. Many express their sadness that she is leaving and say they hope she is happy in her marriage.

HIDDEN IN FRONT OF YOU

Bridget turns to Matt's three contractors.

She says, "I appreciate your presence. I noticed that we did get a visit from those two. Would you please stay until Mr. Lee's folks have their stuff removed? After that, there will be fewer people. I believe my people can handle things then."

All three nod, yes.

The home is almost empty. The guests have left, and the caterer's equipment has been removed. Bridget thanks the three operatives for staying. She still has her own weapon plus Julien, and Josey has theirs. By the two McCarthy operatives entering the home, Bridget got a good look at who Arnold must deal with. They appeared arrogant and a bit irritated. They knew that they were dead at the first sign of them starting trouble.

58 - BRIDGET'S TRANSFORMATION

Julien has been in a stand-off mode concerning Juliet for the most part during the last several months. Juliet's changes in hours and days have interested him, yet he has not said a word.

Julien and Juliet are sitting on the small couch in the office TV area when Julien says, "Is it time for us to talk as we used to? Are there things that you may need to share with me?"

Juliet says, "Daddy, you know that I am seeing Arnold. It began as I started being an assistant and a part-time caretaker for him. The more I saw him, the closer we became. We want to get married. As things quiet down, I plan to move in here with him. He is everything I want in a man."

He has one more dangerous task to complete, the two contractor leftovers from the McCarthy Group. Those two even came to the barbeque party today, looking for Arnold."

Julien says, "Bridget gave me some hints and said you two were considering marriage. You have made a good choice, my lovely daughter. It's time for me to say goodnight and head for home."

Julien leaves as Sid comes in the back door.

Sid begins by saying, "I am taking some of the leftovers home. They are too good to leave here. Tomorrow is the day we say goodbye to Bridget, my beautiful daughter. Your surgery is scheduled for 10 a.m. No eating in the morning. Juliet, you will drive her to Dr. Neel's office and get her there by 8 a.m. They want to keep her overnight for at least one night. You can plan on bringing Arnold home in the late morning of the next day. Juliet, you will be his official nurse and caretaker. You will have a direct line to Dr. Neel's office in case you need any help."

Juliet and Alissa are the last to leave, and they give Bridget a big hug and kiss before leaving.

Bridget is thoroughly exhausted from the day. She climbs

into the silk sheets early in the evening and is falling asleep as she crawls into bed. Even with the excitement of tomorrow's surgery and getting back to being a male, she quickly falls off to dreamland.

Morning arrives quietly with the weather in a typical San Francisco calm. Bridget is sleeping soundly when. Juliet comes early with her own intentions. She undresses and crawls in between the silk sheets with her lover. Juliet lays there with her lover and arouses Bridget until she wakes up. They both enjoy this time of passion together. In the end, they are together with their arms and legs wrapped around each other. Today Bridget disappears, and Arnold returns, the big day both have been looking forward to.

They both take showers, and Juliet applies her makeup. Bridget just brushes her teeth and slides into some of Arnold's comfortable slacks, tennis shoes, a loose shirt, and a sweatshirt with a zipper and pockets. Bridget's hair is still long, but Sid can cut that later. Bridget sneaks a half cup of coffee before Juliet catches her. Within minutes they are off to Dr. Neel's office in Juliet's new car, the pink Mercedes.

Juliet says, "Are you going to be worth keeping once you are a male again? Changing gender might be tough. You have done so well as a girl."

Bridget says, "Do you prefer running around with me as a girl?"

Juliet says, "You got me there. Alissa would understand, but my father would have a fit. I am sexually attracted to a man. What would I do? I am used to those "C" cup tits bouncing against me when we make love."

They arrive at the clinic. Juliet parks the pink Mercedes by the front door. As they walk into the clinic, the entire staff is waiting for them.

Dr. Neel walks up to Bridget and says, "Ready to be called Arnold again? I will perform some facial changes to help you not look so much like a female. The length of time you are in pain should be less than before. Also, the recovery time should be shorter. Juliet, we should have Arnold ready to go early afternoon tomorrow. For the last few weeks, we have raised his level of testosterone."

Juliet is asked to go home for the day. Bridget has not eaten except for the half a cup of coffee she snuck and has passed any leftover stool. At 10 a.m., Bridget is waiting in the surgery room with everything hooked up for surgery. The anesthesiologist arrives. She administers the necessary medication for the first step of the operation. Bridget begins to feel a bit calmed down and a little sleepy. When the surgeon arrives, the anesthesiologist ups the dose. Bridget becomes unconscious.

The surgeon works on each side of the face separately, first on the left side, then the other. Sixty to sixty-five minutes per side is as long as it takes. After a short break, comes the implant removal. The surgeon uses a scalpel to make an opening so the implants can be removed. He works on each side separately. When the surgeon is done, the anesthesiologist starts Bridget's reversal. By the time the surgeon has completed closing the incisions, Arnold starts showing signs of awareness. Arnold is wheeled into the recovery room to finish waking up.

Hours later, Dr. Neel comes in for a discussion.

He says, "Everything went well. There should be no problems with this surgery."

As soon as Dr. Neel leaves, Arnold falls asleep.

The next day Juliet arrives at about 2 p.m.

As she walks into Arnold's room, she says, "I can see you have been worked on."

The medical staff wheels Arnold to the waiting pink Mercedes. Arnold has less pain than before because of the pain medication. Arnold's face is bruised and sore, and his chest area is tender.

After Juliet parks the Mercedes inside the garage, she assists Arnold into the kitchen area where she sits him down. She fixes him a full breakfast and his favorite coffee. She then walks him into the bedroom for a nap.

As the end of the week approaches, the pain has reduced and is no longer impeding his movements. Dr. Neel said that breast removal went well and was trivial. A few days at home and Arnold is already feeling that he should be finalizing the day with the two contractors. He does not want to wait. Yet his strength and stamina are not up to par, so he is forced to wait.

Seeing that Arnold is home, Sid knocks at the back door.

Sid says, "Do you feel well enough for me to do your hair, or shall we wait?"

Arnold says, "Let's wait."

59 - REVENGE

Within the first week, Arnold is venturing out. He is testing the responses of the Jaguar.

Arnold calls Nick, who answers, "Nick, here, how may I help you?"

Arnold says, "Nick, I am back. I have been road testing the Jaguar.

You have done a great job prepping me for my next chase, which will be a more critical chase than any of the others. If I drop the car off, can you give it a once over recheck? I will be putting it through one of the most demanding chases of my life."

Nick says, "Arnold. I am always available to you. Just set the time, and I'll do whatever checking you want me to do. Drop the Jaguar by.

It should take only a few days. You have been running on consumer ethyl, but I have some 110-octane tetraethyl fuel here, and you will really notice the difference in performance with the tetraethyl. I also have a couple of additional ideas that you will appreciate."

Arnold says, "I'll be there. It sounds good."

Arnold gets off the phone. He feels like jumping up and down with enthusiasm, yet the pain is still too severe.

Juliet says, "What is up with you? You are still trying to heal and recover."

Arnold says, "We are going by Nick's place later to drop off the Jaguar for a little upgrade. You need to follow me there in the pink Mercedes. Nick will be keeping the Jaguar for a few days."

Arnold is planning for his chase event. When is the best time to schedule this chase? Weekends are not good because of the type of unskilled Saturday and Sunday drivers on the road. Picking a day means choosing the quietest part of a day as possible. That would be on the early side of a morning

HIDDEN IN FRONT OF YOU

during mid-week, say Tuesday morning. By parking Arnold's car next to Alicia at 8 a.m., those two contractors will see it and be ready to go after Arnold. The chase could start before 9:15 a.m.

Sid comes in the back door and says, "What's for lunch?"

Arnold calls Sergeant Brown.

He answers, saying, "Hello, Sergeant Brown."

Arnold says, "I've had some minor break-ins on the Alicia lately. I plan on being on the boat on Tuesday at 8:30 a.m. Would it be possible for you to meet me there at 8:30 so we can look into this?"

Sergeant Brown says, "Certainly Mr. Pierce, but I am parking my car across the street, and I will jaywalk over to the Alicia."

Arnold says, "I'll be required to write you another ticket. As an officer of the law, you need to set a better example for us citizens. I hear that you enjoyed the short ride with Bridget. I do not hear you crying about that."

Brown says, "That woman is crazy. She committed multiple violations and said she was going slower so she could break in a new engine. Driving that car on our roads is a violation in itself. With a top speed over four times the legal driving limit, you are a real menace. See you on Tuesday." Click goes the phone.

Arnold says to Sid and Juliet, "That takes care of getting him to Alicia. He is going to be screaming at me after the chase."

Arnold comments, "I am concerned about my entry onto the Alicia before Sergeant Brown's arrival and without being spotted by the mafia assassins. Alicia is pointing south-southwest and is the first boat when looking from the restaurant. Josey and Julien will have the Jaguar parked next to Alicia by 8 a.m. If I can get on the Alicia well before 8 a.m. and into the cabin without being spotted, I can make some coffee and be waiting for Sergeant Brown. That will make it all appear normal to Brown."

Sid says, "Why don't you just turn the two contractors into the authorities?" Arnold says, "I think that option would allow the mafia to hire several more assassins. These new assassins would not be known to me. That would allow them to attack me from my blind side with me not having any protection. I would be back where I started."

Sid responds, "Yeah, I guess that's right. No gain there."

Arnold drives to the Alicia Friday morning at about 6 a.m. After stepping onto the walkway, he walks alongside the boat climbing on the Alicia midship. Staying low, Arnold crawls around to the doorway. He unlocks the cabin and enters. It took 45 seconds to complete this route. On Tuesday, it will be well before the assassin-contractors show up for work at 9 a.m. Arnold plans on bringing two 44 Magnums and the snub-nosed 38mm with the new barrel. He has several six quick round loaders plus extra rounds. The snub-nose will be in an ankle holster. The first 44 Magnum will be in a chest holster, and the second 44 Magnum will be resting on the shelf by the cabin door. All rounds have hollow point bullets and the highest grain load available. Everything before Sergeant Brown's arrival seems to be set in place and workable.

Day after day, Arnold is improving. Most of the incisions have closed and are no longer bleeding. The chest tenderness has reduced to an acceptable level. Arnold's exercises are less painful. He feels quicker on his feet, but his balance is not 100 percent. His enthusiasm keeps growing each day, and he wants a conclusion to this turmoil in his life.

Sid has come by to give him a haircut. He leaves Arnold's hair a little longer than before and dyes it as close to his natural color as possible. Arnold makes plans with Juliet to visit the firm's office on Monday just before the big chase

HIDDEN IN FRONT OF YOU

event. Together they will take the pink Mercedes. Mikey will let it slip in the afternoon that Arnold visited the office this morning. Mikey is told not to go to work on Tuesday.

The Sunday before the office visit, Arnold feels close to 100 percent. His strength is up to par, his stamina has improved, his balance seems reasonable., and his agility has almost entirely returned to 100 percent. But he realizes a hand to hand fight would still be to his disadvantage at this point in his recovery. As significant as the recoil is, he feels he has the strength to handle the two 44 Magnums. The recoil is going to be hard to control without using both hands to hold the weapon.

Arnold looks through his male clothes that have been in storage. Upon putting them away, Sid had them cleaned or washed then hung in portable closets. He chooses two. One he will wear to the office on Monday. Going to the office makes him feel slightly uneasy. He does not want to endanger anyone's life by letting the staff or outsiders know of his female impersonation. He knows the two contractors at the restaurant want to kill him. There could be more. The threat will hopefully lessen over time.

Arnold and Juliet take Sunday afternoon off to see Nick and pick up the Jaguar. They drive the pink Mercedes to Nick's shop.

Nick says, "I am ready for you, crazy guy. Since you are going to put this car through some extreme paces, I have made some additional modifications. I changed the factory plug wires to solid wires to reduce any chance of failure. You will get static on your radio from these new wires. I installed some anti-radar bulbs under your hood. The cops will have a tougher time verifying your speed. At the speeds that I think you will be driving, your fuel consumption will increase significantly. I have molded an additional gasoline tank into your trunk. It may slightly change your weight ratio from the front to aft. This tank has an additional gauge, and it will automatically drain directly into the original tank. You had the finest street tires. I replaced them with racing tires with the highest reliability that I could acquire. I know I will hear about this run on the newscasts. You sound so positive you are going to do it. I drained the ethyl gasoline and filled both tanks with the tetraethyl. It is above 110 Octane. You are all set to go, my friend. My heart will be with you on Tuesday. You will be the fastest vehicle on the road. Please remember you are not indestructible. By the way, Arnold, there were 26 bullet holes in that crushed jaguar, not fifteen."

Arnold says, "I guess that I miss counted or did not see them all. Thank you, Nick. I always have confidence in your work."

Arnold drives home for the night, occasionally testing the improvements.

Juliet leaves to pick up Alissa. Juliet will return in the morning. Tonight, she and Alissa are visiting with Julien.

After having a light dinner, Arnold goes off to bed at an early hour.

The next morning's weather has a slight breeze and mild fog, which is typical for this time of the year. Marin County will be warm yet not hot. The bridge will have that pleasant fog odor.

Arnold has taken a shower, dressed, and made breakfast before Juliet arrives. They will be taking the pink Mercedes with Arnold driving.

Keeping an eye for operatives, Arnold drives slowly out of the garage. No, 911 is waiting. Off they started for the bridge. As they cross the Golden Gate, the fog odor holds true. Up to and through the tunnel, the weather becomes dryer and warmer. The trip takes under thirty minutes. Arnold pulls into the parking space.

Some bandages are still visible. Arnold tries to walk a little

HIDDEN IN FRONT OF YOU

slower and cautiously when entering the reception area.

Matilda says, "Mr. Pierce, welcome back. It is so nice to see you. Jennifer will most likely have your morning coffee and pastry ready."

As Arnold approaches Jennifer's desk, there Jennifer is holding his coffee in one hand and the pasty in the other.

With her eyes tearing some, she welcomes Arnold by saying, "It is so good having you back with us."

As she places the coffee and pastry on his desk, Jennifer turns to hug Arnold. She walks back to her desk. Arnold continues drinking her excellent coffee.

Arnold then walks over to HR.

Arnold says, "I am looking for Cecil."

A person dressed as a man walks up to Arnold.

They shake hands, and Cecil says, "Welcome back, Mr. Pierce. It is good to see you here in the office."

Arnold says, "How is your change of life going. Are you happy? Is there anything I can do for you?"

Cecil says, "From your directions through Bridget, everything is wonderful. I am who I want to be. I live a pleasant life, and I feel safe here in this firm."

Arnold says, "We are pleased about your happiness. I hope you stay with us as long as you care to. It is exciting to me that we were able to help you. Please always feel welcome here. I must visit with others, so see you later."

Arnold walks away and feels warm and satisfied that Cecil is happy. He stops by Claire's office. Claire sees Arnold jumps up, runs over, and gives him a big hug.

Claire says, "It is so good to see you. You look like you have mostly recovered. You do look healthy, but how do you feel?"

Arnold says, "I am on the last part of my recovery. No permanent damage like Frank's. I am building my strength back up, and my stamina is returning. Do you have enough work now? Bridget was telling me that you were feeling underutilized."

Claire says, "All is better. We have increased our client base, and I have had the opportunity to take on some new cases. I am busy and pleased. Thank you for asking. I hear that we may get Rita and Harriet back again, how exciting."

Arnold says, "It has been good seeing you. I must say hello to others. See you later."

Arnold makes a quick stop at Jennifer's desk.

He says, "Please call Mikey and tell him to let the contractors know about my office visit and that I have gone to the City Hall in San Francisco. Also, let him know that he is to call in sick tomorrow."

As Arnold enters Julien's office, he says, "Either Juliet goes with me now, or maybe you could drop her by my home when you quit for the day. I am driving her car."

Julien says, "There's not much for her to do today. She may as well go with you now. Have a good time. It is good to see you up and around. My thoughts will be with you on Tuesday."

The last stop before leaving for the day is David's office. The door is open, so Arnold walks in. David looks up and starts smiling. He then reaches across the desk to shake hands.

David says, "It is great seeing you. I have missed you for these many months. You look like you are still recuperating, but you're looking well. Mikey is settled in at the restaurant. He is studying and doing some work for me here in the office. So far, he is looking good."

Arnold says, "That is good to hear about Mikey. I believe he has potential."

"David, I have a hazardous event tomorrow. Two leftover contractors are looking to kill me. I am going to end it tomorrow. I have a working plan, the Jaguar is ready, and I am ready. I will have one hell of a fight on my hands. As always, you are the executor of my personal items. Please take care of things if I don't make it."

David says, "I thought that mess had been cleaned up by now."

Arnold says, "These two were in transit during the event. They hold a grudge for losing all that power and easy money. They blame me for the death of some of their family members. There are murder warrants on them, they are anxious to kill me, and this is the only way I know how to get rid of the threat permanently. Hope to see you soon."

Arnold decides to have some lunch before leaving San Rafael. Arnold and Juliet go to the same restaurant where Julien's party was held. The chef has a roasted beef rib for the lunch special.

Arnold says to Juliet, "I feel the need to visit tomorrow's expected roadways. I have checked them out before, but refreshing my possible paths today will reinforce my memory."

Juliet says, "I am worried for you, my love. You are not quite up to par. You have a threat that is known to be excellent at what they do. I hear that he is so big and strong that even you could not beat him in the ring."

Arnold says, "I have considered all of that, but I have no choice. He is coming after me, no matter what. I have plans to take away as many of his advantages as possible and give myself a fighting chance. He is not aware that I know of his presence and intent. If he did know, I would be foolish in approaching him tomorrow. He is also acting impatiently. It was foolish when they walked into my home during the barbeque, and it showed their anger and arrogance. That is not clear thinking, and it isn't proper planning. Do you agree with that?"

Juliet says, "Yes, I do agree with your thoughts and your

evaluation. You are my life, and I don't want to live without you. Alissa needs you and loves you too. She is always talking about you."

Arnold says, "I promise to give myself every advantage. That was a good lunch. Let's go review the landscape."

Driving south then north on the 101 is a good start. Arnold tests some of the shoulders for stability. In some places, Arnold ventures out onto the highway medium to check for firmness and control. Arnold drives through several possible 90 mph U-turn sites. They each give him more room than he had when he performed that maneuver in years past. Within a few hours, he has checked out most of the roadway. They head toward Filbert Street. Arnold feels he is going to rely on some of his previous driving experiences that he hopes this contractor does not have. He also feels comfortable in his assessment with the recallable memory of the roadway and truck stops. Arnold plans to take many of this guy's advantages away from him.

Juliet says, "I understand your preparation, and your need to follow through with this. To me, it is scary. I fear for your life."

Arnold says, "I would not bother with this part, but I have no choice. These two are coming after me no matter what I would do to avoid them. Sid wants me to turn them in, but then there would be more replacements that I don't know anything about."

Back at the Filbert house, it is just the two of them. They have a high protein and low alcohol dinner. They finish the meal with a dessert made with fresh blueberries, raspberries, and strawberries.

Arnold says, "Tomorrow is early to rise day. All the emotions are roaming around in my head. Part of me is looking forward to the day. Other parts are reluctant to start the day. I want this behind me. Am I good enough to

HIDDEN IN FRONT OF YOU

control the event and come out the victor? There is so much more, so let's leave it at excited and scared. Let's plan an early to bed, some time for us, and a good night's sleep."

Arnold is not aware of Juliet tearing in fear. She doesn't know what life would be like without him. Through the night, she continuously wakens and holds on to him to help him sleep peacefully. Her emotions are too active to let her sleep well.

When Juliet wakes up in the morning, Arnold is not there. She climbs out of the silk sheets and starts looking for him. He has made some robust coffee, had a full glass of grapefruit juice, and is taking a shower. When Arnold sees Juliet, he says, "Good thing I don't need makeup today. I am too worked up to do it correctly."

He puts on heavy work pants and boots. Over his chest, he put on a t-shirt made of 50% wool then a standard long sleeve wool hunting shirt. He places the bulletproof vest and a dark jacket by the door to the garage.

Josey and Julien have already picked up the Jaguar. At the last minute, Arnold had Josey remove the convertible top. The Jaguar will then be pointed in the direction Arnold needs to start from. The 911 is always parked in the employee parking lot across the street. The Jaguar will be in position long before it is required and warmed up from driving it over from San Francisco. It will be full of the tetraethyl gasoline for that extra thrust and RPMs.

Arnold is driving as he and Juliet leave the garage. They cross the bridge and head for Tiburon. They are both quiet. Arnold is tense, and Juliet is frightened that she might lose her soon to be husband. There is nothing either can say that will change the day. Arnold parks the Mercedes. He puts on the bulletproof vest and the jacket that has both side pockets full of 44 Magnum cartridges. He kisses Juliet and says, "See you soon."

As Arnold is walking away, Juliet is crying so heavily she can't see to drive.

Arnold puts some extra cartridges into the center console of the Jaguar. He then runs to the cabin. Arnold unlocks the cabin door and enters. He picks a spot near the door that will keep him partially hidden from the restaurant roof position. He has one 44 Magnum in his shoulder holster and the second one resting on the carpeted ledge just inside the doorway.

Sergeant Brown arrives on time at 8:30 for their meeting. He parks across the street then jaywalks to Alicia.

Arnold says, "Good morning to you, my jaywalker friend. I guess another ticket is appropriate."

Brown says, "Is that all you can come up with this morning?"

Arnold sees the 911 arrive across the street. Both contractors spot the Jaguar, and they hurry into the restaurant. Within minutes they are standing at the opening peering down at the Alicia.

Arnold says, "Recently, I have noticed things missing here in the cabin. I have received a few phone calls at home that make no sense to me. Today is my first full day back here since the accident. You can see that the lock has been tampered with. Things are missing or moved."

While they are talking, Josey steals the red light from Brown's car and places it into the Jaguar. Both Julien and Josey stay out of harm's way by remaining parked several hundred feet south of the Alicia.

Arnold peaks out the cabin door. He sees the big guy uncovering the rifle. The little guy is standing behind some plywood with two pistols drawn. The guns appear to be 38-caliber semi-automatic pistols, with fifteen or sixteen round magazines. The little guy suddenly begins firing at where he thinks Arnold should be. While Arnold and Brown are

HIDDEN IN FRONT OF YOU

staying out of sight, Arnold shows himself then darts back to a safe position. Arnold fires six 44-magnum rounds into the smaller of the two. The shorter guy is now draped over the plywood panel bleeding and dead.

The big guy is looking for Arnold through his scope. Arnold obliges him by showing himself one more time. The guy sees his partner dead and decides to run. The big guy leaves his position and runs to the 911 holding only his handgun.

Arnold checks Sergeant Brown. He has a clean hole in his side.

Arnold says, "It is only a flesh wound. A little more blood than you would like, but you are fine."

Arnold helps him walk to the Jaguar. The big guy is having trouble getting the key into the key slot. Arnold has both 44-Magnums loaded and ready. Brown is standing next to the Jaguar and exchanging shots with the big guy and gets hit again.

The 911 is only across the street. Arnold fires six rounds and flattens three tires then reloads the 44 Magnum. He lies down on the pavement next to the Jaguar. The big guy jumps behind the 911 and continues firing. His shots are inaccurately aimed mostly at Brown. One of Arnold's shots hits the big guy, and he falls. As Arnold is walking across the street, the guy tries to lift his weapon. Arnold reshoots him, and he is laying there dead.

When the police arrive, Brown explains how Arnold saved his life, and then he described the firefight. Upon their request, Arnold shows the officers his gun permits.

Arnold walks into the restaurant and calls Jennifer.

He says, "All is fine, it is all over. Please tell Juliet."

60 - PEACE AND TRANQUILITY

Arnold walks back to his Jaguar. A sense of calmness has taken over his emotions. All known dangers have been taken away. He can drive the streets without continuously checking for hazards. He may now continue the profession he loves in a harmonious work environment. He is a trial attorney, pursuing more time in the charity work and, most importantly, someday being the father along with Juliet of a loving family with beautiful children. The firm can go back to its original configuration established by its originator, Jules Voisinet. His plans for his personal life can now be realized. From his life almost being destroyed, he now feels free to put his life into the proper order.

Instead of driving home, he stops off at the firm.

Matilda has gone. Jennifer is still at her desk.

Jennifer sees Arnold walk into her area.

She says, "Juliet shared with me her involvement with Mr. Pierce during his recuperation. You have found yourself a beauty."

Arnold says, "Thank you, Jennifer, I agree. Let's have a luncheon tomorrow here in the office using the same caterer. This way, I can say a few words."

Jennifer says, "One of which is an announcement that you are getting married. Juliet shared that with me too."

Arnold says, "Yes, I am excited."

As Arnold is wandering around with this pleased look on his face, David Worth asks him to step into his office.

Arnold says, "That would be a pleasure for me, David. I hear that she is doing well."

David says, "You have a marvelous contractor in Alissa. She is competent in researching her plans, absorbs favorable opinions, and she carries out the event with an efficiency seldom seen in most. Basically, Alissa is working at a high level. She has become a close friend of Naomi. Working together with Naomi, she has everyone amazed, including Dr. Keane. We are fortunate to have her working with us."

Arnold feels both pleased and proud of Alissa.

David continues, "At first I considered it to be an improper request to the school to allow a guard dog on campus as a service dog. But my opinion was wrong. The dog, Salty, plays and acts friendly with all the students and teachers at the school. He will be performing or running around until an outsider appears in the immediate area. Then he runs to Naomi, sits down next to Naomi's, and waits there for Naomi's instruction. It is exciting to watch."

"Alissa took hold of this assignment and has run with it. Alissa, Naomi, and Dr. Keane have now started working with a third individual. This time it is a boy. Alissa and Naomi have been working closely together. Their achievements have been amazing. They both have found their life's work. Naomi wants to become a general practitioner with special psychological training in child abuse cases, similar to Dr. Keane. She wants to help abused children."

"Alissa wants to become a trial attorney to work in both criminal and abuse cases. Alissa loves both the challenge and confrontation. Alissa performs as well as any contractor we have ever had, including you, Mr. Pierce. You would think that she had done this before. She seeks direction from experienced people, she listens better than most, and she makes her decisions clearly and definitively. Please review her work and meet with her. I know that you will be proud of both her and Naomi."

Arnold says, "David, thank you for sharing this information. I agree Alissa is a special person."

As he walks out of David's office, Arnold now feels like strutting around bragging about Alissa and Naomi. More than anyone, Naomi can understand the trauma these young people experience. Working with Naomi must have been a real eye-opening experience for Alissa because her objective has now become creating solutions for the abused. From their conversations and the meetings with Dr. Keane, Alissa can appreciate Naomi's traumatic experiences.

Reaching Jennifer's desk, Arnold says, "Mrs. Hastings. What is your opinion of Alissa concerning the contractor's work she is performing?

Jennifer says, "Alissa has come to me for advice, review, some assistance in her decision making, and then implementing her decisions. She hears everything a person says. Alissa weighs all options known to her before making a final decision. She is extremely aware of people's opinions and how to deal with each one of them. I have heard that she is doing an outstanding job."

Arnold thanks Jennifer for her opinion.

Arnold walks to his office and calls Sid, "Sid here."

Arnold says, "Long ago, you said you had access to a large selection of jewelry. Do you still have that access?"

Sid says, "Mr. Pierce, you are a little late. I have been discussing this with a beautiful young lady for quite a while. There is a collection that she has viewed and prefers. When you have some time, I will allow you to view the collection. You should have had this figured out many moons ago. Let me know when you are ready. Bye."

Arnold leaves the office and heads to the garage. On the way home, his first stop is the restaurant next to Alicia. He walks in and asks for the maître de'.

The man walks up to Arnold, saying, "You are a hero. Sergeant Brown says, you saved his life."

Arnold says, "I came by to discuss two things. One is to upgrade your exterior wall with a new coat of paint and to construct a blockage to the roof area. The second is to request having a fully catered reception dinner by you folks

HIDDEN IN FRONT OF YOU

here at this restaurant. I'm going to rent the old church on the hill just up from downtown."

The maître de' says, "I do appreciate your willingness to repair the damages. We would be honored to have your wedding party here, sir."

Arnold says, "I'll have my office work out the details. I'll be talking with you soon. A lady called Jennifer from my office will be taking care of the particulars."

A short drive to the small church on the hillside takes five minutes. He learns the phone number of the real estate office that manages the building from a maintenance caretaker. He will assign that duty to Jennifer. Two errands down.

He drives home, knowing that he will be eating alone tonight. Arnold chooses a large glass of port, and he will also need some relaxing music. He selects a tape with background music by Beethoven. They include soft piano sonatas, melodies, sounds of water running over rocks, and birds chirping.

Meanwhile, Julien gets to Juliet's home by 7 p.m. He walks in and gets a big hug from Alissa. She has brought home some of last week's artwork. Grandpa and Alissa sit on the couch, viewing the artwork. Some are in pencil, and some are in watercolor. Julien is impressed.

Alissa says, "I want to show these to Arnold. He may like them too."

Julien says, "I'm sure he will like them. These are great. It is a fun hobby to have."

Juliet yells, "Dinner is ready. We are having filet mignon, mature red mashed potatoes, asparagus, steamed beets, steamed string beans, fresh strawberries for dessert, and seltzer water."

After cleaning up, the three watch a movie and have some ice cream.

Alissa says, "I miss Arnold."

Juliet says, "We had a little difference of opinions this week. In a relationship, communication and compromise are two of the most important parts of getting along. I think the world of him. We will have it settled by tomorrow."

61 - THE PROPOSAL

The fog is typical for the Bay area. Some broken clouds are on the horizon. Arnold stays in bed, thinking about how the day will turn out. Coffee is first. He sips on his coffee while reviewing yesterday. He finally takes a shower and brushes his teeth. He no longer has a beard to shave. No need to play with makeup, no lipstick to apply, no nylons stockings, just throw on some men's clothes for the day. He thinks how easy men have it.

For breakfast, he has corn pancakes, two poached eggs, a large slice of ham, raspberry jam, fruit, a glass of grapefruit juice, and more coffee. This should hold him through mid-afternoon.

Sid walks in, saying, "I heard you are in deep shit at the office with Miss Beautiful. I do agree with Julien that you seem to learn everything the hard way. The Bridget thing should have started months earlier, but you were stubborn and set in your ways. You were fortunate people cared for you, and we're looking out for you. Now review this collection of engagement rings. I have Juliet's favorite styles on the left. I believe the second and third ones are the best choice."

Arnold chooses the second one.

Arnold says, "Thank you, as always, for your support. You have been a significant part of our success. I am proud to call you, my friend."

Sid says, "See you later, stubborn one. I'll send you my bill."

As Arnold drives out of the garage, no eyes are watching. The Lombard traffic from the left is heavy since there are so many are going to work. He turns onto Lombard northbound toward the bridge. Crossing the bridge was scented with that familiar smell of fog. After the bridge and through the tunnel, he enters a new world of no fog along with warmer air, the beginning of Marin County.

He drives slowly. He is not looking forward to another possible confrontation with Juliet, like the one they had yesterday. Up he goes in the elevator. As he enters the waiting area, he walks softly and quietly. Matilda says, "Good morning, Mr. Pierce."

Arnold nods a good morning. He feels that the entire office has heard of yesterday's outburst. As Arnold passes Jennifer's desk, she hands him his coffee with no pastry. He then enters the silence of his office.

Arnold walks out to Jennifer's desk and says, "Have the offices been prepared for both Rita and Harriet?"

Jennifer says, "I made an executive decision on both of those issues. I had the two offices near Mr. Love's office repainted and welcomed back signs installed. I left Juliet in Julien's office, but I added a nameplate for her."

Arnold walks into Julien's office. There is no Juliet.

Julien says, "She was contemplating not coming in. Later she called to say she is on her way. What did you do to piss her off?"

Without answering, Arnold walks back to his office. In his office, he is doing nothing. He is moping.

As he wanders out to the lobby, Matilda says, "She is here, Mr. Pierce."

That gives him a little spark of hope.

As he approaches Jennifer's desk, she says, "You are to wait for her in your office. Juliet will be with you in a few minutes."

Jennifer calls Juliet, "Arnold has returned."

Juliet walks into Julien's office and sets her coat and purse down. She leisurely walks to the lady's room and returns. Julien is watching without saying a word. Juliet knows Arnold is in his office alone. With a feeling of confidence, she walks into Arnold's office and sits down.

HIDDEN IN FRONT OF YOU

Juliet says, "Yesterday, you implied you and me. That equals two. You now have a woman in your life that is dedicated to you, and we have a family. Yes, I am pregnant. For us two, it must be one. I can't have this any other way."

Arnold jumps to his feet and runs over to give her a big hug. He is so happy that he is tearing.

Juliet says, "Do I get your commitment to this agreement?" Arnold says, "I will agree willingly. I have one more thing to offer." He pulls the box from his coat pocket and presents it to Juliet.

Arnold says, "Will you marry me as soon as possible?"

Juliet says, "Let's drive to the Cliff House. I have my reasons and have made reservations."

They leave the office get into the Jaguar.

She says, "There is no hurry, Mr. Pierce. You can drive the legal speed."

Arnold knows that when Juliet makes up her mind, it is permanent. She reaches over to hold his hand.

Juliet says quietly, "I love you, Mr. Pierce."

Not another word is said. Arnold is worried, yet he is enjoying her presence. Juliet appears happy while enjoying the scenery. It is a mid-weekday with few tourists and light traffic. There is a parking space close to the Cliff House. After parking, Arnold runs around to open Juliet's door. Since Juliet had made reservations, they just walk right in. They arrive on time.

She addresses the maître de', "Sir, my reservation is for the second table at the north end of the window, looking west."

He answers, "Yes, Ma'am, we have that table ready for you."

Juliet says, "Why this restaurant, why this table and why today? At this table is when I decided I would marry you if you would ever ask. When we were here before, I realized I wanted you beside me for the rest of my life. Now that we have the oneness issue settled, we can continue."

Arnold is without words for the moment.

He says, "I don't know where to start."

Juliet, while laughing, says, "What good is a trial lawyer without something to say. Is this a day of miracles? You have not lost your vocabulary, Mr. Pierce; you're just at a loss for words. Don't worry; it will return soon."

He says, "Will you please marry me?"

She says, "Yes, I will marry you, Mr. Pierce."

Arnold jumps up and shouts, "Excuse me, folks. I just asked this beautiful woman to marry me. She said yes. How lucky can a man get? Thank you for listening."

As he sits down, there is a round of applause and whistles.

Juliet says, "You are a silly boy. No wonder I love you so much."

He says, "I found a little church on the hill in Tiburon. I have also looked into hosting our wedding reception at the restaurant next to Alicia. I now see that what I did was completely unfair to us. I have been operating so much on my own for years that I let you down. I will never do that again. We can go by the little church to see if you think it is appropriate."

As they finish their dinner, they are both pleased, and their happiness is apparent in their faces.

Arnold says, "We may want to come here once in a while to celebrate our anniversaries."

Arnold pays the maître de' then hands him an additional fifty dollars tip to share with the rest of the staff as he sees fit.

The maître de' says, "I have read Mr. Little's articles in the Chronicle. I'm proud to have you as a patron. Your work and integrity are an outstanding example for the rest of us. Thank you. You have a beautiful ring their future, Mrs.

HIDDEN IN FRONT OF YOU

Pierce."

Within minutes they are back at the Filbert house.

Arnold using the house phone calls Julien at home, "Tom Cat, please bring Alissa and yourself to my house. I have something I have wanted to say for months."

Julien and Alissa arrive within fifteen minutes. They are both wondering about this sudden request. As they sit at the kitchen table, there is a glass of port poured for each. No one is speaking. Each has taken a sip of the port.

Bridget says, "With the war and the lawsuit in progress, one thing has been overlooked. Juliet and I have been discussing a topic, then it seemed to get missed in our execution of this war. Alissa, I want to adopt you as my daughter."

Julien is without words, and Alissa is in tears. As Alissa regains her composer, she tries to talk yet can't. It takes a few minutes for her to starts talking.

Alissa says, "You two make me so proud. I can now be the older sister of all those little Pierces that mom is going to deliver. I want to change my last name to Pierce. I love you two. What a beautiful family to be a part of."

After discussing the new turn in events, the three leave for the evening. Arnold is pleased he did not let this slip through the cracks.

62 - THE WEDDING

As the sun rises in the early morning, it was easy to see that it was going to be a mild day. The rain was light yet consistent. No fog and a soft breeze were in store for the Bay Area today.

Arnold calls Nick as the coffee is brewing.

Nick answers, "Nick, here."

Arnold says, "The Jaguar works perfectly. The Jaguar was superior to anything I have ever driven."

Nick says, "I'll be at your wedding and reception. I read in the Chronicle that you killed two guys with murder warrants with your 44 Magnum, and you saved a cop's life. Did he really complain about being shot? See you, lover boy."

Bridget and Juliet fix breakfast together. Both are thrilled with the thought of their marriage.

Arnold says, "There will be a small meeting with a catered lunch today, so we should consider a light breakfast."

They stop by the church on their way to the office. Juliet knows that it would be at least a four-month wait to get a full-sized church. This quaint little church is the typical late 1890's style. For its years of service, it appears to be in moderately good shape. Juliet loves it, and it is available from 8 a.m. until 2 p.m. the following Saturday. They also meet with the restaurant maître de' to confirm the date with him.

With the date and time set, Arnold calls Josey, "Josey here."

Arnold says, "Josey, I would like you to send a diver under the Alicia to check everything out and fill in the bullet holes and cracks. I plan on using the boat for a long voyage."

Josey asks, "What's up?"

Arnold says, "Be at our office luncheon today, and you will find out then."

Arnold and Juliet each drive their own vehicle. As they both walk into the lobby, the staff is waiting for things to explode. They both walk casually to their respective offices.

Juliet says, "Daddy, I am about to move in with Arnold. You will understand at lunch."

Juliet walks over to Jennifer's desk and removes her left-hand glove. Jennifer jumps out of her seat and hugs Juliet.

Juliet says, "Please keep this quiet. Arnold would like to announce it to everyone at one time."

She puts the glove back on her left hand.

Jennifer prepares the coffee and pastry then enters Arnold's office.

Jennifer asks, "What kind of devilish plans do you have for today? Are you staying out of trouble? I saw the ring. It is beautiful. We girls cover for each other."

Arnold says, "Please don't let the cat out of the bag. I want to end the meeting with our announcement."

Jennifer says, "You have a call from Mr. Little."

Arnold says, "Arnold Pierce here, how are you, Mr. Little. That was fine work with those articles."

Mr. Little says, "I have a nice piece of news for you. Sean McCarthy, Kevin's brother, has been arrested and deported to Ireland. He arrived at the San Francisco Airport and was arrested later that same day after causing an accident in Marin County."

Arnold replies, "Thank you for the good news. I have some news for you, sir. You will need to be here for our office luncheon to hear it."

Little says, "I'll be there. See you then."

Arnold holds a quick meeting with both Harriet Williams and Rita Kennedy.

As the meeting starts, Arnold says, "Harriet and Rita, I am very pleased to have both of you back with us. We can certainly use your expertise and fine work. We are looking forward to your presence. Harriet, can you stand seeing Mr. Spence every day? Remember, he is our Alley Cat."

Harriet says, "Mr. Pierce, you got us together while the firm was in the middle of the McCarthy war. It now looks like you have eyes for Juliet."

Rita says, "I am in debt to you. I knew the guards were reporting to McCarthy, and you were forced to wait. After all that, you followed through. Thanks to you, Mr. Pierce, everything is clear for me to get my full life back again. I am positive that I will enjoy being here with you folks again."

Arnold says, "If I had known about Mr. Williams earlier, you would never have left. I apologize for my blindness. We will make it up to you, I promise.

I do have one more announcement. Juliet and I are getting married on Saturday next weekend. Jennifer will get the invitations to you this week. I hope you both come to the wedding. That is all for now."

Arnold walks to Jennifer's desk.

Arnold says, "We need to meet. Please bring some fresh coffee."

Jennifer enters with two fresh cups of coffee. She closes the door and sits across the desk from Arnold.

He says, "Thanks for the office upgrades and name tags. Good thinking. Harriet seems to have guarded herself well. We owe her a great deal in assisting us with Rita's case. I feel somewhat responsible for the harm done to Rita. She seems to have been caught in the middle of a bad situation. I would like you to review her loss of property, loss of monies, and any other damages she has suffered. Possibly, we can reimburse her to some degree. I do not have the time to get involved. I also feel that you may be able to put yourself in her shoes better than I. The firm will assume the cost of getting her released. I feel she may open up to you more than she would to me. Remember, she is the victim."

Jennifer agrees to Arnold's request, and Arnold continues, "The other day, I was an ass. I acted like a man without a

HIDDEN IN FRONT OF YOU

partner. Juliet was correct and reminded me that I must change my actions. She is right. I have a wonderful woman, a marriage, a family, so I had better know what comes first."

Jennifer says, "Family, would you be a little more descriptive?"

He says, "We have one on the way, mums the word."

Jennifer says, "I can now understand why she was so mad at you. You were really in the wrong this time."

Arnold says, "I didn't find out she was pregnant until yesterday. I had the ring, the church, and the reception already planned. We went by the church together and agreed upon the reception site. Please get out the invitations to everyone we deal with. I prefer that no one feels left out. The date is the second Saturday from today."

Jennifer stands smiling brightly and returns to her desk.

Arnold calls Sergeant Brown, "Brown here."

Arnold says, "After saving your life. I guess your jaywalking violation will need to be added to the list. That is gratitude for ya. You were crying about a couple of small bullet wounds. I still want to know if they hire babies for officers in Tiburon?"

Brown replies, "Did you set me up, you son of a bitch?"

Arnold says, "Tiny little flesh wounds and you are crying. Should I have let him shoot again? You are invited to my wedding. Shall I drive over to pick you up? I know how to drive a taxicab. Hope to see you there."

Brown says, "Even if I am on duty, I'll be there."

It's around 11:50, and people are starting to congregate near the main conference room for the luncheon. The caterer has everything ready for an enjoyable lunch. Jennifer has made sure that all things are in order. The conference room is large enough to let each person sit while eating lunch and listening. The caterer has brought along two extra assistants to service the group. Prime rib is the choice of the day, along with steamed and raw vegetables. An assortment of antipasti items, fruits, and cheeses are offered. Arnold waits until most of the individuals have finished their main meal and are starting to dive into the desserts and coffee. There is lots of talking, joking, and laughter. They are a happy group.

Arnold stands and taps a glass to get their attention.

Arnold says, "Welcome to you all. Most of you were either on the front lines or supporting the firm and realize the dangers that we all faced together. Your support and hard work helped us gain control of our future. We also have some guests. Mr. Little, who has presented a clear and honest picture of our work with the morning Chronicle of the City of San Francisco. I have one more article for him to write. We have Judge Brass, who assisted us all in repairing the city problems. Then we have Mr. Fish, our new Police Commissioner, who has shown great leadership assuring us a good future. Josey, you are not forgotten for always being there for whatever needs to be done. We want to remember Jennifer, who was promoted to first level management of the office. Her value is easily seen by all the improvements here in the firm. It is hard to count the many, many things she does that improve this office every day. Based on that, the firm has provided Jennifer an additional two weeks with pay, two round trip tickets to Hawaii with all expenses paid. Josey is working on Alicia in preparation for an ocean voyage up and down the Pacific coast. For Bridget, she has found her man and things are going well. She stayed as long as she could. Juliet is the one that assisted me in recuperating. She fed me, worked on my injuries, delivered my notes to Bridget to help in the guidance of things. Also, she personally assisted Bridget in multiple assignments. Many were ones that were essential to our success. Folks, let me take a short break."

HIDDEN IN FRONT OF YOU

Arnold walks off to the men's room.

Then he finds Juliet and says, "When we sit down, please sit beside me."

Then he finds Julien and says, "What do you think so far, Alley Cat?"

Julien says, "Now you are going to have her move in with you. I am not quite content with that. You are a good guy. She could do worse. Please honor her."

Arnold says, "My friend, I do have her honor on my mind. Please trust me?"

Julien says, "Okay, for now. Remember, Matt trained me too. I could come after you."

Arnold says, "No worries. We should work out sometime, just because you need to behave yourself."

Arnold starts the meeting again.

He says, "Josey is fixing Alicia for a several weeks cruise up and down the Pacific shoreline."

Arnold has Juliet stand with him.

He continues, "About ten days from today, on a Saturday at 10 a.m., we will be married in that little old church up on the hillside in Tiburon. The reception will be held at the restaurant beside Alicia in Tiburon. From that site, Juliet and I will sail away on our honeymoon. Julien, you get Alissa's company for those two weeks. It sounds like a win-win situation to me. Hope to see you all there. Thank you all for your support and assistance. When I walk into the office, I feel that we are more family than just people working together."

The meeting ends with applause and whistles.

During the following week, Arnold has what furniture and specials items that Juliet wants to retain moved to his Tiburon home's garage. They have Juliet's house repainted, upgraded, and then put it up for rent. With housing in demand, they have no problem picking some good tenants at a favorable price. The Tiburon second bedroom now becomes Alissa's. She has no problem filling it with her favorite toys, dolls, furniture, and pictures. Arnold and Juliet still get silk sheets.

The old church fits the bill. It could stand some upgrading. Arnold hires Joe, Alissa's boyfriend's father, for the work with the commitment that both Otto and Alissa give him a hand in the work. They can fix failing pieces of wood, stain the seats and handrails and refinish the flooring. It still looks like the late 1890's style but in better shape. The church also gets some outside tender loving care. Arnold is having many people park at the reception using a provided bus to get to the church.

Josey finds the Alicia is in reasonably good shape. There only a few minor repairs required. There is a significant number of barnacles that will make Arnold dry-dock the hull sometime soon. It is not necessary to remove them for this honeymoon trip. Running gear, shafts, rudders, and anchors seem to be sound. No bullet holes were below the waterline, but there were several holes near the cabin and on the deck. Those had to be repaired and repainted. Josey knows the boat. He takes each sail out to inspect them, verifies the emergency equipment to be in good shape, and then replenishes the freshwater. The free emergency gear is checked and tested. The automatic steering, radios, and emergency signal gears also get checked out. Josey has the work completed three days before the wedding.

David Worth says, "I can now see how you kept such a close eye on the firm. It was not obvious that Juliet was the go-between. She did spend a lot of time with Bridget. It looks like I am CEO until you return. Juliet is a good choice. You are a lucky fellow."

Julien walks up to Arnold and says, "Trust you! That is like wrestling with an alligator. She will keep you straight."

HIDDEN IN FRONT OF YOU

Arnold says, "That is one of the reasons I want to marry her. We have made a pack. That is to be a unit. Like she says, "we" that means "one." You might as well trust me, Gramps. Soon we will be related. Now that is scary. I have chosen you for the best man along with Josey and Sid, to stand with me. Juliet has chosen Alissa, Jennifer, and Matilda. You and Alissa will be my only relatives that I am not married to. You are a welcome old man. You may thank me later."

Arnold's life is back to normal. His health is good, and he is feeling happier than he has felt in many years. The firm is running like clockwork, personnel is comfortable, and they all seem pleased with their assignments.

Jennifer is receiving a lot of replies about the wedding. Arnold and Juliet have agreed on the main course, the desserts with the restaurant's maître de'. Mikey is given the day off so he may attend, and he was encouraged to bring a girlfriend. He chose Naomi. Sid has agreed to oversee the painting and remodeling of Bridget's all pink home to a family home while they are on their honeymoon. Mr. Little's article on the wedding has encouraged many to send or call with congratulations. Every day, both Juliet and Arnold are glowing with happiness. The increase in clients has filled Harriet's and Rita's calendar. The world that Arnold had at once before has returned.

Days go by slowly for Arnold and Juliet as they wait for that magical day. Each day seems more exciting. They agree that soon they will be together as one in every sense of the word. As they look back over the last months, the two of them have gone through hopefully the worst they will ever see. This experience has brought them together as one. Daily they find themselves keener for the other's feelings and ideas. A closeness has developed between them that they both want and need from each other.

The night before the wedding, Juliet stays at her home to finish working on her wedding dress. She has taken parts of her mother's and grandmother's wedding dresses to fit her taste. Both are similar, yet there were parts from each that she preferred. The three dresses for Alissa, Jennifer, and Matilda, Juliet, made herself from scratch. Arnold purchased an appropriate tuxedo and suits for his three men standing with him.

The day finally arrives. Arnold is up early with coffee first, as usual. Julien has offered to transport Alissa and Juliet. Sid will drive Arnold. Arnold showers and partially dresses. With the reception and all its food, he fixes a light breakfast.

He remembers to get the letter from Alicia out of storage. It has been hidden there for years. He stuffs it into his inside jacket pocket. His memory of the last months makes him put the 38-caliber snub-nosed in his ankle holster. He and Sid drive toward Tiburon around 8 a.m. Arnold walks into the church at 8:30 a.m.

Joe, Otto, and Alissa have done a great job. The nineteenth-century decor is evident. The people have started to arrive at the church. The bus is there, ready to begin making runs to and from the restaurant.

Arnold rounds a corner and gets a big hug from Naomi.

She says, "This is Sammy's and my first wedding. Alex is in the hospital. He caught one that took him out, and he has a possible concussion."

"It is so exciting that you and Juliet are getting married. You two work so well together."

Mikey and Naomi's parents are there wishing them well.

Arnold says, "Mikey, you have not had a ride on the Alicia. Let's plan a trip after we get back. Thank you for your good work with those two guys at the restaurant."

Mikey says, "I heard you took care of both of them with a 44 Magnum."

HIDDEN IN FRONT OF YOU

Arnold says, "That is true. Sometimes it comes down to that."

Sergeant Brown and his wife show up.

Arnold says, "I presume, with your bodyguard here, that you are not here to arrest me? Good to meet you, Mrs. Brown."

Brown replies, "I wish I could arrest you. You were having such a good time, and I was scared the whole time wishing I was somewhere else. Juliet must love you to marry such a wild ass man. I hear you wrote me another jaywalking ticket, plus you put the notice of it into the local weekly paper. Then you had a short chat with some Tiburon council members."

Arnold says, "Hell, Sergeant, what are friends for. I stopped the guy from putting a deadly hole in you. How much nicer do you want me to be?"

Brown says, "You could admit to putting one 38-caliber round in that driver's backside."

Arnold says, "You know better than that."

Jennifer and her husband are there early.

Jennifer says, "Two weeks paid and Hawaii too."

Arnold says, "Jennifer, we could not have done it without your participation. You were a vital link to our success. You must admit that there were some scary parts. Enjoy the islands. You might as well take that husband of yours with you."

She smiles and gives Arnold a big hug.

Parking is getting scarce. For additional people, there is a large balcony. As the church fills the standing room along the back and sides start to become more and more crowded.

Unnoticed by Arnold and Juliet, an unknown woman is standing in the balcony. She is not talking with anyone, and no one near her knows her. Later after their return from their honeymoon, when the guest book is read by Juliet, she sees with love Alicia Holley Cummings as the last entry.

The organ starts playing. Arnold, Sid, and Josey are standing to the right of the minister. The ladies start walking down the center aisle. Julien looks quite proud to be escorting Juliet to the altar and also being the best man.

Soon all are standing on the forward platform. As the minister is presenting his version of the wedding introduction, Arnold is getting impatient to place the wedding ring on Juliet's finger. As the minister is saying until death does you part, he asks Arnold to put the ring on her finger. Arnold is ready in an instant.

Then the minister asks Juliet to place the ring on Arnold's finger, which surprises Arnold. She has found a similar ring for him. The minister then says I now pronounce you man and wife. You may kiss the bride. This is what Arnold was looking forward to the whole day.

They walk to the front door holding hands while they are plummeted by rice. They quickly hop into the waiting limousine and are on their way to the restaurant.

During the service, the restaurant maître de' came to the church to verify the crowd. It was much larger than he expected. He ran back to the restaurant, increased the amount of food his staff was preparing, opened more reception areas, and called in two more servers to help.

Within a half-hour, all the attendees were transported to the restaurant and given a place to sit. The serving of the meal started immediately.

As the couple entered, the crowd applauded.

Julien yells, "She finally made an honest man out of you, Arnold. We all love you, both."

Before sitting down to eat, Arnold and Juliet start dancing in the open dance area. They get many cheers and comments from the crowd.

Arnold says, "Was everything the way you wanted it, Juliet

Pierce?"

She replies, "I feel wonderful, Arnold Pierce. We are finally one."

As they stop dancing and return to their table, Juliet brings out a box.

"When I last saw Holley, we were shopping in downtown San Francisco. I found this wool long sleeve high neck pullover that I thought you would like while on the boat. Holley did not necessarily agree, yet I bought it anyway because I wanted it. Will you wear it for me today, please?"

Arnold grabs the microphone and says, "Excuse me, everyone. I hand this microphone off to Grandpa, alias Julien Spence the Alley Cat, who is now my relative."

"We thank you all for your presence in sharing with us our most important day. Sometime soon, we will be leaving on the boat parked just outside, the Alicia. We plan to visit most of the Northern Pacific Ocean coastal waters along with a few ports. Jennifer and her husband are off for the Hawaiian Islands. Our first night will be at our favorite inlet at the Farallone Islands. From there we will head north. Here is Grandpa."

Julien says, "Several months ago, my daughter said she had fallen in love with Arnold. I agreed it was a good choice but told her to be patient. She tried, but we all fail at times. She fixed his meals, acted as a nanny nurse with his injuries, and acted as a go-between Arnold and Bridget. She basically nursed him back to health. She also became active in some of the events through those many months. Alissa approves, so we have a happy family. It has been an honor for us to go through good times and bad together. I believe we agree it is a family working together. Who is next with words of wisdom for our newlyweds?"

Julien passes the microphone off, and it starts circulating throughout the room. Small groups of conversations spring up here and there. Both Arnold and Juliet try to visit everyone they can as they roam through the crowd together.

After a couple of hours, Arnold and Juliet walk off to change into their sailing clothes. As they return, Arnold is wearing his new wool pullover. They walk back into the reception area, where Arnold grabs the microphone.

He says, "Our sincere thank you for joining us on our day. Stay as long as you want. I have requested that the food and drinks be available until the end of the day."

He hands off the microphone to Julien then he and Juliet walk out to the Alicia.

Arnold unties the mooring lines, engages the motor, and steers the Alicia from its berth. Arnold has the mainsail already set for a slow and comfortable journey to the Golden Gate. They continue to wave to the crowd until they are well out of sight. As they are proceeding toward the bridge, the winds are light, and the fog is moderate.

Arnold has the letter ready for when they are under the Golden Gate. They are sitting as close as possible to each other at the helmsman's position. Occasionally they kiss and hug each other. As they approach the Golden Gate Bridge, Arnold hands Juliet the letter. Juliet is in tears after she reads the letter from Holley. The lady she thought was Arnold's occasional acquaintance was actually the woman Arnold lost in that auto accident years ago. The woman he had spent so much of his early school days with him. There is nothing she can use to understand this phenomenon. Death is death, yet she spent time with a woman that had passed away. She turns to Arnold holding him close.

HIDDEN IN FRONT OF YOU

The letter:

To the woman that Arnold loves. If you are reading this, then it is true. Beyond a shadow of a doubt that he loves you, else he would not have given you this letter.

I can only hope you feel as strongly about him as he does about you.

I am writing this letter to make sure you know one significant thing. I am glad Arnold has found you. I only wish I could have been there to know you.

In some ways, I have been. The thought of you in Arnold's world gives me solace. Knowing Arnold, I am aware of his desires, his respect for others, and his dedication. He will be thoughtful, supportive, and attentive to your every need. I hope that I am somewhere nearby.

Alicia Holley Cummings

The End

Made in the USA
Columbia, SC
17 November 2020